THE **DARK SIDE**
OF THE **SUN**

To: Cliff
Best wishes old
Classmate
Enjoy
Mike D____
Sept 2021.

THE DARK SIDE

OF THE SUN

MICHAEL B. DARDIS

Beaver's Pond Press

— *Minneapolis, Minnesota* —

Edited by Angela Wiechmann
Cover illustration by Margarita Sikorskaia

ISBN: 978-1-59298-781-8
Library of Congress Catalog Number: 2018949407
Printed in the United States of America
First Printing: 2018
22 21 20 19 18   5 4 3 2 1

Beaver's Pond Press, Inc.
7108 Ohms Lane
Edina, MN 55439–2129

(952) 829-8818
www.BeaversPondPress.com

To order, visit www.ItascaBooks.com or call 1-800-901-3480 ext. 118.
Reseller discounts available.

This novel is dedicated to my wife, Nancy. She has provided me with love and support for over forty years. Without her help, this novel would not have been possible.

This novel is also dedicated to all veterans who have recovered from trauma and loss and to those who suffer still.

PREFACE

This novel is a work of fiction. It is based loosely around actual historical events and individuals. All dialogue has been invented, and certain events and individuals have been imagined.

This is the story of people dealing with light and darkness in their lives. This story could be about any of us.

Michael Dardis
Fall 2018

PROLOGUE

THE COLD GRAY OF ROLLING WAVES ON LAKE SUPERIOR brought little relief to the slate sky. Two flickers raced among the limbs of a weathered maple tree. Their yellow tail feathers flashed like a semaphore in the haze. A bald eagle sat at the tip of a birch tree, turning his white head slowly to spy a floating tidbit or a lazy fish. Yes, early spring in the Upper Peninsula of Michigan could be a slow, monotonous process as nature woke from a deep sleep.

Bill O'Brien surveyed the shoreline from the cabin window, sipping a hot cup of coffee. It wasn't quite 6:00 a.m., but it would again be a quiet day. Most of the neighbors had not yet opened their summer camps, so the wildlife had free rein for a few more weeks.

The warmth and crackle of the wood in the fireplace was accented by an occasional pop of pinesap from the burning logs. The fire was welcome company in the quiet morning and took the edge off the cool air in the cabin. The faint wood-smoke scent even enhanced the aroma of Bill's coffee. He inhaled sharply and took another sip from his cup. The brew was dark and strong, with a splash of Jameson to make it as Irish as his ancestry.

A family of mergansers drifted easterly just off the rocky beach. An assertive mother tended to the newly hatched bobs of fluff, trying to teach them about danger, about feeding, about survival, about life. Bill watched the line float serenely past.

Suddenly a splash of water scattered the hatchlings, and the last duckling in line disappeared under the water. A lake trout cruising the shallows was also intent on tending to its survival needs. The great circle of life was so much a part of the culture in the Huron Mountain region of Michigan. Many dangers lurked in the woods and under the cold waters.

Bill sipped his coffee inattentively. A dribble seeped down his chin to his well-worn olive drab shirt. As he brushed the fabric, he noted the name stitched on the pocket: *O'Brien.*

Despite the comfort of the fire, the ache in his left leg reminded him of the sudden cold darkness that had entered his life like the solar eclipses he had studied in his history classes at the University of Minnesota. Ancient Greeks believed that eclipses occurred when the gods were angry and ready to mete out disaster and destruction.

Bill certainly had seen his share of disaster and destruction. But he believed the real meaning was to cast out falsehoods and replace them with truth.

1.

G ROWING UP, BILL IDOLIZED HIS FATHER. Michael O'Brien had the "gift of the Irish" to always see the bright side in hard times. Michael was a fourth-generation Irish American.

Michael's own father, Thomas, was an engineer. Thomas learned to fly at an early age and joined the Lafayette Escadrille, the US volunteer squadron that served with the French Air Service in World War I. He died in a plane crash in 1922, when he was a mail service pilot.

Michael's mother, Kathryn, never remarried. She devoted herself to Michael and his younger brother, Sean, ensuring they pursued an education in Detroit. After Thomas's death, Michael promised he would help look after Sean as well.

Michael was pleased to continue the family tradition of education. He graduated from the University of Michigan with a degree in business just before the United States entered World War II. Michael was also proud to continue the family tradition of flying and military service. He qualified for pilot training and served in World War II.

Sean also applied for pilot training but did not have the right aptitude— nor the right attitude of his older brother. He was assigned to the Eighth Air Force ground crew and was jealous of his older brother being a pilot. Sean's peers in the ground crew did not like him, and he returned the favor. Michael tried to encourage Sean by pointing out that ground support personnel were key to the safety of the flight crews. That did little to buoy his spirits.

While Michael and Sean were serving in England in World War II, Kathryn died back home in Detroit. Michael knew he had to honor his mother's wish and care for his brother.

Also while in England, Michael met the love of his life, Helene Bahr. Helene was a refugee from Nazi Germany. She was a problem solver, working for the British government when they met.

She was beautiful in so many ways. Besides being a slim, attractive woman, Helene was intelligent and cultured. As a young girl, she had traveled to archaeological sites in the Middle East with her father, giving her a unique perspective on family and other cultures. She had also studied archaeology at Heidelberg University in Germany. However, she had lost her entire family in the vortex of the war. Michael helped her through her grief.

After his discharge from the military, Michael and Helene married, returned to the United States, and settled in a small house outside Detroit to begin their life together. Helene was several months pregnant with Bill when they arrived from Europe. William Thomas O'Brien was born on the Fourth of July, 1944, in the Henry Ford Hospital in Detroit.

Sean also returned to Detroit after being released early from his foreign service. Sean did not support Michael's marriage to Helene. As a traditional Catholic, Sean continually chided Michael for "throwing away" their Irish Catholic heritage by marrying a German Lutheran. Michael and Helene tolerated Sean's outbursts, but there was continual friction in the family. Despite Sean's behavior, Michael still felt responsible for his younger brother. He tried to coach Sean, and he often overlooked Sean's rude remarks, much to Helene's increasing chagrin.

Michael found a position working for the Flying Tiger Line airfreight company in Detroit. He eventually found a maintenance position with the Flying Tigers for Sean, just to keep him close. For fifteen years, Michael flew all types of aircraft around the region, delivering everything from machine parts to frozen food. Whatever was required, he was there on time and ready for his next assignment. Michael also used his university business training to help improve the company's delivery systems.

With three young children—Bill, John, and Jackie—in the household, Helene was happy with her new role as educator and guardian. She pushed her children to excel but respected their individual capabilities and interests. She refused to accept common theories of the day on race, religion, and politics, and she became active in a variety of social welfare organizations. An outspoken woman, she got to her point quickly and clearly, without being rude. She taught her children to listen to the opinions of others who did not agree with them.

Helene was the touchstone for the children and often their confessor. However, she was always careful not to undermine Michael's role as husband and father. Although Helene ran the household, Michael was a man of solid principles. He was not averse to guiding the children when they strayed from his desired path—which of course happened frequently. Helene would smile and watch as Michael calmly pointed out the lessons to be learned from the mistake.

Helene tirelessly supported the family—especially with her uncanny ability to find items Michael and the children mislaid or to solve problems without batting an eyelash. Michael often deferred to her on family decisions, which made them the perfect team. Michael's only complaint was that Helene finished the weekly crossword puzzle—in ink—before he could even see it.

Michael was closemouthed about his military experience until Bill turned sixteen. They were doing routine maintenance together on Michael's twin-engine aircraft when Bill asked, "What did you do in the war, Dad?"

Michael cleared his throat and took stock of his oldest son. More than one person had commented that they could tell at a glance that Bill was Michael's son. Bill had grown up quickly this last year and now stood nearly eye level with his father.

Setting down the wrench he had been holding, Michael wiped his hands on a rag. He ran his hand through his short dark-brown hair and told his son the story of his combat experience.

Michael had survived twenty-five combat missions and earned an early return to the United States before the war in Europe ended. So many of Michael's friends died in that war. Michael expressed sadness about the massive destruction his bombing had caused in the civilian areas. However, he was also sure it had been the only way to end the war.

He told Bill, "War is the most tragic and useless thing man can do. But at times, it is necessary, and it was necessary then."

Even at that young age, Bill was amazed that his father was not hardened by those horrors, as were so many other veterans of war.

Michael always encouraged his children to do the right thing regardless of the cost. Bill promised his parents he would take care of his younger siblings, John and Jackie, much as Michael had tended Sean. At one point, Bill successfully took on a much larger bully trying to take young John's lunch money. Bill looked forward to always being there for his siblings, even if they didn't want his help.

The love between Michael and Helene was easy to see. They often strolled hand in hand down their street in the Detroit neighborhood, embarrassing the children with their show of affection. The kids always stayed several steps in front of "the lovers." Bill, John, and Jackie often spied on their parents snuggling together on the front porch swing. They saw Michael running his fingers gently through Helene's silky brown hair as she rested her head on his shoulder. When they exchanged a brief kiss, Johnny commented, "Eeeew!"

Sometimes Michael would find Helene lost in contemplation, remembering the family she had lost during the war. He would gently remind her of the loving family she had now and how important she was to their happiness.

Bill hoped he would be as loving and patient as his father.

2.

IN 1961, BILL'S FATHER GOT HIS BIG BREAK and started M. O. Airfreight. By this time, Michael had many connections in the airfreight business, so he asked a friend to arrange a meeting with a representative of the Ford Motor Company. Michael hoped his military service and familiarity with the B-24s produced at Ford's Willow Run plant would help him get a foot in the door and gain a contract to carry critical auto parts to the various Ford plants around the country.

After a few months, the meeting was arranged at the Ford Motor Company headquarters in Detroit. Michael was pleasantly surprised it was with Henry Ford II.

Michael greeted him enthusiastically. "I'm so happy to meet the family responsible for producing the fabulous B-24 aircraft I flew in the war effort."

"Mr. O'Brien—or would you rather I call you Michael?"

"Mr. Ford, please call me Michael."

"Michael, I'm in turn happy to meet the pilot of my father's first B-24 from the Willow Run plant. Your representative mentioned your service when he called, and we were able to confirm that your plane was indeed the first B-24 that came off our production line at Willow Run." He smiled. "Our family was very proud to serve the United States and its wonderful servicemen through the production of the B-24s. I'm especially pleased—as I know my father would be if he were alive today—to know those planes brought you and so many other men home safely."

Henry directed Michael to a set of nearby chairs. "Please sit down. Tell me about your family."

"My wife, Helene, was born and raised in Germany. I met her while I was with the Eighth Air Force in England. We have three children. Overall, we have been blessed."

"Michael, you are truly fortunate. I'm pleased that your wife has a German heritage." Henry beamed. "Before the war, my father had a very bright and capable young German man working in the aircraft design branch of our company. Perhaps he helped design the aircraft you so proudly flew."

Henry leaned forward in his chair, ready to talk business. "I was meeting with our shipping division vice president when your representative called. It was timely. We've experienced some delivery problems with critical parts. We're in the process of considering another contract. Tell me about your company."

The rest of the meeting went well. Michael stressed some of the innovations he had instituted into his business that would allow the Ford Company to save time and money in moving critical parts around the country. The meeting ended with a handshake and Henry's assurance that Michael would receive a contract proposal soon.

A month later, Michael was thrilled to receive a contract to move auto parts across the country. This was a major achievement for his fledgling company. It greatly expanded M. O. Airfreight. Michael busied himself with his booming business. The family was prospering, and the small house in Detroit was bursting at the seams.

By early summer, Michael decided to move his business to a charter hangar at Wold-Chamberlain Field in Minneapolis, Minnesota. It was a more central location for shipments, and it provided space for three more aircraft. He hired four more pilots to keep up with the demand. Now, two pilots could trade off flying duties on longer cross-country flights. His business continued to grow as he serviced the Detroit and Saint Paul Ford Motor Company plants as well as handled other corporate contracts to both the East and West Coasts.

Michael was also glad to get Sean out of the Detroit area. Sean had started gambling, and some of his friends were questionable. Michael worried they were manipulating Sean into more serious trouble beyond the occasional bar fight.

Michael offered Sean a position supervising the loading and unloading of shipments at M. O. Airfreight. After much discussion, Sean finally agreed to come to Minneapolis to work for Michael, but he maintained an attitude that kept his peers at arm's length.

With 160 acres of rolling meadow and old-growth oak trees, a small farmstead just north of Minneapolis provided the clean air and open area Michael's growing family needed. It was also large enough to accommodate a private landing strip. Michael kept a small twin-engine aircraft for family vacations and air-commuting to work. It was the perfect location for family and business.

Bill matured quickly on the farm. He was proud of his parents for what they had accomplished, and he respected their views. He enjoyed the farm more than the urban environment in Detroit, with bullies on every street corner.

Because Bill was the oldest, most of the chores fell to him. He was up at daybreak every morning to feed and water their small herd of cattle and horses. It was also his job to wake his brother and sister so they could feed the chickens and rabbits before school. After school, the one-acre garden always needed to be weeded or the lawn mowed.

Uncle Sean frequented the farm at dinnertime, but Bill didn't see him doing a lot to earn the meals. When he did do farm chores or help Michael with maintenance on the airplane, he was grumpy and didn't seem to get much done.

Then there was Bill's homework. English homework came first—he just wanted to get it out of the way. He disliked all the reading and writing. His Conversational German class was interesting. He found practicing with his mother fun, seeing as it frustrated his siblings, who couldn't understand what they were saying. Bill always left math and science for last. He excelled at both and was in advanced classes. If he did math or science first, he tended to get engrossed and run out of time for the other assignments.

With the kids taking care of the outdoor chores, Helene had time to make breakfast and fix lunches for school before loading the children into the Ford Galaxie 500. She dropped Bill at high school, John at the nearby junior high, and Jackie at her elementary school.

Done with her chauffeuring for the morning, Helene then started her errands. Some days she had grocery shopping or needed material to make new clothes for the family. She would also attend various meetings in the afternoon before picking up the children and heading home to start supper.

Many days, she would stop and visit her cousin Rudolph, who lived on a hobby farm nearby. He received occasional updates from relatives still in Germany. She relished the chance to stay in touch with her heritage.

The O'Brien family was very close. They loved to travel the Midwest to various air shows and fly-in breakfasts on the weekends. In June, they never missed their annual vacation to the Experimental Aircraft Association air show in Wisconsin. Michael and Bill would cruise the show, chatting with pilots and designers about the latest and greatest inventions. Helene kept track of youngsters John and Jackie as they ate cotton candy and watched the aerial acrobats screaming overhead in ever-more-dangerous stunts.

3.

DURING THE SUMMER OF 1962, Gene Cummins, a friend of Michael's, hired Bill for a surveying company. The job would help him save for college at the University of Minnesota next year. Hopefully, it would also allow him to go to the senior prom and get that shiny new red Chevrolet convertible he had coveted ever since he passed his driver's test.

He was proud of his new job and his independence, but it came at a price. He found himself with a dilemma when the family decided to fly to Denver for their summer vacation. They planned to stop and see Michael's old war buddy, General Fredrick Schwartz. He was one of Michael's close friends from the Eighth Air Force and now an instructor and pilot at the US Air Force Academy in Colorado Springs. For Bill, thoughts of seeing Pikes Peak, the academy, and the Rocky Mountains had strong allure, but so did the almighty dollar. His bank account won out.

Before the rest of the family piled into the twin-engine and headed west, Bill pulled out his Brownie camera and snapped a photo. Helene said she would call Bill when they arrived in Colorado and give him the highlights of their flight around Pikes Peak. Then he was left on the side of the runway, waving good-bye.

While the family was away, Sean agreed to help Bill with the morning farm chores. Bill found his uncle helpful but cold and silent. Fortunately, Bill knew how to get the farmwork done without a lot of conversation. He was glad when he could gun the Ford down the driveway and head off to work.

Bill was helping Gene complete surveys for the Federal Aviation Administration (FAA) on a new runway planned at Wold-Chamberlain Field. At noon, the workers headed into the surveying office trailer for lunch. Bill checked the message board just inside the door, hoping there would be word from his family. He could already hear his little brother and bratty sister gloating about the beautiful Rocky Mountains and all he was missing. There was no message yet.

"It's a cooker out there today, hey, Bill?" Gene pulled off his hard hat, wiped his brow with his sleeve, and untied the bandanna from his neck. He wiped the brim of the hat and put it on the shelf labeled with his name.

"Sure is," replied Bill. "It would be nice to get some rain out of that sky to cool things down. I'm keeping the livestock close to the barn, so I can be sure they stay watered."

"Good idea. Michael is lucky he has a boy with some sense to watch the place while the rest of them go on vacation," praised Gene. "My kid don't have the brains God gave a doorknob!"

Bill laughed and took a large bite out of a peanut butter sandwich his mother had packed. He smiled as he remembered her handing him the bag, saying, "Here are three sandwiches. Three's a crowd, but I want to make sure your stomach is crowded with something. We won't be back for a week, and I know how much you like to cook!"

Gene broke Bill from his thoughts. "You heard from yer Dad yet, Bill?"

"No. I was hoping there would be a call by now."

"You know your pappy. He's probably got the family flying circles around Pikes Peak before they head in to Denver. That's a place you really wanted to see, right?" Gene chided him with a twinkle in his eye.

"Yeah." Bill smiled back, starting on his second sandwich. "I'll get there another year—when I don't have an ogre for a boss!"

"Ogre, huh? Then polish off that sandwich, and let's get back to work!" Gene put his hand on Bill's shoulder and gave it a light squeeze.

Gene thought it was certainly nice to see how Bill had grown and matured. Michael and Helene had done a great job. He wondered where he had gone wrong with his own son.

The two men grabbed their hard hats and headed back into the afternoon sun. The temperature and humidity seemed even more oppressive than they had earlier.

"Bill, this may be an early quittin' day," Gene predicted. "I'll pay you for the whole day, but I don't want a case of heatstroke on my hands."

That suited Bill fine. He still had to get home and tend to the livestock before searching the refrigerator for dinner. Sean helped out only in the morning, seeing as Bill had plenty of time to finish the evening chores.

Bill pulled the Galaxie 500 into the garage and headed directly to the barn to feed the livestock. A storm was definitely brewing. He tuned the barn radio to WCCO-AM to check the weather forecast. If this turned out to be a serious storm, he would need to bring the animals inside. Last time, he forgot to bring them in before the storm hit. He was out until midnight in driving rain and lightning, trying to round up the terrified cattle scattered across the pastures.

I learned my lesson, he reminded himself.

According to the broadcast, the heat and humidity had cooked up some severe storms and possible tornadoes coming across the North and South Dakota borders. That was the general line for a bull's-eye on the farm. He quickly fed the rabbits and chickens and double-checked the latches on their pens. All secure.

The horses were stomping in their stalls, looking for dinner. They would have to wait until he got the cattle under cover. Riding bareback on Goldy, his favorite palomino, Bill rounded up the cattle and directed them into the barn. Like a herd of Pavlov's dogs, they headed to their stanchions without objection and waited to be milked and fed.

He stabled Goldy, fed and watered the horses, then tended the cattle. By the time he had finished hand-milking and feeding the cattle and then storing the milk cans, the rain had started in earnest. Time to check the answering machine for messages and dive into the refrigerator for any special surprise his mother must have left for dinner.

The message light was flashing, so he pushed the Play button.

"Hi, honey—this is Mom. It's about ten a.m. Dad decided to surprise us with a stop in South Dakota to see Mount Rushmore, so I thought I would give you a quick call. Check the freezer for dinner. I made you TV dinners for each night. Preheat the oven to three hundred fifty degrees, open a corner of the foil, and give it about thirty minutes. I didn't label anything, so each night will be a new surprise. Enjoy! We love you!" *Beep.*

"Beep back at ya, Mom," Bill said, grinning.

His stomach growled its displeasure at his delay. He pulled open the freezer door. Sure enough, there were ten foil-wrapped plates stacked in front.

"Ten?" Bill laughed out loud "You're only off for a week. You always overplan, just like Dad." He then mimicked her expected singsong response, "Better to be safe than sorry."

Bill set the oven temperature, opened the corner of the foil on his mystery selection, and popped it into the oven. He set the timer for thirty-five minutes—mentally adding the preheating time—then turned on the TV and headed for the couch.

"This is a dangerous storm," the newscaster was saying as the TV came to life. "Stay indoors until the threat has passed. Again, a tornado has been reported on the ground in Glencoe, heading northeast at about thirty miles per hour."

Bill calculated that the tornado would pass a good forty miles north of the farm, but they would still be in for hard rain and strong winds. He would need to check on the animals before he headed to bed tonight.

Glancing at his watch, he realized it was nearly eight—seven in Denver's mountain time zone. They should have landed by now. His mother had promised to call when they arrived. Even the stop in South Dakota should not have delayed them this long. His mother loved flying nearly as much as his dad did, but not in bad weather and not in the dark. If they made any other sightseeing stops, they may have been forced to stay somewhere other than Denver for the night.

Bill hesitated calling the FAA to report the plane overdue, but he had a feeling of dread. Bill knew his dad always filed a flight plan. The problem was, Bill hadn't seen it. He didn't know from where they might be overdue. A false report with the FAA could be costly for a pilot. Nonetheless, he was worried.

Finally, he went to the corner desk, picked up the phone, and placed a call.

"FAA Flight Status—Decker speaking."

The military-style response startled Bill at first.

"Oh, yeah . . . hi," Bill stammered. "I need to check on a flight heading toward Denver."

"*Toward* Denver or *to* Denver, son? Big difference."

"Yes, I realize that. But I don't quite know. I haven't seen the flight plan, but I know my Dad left our farm strip at six a.m. and stopped in Rapid City, South Dakota, around ten a.m. I believe their final destination was Denver, unless they changed plans."

"Well," Decker said, "I can't do much without his tail number. Do you have it?"

"Sure!"

Bill rattled off the number, then silently admonished himself. What an idiot! Not mentioning the tail number was like telling the police to look for a blue car in Minneapolis without giving them the license number.

"Hang on a second, and I'll check the flight plan."

The second seemed to drag to hours. Finally, Decker came back on the phone.

"Looks like they planned the first stop in Rapid City, then a flyby of Pikes Peak and a landing in Denver by six p.m. central. Tomorrow they planned to fly to a private strip near the Air Force Academy. And you say you haven't heard from them?"

"No." Bill swallowed hard as he answered. "It's my mom, dad, brother, and sister in the plane. Dad always calls if he's delayed."

"Well, give me your phone number. I'll do some checking on the route. Your dad sounds like an experienced pilot. With that storm coming across the country, they may have tucked into a small airport to wait it out. Some of those don't have a phone connection available unless the tower is open. Just looking at the fuel he had loaded, there is more than enough to fly a hundred miles past Denver. I'll let you know as soon as I hear anything, and I'll be sure to tell them to call home."

Bill thanked Decker and placed the phone back in its cradle. He tipped the chair forward so he could lay his head on his arm draped across the desk. He stared in a daze at the radar pattern on the television screen. The announcer described the storm raging outside while Bill tried to deal with the storm raging inside his chest.

A loud beep caused him to jump, knocking the chair over. Dinnertime.

Bill waited anxiously all night. The storm passed about midnight, and he checked on the livestock. Back inside, he lay on the living room floor in front of the television. Somehow the light and chatter, regardless of the programming, was comforting.

Bill was half asleep on the floor at 7:00 a.m. The television was still on, showing pictures of last night's storm damage. Some buildings were flattened and a few trees downed. Fortunately, there was no loss of life.

Bill rubbed his eyes and realized he still had not heard from the FAA. He heard a car pull into the driveway and looked out to see Sean heading into the barn. If he did not join Sean quickly, he would receive a tongue-lashing. Sean took every chance to admonish Bill for being lazy and unworthy of his family and the benefits of the farm.

Bill pulled on his boots and jacket and was heading to the door just as the phone rang. He grabbed the receiver before the second ring.

"Hello? O'Briens," he nearly yelled into the phone.

"Is this Bill O'Brien?"

"Yes."

"Bill, this is Jack Tucker in the Denver FAA office."

"Yes—did you hear from my family?"

"Bill, they flew off course in the storm and skirted south of Denver. The tower radar tracked them for a brief time last night but then lost the signal. We spent the night checking small airports in the area for any possible landings. At first light, we sent up a search aircraft and found the plane clinging to a mountainside." There was a pause. "I'm sorry, son. There were no survivors. They were killed on impact."

Bill dropped the phone back on its carrier and fell to his knees. A low wail started deep within him and finally released like a siren.

"What is all this ruckus about?" Sean growled as he came bursting in.

Bill told him through his sobs. Sean grabbed the phone and called Helene's cousin Rudolph.

"Just get over here and handle things. I got morning chores to do, and he won't be much help."

Rudolph arrived in less than an hour. He rushed into the house and found Bill still sitting on the floor in a daze. The morning news was still droning away on the television. Rudolph turned off the TV, then tenderly reached down and put his hand on Bill's shoulder. He knelt beside him to recite the Lord's Prayer for the lost family.

Rudolph called Gene and told him what had happened. "Bill won't be showing up for work today," he explained. "In fact, he may not be in for a few more days. He's the man of the house now, and there are things that need taking care of."

Gene was nearly speechless. "You tell him to take all the time he needs," he finally said. "And let me know if I can do anything. Thank God you're there to help him out."

Rudolph helped Sean with the chores and sent him on his way. A lot of details needed to be handled to recover and return the bodies to Minneapolis for a proper burial. A representative at the Denver FAA called and agreed to contact the funeral home and make arrangements for transport and transfer of the family's remains. He also gave Rudolph the number for General Fredrick Schwartz, who owned the private strip Michael and Helene were scheduled to visit.

"I guess I'll start a family graveyard on the farm," Bill told Rudolph as they walked to the car. "There's a stand of pines on the hill that forms a nice windbreak. I can add a white picket fence and some flowers around the outside. It will look nice from the house."

Bill stopped beside the car and swallowed the lump forming in his throat.

Rudolph took Bill to the local funeral home. Bill was glad Rudolph was there for support. He wavered between wanting to just run away and wanting to take control of his life and the farm and make the best of what life had dealt him.

When they arrived back at the farm, Rudolph called the general, who offered to recover and store the wreckage in his hangar. Reports said the plane might be reparable, if Bill had an interest.

"Michael and Helene were good friends," General Schwartz added. "If there is anything else Bill needs, please let me know."

Rudolph agreed to the general's offer. It was comforting to know Michael and Helene had a far-reaching circle of friends willing to help Bill.

"I guess I'll have to quit my job and take over the farm full-time," Bill said. "Dad's got some good, dependable staff on at the freight company. At least I won't have to worry about that for a while."

"Bill, take your time," advised Rudolph. "I'll help you with anything you need."

They heard a car door slam. Sean walked into the kitchen as though he owned the place and poured himself a cup of coffee. He apparently had something to discuss. He poured another cup of coffee and handed it to Bill.

"William, we need to talk in the office."

He ignored Rudolph, turned, and walked to the small office off the kitchen. Sean waited for Bill to follow, then closed the door on Rudolph.

"You need to know that a few years ago, when your dad's business started doing really well, your dad and mom decided they needed to name a guardian for you kids in case anything happened. Well, they asked me, and I said yes. I said I would do anything I could to help the family. I've got the paperwork back home that gives me power of attorney for the business, the farm, and the family finances as well as guardianship of you kids until you're eighteen."

Bill listened carefully to this revelation. Slowly he realized that Sean was taking over everything. Bill was not the "man of the house." He was back to being a seventeen-year-old farm kid without a future. He would not control the farm nor the family business.

Sean also explained that while Rudolph and Bill were talking to the mortician, he had contacted the O'Briens' minister and made funeral arrangements at the local church.

"But I was thinking we could bury them here on the farm—"

"No," Sean interrupted. "We'll bury them proper in the church cemetery, even though it's a Lutheran cemetery."

Bill turned and looked out the window toward the stand of pines he had envisioned as the family gravesite. He realized Sean was controlling everything. Bill couldn't even decide the burial of his family.

The next week was a blur for Bill. He did morning chores but could not face going to work for the surveying company. The thought of working at the airport and seeing the planes come and go as they pleased brought him a new rush of dread. He had always wanted his dad to teach him how to fly so he could follow his footsteps into the air force and maybe have an aeronautical career. That was the last thing on his mind now.

The family funeral was conducted at Hope Lutheran Church, where Michael and Helene were regular members. The four sealed caskets were lined up like dominoes. Pastor Erick Johanson prattled on and on about how they had gone ahead to prepare the way for everyone to follow . . . they were not dead, merely sleeping . . . they would rise again. The hymns didn't offer Bill much comfort either. In fact, Bill twitched as he endured the congregation's off-key droning, punctuated by Sean loudly finding an occasional note.

Hundreds of people attended. Some were from the nearby community, perhaps mostly interested in the spectacle of the tragedy. Many employees of M. O. Airfreight arrived and sat together near the back of the large sanctuary. There was even a representative from the Ford Motor Company in Detroit.

Rudolph sat on one side of Bill. Gene was on his other. They were the only comforting sources in the whole chapel. The rest of the attendees were a blur to Bill. He counted the number of pieces in the stained-glass windows to keep himself from jumping up and running, screaming, from the service.

The burials were done according to Sean's instruction. A single headstone would be erected in the next month, marking the end of Bill's family. An air force honor guard presented the American flag. Surprisingly, Sean deferred the honor of accepting the flag to Bill.

In the following weeks, Sean locked up the family bank account, transferred the farm into his name, and filed papers to make himself the new president of M. O. Airfreight.

Rudolph approached Sean on several occasions to offer assistance and act as a bridge between Bill and Sean. On each occasion, he was rebuffed. Sean was clear that Rudolph should not interfere with the business or with anything else regarding the guardianship of Bill.

"This is family business, and you stay out of it!" Sean replied.

Despite Sean's attitude, Rudolph vowed to look after Bill the best he could. He quietly monitored how Sean was conducting his responsibilities.

Though still stunned, Bill needed to return to work. He asked Gene if there was another assignment that would take him away from the airport. Gene was more than understanding. He found a position on a crew working to improve a ramp to Interstate 35W connecting Minneapolis and Saint Paul with Duluth to the north. Although Bill was working and saving money for his college education, the work was repetitive and not very interesting. Very little seemed interesting to Bill now.

4.

ARRIVING BACK AT THE FARM ONE EVENING after work, Bill saw a strange pickup in the driveway. When he walked into the kitchen, he found Sean and another man sitting at the table sipping coffee and telling stories.

Sean looked up. "Pull up a seat here, Bill. I want you to meet Jesse Morgan. He's a real estate man from Saint Paul. He's going to help with the sale of the farm."

Bill stood by the chair in stunned silence. "He's going to help with *what?*"

"I'm selling the farm. There's too much to do between the farm and the business, and you can't be staying here alone. And what will happen when you go to college? We can't hang on to this. Besides, Jesse thinks I can get a good price for it in the current market."

Bill bristled at Sean's cold, harsh decision. It ripped away the last remnants of Bill's hold on his family memories.

"You can't sell my home! I was raised here. My mom and dad built a life for our family here. I'll quit the surveying job and take on the farm full-time for the rest of the summer. I can drop out of school and farm for a living. I don't want to lose this."

"Son, we must do this for several reasons," Sean assured him. "Besides, the paperwork is done, and the signs go up tomorrow."

Bill bristled again. He felt rage building in his chest as he looked at the smug little man his father had entrusted with his family.

Bill glared at Sean in anger. "Don't you ever call me 'son' again! I am not your son and never will be."

Sean stood up quickly, knocking over his chair. "Don't use that tone with me, William," he lectured. "I need to sell the farm to pay for the funeral expenses, the mortgage on the farm, and some debts M. O. Airfreight has accumulated recently. You don't understand the business world. There will probably be some money left to add to your college fund. I'm trying to do the best I can for you, but there are expenses that need to be paid. I take seriously my pledge to your parents to do what I can for you."

Bill said nothing further to his uncle. School would start in a few short weeks, and then in just five months, he would turn eighteen and be free of this "guardianship." Whatever his father had seen in Sean to trust giving him control of the business and family was hard for Bill to understand in light of these decisions. Bill could hardly stand to be in the same room with his uncle. All his remaining joys were being destroyed just as completely as his family.

Bill would never again consider Sean as family.

As fall approached, Bill prepared to start his senior year in high school. Sean met Bill in the barn while he was finishing the milking one evening.

"The farm sold, Bill," Sean explained. "It closes next month, and you'll have to move out by then. You're welcome to come live with me at the apartment."

Bill cringed. "I'll find my own place, you son of a bitch."

Sean shrugged, knowing it may be best to not further antagonize Bill. "Your mom's cousin Rudolph said he had plenty of room on his hobby farm too. You just need to decide."

Bill did not hesitate. "I'll live with Rudolph."

"That's fine with me, William. I'll set up a bank account you can use to pay Rudolph for your expenses. I'll deposit some money in that account each month, if there's any profit on the business."

Bill felt sure there would be an abrupt end to the funding if money got tight. In fact, Bill broached the subject with Rudolph one night over dinner a few weeks later.

"I'm sure you're aware that M. O. Airfreight is not doing well under Sean," Bill began.

Rudolph nodded knowingly. "Yeah. I've heard rumors."

"I guess what I'm trying to say is, I think Sean is siphoning off funds for his own use. I can't help but think he'll file bankruptcy someday soon, and that will be the end of my funding. I won't be able to pay you for my expenses, let alone pay for my education."

Rudolph poured another cup of coffee for each of them, then sat back with a fatherly look. "Bill, I took you in as family," replied Rudolph. "And as family, you are welcome here anytime—I do not need compensation. Actually, the money you have been paying me has found its way into a schooling account for you."

Surprised, Bill stared at Rudolph. "I don't understand."

Rudolph smiled and put his hand gently on Bill's shoulder. "You are family," he repeated. "Plus, I enjoy having you here. Since my daughter, Jessica, headed off to college three years ago, the house has been a bit empty. I will help you find a job and help you with your university education, if that is what you want to do." He beamed at Bill. "Your mother and father were prouder of you than you will ever know."

But then Rudolph's warm smile hardened a bit.

"If Sean is mismanaging the money, his fortunes will come to an end," he said. "What goes around comes around. That will be the end of it for him, but not for you. I have been monitoring—and will continue to monitor—both the airfreight business and the probate court proceedings to ensure you are not being cheated. So far it looks like Sean has not been dishonest—he just hasn't made very good business decisions. He was never that bright. He looks to be in over his head. He works hard but always seems to come up short. Fortunately, the other people at the business are doing all they can to offset his shortcomings. He's not an easy man to work for, but many of the employees were very loyal to your father. They're hanging on to help protect the company for you. I'll try to stay in touch with the guys there and see what I can do to help. Who knows—maybe Sean will end up selling it cheap, and you can move in on him."

Bill leaned forward, stared at his coffee cup on the table, and vowed to redouble his efforts to help Rudolph in any way he could. He would pay him back in some way for his kindness.

Bill worked hard in school during his senior year. He excelled in math and science and even started to enjoy English to a small degree. He also continued taking German. Bill practiced with Rudolph whenever he got the chance, but he could not find the joy he had experienced when he bantered with his mother.

Rudolph had been a wrestler, and he encouraged Bill to try out for the sport. Because Bill had been working on the farm all his life, he had good upper-body strength and balance. Now, he just needed a coach to help him with his technique. After weeks of intensive training and workouts, Bill made the team. Rudolph kept him on a strict diet to help him maintain his weight and build his strength.

The sacrifices paid off. Bill competed as a middleweight in the district tournament. Although he placed only third, Bill was proud of the accomplishment and proud to be part of a team. He was pretty sure his father would have been proud too.

During the first heavy snowfall of the season, Bill came home to find a letter waiting on his bed. He saw the return address: University of Minnesota. His heart skipped a beat. He held the unopened letter to his chest, willing it to be good news.

"Open it, you dope," Rudolph admonished him from the doorway.

Bill jumped at the sound of Rudolph's voice, then grinned and tore the envelope open. He had been accepted to the University of Minnesota and would be in the freshman class of 1963.

Several of Bill's classmates had also received acceptance letters from the university. They would all start together in the fall. Each of them had different dreams and aspirations. At least Bill would have a support network when he started the next chapter of his life.

Still, Bill knew he would always have a void in his heart, a void only his true family could fill. The darkness of losing his loving mother, hard-working father, bothersome brother, and bratty sister made him feel vulnerable. He had learned much from his parents. He had loved flying with his father. He had learned to relish his German heritage with his mother. She also taught him to treat others—such as his brother and sister—with patience and understanding. He realized how lucky he had been to have them all in his life, even for a brief time.

As the bright-eyed freshman lined up for class registration, a poster caught his eye. Another uncle, this time Uncle Sam, had plans for him. He pointed out, "America Needs You to Volunteer and Do Your Military Duty." Draft calls for military service were increasing. Bill knew he had little chance of dodging the call, seeing as he had no one to support him at his local draft board. Besides, he did not want to shirk his responsibility. He thought of the few times his father had proudly shared his service stories. He was determined to honor his family.

Plus, if he served his time in the military, they would pay his college debt. It seemed like a good deal. Bill still received a meager payout from the trust fund Sean established, but that money was coming to an end. Sean said the sale of the farm had not netted what he had hoped. The business was still active but not thriving as it had been with Michael at the helm.

Bill decided to join the ROTC program and serve as an officer instead of just an enlisted grunt. At least being an officer would provide some advantages in leadership, education, and job opportunities after his tour of duty. The big decision was choosing which branch. He still could not work up an interest in flying, so the air force was off the table. The navy ROTC program was full, so he signed up for the army ROTC.

Bill enjoyed his time at the university. He lived in the Pioneer Hall dormitory with his high school friends. They all complained about the dorm food, although they ate everything in sight. They tried to date girls in nearby dorms but were mostly unsuccessful.

He was also involved in a number of intramural activities. Bill tried his hand at boxing, karate, basketball, and even dancing. Although he was never particularly great at any of them, the activities kept his mind sharp and his body fit.

Before his second year, he declared a double major in geography and business. He felt good about his job prospects once he completed his service with the army. He enjoyed the two ROTC summer camps he attended—yet he knew that Vietnam cast a bigger shadow over that future than when he had entered the ROTC program.

Bill's friends helped him enjoy the carefree life on campus. He was finally starting to move away from the despair of all he had lost. He even met Barbara, a beautiful girl, at an off-campus dance. She was warm, kind, and caring. In addition, she was very attractive.

In 1967, Bill graduated as a second lieutenant in the United States Army. The buildup in Vietnam had exploded in the last two years. His friends were being drafted—or were trying to dodge the draft with college deferments.

Bill was given the choice of army specialties: infantry, artillery, or engineering. Infantry would be hard hand-to-hand jungle warfare. No thanks. Engineering required more education than he had taken. Artillery seemed the obvious choice. He was looking forward to using his college skills.

After the graduation ceremony, there was a class picnic at Minnehaha Park in south Minneapolis. His friends and their relatives were gathered around the grill. His "girl," Barbara, was there, looking great as usual. The sun glinted off her blond hair and flashed deeply in her amber eyes. She had a sense of humor that kept Bill smiling from ear to ear as he munched a hot dog and dreamed of their future.

They had been dating off and on for two years. He was truly smitten. Barbara had also just graduated from the university with a degree in social work. She was openly apprehensive about his involvement in the military and the probability of a tour in Vietnam, but he thought they could work through these issues.

Bill and Barbara briefly stepped away from the party hand in hand. They spoke in the quiet affection only young lovers seem to speak.

"Barb, you know I love you, don't you?" Bill asked, thinking he knew the answer.

"Yes. I've known for some time. And I do like you a lot. You know I'm not seeing anyone else right now." Barbara stared off at the water cascading over the falls and pursed her lips. "But there's so much unknown right now. You have a three-year military commitment. The Vietnam situation is only getting worse. You'll probably have to go. I just don't know how we can overcome all that."

"If we really care about each other, it will be fine," he responded. "Others have gone through this too and are working it out."

They left the issue unresolved, kissed, and made their way back to the party.

Bill had until September before he had to report to Fort Sill, Oklahoma, for artillery school training. He wanted to spend much of this time with Barbara planning for their life after the military—or maybe during the military. He wouldn't mind being a married officer.

But Barbara surprised him with other plans. During a dinner date a week after graduation, she made a fateful announcement.

"Bill, my parents have agreed to pay for an extended trip to Europe for me. I'm leaving next week with a girlfriend. It will give both you and me some time to think about our future."

There was very little Bill could say other than to wish her a great trip. He lost his appetite. The rest of the date consisted of small talk about friends and current events.

As Bill drove home, the night felt much colder than normal for late summer. Deep down, he knew this could be the end of the relationship. Here was another person he had lost. It brought back much of the gloom from five years before. The drive back to his apartment was slow and dark.

Bill had met Barbara's parents on several occasions and had freely discussed his military plans when they asked. At the time, he thought they understood how much he cared for their daughter. Now he knew they were using this trip to keep their daughter from making what they considered a mistake with him. That made him even more resigned. He didn't know if there was any way to fight this decision. He didn't know for sure whether he wanted to fight it. But he did know the relationship was slipping through his fingers like sand.

It was a particularly lonely summer with Barbara in Europe. She returned a week before Bill had to leave for Fort Sill. Bill took her out to dinner. She looked even more stunning than usual, but she also seemed more distant and less affectionate.

Bill had arranged for a lovely dinner at the Flame Room in downtown Minneapolis. On the drive to the restaurant, he tried to engage Barbara in conversation. Her responses were curt. Finally, he just asked her about her trip.

"It went well," she said. "I'm glad I was able to go. I met some wonderful new people, both Europeans and fellow Americans." She looked out the window. "I'll fill you in more at dinner."

They were seated promptly at a romantic corner table. The roving violinists came by and asked for any favorites the couple would like to hear. Bill suggested they come back in a few minutes, to allow them time to talk.

"Barb, why don't you tell me what's bothering you?"

Barb turned to watch the violinists as they walked away. She sipped her water. "All right, Bill. While I was in Europe, I had a lot of time to think about our relationship. I had a chance to meet new people, and they opened my eyes to so many things. I'm not the same person you knew before."

A waiter came by their table. Bill ordered a bottle of wine as Barbara stared out the window at the lights of the city. When the wine was served, she picked up her glass and held it gently in both hands.

"The people I met are so totally against the war in Vietnam. I really question what we are doing there. I'm concerned about what you might have to do there."

Bill took a sip of his wine, then started to respond. Barbara raised her left hand to stop him.

"I met an American businessman in France. His name is Robert. I honestly don't know if there's a real relationship there. But I want you to know I'm going to California next month to visit him and see if he feels the same way I do."

Bill now saw the reason for Barbara's change in attitude. She was a "man magnet." She could literally have her pick when it came to men.

"I still have feelings for you," she said, "but I need time to sort out these conflicts."

Bill knew he would likely compete with men of wealth, connections, and security throughout his life. He had none of those to offer. He did not kid himself on his future chances with Barbara, but at least she said she was still thinking things through. He wasn't totally out of the picture. Some chance was better than no chance.

Better to change the subject.

The rest of the evening passed with small talk. The roving violinists never returned—a fitting comment on the evening. Bill paid the bill and drove Barbara home.

5.

I T WAS RAINING THE MORNING BILL RODE THE BUS to the airport for his flight to Oklahoma City. The bus arrived an hour before takeoff, which allowed Bill time to purchase a magazine and some snacks. The flight was on schedule.

Shortly after takeoff, the aircraft banked into a haze of white. The small window by his seat streaked with windblown rain, and the world was rendered invisible. He was enveloped in that same invisibility. He felt the first pangs of apprehension. The cloud bank stretched through Nebraska and Oklahoma, parting only briefly as they started the descent.

After they landed in Oklahoma City, Bill boarded a bus for Fort Sill. The feeling of anonymity remained. He was about to become a very small cog on a very large wheel.

Fort Sill had a history as an old US Cavalry post. Many Apaches were imprisoned at the fort near the end of the nineteenth century. The post was in the middle of nowhere. The fort buildings and open fields stretched as far as the eye could see.

I guess you need a lot of room to fire cannons, Bill mused.

Bill was assigned to a room in officers' quarters. His roommate was Lieutenant Dale Patterson.

"Dale, where do you call home?" Bill asked.

"Born and raised in Lansing, Michigan, and proud of it."

Dale was a recent graduate of the University of Michigan. He was a history buff and loved the outdoors. In Michigan, he had spent many summers guiding fishing trips in the Upper Peninsula and on Lake Superior and Lake Michigan. He said he enjoyed his family's camp in the Huron Mountains.

"What's a 'camp'?" Bill asked.

"You Minnesotans would call it a 'cabin.' But we like to enjoy more than just the physical building. Our camp has a distant view of Lake Superior, but it's right on a great trout stream."

Bill had seen Lake Superior from Duluth during one of his forays to northern Minnesota. He remembered it as the only body of water classified as a "lake" that didn't seem to have an opposite shoreline. It was like a small ocean.

The Field Artillery Officer Basic Course was a refresher on subjects they had taken in their university ROTC classes, but it was also a concentrated focus on artillery procedures. It was meant to teach them how to behave like officers in the artillery. The instruction centered on the use of artillery, including laying of the gun (setting up the artillery piece to shoot), map reading and plotting, calling in artillery as a forward observer, and, of course, familiarization with various weapons. Together Bill and Dale worked with a wide variety of guns and howitzers. They trained on 105mm howitzers, 155mm self-propelled howitzers, 175mm guns, and 8-inch howitzers.

In addition, there was daily physical training (PT) that included running, completing an obstacle course, and marching. They also got some experience directing enlisted personnel going through artillery training.

The roommates became fast friends and enjoyed challenging each other at every turn: Who could put in the best time on the obstacle course? Who could do the most push-ups during PT? Bill seemed to have the edge physically because of his wrestling, karate, and boxing training. However, Dale often bested Bill on the artillery fire drills. Dale seemed to have a natural gift for quick and accurate calculations. This only made Bill work harder on his technique.

Occasionally, they were given off-base passes to neighboring Lawton. Lawton was a small army town with all the temptations of wine, women, and song. Dale and Bill tended to avoid the women and song but saw plenty of the wine. They spent many nights in the Impact Zone, an area of town with many bars. Bill and Dale just shook their heads and laughed when they found out why it was called the Impact Zone. It was rumored that a confused second lieutenant had dialed in the wrong firing coordinates during training and blasted the area. Everybody claimed they knew who did it, but no one ever named names.

The initial training lasted twelve weeks. Bill, Dale, and the other trainees would then be allowed leave for Christmas and New Year's. They would be due back to Fort Sill in early February 1968. At that time, they would be given their post-training assignments. It was now pretty clear where they would be going, but at least they would have some time to visit friends and enjoy themselves first.

A few days before leave, Bill stopped to look across the grounds at the setting sun as he walked back to the barracks after a five-mile run. "Dale, where are you headed to?"

"I'm going to Lansing to snowmobile and cross-country ski. I expect it'll be the last time I'll enjoy cold for a long time." Dale wiped his sweating face on his sleeve. "Where are you going?"

"I want to see what's up with my friends back in Minneapolis and see if there's any hope with my girl, Barbara."

Bill was truly looking forward to catching up with his college friends. He hoped Barbara would also be home for the holidays. He had received only one letter from her since he had been at Fort Sill, but there was always hope.

Back in Minnesota, a fresh layer of snow had fallen. The streets were plowed, but everything was so white, bright, and pristine. That was what he was missing in Oklahoma—just snow. In Oklahoma, they had ice storms. The hazardous conditions caused fully loaded military trucks towing howitzers to slide off the roads.

He also missed the bright colors of home. In Oklahoma, the fields were brown, uniforms were olive green, buildings were either tan or gray. It was nearly a monochromatic landscape. Even Christmas decorations didn't help. Holiday lights didn't look right on dirt and grass. There was something about the holidays that just screamed for bright lights against white snow.

Much had changed for Bill's college friends since he left. Eugene had gotten a great job right out of college and was planning on getting married in the spring. Dennis was entering a seminary to become a minister and was marrying his long-time sweetheart. Another friend had married before graduation, and they were now expecting their first child.

Bill was proud of his own achievements but also jealous of the normal, pleasant lives his friends were already building. He felt he had to start his life over. He simply hoped to *have* a future after his time in the army.

Gary's changes were different. He was the only one of Bill's classmates walking the same path Bill was now on. Gary was already in Vietnam with the air force. He had dropped out of the university in their sophomore year and was in his fourth year of a six-year enlistment. Bill hoped he was safe. He hoped they both would be safe and he would be able to greet Gary when he returned.

Barbara was back in Minneapolis briefly to see her family for the holidays. Bill met her for dinner at a local restaurant.

"It's been a few months since we've last talked," Bill started. "I got only that one brief letter from you while I was in training. How have you been?"

Barbara sat back in her chair and met his eyes with a steely stare. "I'm still sorting things out, but I know I'm totally against the war. I'm active in the antiwar protests in California."

Barbara paused and looked at Bill. When he didn't respond, she continued.

"I can't support the war or those fighting in it! I'm sorry."

Bill finally took a deep breath and looked into her eyes. He had changed too since his college days only a few months ago.

"I'm so sorry to hear you feel that way. But many of the men and women going to Vietnam have little choice. In most cases, they either go to fight, or they go to jail. Some of us do choose to serve our country. I hope to help more of those men and women return to their homes and families safely. I don't support war, but I made a commitment, and I need to fulfill that commitment."

Bill licked his lips and continued. "I hope you're successful in helping stop the war, but I don't have a choice except to serve. I expect to be sent overseas as soon as I return to Fort Sill. Please keep an open mind and an open heart to all of us over there. We'll need it." He paused. "By the way, I still love you, whatever you choose to do."

"I'll try to keep a prayer for you," said Barbara, looking down at her hands wringing the napkin in her lap. "But I am so against the war that it's hard to condone what you're doing. I'm also still trying to resolve my relationship with Robert. He's asked me to marry him, but I'm not sure it would work out."

Although he and Barbara had dated exclusively for two years, Bill realized they had never really known how different they were from each other. They had never talked about the really big issues in life. They had been like children, without a need to make hard choices or ask hard questions.

Back then, he was a kid without a family, working his way through college and trying to stay ahead of the military draft. Now, at best, he was looking like cannon fodder for Vietnam. He had certainly matured, but what else did he have to offer her?

Barbara was the daughter of a wealthy business executive who provided her with everything she needed. Apparently, she wanted, needed, and was influenced and impressed by someone who could provide immediate financial support and emotional attention. She was fickle and impressionable. She had not been required to make or live with any hard decisions. Now she was floundering.

Barbara had many admirable features. She was beautiful, kind, and intelligent. She had that wonderful soft sense of humor. Bill would miss all that. He still loved her. However, he now realized he wasn't really losing her, because he had never really known her. He had only his memories of what she had meant to him. He wondered if anyone else would brighten up his life as much as she had for the time they were together.

Bill paid for the dinner, and they left without exchanging another word.

At Fort Sill, the news from Saigon was no better. The Tet Offensive was in full swing. The country seemed overrun by Vietcong and North Vietnamese troops. Fighting was spreading everywhere. Even the American embassy was being attacked. American casualties were high, with reports of several thousand dead and wounded. This was a military and political disaster.

Based on this news, Bill was not surprised when his orders came through for Vietnam. He and others left Fort Sill by bus, then flew out of Oklahoma City. Bill wondered how many would make the return flight.

6.

THE MILITARY TRANSPORT LANDED AT Travis Air Force Base, near San Francisco. They were bused over to the Oakland Army Base, where they each received basic jungle gear along with an M16 and ammunition. It seemed as though they were preparing to fight as soon as they got off the plane in Vietnam. They spent two days getting a host of nasty and painful injections and sorting all their gear. They then departed from Travis.

They landed in Hawaii for refueling. There was no time for touring. Bill saw the inviting waves crashing on the pristine beaches and promised himself, *Someday I'm going to swim in that ocean!*

A quick stop was made on Wake Island, a tiny aircraft carrier island in the middle of nowhere. It was the scene of a battle the United States lost to Japan in the early days of World War II. Perhaps that was an omen of things to come. The aircraft refueled for the final leg of the flight into Tan Son Nhut Air Base near Saigon, South Vietnam.

Bill was amazed by the strange view out the window as the plane banked on its final approach. The landscape looked like a *National Geographic* television special. Houses built of bamboo with thatch roofs sat perched on stilts. Rice paddies spread for miles, their surfaces rippling. Palm trees waved serenely in the tropical breezes.

It doesn't look so bad, thought Bill hopefully.

The stewardess opened the door and waited for the stairs to be driven to the edge of the plane. Bill felt the oppressive heat creep into the cabin like a hot, steamy wool blanket. As the soldiers slowly inched down the aisle to the exit doors, with the officers in the lead, Bill saw the sad eyes of the stewardess. She didn't welcome them to this destination or tell them to have a good day. She just said, "Be safe and return to us."

As Bill stepped onto the aircraft's staircase, the air was like acid with the smell from the barrels of burning feces near the end of the runway. This was the preferred way to eliminate human waste. That smell mixed readily with diesel fumes from idling vehicles and the exhaust of burned kerosene from aircraft. Bill instinctively covered his nose and mouth with his hand.

A line of troops queued up, waiting to board the same plane Bill and the others were exiting. The outgoing flight was the "Freedom Bird," heading for the United States. That flight was the dream of every soldier in Vietnam when his tour of duty was completed.

The departing troops displayed a contrast Bill would later understand. Some soldiers wore wrinkled green uniforms with scuffed boots; others were in clean, pressed uniforms with spit-shined boots. Some had pale complexions; others were heavily sunburned with bleached hair. Bill would learn to recognize these differences between combat troops and rear echelon troops.

Many of the men with the faded and wrinkled uniforms slumped and looked furtively around the airport perimeter. They reminded Bill of chickens when a hawk was flying lazy circles overhead. The hollow, foreboding look on their faces would remain with him for a long time—even after leaving Vietnam.

Bill followed the arriving group to the supply depot. The clock on the wall declared it was 1630.

Hmm, four thirty in the afternoon. I wonder what time it is in Minneapolis right now. He had already started to lose touch. *It's a different world. Hell, it's a different planet*, he thought.

The depot provided the incoming troops with the rest of their field gear: helmets, ammo belts, and pistols. Once they had collected their rifles and ammunition as well as their provisions to add to their personal duffel bags, they were herded into a bus with armor on the side windows. The armor was needed to protect against hand grenades being tossed through the bus windows. This was Bill's introduction into a war without a front line.

After a short bus ride, they arrived at the Long Binh army base near Saigon. There they went to the replacement depot (repo-depo), where they stood in line for their in-country assignments. Bill learned he would be rerouted to another repo-depo at Cam Ranh Bay for his assignment in the Central Highlands area. That transport would occur the next morning. He would receive some replacement training there as well. For now, he was directed to the officers' barracks.

The bunk beds in the barracks were placed only three feet apart. It was a sea of metal dotted with rolled-up mattresses. One green metal trunk was positioned in the gap at the head of each bed, and one was set at the end.

Orders were barked from an anonymous body: "First come, first serve. Secure your gear in your trunk. Make your bed. Dinner will be at the mess in thirty minutes. Follow the line on the floor to the mess area. You will have one hour to eat, then you must return to your quarters. Lights are out at twenty-one hundred. Welcome to Vietnam, gentlemen!"

The next morning, Bill flew to the repo-depo at Cam Ranh Bay. There he spent some days adjusting to the climate of Vietnam—including two days of rampant diarrhea. He also received more focused instruction on the military chain of command in Vietnam, tips on firing and caring for his M16 rifle in a jungle environment, a review of air-ground support techniques, a Geneva Conventions refresher, and an overview of mines and booby traps, base camp security, and unit patrolling methods. At the end of his training, he was assigned to the Third Battalion of the Twelfth Artillery of the I Field Force in Pleiku.

The flight the next day was in a twin-engine transport called a Caribou. It was specially designed for short takeoffs and landings to accommodate the runways all over Vietnam, or in-country, as it was known.

They landed at Pleiku, the headquarters of his unit in the Central Highlands of Vietnam. The airfield and base had survived a major attack the night before. Numerous shell holes surrounded the airstrip, and several buildings were still smoldering. The signs of destruction were unsettling as they came in over the countryside. Unfortunately, that was to become the new normal for these soldiers.

The officers were ushered to the office of the battalion colonel. He welcomed them, then handed out their assignments. Bill was told to report ASAP to the battery stationed at Firebase Thunder, an old French army base. Bill was flown to the small base by helicopter. Normally, transport would have been by truck convoy, but the convoys had been attacked on a regular basis in the past few weeks.

The firebase was about forty kilometers southwest of Pleiku. This was a heavy artillery battery with four guns. The 175mm guns and 8-inch howitzers were capable of launching a 150-to-200-pound shell nearly twenty miles with fairly good accuracy. In addition, they had a mortar and two quad-.50 caliber machine gun trucks for perimeter defense. There were 150 men on the firebase. Bill would be the third officer.

Bill met with Captain Charles Smith, the battery commander. Smith was on the last two months of his tour. Bill had been assigned as a forward artillery observer to work with American and ARVN infantry in the area. ARVN, or the Army of the Republic of Vietnam, were the South Vietnamese, the "good guys." The forward observer's job was to call in supporting artillery fire from the battery when needed. He would go where the infantry went. In other words, Bill ended up in the infantry after all.

So much for my careful consideration in joining the army artillery, Bill thought. *I should have joined the navy to see the world.*

Apparently, many second lieutenants in the artillery spent the first six months of their tour in the field and the rest of the time—if there was any—at the firebase. Bill was to leave the next day on an operation with the South Vietnamese unit. Specialist Paul Duncan—an enlisted radio operator, or RTO—would assist him and familiarize him with the maps of the area and codes for the radio.

Bill did not sleep well that night. The rustling and scratching of rats running around the compound didn't help. He learned that the mosquito netting around his bunk was more useful in keeping rats from running over him than it was in keeping mosquitoes out.

The next day at dawn, the troops boarded helicopters for an airlift about ten kilometers from the firebase. Before they left, Bill met Captain Vehn of the ARVN unit. Bill was told to stay close to the captain during the mission.

The temperature held in the low hundreds, and the humidity seemed to drip out of the air. Each soldier, including Bill, carried four canteens of water, ammunition, a rifle, several grenades, and some rations. Bill also had his service pistol, maps, and compass. Duncan carried the backpack radio. As they boarded the Huey helicopters for the airlift, a barking ARVN lieutenant made sure to remind them to keep the rifles pointed downward.

The flight lasted about fifteen minutes. They could see artillery shells slamming into the trees and brush around the landing zone. Although this alarmed Bill at first, he found out this was a precautionary friendly fire bombardment for the landing. As they landed, there was no return fire from the jungle.

They unloaded, formed up, and moved off into the heavy jungle. The vegetation was dense, dark, and still. The smoke from the bombardment was thick, irritating Bill's eyes.

They moved about two kilometers into the jungle with careful steps. They had been trained to look for booby trap mines and trip wires. It was a hard, hot slog for someone like Bill, who was not used to the climate. Bill quickly emptied one of his canteens, pouring some of the water on a kerchief so he could wipe the sweat from his eyes.

Next time, I'll wear a headband, he said to himself.

Although the day was hot, it was uneventful. At dusk, they stopped. Bill called in protective coordinates to the battery. In case they were attacked that night, the firebase could fire quickly on the locations Bill had designated on his field map.

Once the claymore mines were planted around the perimeter, it was time to get some sleep. Bill huddled in his foxhole. He didn't sleep well that night either. The sounds of the jungle, the insects, the heat, and the darkness played tricks on all his senses.

The sky exploded at 1:00 a.m. A hail of mortar shells rained down on the company. Cries and screams echoed in the darkness.

The sound broke Bill out of a light slumber. *Where the hell did that come from?* he thought. Then his training kicked in. His hands shook as he flipped off the safety on his M16. He took a quick breath and checked on Duncan.

"Give me the radio, Duncan." He knew his next job might be to call in the protective firing from the firebase.

Then they heard the sound of a bugle. The chatter of AK-47 assault rifles and rocket-propelled grenades (RPGs) seemed to come from all sides. The ARVN troops returned fire, triggered their claymore mines, and fired flares to illuminate the perimeter.

Bill called in for support from the firebase. Within minutes, the first 200-pound shell landed near the perimeter, right at the first protective coordinate Bill had plotted on his map. Tree branches and body parts began landing everywhere.

Bill was working methodically now. He blocked out his fear and talked the shells closer and closer. A helicopter gunship pivoted overhead. Bill directed the rocket and machine gun fire around the perimeter, getting ever closer to the company.

Suddenly, he saw two figures run out of the jungle toward him. The first was armed with an AK-47; the other carried a satchel charge. They had slipped through the perimeter and were coming directly at Bill and Duncan. No one else seemed to have noticed them.

Bill had never fired at a person before. Could he kill? He knew he had to shoot. He hunkered down in the foxhole next to Duncan and sighted on the figures.

In an instant, he fired half the ammo clip at the first figure. The dark shape flipped over backward. Bill could see the attacker's body parts being ripped off by the impact. Bill knew that rounds from an M16 tumble when they hit flesh—they do terrible damage. The sight of that man coming apart would remain with Bill for a long time.

Bill emptied the remainder of his clip at the second figure. The man stumbled but still pulled the detonator cap on his charge. The explosion detonated less than fifty feet away, knocking both Bill and Duncan into the air and out of their foxholes.

Bill's face was burned and his shirt shredded. His helmet landed several feet away. His ears were ringing. Duncan had taken pieces of debris in the face and was bleeding profusely.

Bill ran his hand over his face and felt for his helmet. *Is that blood or sweat?* he thought. He quickly checked his own body for injury. His ears were ringing and his vision was blurred. He was in shock, and the explosion was only part of the reason. He was painfully aware he had just killed two people.

Bill slowly recovered, then scanned quickly for any other incoming attackers. He saw none. But he did see his rifle ten feet from the foxhole with pieces of shrapnel embedded in the stock. He grabbed the M16 and pulled Duncan back into the foxhole. The M16 was still functional, so Bill loaded another clip. He pulled out his field first aid kit and tried to dress Duncan's wounds as well as he could while calling "Medic!"

Small battles still raged on the outskirts of the perimeter, but the main battle appeared to be over. Bill retrieved the radio gear, which had been blown to the edge of his foxhole. He was surprised that it also appeared nearly undamaged. Bill put his hand on Duncan's chest, leaned back against the dirt wall of the foxhole, and waited for assistance—or another enemy attack.

Dawn arrived slowly and lit an eerie sight. The hot, humid air prompted the slow rise of green and white smoke from the shell craters. The humidity concentrated the sweet smell of rotting vegetation—tropical trees and flowers torn and thrown about by shells—mixed with the residue of burned cordite. It was like a shroud hanging over the dead and living on the battlefield.

The landscape had been upended. Large craters had blown gaps in the jungle surrounded by smoldering trees and brush. There were body parts and gear lying everywhere. It was impossible to distinguish friend from foe.

The ringing in Bill's ears was beginning to soften, but no other sound seemed to take its place. At home, in Minnesota, he enjoyed the sounds of the birds chirping when he awakened at dawn. The lack of noise in the middle of the jungle now just added to the eeriness of the tomblike setting.

The enemy had melted back into the jungle. There were fifty to sixty Vietcong bodies, or parts of bodies, lying within view. Some had attacked alone, some in groups. The scene grew more surreal as Bill saw some of the ARVN troops cutting souvenir patches from the uniforms of the dead enemy soldiers. Some also took the ears from the dead. Enemy soldiers who were wounded too severely to be questioned were executed with a single shot to the head.

Word came that medevac helicopters were inbound to pick up the wounded. The ARVN soldiers were clearing downed trees to make a landing pad. A single medevac helicopter arrived, carrying an ARVN general and two women. The general gingerly jumped out of the helicopter and spoke briefly to Captain Vehn, who reported that the friendly losses—dead and wounded—amounted to only thirty out of two hundred.

"Not bad, Captain. Not bad at all," praised the general with a smile.

He boarded the helicopter and left without taking any wounded. Bill looked on in stunned silence at the general's lack of concern for his own wounded troops.

Other medevac choppers finally arrived, and the transport back to the base hospital began. As Bill boarded a chopper, adrenaline finally caught up with him. He started shaking, and he started to feel the pain from his wounds. His ears were still ringing.

God, will I lose my hearing from this? he thought.

Riding in the helicopter, Bill had a better chance to check himself out. He looked as though he had been put through a shredder, and his left hand was burned. His shirt was charred and torn to pieces. He was lucky. He was still alive—one of the walking wounded.

When they reached the hospital base, Bill was ordered to wait in the medical tent, where a medic directed him to a chair while the staff worked on the more severely wounded. Eventually, the medic returned.

"You've got second-degree burns, sir," the medic said, quickly slathering lotion on Bill's burns. "Those will heal in a couple of days if you continue to use this salve," the medic instructed. "Get a new uniform over there," he ordered, pointing Bill toward the supply office. The medic then rushed on to his next case.

Bill wondered if every day would be like this. He had killed two men with his rifle, helped kill nearly sixty Vietcong soldiers with the artillery, yet helped save the lives of not only himself and Duncan but many ARVN troops.

Damn, he thought. *What a rush.* He was still shaking. He really needed a three-finger shot of Jameson to pull his Irish ass together.

Bill pocketed the salve and checked his face in a mirror. He could see the cuts in his scalp. He ran his fingers through his hair, raking through the particles of grit.

What the hell? Who cares? he thought and shrugged. He wandered toward the supply office but was stopped on his way across the compound by a battalion first sergeant.

"Why are you out of uniform?" the first sergeant demanded.

Bill looked him in the eye. "Sorry about that, First Sergeant, but the laundry people put too much bleach in the wash."

The infuriated first sergeant got right in Bill's face and demanded to know his name and unit.

Bill managed to find and unfurl the small remaining piece of his fatigue blouse with his name and lieutenant rank.

"So, First Sergeant, you can now salute me," Bill snarled.

The first sergeant snapped to attention and responded with a red-faced salute. He wandered off grumbling, "Goddamn snot-nosed officers have no respect for the real army."

Bill had almost reached the supply office depot when he was again challenged, this time by a fellow second lieutenant. This lieutenant was so clean he sparkled. Bill ignored this officer entirely and entered the depot. But the lieutenant followed, still demanding that Bill come to attention and give his name and unit.

Just as he'd done with the first sergeant, Bill looked the second lieutenant straight in the eye.

"I'm a second lieutenant too, and I'm in no mood to screw with you. I've already killed two men today. If you don't get out of my face, I'll gladly make it a three-fer." Bill reached for his side arm to emphasize his point.

The other officer looked at Bill bug-eyed and quickly vacated the scene.

"What's wrong with these people?" Bill growled out loud. "Can't they see the tatters and gunpowder burns? Can't they smell the smoke and jungle mud? Hell, I'm lucky to be alive."

"What's that, sir?" the supply sergeant responded.

"Nothing. I guess I need a new uniform. Got anything other than olive drab?"

"Can't help you there, sir. But I guarantee we have your size and it will be clean."

Bill appreciated the touch of humanity and gratefully traded in all but the tattered name and rank. If he had to operate in this environment, he would obviously need it until it was replaced.

Bill changed into the new uniform, pinned on his tattered name and rank, and found the officers' club. His pinned-on patch just barely got him past the MP at the door. The club was packed with captains, majors, and colonels along with nurses.

It's just like date night in the States, he thought. *Ain't war grand?*

The dark burns on his face and hand did not attract other officers' rebukes, only their stares. A few drinkers mumbled suggestions about improving his appearance as an officer. He realized that in this crowd, he was so far down the military pecking order that he might as well have been a private.

He didn't let his inferiority get the better of him. At least as an officer, he could still stand at the bar and get his three fingers of Jameson instead of the green beer the enlisted men were allowed. He downed the drink in one gulp.

Then he realized he should find food and a bunk before his head was ringing worse than his ears. The officers' mess was serving steak tonight. It was a bit tough and overcooked, but steak nonetheless. He would enjoy this. Who knows—it might be his "last supper."

After his meal, he was directed to the officers' hooch for a bunk with real sheets and a pillow. It was almost a real bed.

Tomorrow he would be ordered back to the battery. Tonight he would sleep. He would write to Rudolph another day—that is, he prayed he would live to see another day so he could send a letter.

At 0600, Bill was rousted out of his first sound sleep in weeks. He had thirty minutes to grab breakfast and hop the resupply chopper back to the firebase. As he settled into his seat, he glanced around at the few other soldiers heading back to the base. Sure enough, they were surrounded by ammunition, food, ice, and beer.

As soon as the chopper landed, Bill reported to Captain Smith. He greeted Bill warmly.

"Nice job for your first time out. To be honest, we were worried for you and Duncan. Why don't you take a couple of days to rest up and get used to the base? We're planning a special mission in a week and will need you ready for that. You come highly recommended by the battalion."

A special mission, huh? Bill thought.

This could hardly be a good thing. He certainly wouldn't be holding a general's briefcase.

He sauntered off to make the most of his time. As Bill wandered around the firebase, he talked with the enlisted members of the gun crews. It was an eye-opening venture.

Bill learned there was no saluting outside of buildings on a firebase. Being on the front lines, they didn't want salutes to identify the officers to a watching sniper. Formal gatherings were also avoided. Keeping the troops spread thin would prevent a large kill if a lucky enemy shell landed inside the base perimeter.

The men working at the firebase were generally young. Bill estimated them at nineteen or less. He scoffed at first. But then he realized he really wasn't that much older at twenty-one. The men were friendly but guarded and mostly dismissive of officers. They did their job well in this hot, dusty, yet damp environment.

Each of the artillery pieces had a gunnery sergeant, usually an E-5, or buck sergeant. The buck sergeant recognized the visible burns on Bill's face and hand.

"I see you were on the receiving end of at least one of our payloads."

"No, a Victor Charles almost got me with a satchel charge," Bill said with a slight grin, using the military code for VC, or Vietcong. "But I really appreciated your accuracy on my protective coordinates the other night. You saved all our asses."

Bill stopped in to the fire direction center (FDC) to get a better feeling for the group he would be working with. He thanked the officer in charge for the accuracy of the supporting fire.

Most of the radio operators in the FDC had at least a few years of college under their belts. They were a bright group. They had to be—their plotting and range information meant life or death to the troops in the field. Their radios allowed them to monitor several separate units. One of the radio operators told Bill they could even hear radios in Korea if the atmosphere was just right. The FDC team's professional nature encouraged Bill. He knew if he needed them again they would be there to help.

"Tell me about the forward observers," Bill asked the FDC officer.

"The short answer is, they are in high demand, sort of like the helicopter door gunners," replied the officer. "Both positions tend to be short lived, if you get my drift."

Bill nodded knowingly. *Heard that before*, he thought. He once again wished he had joined the navy.

A week later, a helicopter arrived with a colonel from the Fourth Infantry Division. Bill was summoned to a meeting with the colonel and the battery commander. As Bill arrived, he saluted, seeing as they were inside a building.

The colonel returned the salute with some reluctance. His clean and pressed uniform was a marked contrast to Bill's "jungle casual" look. He looked Bill over with some disdain but held his tongue.

"O'Brien," the colonel said, breaking the silence, "you will be assigned as forward observer on our next recon-in-force mission. We're taking a company from the Fourth Division into the area north of Pleiku and south and east of Kontum. Intelligence indicates that the Vietcong are moving from Cambodia for an attack on Kontum. This attack will be stopped at all cost."

The colonel continued. "You and your RTO will come back with me to Pleiku today. You will meet up with elements of the company in Pleiku for liftoff tomorrow morning at zero six hundred hours."

"Sir, my RTO was wounded. I will need another one assigned."

"Okay. We'll get a replacement from the company. Any other issues?"

"No, sir."

"Okay then, Lieutenant—get your gear. We leave in ten minutes."

"Yes, sir."

Bill snapped a quick salute, then dashed back to his quarters. He gathered his rifle, ammunition, and other gear; slammed his helmet on his head; and joined the colonel on the helipad.

All he could think was, *Why me? Well, at least I should be able to get a decent meal and a drink before the big show tomorrow.*

7.

A FTER A COUPLE OF DOUBLE SHOTS OF JAMESON, Bill spent another night at the base near Pleiku. In the morning, he found elements of the company gathering for the airlift to the landing zone (LZ). The flight was longer than his first lift with the ARVN troops. These were all American troops. Most were younger than he was. The group was nearly a fifty-fifty mix of black and Caucasian, all with a wide-eyed, first-time look in their eyes.

This time, there was no preliminary bombardment as they came in for landing. They went into the LZ cold but did not take any fire. The flight of twenty-eight helicopters dropped down into the LZ four at a time, so at least twenty men were on the ground with each cluster of landings. In total, there were 160 men in the company, but that was about forty men less than the usual force levels.

Captain Rob Martin, the company commander, was a two-tour combat veteran. In addition to Bill, the group included Lieutenants Jones and Hanover, two platoon leaders who had just arrived from the States. Lieutenants Peters and Anderson, both seasoned, led the other platoons.

"O'Brien, you'll stay with me," ordered Captain Martin. "Jones, you and the first platoon will advance with us. Hanover, Peters, and Anderson, you'll take the other three platoons and advance to the left and right, keeping off the trails. Any questions?"

There was a quiet muttering of "No, sir" as the units moved out into the jungle.

Officers and RTOs were always prime targets, so they moved in the center of the formation. From his central vantage point, Bill saw that the unit was carrying powerful weaponry in addition to their forty-pound back-packs with seven days of rations and the usual supply of water. One man in each squad was responsible for an M60 belt-fed heavy machine gun, which provided maximum firepower.

Glancing to his left, he noted several soldiers carrying M79 grenade launchers capable of firing 40mm rounds up to three hundred meters. Others were toting disposable rocket launchers. In addition, each soldier carried an M16 rifle, and all noncommissioned officers (NCOs) and officers carried pistols.

The true purpose of the mission was painfully clear. They were to search out and confront the enemy forces. They assumed those forces would also be heavily armed and possibly dug into protective positions. Once they found the enemy location, they were to return fire as long as necessary to hold the position until the artillery from the firebase and the air force could destroy the emplacement.

We're just the cheese in the rat trap, Bill mused glumly.

The first six hours passed event-free. The troops pressed on through the jungle with only the annoyance of the colonel's command helicopter hovering overhead to pass occasional directional change orders to the captain.

Bill gritted his teeth and fought to keep his nerves under control each time the chopper approached. *What the hell are they thinking? We're out here stomping through the jungle, trying to sneak up on the enemy, and that helicopter keeps advertising "They're over here—over here!" It's just a game to them.*

Early in the afternoon, the point man raised his clenched fist and dropped to one knee. The unit was well trained to recognize this signal to stop in their tracks. Immediately, intense automatic-weapon fire ripped into the unit. Men in front started to go down. Bill could hear screams from both flanks, indicating the other units had also been hit. Fire was returned, but the enemy was well concealed. Most of the shots had no effect on the level of enemy fire.

"Red One, this is Red Two. We're taking fire," the captain reported. "The unit is pinned down with heavy close-in fire. Request a retreat to regroup."

"Captain, you will move forward now," ordered the colonel from his helicopter. "Make them commit their major resources."

The enemy fire continued from the right and left of the first platoon. Peters was dead, and Anderson was badly wounded in the first assault and was in way over his head.

"Jones!" Hanover barked over the radio. "Git yer ass over there and take over command. First platoon, dig in now and hold your ground."

Jones grimaced but slithered off to the left to intercept the other platoons and take charge of what was left.

"Red One, this is Red Two," Captain Martin yelled into the radio to be heard above the noise of the battle. "We are pinned down and have taken heavy casualties. Two platoon leaders are down. We are digging in for defense, but we're facing a large force at our front. We're unable to move forward. We have heavy casualties. We also see signs they are attempting to flank us. Over."

"Red Two, do not stop. There is only minor enemy activity in your front," ordered the voice from above.

Captain Martin shot a bewildered look at Bill. His face was covered with dirt, sweat, and soot. The smoke from the shooting filled the air like fog in San Francisco. The stench of burning flesh from the wounded and dying drilled through Bill's nostrils, making him gag. The cries of the wounded echoed all around him.

As Bill looked up at the command helicopter, he saw a series of green tracers arcing toward the craft.

"Red Two, this is Red One," the radio barked. The sound of machine gun fire hitting metal was audible on the broadcast. "We are being fired upon and taking evasive action. Do the best you can. Out."

With that, the helicopter banked and disappeared.

Bill hit the ground just as bullets whizzed overhead, shredding large branches off the trees. *Looks like the rat ate the trap* and *the cheese on this encounter*, he thought as he spit out a mouthful of jungle mud.

Captain Martin continued directing the men. "Dig in, work together, back-to-back. Try to protect from all directions."

Suddenly, Martin buckled and fell next to Bill. Bill reached for the captain instinctively to check his wounds. As he rolled Martin over, only a portion of his face was still attached.

Bill gagged and looked away in horror. He flattened himself closer to the ground. *Officers are always prime targets*, Bill remembered. Would he be next?

The first platoon was now under Bill's command. The other platoons were in the same danger. They reported their positions and followed procedures to close ranks. Bill knew he needed to keep the enemy from separating the platoons and starting a flanking attack that would destroy them piecemeal.

Bill hollered to his men to dig in and cover, then he motioned to his RTO to give him the map. His history studies and classes at Fort Sill about enemy engagements were about to pay benefits. He decided to employ a version of the "rolling barrage" used in World War I. The platoons were still well within range of the three supporting firebases. He calculated firing sequences for each of the artillery units to cover all the platoons, then he grabbed the radio.

"Red Leg One, Two, Three. This is Red Leg Four fire mission. Danger close!"

"Danger close" meant the shells would land close to friendly troops. Some of his men may die from friendly fire, but the whole company would surely be overrun if the firebase did not intercede.

"One round smoke on these coordinates," Bill continued.

He read off the coordinates he had calculated and sent along a silent Hail Mary. *I'm not Catholic, but it can't hurt*, he thought as he buried his head in the mud and waited for the concussions.

"Rounds on the way" was the last thing he heard before the smoke rounds from the three firebases fell nine hundred yards out. He quickly calculated the next coordinates to begin walking the fire forward. This would either cause the enemy to break off the attack and flee, or it would move them directly toward the company, where they were dug in and waiting.

"Red Leg One, Two, Three—fire for effect one volley at my last coordinates and then drop another hundred for one volley."

Bill buried his face in the mud as twelve 105mm rounds and six 200-pound, 8-inch shells slammed into the jungle nine hundred yards distant. The smoke had just started to drift when eighteen more shells landed only eight hundred yards out.

Screams echoed in the jungle in front of him. A secondary explosion indicated that a large ammunition dump must have been ignited.

"Drop two hundred and fire—danger close," he continued.

Minutes later, eighteen more shells landed six hundred yards out. The enemy fire had slackened but had not quit entirely.

"Danger close, all batteries drop one hundred and fire," Bill ordered.

Surprisingly, time seemed to slow down. It helped him mentally relax and focus the adjustments needed for the bombardment.

Soon another salvo of shells fell five hundred yards out.

"All batteries drop one hundred. Fire for effect. Danger close," Bill continued the orders.

The next salvo struck at only four hundred yards out. The concussion shattered a tree to Bill's right. It crashed to the ground on top of two of his men, killing them instantly. Bill gasped in horror. They didn't even have time to cry out.

Some of the enemy charged out of the jungle in desperation but were mowed down by the company's machine guns.

Suddenly, the jungle was quiet except for the occasional gasp or cry of "Medic!" Smoke billowed around the trees like snakes looking for a next victim. The sickening green of the jungle had changed instantly to black destruction as far as he could see. Fires burned like so many campsites on the Fourth of July.

Bill's senses were screaming. His ears were ringing. His eyes burned from the sulfur-and-smoke-drenched air. He coughed and realized his nose was plugged with mud. He blew it out in his hand and was startled at the deep-brown glob mixed with bright-red blood.

He grabbed the radio again. "All batteries, Red Leg Four hold fire." He readjusted the frequency and called the other platoons. "Status check. Report!"

All platoons had suffered severe casualties. Bill gave the order that should have been given long ago: "Fall back with the dead and wounded."

This fight was over. The enemy did not follow. Either they were dead or they had melted back into the jungle. Still, Bill called in artillery fire on the flanks of the company to cover their retreat.

He helped gather the dead and wounded from his own platoon, and they started the slow retreat back to the evacuation site. Bill carried the body of Captain Martin. En route, he called for the radio.

"Red Leg Four requesting assistance clearing LZ for evacuation."

The Cobra airships and air force were more than happy to oblige, shattering the jungle surrounding the LZ.

As the medevacs and other choppers came in, Bill took account of the damages. The only officers still standing were he and Lieutenant Hanover. Captain Martin and Lieutenant Peters had died from their wounds. Lieutenants Anderson and Jones were still alive but critically wounded.

Fifty American soldiers had been wounded and fifteen killed. This meant almost half of the company was either killed or wounded.

Bill felt guilty. He was unwounded except for a scrape on his chin and a bruise on his arm. How could he not be wounded? His mind could not comprehend what they had just been through. It would take time to recover from this one. His wounds were internal.

The colonel who flew off when his command helicopter came under fire never returned. In fact, by the time Bill returned to base, no one seemed to want to talk about the colonel or where he went. One of the battalion officers joked that the colonel had been rotated back stateside to command a motor pool in Texas.

The new company commander replacing Captain Martin recommended Bill for the Silver Star. Better yet, he recommended that Bill take five days of leave to an in-country R-and-R center in Vung Tau, just south of Saigon.

The recon report praised Bill further for over one hundred Vietcong killed and the destruction of their base camp. He found little comfort in that report. So many of his own men had been lost when the trap snapped shut. That price was too high, and the purpose of the war was still unclear.

Bill had been assigned to two hairy operations already in his first few months at the battery. At this rate, he would run out of luck very soon. He would appreciate the time at Vung Tau. He needed the rest. Maybe he could even write some letters to Barbara and Rudolph and get some sleep in a clean bed.

— LAKE SUPERIOR, 1972 —

8.

THE *SPIRIT OF SUPERIOR* WAS A NEW research vessel designed for water-quality research and underwater surveying. At over eighty feet, she could handle most of what Lake Superior dished out. The four crew and five scientists were well equipped to spend several months on assignment out of the Duluth, Minnesota, harbor.

This voyage in 1972 had taken them around the tip of Michigan's Upper Peninsula and down the long lake to an area just off Whitefish Point in Michigan. The busy shipping channel heading into the locks at Sault Ste. Marie was just southeast and required constant vigilance on the radio.

Their assignment was to map and sample a selected portion of the lake floor. An experimental sonar array was dragged behind the vessel, capturing high-resolution images. The data would be sent to Large Lakes Observatory at the University of Minnesota–Duluth to form a mosaic of the lake floor after all the pieces were put back together. The laboratory in Duluth could then compare it to previous data to identify any new hazards or sediment pollution issues.

Because they were unable to anchor in the extreme depth, First Mate Angela Stevens needed to pay close attention to the loran to determine their location. She also had to consider the weather. If needed, she would mark their location and advise Captain Dave Hicks to head for cover deep into Whitefish Bay.

The lake was gray and foreboding this morning, with freshening breezes and waves cresting five to eight feet. That combination generally led to a strong nor'easter coming down the open lake expanse.

"We need to mark and pull in after this pass," Angela advised. "The weather is starting to take shape. Perry, plot a course for Whitefish Bay."

Navigator Perry Sorenson nodded and without hesitation bent over the charts.

The *Spirit* lumbered toward the final coordinates on the far eastern corner of this pass. She bucked over the increasing waves and dragged the sonar array for one more pass. Angela glanced at the picture on the sonar screen across the cabin. One moment, the depth would register sixty feet, then suddenly they would clear a lip, and the sand and rock bottom would pitch to four hundred feet or more in depth.

Captain Dave Hicks had been on Lake Superior all his life. He loved her fickle moods—one moment calm and serene, the next raging with fury. The lake was so big and impenetrable that it seemed like an inland ocean. He had been hired to sail the *Spirit* six years ago and had managed to hire many crew members he had worked with on other ships. They had been on this assignment for several weeks now, and the crew worked well together.

He was also happy to be trying out the new experimental sonar array. This was a recently demilitarized version of the type used by the US Navy. The screen allowed Dave the ability to watch the sonar image in real time, rather than wait to review a recording later. He reveled in the clearness of the water and watched the detail slip by like an underwater television special.

In the past, they had surveyed over a dozen shipwrecks across the lake. Some of these dated back to the early nineteenth century. Some were more recent, such as the 1920 sinking of the *SS Superior City*, lying in 230 feet of water. Dave scanned the graying skies and thought of all the people who had lost their lives on this lake. It could extol a terrible price in an instant, regardless of the size of the vessel.

Just after noon, a puzzling image came on the screen. A wreckage rested at about two hundred feet. It was definitely metallic, and the bulk of the structure was concentrated in a single area. But it didn't look like any ship he had ever seen. Two equal-sized metal expanses radiated out in opposite directions and at right angles to the central mass.

Dave walked over to another screen, where he could call up an instant replay of the scene in slow motion. Yes, it was unmistakable now. It wasn't a ship. The wreckage was an airplane. And it had been there awhile, judging by the drifted sand and sediment banking against it.

They reached the end of their grid run. They would need to return to the wreckage for a better reading, but the weather was an issue. Although Dave was curious about the object, he respected Angela's decision to head to Whitefish.

"Mark the loran location and retrieve the sonar," he ordered.

The crew jumped into action. Perry provided the proper headings, and the large vessel turned south, heading for Whitefish Bay for cover from the brewing storm.

As the rain pelted the windshield, Dave turned control of the wheel over to Angela and moved to the reference books in the corner of the cabin. The books listed ships and planes that had sunk or crashed in the area. Several aircrafts had gone down, but the crash sites had been located on land. Even going back to the early twentieth century, he could not find any reports of missing aircraft.

Dave made a screen print of the best image from the sonar replay and sent it by telephone fax to the coast guard base in Marquette, Michigan. He asked if he should continue their current assignment tomorrow or include a more detailed pass of this particular area to get additional information regarding this possible aircraft.

The reply came before they reached safe harbor. He was told—no, ordered—to continue his current assignment the next morning and make no attempt to identify the object. "You will be contacted shortly by the proper authorities" was the curt response.

The nor'easter was organizing now and would be heard and felt within the hour. Retaking the wheel, Dave pushed hard to get his ship and crew into Whitefish Bay for the night.

FBI agent Daniel Hogan turned on the phone-answering service, trying to disengage from his job long enough to enjoy a late dinner with his wife, Sally; son, James; and daughter, Marcie. Both kids attended a small private elementary school near their home in Marquette. James was twelve years old and generally more interested in sports than schoolwork. Marcie, at ten, was always engaged in reading, writing, and just learning in general. They seemed direct opposites.

Tonight, however, James and Marcie were both excited to tell about their school project. The teachers had asked the students to pick a subject from World War II for their class to study. At the end of the year, they would present the results of their study. They could do a play, draw a mural, or write stories. The teacher would decide what was appropriate for their grade level.

As Dan dove into the meat loaf and listened to the chatter about the school projects, he heard the ring of the answering system as a message was delivered. But this was family time—phones were not answered. He ignored the call for his attention. Another ring and message, then another, finally stopped the conversation at the table.

"Dan, you're not going to get that, are you?" Sally admonished him. "Can't it wait until after dinner?"

As he debated, the phone rang again. He finally sighed and got up to answer it.

"Yeah, I heard the message come in," he responded to the caller, "but I'm having dinner with my family, and that takes precedence." He listened and nodded, and his expression grew more concerned. "I'll be there as soon as I can," he said, then hung up.

"Sorry, Sally—I have to head back to the office. Something urgent has come up." He shrugged in apology. "Maybe I can take a meat loaf sandwich with me."

"Go get yourself ready. I'll pack it up for you," said Sally, pushing herself away from the table.

James and Marcie both looked down at their plates. The excitement of the school project was all but forgotten.

When Dan arrived at the office, he met the grim face of Special Agent Glenn Bauer.

"We have a problem, Dan," Bauer declared. "Unfortunately, it's both political and environmental. This issue goes right to the top."

"Wait," Dan responded. "Do you mean the Pentagon?"

Bauer raised an eyebrow. "Yep, from the air force chief of staff. And it needs to be dealt with quickly."

— MICHIGAN, 1910 —

9.

O
TTO SCHMIDT IMMIGRATED TO THE UNITED STATES from southern Germany in 1900. He was the most mechanically skilled of the three brothers in his farm family. However, because he was the youngest, he would not inherit the farm from his father. Otto found work in the New York City area and lived there for a time as a laborer. He met his future wife, Emma, while living in the city. By 1910, they had three sons, each separated by just a year.

The auto industry was beginning to grow in the Detroit area. This was where Otto's mechanical skills could provide a bright future for his family. He found piecework in a succession of automobile manufacturing plants. These were small custom shops with a lot of handwork. Otto became very skilled at filing and grinding metal. He was pleased that his experience on the farm in Germany and his vocational training in the German schools were so useful.

The Schmidts were a close family. They enjoyed going on picnics and to picture shows at the new black-and-white cinema whenever possible. Otto was a firm believer in education. He insisted his sons learn to speak proper English as well as learn fluent German for their heritage and Latin for their Catholic religion. Otto and Emma also took English classes at the German American center nearby as well as at any sites with classes after working hours.

Although Otto had left Germany, he was still proud of his native country and Otto von Bismarck's conquest of France in 1871. Otto had always hated the French. "Dem Frogs!" he would say. He was also not fond of Jews or Negroes. Although Otto valued education, he was not broad-minded. Of course, he was not alone in these opinions.

Otto and Emma's sons—Johann, Fritz, and Albert—were boisterous children with a lot of friends. They were active in church activities and in German youth groups, which dominated the lives of the German immigrants in the area. The brothers had fine marks in math and science classes. Overall, they were a tribute to their parents' educational focus.

Before the eldest brother, Johann, was ten, America entered World War I. The European war came home quickly to German American families in the United States. Overnight, the German Americans were suspected of being enemy aliens. Teaching the German language or speaking it in public was forbidden. German Americans were also forbidden to meet in groups. The families were isolated, suspected, and investigated for the slightest reason.

Otto feared for his job in the auto industry. Indeed, he did lose his job after a few months. Times were hard on the family.

When the war ended, things began to stabilize, but Otto never recovered from his anger at the way his adopted country had treated his family. He obsessed on the topic some nights at dinner. Even after he found a new position at the Ford Motor Company, he still felt betrayed. When Otto read about the Treaty of Versailles, he was indignant about the blame heaped upon Germany.

"They say the war was all Germany's fault," he would say. "It is not fair and totally untrue. The Western powers were equally to blame, along with Russia. They don't admit this now because they won the war."

Only the relative prosperity of the 1920s tempered Otto's fixation on the war. In the meantime, his three sons continued to do well in school, graduating with high honors, which allowed them the opportunity to continue their education at a university. Otto tried to interest at least one of the boys in the automobile industry. However, they were all more fascinated by airplanes.

After high school, Johann got a summer job cleaning the waiting area at the local airport. The job gave him access to all areas of the airport. While he waited for the next passenger flight, he loved to sit in the tower and watch the private airplanes come and go. He pored over the navigation charts, plotting imaginary journeys for himself. He also studied the airport plans. This wasn't just a building and runway dropped on the landscape. It was carefully planned, taking into account the terrain, the wind direction, and the weather. Even the buildings were thoughtfully aligned so the tower could track airplane traffic on the ground and in the air.

Johann attended the University of Michigan and studied a combination of aeronautical and civil engineering. After graduating in 1929, he got a job with the Aeronautics Branch of the Department of Commerce, inspecting and ensuring the safety of airports in Michigan. He dreamed of building his own airport.

Fritz was eager to obtain his private pilot license after high school. He gloated to his younger brother, Albert, when he got a summer job flying airfreight around the Midwest. Fritz was proud but stubborn. He always looked for a challenge but was easily manipulated into daredevil stunts. His quick thinking and reflexes allowed him to survive whenever incidents went bad. However, it did not deter him from further experimentation.

Fritz was pleased to be accepted into an aeronautics program at Purdue, where he delved into aircraft design and tolerances, reveling in promises of longer and faster flights. He returned to his flying job every chance he got during college. In 1931, Fritz graduated with a bachelor of science degree in aeronautical engineering. He had accumulated more than two thousand flying hours. In addition, the airfreight job provided him with valuable experience in single- and multiengine aircraft, including the Ford Tri-Motor and Douglas DC-2.

"I think I could fly a desk if it had a motor and wings," he bragged.

After Albert finished high school, he joined Fritz flying airfreight. When he started his education at the University of Minnesota, he managed to find a similar job flying out of the Minneapolis area.

At five feet nine inches, he was shorter than his brothers. Fritz called him the "runt of the litter." Albert was studious and not as adventurous as his older brother. He learned by watching others as they succeeded or failed, and Albert's brothers were excellent role models—for both extremes. Rather than spend extra hours flying, Albert opted to take additional credits to speed up his schooling. His jobs were generally limited to flying in Minnesota, yet he still earned over 1,500 flying hours before he graduated in 1931 with his aeronautical engineering degree.

Otto and Emma were justifiably proud of their family. They had created the true American dream with a good life in Detroit and three well-educated and employable sons.

The stock market crash of 1929 and the Great Depression affected not only the financial life but also the secular life of the Schmidt family. Otto's job was always at risk. As Ford reduced Otto's hours, he grew more and more despondent at the failure of democratic capitalism. He saw the numerous unemployed people, the soup kitchens, and the beggars in the streets selling anything they owned just to feed their families.

Otto looked to the Friends of the New Germany for support. This group was dedicated to the support of the new Deutsches Reich of Adolf Hitler and all things German. Otto participated in marches and rallies and encouraged the family to attend with him. It seemed as though only the authoritative governments of Germany, Italy, the Soviet Union, and perhaps Japan had an answer to worldwide depression. Germans were working and proud again. They had thrown off the unfair restrictions of the Treaty of Versailles. The new Germany was powerful. Even Charles Lindbergh and Henry Ford accepted medals from the German state.

Johann was happy with his position at the Detroit airport. He worked hard and kept his head down. Fritz and Albert, however, shared their father's enthusiasm for the new Germany. They had no time for Jews. They firmly believed the Jews had sold out Germany in 1918 and were the real cause of the war. The French, not to mention the godless Soviet Communists, were the cause of the world's unrest.

Fritz and Albert told Otto they wanted to immigrate to Germany. They wanted to help the cause and find work in aviation. Otto encouraged them to contact the German consulate in Detroit to see if that was possible.

The consulate was enthusiastic about helping them. It provided them with contacts for employment in the expanding German civil aircraft industry and Deutsche Luft Hansa, the main German commercial airline.

In the late summer of 1935, the *SS Bremen* sailed out of New York with the two brothers on board. It docked in Hamburg, Germany, in September.

Fritz was eager to start a new life in his father's native country. Albert was a bit more reserved but, as usual, followed Fritz's lead. They were pleased that their German was quite good. However, they spoke with an unusual accent, a product of their father and a teacher who was an immigrant from southern Germany. After a couple of attempts, they generally managed to be understood.

After collecting their belongings, they hailed a taxi and headed over to the Deutsche Luft Hansa office. They had received their instructions in Detroit and met Herr Straus at the Hamburg office. Straus arranged transport by plane to the Berlin Tempelhof Airport, where the main Deutsche Luft Hansa headquarters was located.

The brothers had some time before their flight to Berlin, so they instructed the taxi driver to take the long way to the Hamburg airfield. Everywhere they went, they saw the Hitler salute and brown-uniformed men and women with the signature black swastika. Many shops were closed and marked with large signs: *JUDEN UNERWÜNSCHT*, which meant "Jews unwanted" or "undesirable." Other shops had the word *JUDEN* scrawled in red paint across the windows. Fritz was thrilled. Albert was watchful.

The roads to the airfield were good, wide, and clean. The people seemed happy and enthusiastic. They stopped at a beer hall outside the airport and enjoyed their first true German beer. It was delicious.

"This already feels like home," Fritz reveled. "I could drink a lot of these beers."

Albert had to agree he was warming to the country. However, he was trying to make sense of the threatening signs on the shops versus the joy he was seeing in the streets.

The flight to Berlin was a little over one hundred miles. The three-engine Junkers Ju 52 covered the distance in just over an hour. Fritz noted that the Ju 52 was very similar to the Ford Tri-Motor. It was the backbone of the Deutsche Luft Hansa fleet. Although it was slow and noisy, Fritz was sure they would be right at home in that cockpit.

At the Tempelhof airfield, they were directed to the Deutsche Luft Hansa headquarters, where they were surprised to see a mix of civilian and military people. They were ushered into the office of Herr von Gablenz, the operations manager.

Von Gablenz greeted them with a *"Heil, Hitler"* salute. The brothers returned the salute and sat as directed while von Gablenz evaluated their flight credentials from America. Both brothers had a substantial number of hours flying multiengine aircraft. Their skills were badly needed by Deutsche Luft Hansa, seeing as the military had hired away many of the similarly skilled pilots.

Von Gablenz immediately hired them, pending a flight check with the chief pilot, Captain Rolf Gelen. Their salary was excellent at fifteen hundred reichsmarks a month, which was over $150 US. Raises would follow if they qualified for other aircraft and duties.

The brothers were scheduled for flight checks the next day in the Junkers Ju 52. They were shown to the transit pilots' lodging nearby to settle in for the night. After a good night's sleep, the brothers easily qualified to fly the Ju 52. Fritz even showed the chief pilot some deft handling on a crosswind landing. Gelen would remember the brothers' skills and mention them to others in the future.

After a few days, Fritz insisted they needed to rent a spacious three-bedroom apartment near the center of Berlin. As Deutsche Luft Hansa pilots, they received a special rate for their rent and an advance on their first paychecks.

"Why not live it up? We have the money. Let's enjoy ourselves," Fritz exclaimed.

Albert finally started to relax, and both boys began to enjoy their new lives.

Deutsche Luft Hansa was Europe's largest air carrier. It aggressively improved air service all over Europe. It was also the first airline to offer overnight service, develop instrument flying for takeoffs and landings, and pioneer the use of radio-direction finding and VHF beacon remitters to allow safer and more accurate location and route determination. As their headquarters, the Tempelhof airport was the first to use lights on the airfield to enable night landings. Deutsche Luft Hansa was busy testing the use of a catapult to launch aircraft from ships. This would later pioneer airmail delivery to the United States.

The brothers knew they were joining an elite air service company, but they were not yet aware of the underlying politics of air travel. Deutsche Luft Hansa was about to merge into the Reich Air Ministry—the Luftwaffe.

Although Fritz and Albert were close, they were different in many ways. Both had the much-needed traits to pilot multiengine passenger aircraft. But while Albert was content to ferry people across Germany, Fritz longed to fly single-engine fighters. He loved some of the new aircraft coming off the drawing boards back in the United States. However, he too was content with multiengine passenger planes for the time being, particularly if he was paid well.

Fritz and Albert spent the first four weeks of their employment in training on the radio-direction, VHF, and route-keeping devices. They practiced night takeoffs and landings. They were introduced to a wide variety of aircraft. They learned to fly the Junkers W 34 and Junkers G 38—the largest aircraft in the world at that time. In addition, they trained on the Heinkel He 70, as well as the Douglas DC-2 and Boeing 247. Although German aircraft were preferred, some American aircraft were purchased. The brothers were getting a workout. It was almost like basic training in aircraft, technology, and tactics.

They did have some time to play, however. Their flat in Berlin became a gathering place for pilots very interested in these American brothers who had returned to Germany. Questions abounded: Was the United States as decadent as they read about in the papers? Were the Jews really free to work and travel? What about the Negroes—did they have tails, and were they free to roam about the country?

Many of these raised smirks from Fritz and Albert, but they answered the serious as well as the absurd questions. Although the brothers were no lovers of Jews or Negroes, they had not thought about restricting either group the way many of their current friends felt necessary.

Fritz and Albert developed friendships with many shopkeepers in the area. That provided plenty of beer, wine, sausage, bread, and cheese for all. The people in the streets and the shops looked more alike than not. The brothers did not see the racial mix so prevalent in the shops of Detroit.

Fritz organized all-night parties in their apartment with a large and expanding cast of characters. Albert reluctantly agreed to cohost, though he did enjoy meeting the musicians, actors, and actresses who frequented the parties. For Fritz, the best guests were the political figures and military officers.

Then there were the girls! They were tall blond and brunette beauties from all over Berlin. It was only natural that first Fritz and then Albert easily developed relationships with these women. It helped that the young pilots were handsome, with dark hair and piercing dark eyes. In addition, they wore dashing Deutsche Luft Hansa uniforms and had money and a great apartment.

Fritz became very fond of his latest girlfriend, Elisa Petter. She was a tall blond with deep-blue eyes. She was a classically trained pianist and a graduate of the Prussian Academy of Arts. Elisa's father, Petra, had worked for the German government during World War I. She had a wide variety of friends she always invited to the parties. Fritz would gladly agree to include her friends, saying, "Beauty, intelligence, and loved by all!" He loved her and was pleased that his friends were jealous when they saw her on his arm.

Albert preferred the quiet, studious types. They rarely attended the parties, so he searched them out at libraries and seminars. He met Freda Fromm at an archaeology seminar in Berlin. Freda's father, Rolf, had been in Egypt and at other Middle Eastern sites for the German Archaeological Institute. He was a professor at Heidelberg University.

Freda was quiet, attentive, and very intelligent. Whenever Albert invited her to their parties, she would twirl her silky brown hair thoughtfully through her fingers as she'd ponder the partygoers' discussions. She noticed everything and often took contrary positions just to get the conversation flowing.

Albert loved Freda, but he decided it was best for them to skip the gatherings if there were Nazi party members in attendance. Her favorite topic was to question the superiority of the Nordic race. That caused some embarrassment and strange looks from many of the political attendees. Albert tried to avoid this scenario as much as possible.

He often thought he should have avoided her altogether. However, he was like a moth to Freda's flame. She was provocative, and he was drawn to her and her spirit. When she loved a topic, her eyes would glow like a hundred candles. And woe to the person who disagreed with her.

When they were not in training, Fritz and Albert were assigned to regular airline routes. They rarely flew together and often were in the copilot seat. Even so, they were familiarizing themselves with the routes and the aircraft.

While chatting with some Luftwaffe officers in a café near the airport, Fritz and Albert discovered they were earning nearly the same wage as a Luftwaffe captain. They also discovered they could earn extra pay for flying routes outside Germany. Deutsche Luft Hansa served over twenty-five countries. They could live very nicely on this money and even send some home to their parents in the United States.

As their experience and expertise grew, the brothers' regular assignments expanded outside Germany. Fritz flew many routes to the Soviet Union, mainly Moscow and Leningrad. He grew to dislike the Communists even more on these trips. In his opinion, they were abrupt and secretive. *I certainly wouldn't invite them to one of my parties,* he thought. He also came to agree with German news reports that the Communists were the main threat to Germany.

Rome and Milan were great for the food, but he judged Italy as generally sloppy and dirty. Not up to his German homeland. The one good thing about Italy was the rail service. It was always on time. Fritz could hop the train, enjoy a good meal in town, and return for his flight without fretting about being late.

However, his favorite destinations were Warsaw, Poland, and Düsseldorf, Dresden, and Cologne, Germany. That kept him closer to home and Elisa.

Albert was assigned routes to western European cities such as London, Paris, Marseilles, Toulouse as well as major cities in Sweden, the Netherlands, and Belgium. These flights provided him access to differing opinions on the cultural and political situation developing in Europe. He loved to discuss these situations with Freda. However, he was surprised that, in many cases, she was already well aware of these developments and opinions.

She would tell him, "Albert, you and your brother are so naive about what's going on in Germany. Germany is a dictatorship. More and more freedoms are being restricted and even eliminated. I feel we are coming to a terrible end."

Fritz and Albert often compared notes on their return from trips outside Germany. Western Europe seemed disjointed, unsure of what direction to take. Those governments rose and fell in days. Eastern Europe was always under threat from the Soviet Union, and it was as disorganized as the west. No nation seemed as well orchestrated and as well equipped with answers to current problems as the German Third Reich.

However, the United States and western Europe still offered the "decadent" pleasures of food, drink, and music. The French offered fabulous food, champagne, and perfumes. The American culture provided Europe with music along with cheap, rich-tasting cigarettes. Pilots could purchase and resell any of these items at an immense profit back in Germany. This little side business nearly doubled Albert's monthly revenue. It allowed him to substantially increase his savings as well as send money back to his parents.

Although Germany in 1937 was clean, confident, and seemingly self-assured, noticeable changes were occurring in the streets, particularly in Berlin. Air raid protections were quietly being added to key Berlin office buildings. Antiaircraft guns were mounted on rooftops. Sandbags and concrete reinforcements were arranged to protect important buildings, such as telephone exchanges and electric generating plants. More new aircraft were moved to the Tempelhof airfield and to airfields across Germany.

The German population noticed, and they were on edge.

Fritz was thrilled at the sight of a new single-engine fighter aircraft such as the Messerschmitt Me 109. It was a powerful all-metal airplane with tremendous offensive firepower. It was clearly ahead of anything he had seen to date. Fritz convinced an air force officer to let him fly in the back seat of one of the Me 109 trainers. Fritz was amazed by the speed and handling when the officer allowed him to take over the controls.

Albert did not share his brother's excitement at the new offensive weapon. He was still happy to fly commercial flights and take people to new and exciting locations. However, the German military enacted a new requirement that all passenger aircraft be quickly convertible to military use. That meant structural changes, which reduced the number of passengers. Albert was not pleased with the changes due to safety reasons but voiced his opinions only to Freda.

Fritz was now being assigned to flights focused on military expediency and cargo movement in all types of weather conditions. Deutsche Luft Hansa's new slogan said it all: "When other airlines stay on the ground— Luft Hansa flies."

Albert noticed that the population of Berlin had also started to change. Gone were the tradesmen who the Nazis claimed were Jews or had Jewish heritage. Some of the new shop owners were well acquainted with the Nazi leadership and were party members. American jazz was frowned upon. The American records were available only on the black market. Albert got a premium for the records he quietly brought back on his flights from western Europe.

The parties in the Schmidt brothers' apartment had a more somber look and feel. There were fewer entertainers. The musicians, actors, and actresses were afraid to be seen for fear they too would be banned from the country. It was difficult for most artistic people to have a polite conversation with a Nazi ideologue, much less have a debate on issues outside official government policy. The revelers were more likely uniformed Nazi men and women. The views expressed were strict party lines, making opinionated discussions uncomfortable and rare.

Elisa still attended these parties because she was interested in Fritz. But Freda avoided attending altogether, telling Albert she was not comfortable at these events. Consequently, Albert tried to schedule flights on the party nights so he could avoid them too.

By 1937, eighteen months after their arrival, the brothers were each promoted to the rank of flight captain and given a substantial pay increase as well as a housing allowance. The intensity of their flying assignments increased. Fritz most often flew European routes. Albert was appointed to a team developing a means to cross the South Atlantic to South America in preparation for the German Antarctic Expedition of 1938–39.

There were many changes across Europe between 1937 and 1938 as Germany flexed its political and military muscles. Germany and Austria were joined together in the Anschluss. Tensions increased in Czechoslovakia, and finally Germany annexed the country. Germany also continued to assist the Franco rebels in Spain with strong support from the air force.

Albert noticed the high tensions in France and Great Britain when he flew to Paris and London. The attitude of the French, British, and other western European people was becoming more hostile toward Germany. The general fear of war was palpable. Civil defense drills were becoming more common in England. In France, military movements were heightened around the French border fortress with Germany at the Maginot Line.

To the east, the Poles and Soviets were also noticeably anxious and edgy. To the south, Mussolini had Italy at war in Ethiopia, using poison gas and machine guns against the natives armed with spears.

In Germany, the public mood continued to support the German government against what was advertised as the threat from the east and from France. Joseph Goebbels and his propaganda ministry stressed the need for renewed German strength to help prevent war. He continued to highlight the threat from the Soviet Union.

The pace of flights and training increased for the crews of Deutsche Luft Hansa. The Berlin-to-Konningsberg route was used for instrument-only and night-flying training for the air force pilots who flew with the regular Deutsche Luft Hansa crews. Due to this increased training regimen, more accidents were occurring. Between 1935 and 1938, sixteen planes were lost, with seventy-six deaths.

Clearly, Deutsche Luft Hansa was becoming a primary training tool for the new Luftwaffe pilots. Since 1935, Deutsche Luft Hansa had been incorporated into the Reich Air Ministry, and the company's director was already the secretary of state in the ministry.

Training also involved pilots from the Condor Legion, the German air force volunteers who supported the Franco regime in Spain. The legion bombed the Spanish town of Guernica in 1937, with the loss of over one thousand lives.

Fritz and Albert concentrated on doing their jobs well, trying not to become enmeshed in world politics. They retained their comfortable apartment in the stylish section of downtown Berlin, which bolstered their relationships with their girlfriends.

One evening in November, Albert treated Freda to a dinner at the best restaurant in Berlin. They had been dating for over a year, and he decided it was time to ask her to marry him.

She glanced at the ring nestled in its velvet-lined box. "Yes!" she shouted. "I wondered when you would ask me."

Albert's eyes locked on hers as he held her hands. She was such a lovely, intelligent woman. Germany had been good to him in many ways. He had a great job, many close friends, and now a beautiful fiancée.

"You will need to ask my father," Freda reminded him, breaking his reverie. "It's just a courtesy, you understand."

He did understand and nervously agreed, much to Freda's amusement. She decided Albert should come to a family dinner the next week to finalize the engagement.

Albert was as happy as he had ever been. He didn't need a plane to soar.

— MICHIGAN, 1937 —

10.

TTO AND EMMA'S OLDEST SON, JOHANN, was fascinated by the opportunities in the United States. He wanted to continue his education at the University of Michigan and obtain a master of science degree. He also wanted to start his own company after he got that degree. He was not soured on the American dream, nor did he share the extreme views of Otto, Fritz, and Albert regarding Jews, Negroes, or the glory of the new Germany.

Johann had read about the abuses of the Nazi regime. They tortured political oppositionists and Jewish shop owners. They enforced racial purity laws, imprisoning anyone who was not of "pure German bloodlines." He was frustrated with his father for supporting the new Germany and its abuses. Although he had concerns about the rise of Communism and Socialism and what that meant to the Catholic Church, he understood why people were attracted to Communism.

"If Germany was so damn good," he admonished his father, "why did you leave it in the first place?"

Before beginning his master's program at the University of Michigan, Johann met and married Ann Fontaine. It was tough for the newlyweds initially. They both worked long hours, though they managed to start a family with the little time they had together. By the time Johann finished his program in 1937, the family had grown to three children: Thomas, Anthony, and little Mary.

Johann eventually wanted to start his own company developing aircraft guidance systems, seeing as he had done his master's thesis on that topic. Before he could get the business started, he applied for an opening with the Ford Motor Company. They needed help building up their aircraft branch. The position reported to Edsel Ford, Henry Ford's son.

Edsel was impressed with the work Johann had done on aircraft guidance systems in his thesis. The ideas were groundbreaking and very much in the direction Edsel wanted to move the aircraft portion of the company. Edsel quickly extended an offer of employment to Johann.

When Johann told his parents the news, Otto was thrilled. Finally, one of his sons was following in his footsteps with the Ford Motor Company. Johann loved working directly for Edsel and found the job both challenging and rewarding.

When away from work, Johann doted on his children. Thomas, at four years old, looked more like his father every day. He too was enamored with flight. Anthony, nicknamed Tony, was a remarkably quiet and studious two-year-old. Little Mary, the baby, was fascinated by all types of shapes and colors and loved to play with her dolls. Ann was a constant, loving companion for Johann; a mother hen for the children; and a pillar of support for the whole family.

Even with all his success, Johann missed his two younger brothers, Fritz and Albert. He had heard nothing from them since 1936. He knew they were working for Deutsche Luft Hansa, but that was the last he had heard.

The FBI had also discovered the brothers' move to Germany. On a warm summer day in 1937, agents visited both Johann and Otto. They seemed skeptical about the family's loyalty to the United States. Johann worried what this would mean for his job with Ford.

Despite the risks, Otto continued his pro-German political activity, now as part of the German-American Bund. Finally, the FBI raided one of these meetings and arrested several suspected German agents, including Otto.

Shortly after, the FBI agents arrived at the Ford plant at Willow Run and entered Johann's office. They said they were arresting him on suspicion of being a spy and operative, like his father. While Johann was led away in handcuffs, other FBI agents raided his home and confiscated letters and documents to try to prove their case.

In addition, they advised Edsel that the FBI's intelligence unit would analyze Johann's work to see if any information had been supplied to a foreign power. Johann's office was locked and sealed with crime tape. No one was allowed to enter without the permission of the special agent in charge of the Detroit area.

Johann was interrogated at the FBI headquarters in Detroit, then flown to Washington, DC, to be interrogated a second time by FBI senior staff. In the meantime, his family could not enter their home. Every part of it was being taken apart to see if anything had been hidden in the floors or walls. Ann was also questioned and her background thoroughly investigated. She and the children fled to stay with her relatives.

Two FBI agents accompanied Johann to Washington in a private DC-3. They had been with him the last five days. One was extremely antagonistic, trying to get Johann to reveal his secrets and true allegiances. The other was more laid-back. He offered Johann cigarettes and coffee to make the flight more comfortable.

The time in Washington was five more days of interrogation, accusation, and little recognition of the substantial contribution Johann was making to the American aircraft design. It was a "Nazi under every bed" philosophy. Finally, the FBI let him go with the admonition that they were watching him and his family, so he better stay in line. It was the same treatment Otto had said the whole German community had received in WWI.

Furthermore, the FBI did not provide a complimentary return flight. Johann had to find and finance his own way back to Detroit. When he finally arrived home, more surprises awaited. His house had been ransacked not only by the FBI but also by an angry mob of neighbors convinced he was a Nazi sympathizer.

Johann attempted to reach Edsel but was told he was not available. In addition, Johann was told he was no longer employed by Ford, due to the concerns of the FBI.

Only two weeks before, Johann had been a proud American, working to support the American dream. He had had a great job, a beautiful home, and a loving family. Now, he was on the streets and unemployed.

Slowly, the spotlight moved away from Johann. In the next month, he decided to again approach Edsel for a job. He felt he had established an excellent relationship with Edsel while working in the aircraft division, and he wanted to tell his side of the story. He wanted to impress upon Edsel that the FBI had extensively investigated his background and found nothing pertinent. He had no relationship with his brothers in Germany, and his father's ill-advised involvement in the bund meetings had ended.

Johann could feel the country moving toward war, and he wanted to do his part. He drafted a letter to Edsel explaining what he could do to help the Ford Motor Company with aircraft design and manufacture. He felt sure that if war came, the Ford Motor Company would be in the forefront of aircraft manufacturing.

In late summer, Johann received a letter from Edsel's office.

Johann, it was so good to hear from you. I am sorry about the issue that caused you to lose your last position with Ford. I agree it was a result of the aggressive FBI inquiry into your family. Also a factor was the terrible strike at our River Rouge Plant and the "Battle of the Overpass"— the goons under Harry Bennett. It was just a total failure of the Ford Motor Company.

Things are starting to improve here, but for now, I do not have any openings. I would, however, like to recommend you for a job building an airfield in the Upper Peninsula. I came across this opening while talking with a friend of my father's. The task should take about nine months. By that time, there should be some serious aviation design work for you here.

Regards,
Edsel

Johann was elated to receive a response. The temporary position building an airport would be a new and welcome experience. It would take him back to his high school roots, when he worked at the Detroit airport during the summers. And afterward, the promise of an upcoming position in aviation design would get him back into his field working for a man he greatly respected and in an industry he loved.

Edsel included the contact's name and a local Detroit phone number. Johann dialed John Rogers immediately.

"I'd like to speak to Mr. Rogers, please. Edsel Ford gave me his name," Johann explained confidently.

"Please hold for Mr. Rogers," was the reply.

Johann waited impatiently.

"Hello there. This is John Rogers. What can I do for you?"

Johann liked the confident tone of Rogers's voice.

"My name is Johann Schmidt. Mr. Edsel Ford suggested I contact you with respect to the airport being built in the Upper Peninsula."

"Coming from Edsel Ford, that is a very high recommendation," Rogers responded. "Are you available for lunch tomorrow at the Detroit Athletic Club?"

"Certainly. What time?"

"Let's say twelve thirty, so we miss the lunch rush," suggested Rogers.

"I'll be there!" replied Johann.

He was not only excited about the job prospect, but a meeting at the athletic club would also be fantastic. It had been a while since he had been able to afford going there.

Johann arrived early for his lunch appointment. He waited in the parking lot, admiring the architecture. The white building gleamed in the bright sun. The circular drive allowed arriving visitors and members to view the ivy-draped walls with fluted columns a full two stories tall.

At the appointed time, Johann went through the massive front door and approached the maître d'.

"I am expected at Mr. John Rogers's table," he announced.

He was led to a table near one of the large windows. Rogers stood quickly and shook Johann's hand in introduction. Johann winced a bit at the grip. Rogers was lean, fit, and easily six feet tall.

"I'm so glad to meet you," Rogers said as he resumed his seat and motioned for Johann to sit across the table. "Johann—I can call you Johann, right?"

"Certainly," Johann replied.

He quickly took stock of his potential employer. Rogers was well dressed, but his deeply tanned face proved that he spent much of his time outdoors. Johann estimated that Rogers was in his early forties. His short hair was dark, and he sported a neatly trimmed mustache. He looked like an individual who could go from a board meeting to the backwoods in a heartbeat.

"Johann, we have a rush job in the Upper Peninsula," explained Rogers. "We need to complete a four-thousand-foot runway on some land I purchased for a third party near the Huron Mountains. Are you familiar with the area?"

Johann hesitated. As a boy, he had attended a summer camp the bund operated up in the Marquette, Michigan, area. But mentioning the camp connection might negatively impact the job offer.

"Yes, I have hiked and camped in the Huron Mountain area and around Marquette on a number of occasions," he responded.

"Excellent," Rogers replied with a smile. He turned his attention to the waiter standing at a comfortable distance awaiting their order. "Let's order first, then we can get down to business. The lake trout is fabulous here. Guaranteed to be fresh caught!"

They both ordered a salad to be followed by the trout with a glass of Riesling. Rogers continued his description of the job.

"The airport we are constructing will support a nearby mining operation. We need people with local knowledge and advanced engineering backgrounds for this position. You will also need to work long days. We need to get the runway done before winter sets in so the mines can begin shipments in spring."

When the salads arrived, Rogers stabbed a forkful of lettuce and waved it in the air as he continued.

"I see your background is in aeronautical and civil engineering. Edsel said you have experience working with navigation controls as well as airport safety features. This will be helpful for the new airfield—it's in a heavy sand area with some very nasty wind conditions."

Johann was excited about the opportunity. He dug into his salad eagerly. All he could do was nod when Rogers asked, "Can you start right away?"

Johann swallowed his mouthful of salad quickly. "When and where should I report?"

"How about next week on Monday morning? That gives you a week to get your local affairs in order. The flight out of Detroit to Marquette leaves at ten a.m. I'll meet you at the airport, and we can go out to the site together."

"Sounds perfect." Johann finished the salad and washed it down with a sip of wine.

"The basic surveying and clearing is already started," Rogers explained as the waiter replaced each salad plate with a golden-brown serving of lake trout nestled on wild rice. "We've built basic housing units. They're small but clean. We can help arrange lodging for your family in Marquette so they can be closer to your job."

Johann was amazed at the fast-moving operation. *It must really be important*, he thought.

"Sounds fine to me," Johann said. "I'll pack my field gear and be ready on Monday. My wife can check the house rentals in Marquette and get the kids settled."

"By the way, the pay is a thousand dollars a month, as you will be the chief engineer on the project." Rogers smiled at his new recruit, whose mouth was agape in surprise. "That should help with the house rental."

Johann could not believe his luck. He popped a piece of tender lake trout into his mouth and chewed happily.

The next Monday, Johann met Rogers at the Detroit airport. Rogers was now dressed comfortably for work, in jeans and a flannel work shirt. He was a chameleon, able to transform for any required role. The flight was a charter to Marquette and took only two hours. A car was waiting at the Marquette airport to transport them the final fifty miles west to the construction site.

As they arrived at the site, Johann could see that much of the preliminary work on the buildings had been completed. The workers had bunkhouse accommodations in a cluster near the gated entryway. He noted a building labeled "Mess Hall" near the cluster. Farther back on the site was a large house Rogers noted was for the key engineering staff, including Johann.

Johann eyed the construction site and envisioned the runway and the remaining work needed. He would have to complete his calculations and lay out the runway quickly so the grading and groundwork could be finished in the next couple of weeks. The pavement could then be laid and allowed to cure before the inclement weather set in.

Work had also been completed on a large metal equipment building. Rogers explained that this was needed to store incoming shipments and protect equipment. The building was also used for equipment maintenance and would be used to prefabricate walls for the tower structure. As Rogers continued the tour, Johann saw several wooden crates stacked at the far end of the building. The black labels stamped on the boxes read "Mining Equipment."

"In addition to the runway, which is your responsibility," continued Rogers, "we are improving the road to Marquette and the road to the mine site to handle heavy truck traffic. I'll introduce you to the civil engineers and workers a little later. Many of them have come from Switzerland to help with this project."

Johann raised one eyebrow and squinted at Rogers.

"The owner of the airport property joined forces with an engineering company in Switzerland many years ago," Rogers explained. "They hired men with a solid background in establishing mining sites in remote wooded areas."

In the distance, trees were being cut and loaded onto logging trucks. A large grader pushed trimmed branches into a pile. A truck was being loaded with trimmings from a machine that spewed mulch from a spout into a growing pile near an incinerator.

Rogers noticed the confused look on Johann's face.

"We contracted with the Ford sawmill up the road in Alberta, Michigan, to take the logs. The Fords have a very efficient factory and milling town there. They trim and slice the trees for use in the new 'woodie' station wagons. In Alberta, they use the trimmings for power in the sawmill and heat for the town. Here, we have implemented the same kind of system to use the trimmings to power all the buildings. Come on—I'll show you to your quarters."

They walked across the leveled sand field to the engineers' house. Johann found that there were five separate bedrooms, each with a bathroom.

The bedrooms were placed like spokes on a wheel surrounding a central conference room with a large table for discussions. Johann noticed that electricity was also available throughout, which would make late-night design sessions a reality.

Rogers pointed him to a corner room. "That one will be yours."

Johann tossed his pack in his bedroom and returned to the conference table to discuss the project further with Rogers. Johann would be supervising other civil engineers and foremen on the runway project. This building would give them a place to live and work together on the design.

Just inside the doorway was a radio room, where they would receive information on incoming shipments. A telephone line was available for ordering supplies. It could also be used for limited personal calls.

A cabinet next to the radio table was used to store weather data. Before purchasing the property, the new owners had gathered local weather data from the last two years. Johann would need this data to determine prevailing winds and water runoff in order to place the runway properly.

"You've got to take into consideration the prevailing winds off Lake Superior," noted Rogers. "It's only ten miles northeast of here."

In a nutshell, Johann's job was to focus on the layout, size, and quality of the airstrip and direct the other engineers and workmen on building a hangar and control tower. The runway needed to accommodate heavily loaded cargo planes.

Rogers continued his briefing. "The primary aircraft are DC-3s or modified Swiss Focke-Wulf Fw 200 Condors. The landing strip will be used to bring in mining equipment as well as transport out raw minerals to various processing areas around the United States. In addition, the strip may handle some charters and private traffic, so we'll need to build and man a control tower."

Johann studied the preliminary plan crudely sketched on a large sheet of paper on the table. He noted the locations of the engineers' house, the workers' housing cluster, and the large equipment storage building. There was a note in the corner of the plan to add a control tower and an aircraft hangar for cargo plane storage and maintenance. Understandably, the location of these would depend on the runway layout.

Other notes provided some details on the runway. The expected length was four thousand feet. The surface of the runway would have a packed gravel base with a twelve-inch-thick blacktop surface. *This is a serious runway,* Johann thought as he continued to transcribe the notes.

Landing aids were to be included to allow instrument landing at any hour. He had never had the opportunity to fly into an airport with this kind of assistance. He would need to do some serious studying and contact everyone he knew to get leads on equipment and advice on any issues they had found during testing. The lighting would also need to be installed before the winter weather so the runway would be fully usable in the spring. This would truly be a unique airport in America. It reflected the value of this landing strip to the mining operator.

Johann gasped audibly when he saw the budget estimate scrawled on the corner of the plan. The runway, hangar, and tower alone were estimated at one million dollars.

"Wow!" he exclaimed. "That's quite a budget for an airport."

Rogers had been waiting for Johann's response to the budget note. It was satisfactorily appreciative of the effort expected.

"This isn't just any runway, and this isn't just any project," admitted Rogers with a knowing smile. "I'll let you get settled so you can start looking over the plans in more detail. Dinner is at six in the mess hall. See you there."

11.

THE CONSTRUCTION PROCEEDED ON SCHEDULE. Johann spent many long days drafting the plans to scale and studying the weather information to determine the proper layout for the runway. The runway was established in a northeast-to-southwest direction to avoid the crosswinds blowing off Lake Superior and the Huron Mountains to the northwest. Taxiways were set parallel and on both sides of the runway. There was access midway down the airstrip for shorter-landing aircraft as well as at the end for the expected heavier cargo planes. A clear zone was cut and leveled on both ends of the runway to allow an overrun area, in case an aircraft had a problem with a landing.

Johann was allowed to spend brief periods in Marquette, where Ann had rented a small house. Johann's son Thomas loved to explore the edges of the woods out the back door. Anthony loved to watch the birds at the feeders by the window. And little Mary just enjoyed being with her mother in the fresh fall air and sunshine. The air was clean—a total change from the congestion of Detroit. When he couldn't break away for a visit, Johann called Ann and spent more than his allotted personal time on the phone. No one seemed to notice or care.

After three months, the runway was completed and marked, and the lighting was installed. The hangar and tower were in the final stages of construction, and taxiways were ready for surfacing. The project had gone smoothly to this point. The civil engineers from Switzerland needed very little management. They worked well as a team.

Over dinner one night, Johann found out they had actually worked together on developments at the Berlin Tempelhof Airport for Deutsche Luft Hansa. They were able to easily translate the German specifications when trying to work out difficult details. Johann was glad his mother had insisted he speak some German at home. His conversational German had not included engineering references, however, so his vocabulary was stilted compared to the other engineers. But he learned quickly.

Johann became close with Hans, one of the engineers. During a mealtime discussion, Johann mentioned that his brothers were in Germany flying for Deutsche Luft Hansa.

"Actually, I met your brother Albert last year at the Berlin airport," Hans said. "He's married and showed me a picture of his family. He seems very happy and successful."

Johann was elated to get word on his youngest brother and his family.

As construction continued, anything Johann requested was ordered and brought in from Marquette. Included in the shipments were an increasing number of crates labeled "Mining Equipment." Johann was so busy working on the runway project that he never really thought about how they were getting all these items drop-shipped to the center of the United States. He was just glad the mining equipment was trucked up to the mine site as soon as it arrived. Johann needed the original maintenance building to store shipments he received for the airport construction and the instrumentation for the tower.

Near the end of the fourth month, the taxiways were marked, and support services such as fuel and repair were available in the new hangar. Now Johann turned his attention to the instrumentation needed in the tower to control the landing of the aircraft and the runway lighting. The installation and testing of this equipment would be done over the winter months. However, now shipments could begin arriving during the daylight hours directly by cargo plane.

One time at breakfast, Johann asked Hans when the mine would be up and running.

"It takes a long time to get a mine fully operational," replied Hans. "It might be a year or more before we get all the details worked out and can start shipping ore by cargo plane. For now, we truck the ore to Marquette and then send it out by laker ships to Ohio, where it's processed."

Life at the airport work site was hard with long hours but not without its pleasures. When he couldn't take time off to visit his family, Johann enjoyed the outdoor opportunities the area provided. In late fall, Johann bought a hunting license. He hoped to find ducks on the inland lakes or perhaps a deer to help augment their diet. The changing of the leaves tempted him to go for longer forays into the woods to hike and fish. The gold and red leaves of the surrounding oak and maple forests were highlighted by splashes of the brilliant yellow and silver leaves of the birch and poplar. The crisp morning air motivated him to go farther each time he had a chance.

As spring arrived, the final testing of the tower instrumentation and lighting continued. The testing had gone slower than expected, and receiving parts for the new equipment was more challenging than Rogers had anticipated. He asked Johann to stay on for two more months to see the project to a close. Johann was happy to accommodate that request.

Johann found spring fishing in the trout streams of the Huron Mountains particularly challenging. He relished the chance to bring back a creel of trout for their Swiss cook. Although the food they received in the mess hall was generally good, there was nothing like fresh fish.

A steady rain arrived one Saturday, dashing Johann's plans to fly to Marquette to visit his family. With a day to himself, Johann decided to get some extra exercise and walk up into the Huron Mountains where the mine site had been established.

As he hiked higher up the road, he found a place where he could look down and admire the airport. It was truly magnificent. He reflected on the changes to the landscape from when he had first driven in with Rogers nearly nine months ago.

The black runway glistened from the rain. From his high vantage point, Johann could see the sophisticated arc lights marking the glide slope on the northeast approach. The gas and neon lights marked the airfield limits, making it look like a stage awaiting the start of a play. To the southwest, he could see the line of red lights marking the end of the runway and leading to the taxiway on the left.

As he admired his accomplishment, a DC-3 lumbered down through the rain from the northeast and made a perfect landing. It taxied toward the storage hangar and shut down its engines just as a convoy of trucks rushed out to engulf it. The crew quickly began unloading crates. He knew the trucks would soon head up the same road he was hiking. He turned and continued his hike, hoping he could get a look at the actual mine—the other end of the project.

"Halt!"

Johann was startled as he came around a bend and found himself face-to-face with an armed guard standing in front of a gated area.

"No unauthorized personnel are allowed inside the gate," the guard declared.

"I'm Johann Schmidt, an engineer from the airport complex," Johann explained. "I just wanted to see what the mine looked like."

The guard relaxed briefly and reached in his pocket for a chocolate bar. "I'm waiting for a shipment that just landed at the airport. You'll have to leave the area and go back to your quarters." He broke off a piece of the chocolate and munched noisily.

"Well, it was a nice hike, even in the rain," responded Johann, turning to head back down the road. Then he paused and turned back to the guard. "Say, you don't have another bit of that chocolate, do you? I could use a little boost—I underestimated the distance of this hike."

"Here, take this." The guard handed Johann the remainder of the candy bar, then returned to his post. "The trucks should be arriving soon. You need to get moving."

Johann thanked him and turned for home. As he heard the first of the trucks laboring up the mountain road, he decided walking an animal path in the woods would be safer than meeting the convoy on the narrow gravel road.

Johann unwrapped the last of the candy bar and popped it into his mouth. He crumbled the wrapper and put it in his pocket. The chocolate was slightly bitter and had a waxy texture.

"Wow, that's not Hershey's!" he exclaimed as he shifted the bit around on his tongue.

He pulled out the wrapper and flattened it on his palm. The label read, "*Zwei Unzen Schokoriegel—Produkt aus Deutschland.*"

12.

JOHANN WALKED BACK TO THE AIRFIELD, mulling over the candy wrapper. Although the civil engineers he worked with were from Switzerland, Hans had told him about their work with Deutsche Luft Hansa. Perhaps that's where the bar had come from.

Or perhaps there were some Germans among the mine site workers. The workers were rotated out on a regular basis. Johann had gotten to know some of the previous workers. They too had lived in the housing cluster and had assisted with the airport construction. Those workers were mostly local Michigan men of Scandinavian descent. However, he had no direct contact with the newest workers. Most of them now worked only at the mine and were kept separate from the small contingent seeing through the final days of the airport project.

On Friday, Johann advised Rogers that the project was complete. Rogers thanked him for his work and told Johann he could head to Marquette to prepare his family to move back to Detroit before the end of May. Although Johann had not heard from Edsel Ford regarding his new assignment, he was eager to get back to aircraft design, even if it meant living in Detroit.

Johann's call to Ann that evening was filled with hope and excitement at what the future might hold. He would once again be with the family every night. That was something they were all looking forward to.

The next day, Johann packed his bag and hopped a truck bound for Marquette. When he arrived, he raced to the little rental house to see his family. The reunion was boisterous. Ann held Mary and watched Johann engulf the boys with hugs and kisses. Thomas and Anthony filled him in on all the things they had been doing. Mary clapped her hands in glee.

As happy as she was, Ann also felt a pang of regret. She had enjoyed their life in Marquette. Returning to Detroit would bring them closer to their parents, but they would lose the serenity this vast wilderness had provided.

Let's face it, she thought. *I'm spoiled by all this beauty and clean air. But if Johann's job is in Detroit, then we will move back to Detroit.*

Johann surprised Ann by suggesting that before they headed back to Detroit, he should rent a plane so she could see the airport he had built and the beautiful Huron Mountain area. Ann was thrilled with the chance to see where Johann had been working. In addition, a day off from packing would be much appreciated.

In the middle of the week, they dropped off the children with the babysitter and headed to the Marquette airport, where Johann had rented a two-seat Piper Cub. The weather was clear and the wind light, making the Cub a perfect machine for the flight. As he flew west along the Lake Superior shoreline, Johann pointed out the tall expanses of limestone cliffs plummeting to the crashing waves below. Ann marveled at the thick hardwood and pine forests.

"You can't even see the ground underneath!" she exclaimed.

When they neared the airfield, Johann called the tower and advised them he wanted to do a flyby. He was approved. He turned the plane into the flight path for the glistening new runway. The lights flashed as he cruised over the airport at just two hundred feet. From this altitude, the airport looked sleek and beautiful.

Ann was proud of her husband as she gazed down at the airport through misting eyes. "Johann, it's truly amazing that you were able to take that solid forest and create this!"

Johann cleared the airfield and turned north to fly over the Huron Mountains. He could see where the gravel road headed up to the mine entrance, but the view quickly became obscured by the tree cover. In the distance to the east, they saw the glistening surface of Lake Superior. Occasional breaks in the trees opened sights of coursing streams ending in small water-falls as the watershed pushed toward the lakeshore.

Johann thought of the hikes he had taken up to the trout streams and the abundant game he had found in the woods. He wished he could have stayed there and had the opportunity to teach young Thomas and Anthony the ways to properly hunt and provide for a family from what the wilderness offered.

Perhaps fate will intervene, he thought as he banked the small plane southeast and headed for Marquette.

At the end of May, Johann bought his family a new home in Detroit. He had been saving most of his wages and was proud that once again he could afford to buy a house. After they got settled, he would talk to Edsel about his new position and see where life took them.

Otto and Emma, Johann's parents, were excited for the family's return. "Send your Marquette furniture and household items to your new home," Otto said. "We'll arrange to meet the delivery. Take your time getting here. You deserve a little vacation with the family."

Johann happily took his father's advice and booked passage for the family from Marquette to Detroit on the cruise ship *Negaumee*. The passage was sure to be scenic as they slipped east along the Lake Superior shoreline, through the massive Soo Locks at Sault Ste. Marie, to Lake Huron, the Saint Clair River, and their final destination, Detroit, on the shore of Lake Saint Clair.

It was a slow but comfortable way for the family to travel together. It gave them time to reconnect and prepare for their new life. Mary and Anthony were content to sit with Johann and Ann, watching the scenery and other boats pass by. Thomas finally talked Captain Prentiss into a tour of the cruise ship, complete with the pilothouse. The captain even gave him a turn at blowing the boat whistle.

Thomas rejoined the family as they approached the Soo Locks at Sault Ste. Marie. Their ship looked small in comparison to the ore boats waiting in line to traverse the locks. When it was their turn, a large door opened in front of them, allowing the cruise ship to slide into an encased chute. They tied up loosely to the side and waited for another pleasure craft to tie up behind them. A whistle blew, and they could hear water gushing nearby. Slowly the water was released from the chute, and the ship dropped several feet. A viewing window gave people on shore a chance to watch the boats traverse the lock. Anthony was sure it was better to be on the boat instead.

Once the water level in the lock chute was at the same level as the water in Lake Huron, another whistle blew. The boats were untied, and the massive door opened in front of them.

"It's like a huge boat elevator!" squealed Anthony, struggling to free himself from his father's arms.

Johann had to agree. He was fascinated with the sophisticated engineering required to create the "elevator." After looking at a map, he realized this was the only way to move a ship from Lake Superior to Lake Huron. It was ingenious. The ore and supplies traveling from Minnesota and the Upper Peninsula in the north were vital to the industries and cities farther south in the Lower Peninsula, Wisconsin, Ohio, Illinois, and Indiana. He wished he had time to tour the lock and study the mechanism.

But that would have to wait for another trip. He was sure Edsel was waiting in Detroit with a new opportunity for him, and he was anxious to get his family settled. Besides, Thomas announced he was "hungry with a capital *H*!" Johann realized he was hungry too. It was time to grab dinner before bedtime.

The *Negaumee* pulled in to Detroit two days later. The family was tired but eager to settle into their new house. Johann's savings had provided for a large down payment on a four-bedroom home only a few blocks from their earlier neighborhood. Ann's parents had jumped at the chance to help Otto and Emma arrange the delivery of the furniture and personal items. The parents had teamed up to set up the beds, knowing the family would be ready to sleep when they arrived.

When Ann and Johann arrived with the kids, the beds with clean linens were indeed appreciated. Their other meager belongings could remain in their boxes in the living room. Tomorrow was soon enough to make the house a proper home.

Johann's first task the next day was to call Edsel. He leaned against the kitchen counter to make the call while Ann unpacked dishes.

"Mr. Ford. This is Johann Schmidt," he said. "I returned to Detroit with my family just last night. We treated ourselves to a cruise down from Marquette. I thought I would check in with you first thing regarding the aviation design position we had discussed several months back."

"Welcome back, Johann. I hope you had a pleasant voyage."

"Yes, it was nice to have a few days to reconnect with my family. Traveling on the Great Lakes was truly an adventure we will not forget. I was amazed at the lock and dam mechanism at Sault Ste. Marie. I have never seen anything quite so ingenious."

"Sure, it's ingenious," said Edsel with a laugh. "But I can assure you they didn't build it in under nine months, as you did the airport in the Huron Mountain area!"

"Thank you, sir."

Johann blushed a bit and glanced at Ann to see if she had noticed. She had and smiled at him as she washed and stored the dishes in the cupboard.

"About that new position, sir. Has anything opened up?"

"I'm sorry, Johann," Edsel said with regret. "I really don't see anything new coming up here for several months still. There are rumors that the government is going to ramp up the aircraft requirement based on information about growing concerns in Germany and Japan. I'm sure our Ford Company will be a part of the new production, but I can't make any promises at this point."

Johann was not pleased with the delay. "Well, please keep me in mind when the buildup does occur. I look forward to working for Ford again."

Johann hung up the telephone and turned to see Ann staring at him with concern.

"What did he say?" she asked.

"There's no job right now. He thinks there will be a need in the next few months, but there's nothing right now." Johann walked over to the table.

He sat down dejectedly and tilted the chair back. "We certainly have some savings, but I'm not sure how long we can afford to live here if I can't find a full-time position soon."

"Things will work out. They always have." Ann was an everlasting optimist. "Come on—let's get these boxes unpacked."

Johann dragged himself out of the chair and started unwrapping plates while Ann continued to wash the dishes and arrange them in the kitchen.

As the days passed, Johann continued to look for even a temporary job. He knew they would need the money to support the big house—not to mention that his boredom was starting to get on Ann's nerves.

A week later, as Johann was sipping his morning coffee and scanning the newspaper, the phone rang. He grabbed his cup and walked over to answer it.

"Schmidts'. This is Johann. May I help you?"

"I hope I can help you, Johann," Edsel said with a laugh. "I just talked to John Andrews, the operations manager at the Detroit municipal airport. He told me he could use someone to help with aircraft operations for a few months. I'll put in a good word for you, if you're still available."

"Mr. Ford, that would be great," responded Johann with a smile. "I remember Mr. Andrews from when I worked for Aeronautics Branch a few years ago inspecting airports."

"It's only temporary until a position opens here at Ford, but you were my top recommendation."

"I appreciate your faith in me, Mr. Ford!"

Johann contacted John Andrews and started his new job the very next day. To celebrate, he made reservations at the Detroit Athletic Club to take the family to dinner that weekend. The club had an all-you-can-eat buffet on the weekends, and Johann made the most of it. What a meal! They feasted on roast beef, lamb chops, roasted potatoes, fresh green beans, three kinds of pie, and ice cream.

Even little Anthony surprised Johann with his appetite. "Can I have some more of those green beans?" he begged.

Johann was happy to oblige. What a great way to celebrate their new life in Detroit.

After dinner, Johann helped Ann put the children to bed, then took his pipe and headed to his reading chair. He sat with a book open in his lap and gazed out the window into the darkness beyond. His thoughts strayed to the airport he had helped construct.

Little things had bothered him, particularly near the end of his tenure there. Several men arrived on incoming flights and were spirited away to the mine. There were still far more incoming shipments than outgoing. The planes leaving the airport were generally empty. The planes arriving came in after dark and were unloaded quickly. Even some overheard bits of conversations caused him to pause.

However, the job was done. He had been paid well for his efforts, and now he was home with his family.

In late July, Edsel called again. "There are some developments here at the Ford Motor Company that I would like to talk to you about. Can we meet Friday at eleven at the athletic club?"

"I'll speak with Mr. Andrews," responded Johann happily. "I don't think that will be a problem."

"Let me know if something comes up. Otherwise, I will see you on Friday."

"Thank you, sir. I'll see you then."

The meeting was just what Johann had hoped. Edsel started the discussion as soon as the drinks arrived.

"Johann, we'll be building aircraft for the government. We'll be building a lot of them! We need your help to set up the processes to first produce components for a new army bomber, the B-24, and then hopefully construct entire bombers at a new plant being developed at the Willow Run airport.

Our ultimate goal, if we get the full bomber approval, would be to produce one B-24 per day."

"That's incredible," exclaimed Johann.

That level of production had never been accomplished before, but Johann was eager to take on the challenge.

"You would work directly for the vice president of aircraft development, who reports to me." Edsel did not mince words. "Can you start next week?"

"Yes, sir. I'll finish up a few tasks at the airport and be ready to start at eight a.m. on Thursday, if that meets with your schedule."

"That will be great. Now let's dig in before this great lake trout gets cold."

— GERMANY, 1937 —

13.

THE RELATIONSHIP BETWEEN FRITZ AND ELISA was, in a word, complicated. The Petter family had originated in the Volga region of Germany. Elisa's brother, Karl, was frequently involved with groups trying to protect the old German values. The Gestapo, the secret state police, could arrest Karl on a whim. So the family wanted to avoid any additional Nazi Party attention. In addition, they kept a deadly family secret: one of their distant ancestors was Jewish.

Fritz, on the other hand, was a strong, vocal supporter of the new Germany. He was a devout follower of Adolf Hitler. He had recently joined the Nazi Party and was considering joining the rapidly growing German air force. Fritz really wanted to get his hands on the new Me 109 fighter. The plane had a fast, supercharged engine and heavy armor with a 20mm cannon and machine guns. It had substantially greater firepower than any fighter plane in Europe.

Fritz loved Elisa, but she did not fit his idea of the perfect German wife. She was an artist, and her friends were often not really acceptable to "good" Nazi Party members. She enjoyed music, particularly the American Negro jazz that was banned in Germany. Elisa often opined to Fritz her distaste for the repressive policies of the Reich. She was appalled by the Reich's treatment of the Jews, Gypsies, and political opponents, but she was not an activist. She believed, as did many in the German population, that there was little to be done about such things.

Elisa was concerned, however, about the disappearance of some of her more outspoken friends, some with more "flexible" sexual beliefs. Fritz assured her they had merely moved out of Berlin; perhaps they had just relocated in the countryside.

Fritz wanted Elisa to join the Nazi Party, but she did not want to become political. Fritz thought she would look rather striking in a brown uniform with the white-and-red armband and black swastika. But she felt that was too extreme and refused to wear any uniform.

Despite their disagreements over the party, Fritz and Elisa moved in together in an apartment near the one he and Albert had rented when they first arrived in 1935. They talked of marriage but could not firm up a specific date because Fritz had to increase his training if he wanted to get an air force commission.

After several attempts, Fritz procured an appointment with Eberhard Milch, the director of Deutsche Luft Hansa, to discuss his request for a transfer to the Luftwaffe. Milch listened to Fritz's request for a direct commission with interest.

"So you want to be part of the greatest air force in the world," Milch responded. "Convince me you are qualified!"

Without hesitation, Fritz responded, "I am a loyal German who left the United States to support the new Germany. I am a Nazi Party member. I also have a significant amount of experience and flight time compared to most of the pilots in the Deutsche Luft Hansa. I have five thousand hours on multiengine aircraft and have trained many of the air force officers on instrument flying. I also have an aeronautical degree that will be very useful to the Luftwaffe. Besides this, I've had a lot of single-engine flight time when not flying for Deutsche Luft Hansa, including about five hundred hours in the new Me 109. I earned these hours flying with air force pilots over the last two years."

Milch was impressed, not only with the scope of the discussion but also the tone. He ended the session by telling Fritz that a favorable recommendation would be made to the appropriate German air force officers.

Luftwaffe headquarters approved Fritz's request for an officer's commission. Albert wasn't interested in joining the air force, but he was interested in using his skills to test the new aircraft. Key people in the air ministry had already been following the brothers' training. Based on their training and skills in working with so many of Deutsche Luft Hansa's aircraft, they would have the opportunity to do most of the test flying on the world's most modern airliner, the Focke-Wulf Fw 200 Condor.

Initially, the brothers would work with the plane's assistant designer and chief test pilot, Kurt Tank. This airliner was rumored to cruise at almost twice the altitude of existing airliners and had a pressurized cabin. It had an initial range of 1,860 miles. With extra fuel tanks, it could go much farther.

In July 1937, Fritz and Albert met Kurt Tank at the Tempelhof airport. Tank went over the specifics on the aircraft and talked to the brothers about their multiengine experience. He had already reviewed their files, so he knew the basics. He was impressed with the tone and professionalism of their discussion. He could tell these men were good, experienced pilots who also had a solid design background.

They had gone beyond merely flying an assigned aircraft. They knew what topics to address—stall speed, ceiling performance, power curve of the engines, metal fatigue issues, wing lift. They also indicated how some improvements could be made to extend the range of the aircraft. He was happy to have them on board.

Tank was well aware that only Fritz was a Luftwaffe officer. He was now a major with a commission straight out of the Reich Air Ministry. Tank knew that must have been approved by Luftwaffe reichsmarschall Hermann Göring himself.

The difference between the brothers was obvious to Tank. Both were excellent pilots and knowledgeable. But Fritz was a more flamboyant, daring pilot, a quick thinker but not dangerous, while Albert was steady, smart, and analytical in a crisis. Albert had a deeper understanding of technical flying and aircraft dynamics. In short, they were a great complement to each other and would be invaluable at working out the bugs of the Fw 200 prototype.

The first few test flights went off without a hitch. The prototype was powered by four 875-horsepower Pratt and Whitney radial engines. The engines performed extremely well.

However, Albert experienced a sudden surprise during one test flight. As he descended toward Tempelhof field one evening, he expected to see the bright pole arc lamps marking his approach. Usually, green marked the approach, white the touchdown point, and red the end of the runway. Instead, Albert saw pale-green lights for the approach, but no lights for the touchdown zone or the runway end. He would have to land the Fw 200 without the usual assistance. The control tower could offer some support for alignment, but he'd have to rely on his own memory of the runway to control his speed and descent. He didn't have enough fuel for more than one attempt, so he headed down into the darkness.

Albert brought the plane in slowly, chopping off airspeed until it appeared he was near touchdown. But just before touchdown, one of the right-side engines stalled and fell silent. The plane wobbled and came down hard on the runway. The right landing gear collapsed under the shifted weight. The aircraft slid down the runway on its side, then pivoted across the concrete. Metal crunched and screamed against the hard surface. Fortunately, with little fuel remaining, the aircraft did not burst into flames. Albert suffered a dislocated shoulder and broken foot. The Fw 200 was badly damaged but salvageable.

Tank and the Nazi officials reviewed the crash details and praised Albert for an excellent job of getting down at all. Other pilots had totaled aircraft when landing hard on a runway, even in perfect conditions. Some of those pilots had not survived their mistakes. After inspecting the landing lights the next day, the Nazi officials determined the field lights may have been sabotaged by members of the anti-Nazi movement.

Albert was just glad to be alive. Although he had experienced previous emergency landings, nothing like this had ever happened. He was given a 120-day leave to recover from his injuries. He had been assigned to a major mission for the Fw 200 in the offing, but now that mission would go to someone else.

Fritz was named as the pilot to replace his brother. In late 1937, plans were announced for an unprecedented nonstop flight from Berlin to New York City. It would be the first time a craft heavier than air would make this flight.

One week after the accident, Albert hobbled into Freda's house on crutches to have dinner with Rolf and Margarette Fromm and ask for Freda's hand in marriage. The Fromms were a distinguished and scholarly couple. Rolf, in his fifties, was average height and slightly overweight from his wife's excellent cooking. He smoked a hand-carved briar pipe he had received as a gift from an archaeological associate. His face was tight and permanently reddened from many years of working at sites in the Middle East. Rolf's manner was polite but fairly abrupt with strangers.

Margarette was an attractive woman in her late forties. She was neatly dressed and wore her long dark hair braided and carefully wrapped in a bun. Her features were as soft as her husband's were rough. She was pleasant and friendly to Albert as they walked to the sitting room. Her mannerisms and dress were very different from those the cultural ministry recommended and most Nazi Party members followed.

Freda was waiting in the sitting room, nervously twisting her long brown braid between her fingers. She beamed when Margarette escorted Albert into the room.

"How are you feeling, Albert?" Rolf asked.

"I'm fine," replied Albert. "I just need a few weeks to heal my foot. Then I'll be back in the cockpit."

"Don't you think about the danger in your job?" Rolf exclaimed. "My God, you could have been crippled permanently—or even killed!"

At first, Albert was taken aback by the tone of the question. "Actually, flying is very safe. In fact, it's safer than driving a car in Berlin," he responded. "I've flown for many years, and this is the first serious accident I've had."

Rolf seemed relieved. He tapped out his pipe to clean and refill it. The maid came in and motioned to Margarette that dinner was ready.

"Let's go into the dining room, so we can enjoy a nice meal together," Margarette suggested.

Albert was excited not only about getting a home-cooked meal but also about what he planned to say later to Mr. Fromm.

The Fromms' home was large and well decorated. Obviously, they had money and were not afraid to spend it on the comforts of servants and fine food. Everything was first class.

During dinner, Albert found out that Mr. Fromm was a highly respected authority on human evolution. He had been the chair of the archaeology department at Heidelberg University.

"Unfortunately, though, the university recently demoted me for my teachings on evolution. Apparently, my facts conflict with the party doctrine," Rolf said with obvious distaste, oblivious to Albert's political leanings. "I'm continuing to teach my previous curriculum to small groups of students outside the university. Freda and Margarette want me to stop my classes, but I cannot turn my back on the truth."

Albert could see where Freda got her spunk.

The dinner was spectacular. Albert had never tasted wild mushroom soup with such a delicate flavor. The beef roulade, stuffed cabbage, parsley potatoes, green beans, coffee, and wine filled him to the brim. However, he still made room for a slice of the Black Forest cake, which he found out was a favorite of both Freda's and Rolf's.

After dinner, Rolf and Albert retired to the sitting room. Rolf offered Albert a Cuban cigar.

"Thank you, Herr Fromm," Albert said, "but I don't smoke."

"Good for you, boy. I keep them around for visitors, but I prefer my pipe."

Albert did accept the glass of brandy Rolf offered. It was more to steady his nerves than from a weakness for the warming fluid.

Albert took a deep breath. "Herr Fromm, I would like to ask you for your daughter's hand in marriage."

Albert waited. Rolf seemed to pensively weigh the question.

"My boy, few other men would have had the courtesy—or the courage—to come and ask me that question. If you will hold and protect our daughter in what I fear is coming in this nation of ours, my answer is a resounding yes! If you cannot protect her, I would be forced to say no."

Rolf continued in explanation, "Margarette and I have seen many horrible things already. It's becoming more dangerous in Germany every day. It's far worse than you may know. We'll probably be at war in the next two years, and then who knows what will happen. This is a time when people have to stand up for the human values of love and decency. We need to resist the dark forces of evil that are all around us."

Albert was stunned by this frank assessment. He too had noted the shop closings, the increased military spending and presence in the streets. People he knew had disappeared. From the air, he had seen several tent camps growing outside German cities with no stated official purpose. But he did not think things were as dire as Rolf seemed to feel they were. Still, he wanted to reassure Rolf of his intentions.

"Sir, I promise you I will do all that is in my power to protect Freda. In fact, if necessary, we will leave Germany."

"Then I accept you as my son and give you our blessing," responded Rolf. "You also have our prayers for safe passage no matter where you go. You need to know that we have been putting significant funds in a Swiss bank account that can be accessed in case of emergency. We believe it will be necessary to have funds available outside of Germany, if the worst comes. After you marry, you both will have access to those funds."

Albert was struck by the seriousness of what he had just been told. "Sir, I hope we never have to use those funds."

As Freda and Albert headed back home down the dimly lit street, snow began to fall softly. He stopped her under a street lamp.

"Your father gave me his blessing for our marriage."

Freda gazed at him through joyful tears.

"Both of your parents are very concerned about your welfare," he continued. "I will do anything I can to protect you."

With that statement, Freda erupted into both more tears and smiles. "I love you, Albert Schmidt," she vowed. "I love you more than ever before. Let's set our wedding date."

14.

F RITZ AND ELISA DECIDED TO MARRY in November 1937—not long after Freda and Albert's engagement. Fritz announced they would have a very German wedding with a justice of the peace presiding. Albert and Freda and a few of Fritz's fellow pilots would be invited. But the wedding party would consist of fellow Nazi Party members. The wedding would be held in a swastika-festooned conference room at a fashionable downtown hotel.

Elisa reluctantly bowed to Fritz's wishes but felt very uncomfortable with the arrangements and guests. He didn't encourage her to invite her friends. He did not want the Nazi Party members to be forced to rub shoulders with the artistic crowd Elisa had befriended.

Petra and Ruth Petter, Elisa's parents, were invited to the political wedding, but they refused to attend. The thought that Elisa was marrying a Catholic in a downtown hotel covered with Nazi decoration sent them reeling. They could not believe their daughter would agree to be married by a justice of the peace instead of by a minister in a church.

Furthermore, the Petters had no interest in making pleasantries with members of the Nazi Party, where a misstep could mean a knock on your door late at night. They considered Fritz a traitor for coming back to Germany to join the Nazi Party. They had once dreamed of going to America, but due to the nature of Petra's research work, the new German government had prohibited them from departing the country.

The fact that her parents refused to attend the upcoming wedding distressed Elisa at first, then it angered her. But after thinking about it, she realized that they would be very uncomfortable attending. She hoped that with time, they would be able to reconcile.

Fritz, however, wasn't distressed in the least by the Petters' decision. He hadn't even bothered to ask for their blessing—he was pretty sure they would have declined. Fritz didn't even tell his own parents about the wedding. He would tell them in person when he arrived in New York after his historic flight. He planned to send them and Johann some money for train fare so they could celebrate with him.

The wedding was a grand celebration. There were larger-than-life pictures of Adolf Hitler on every wall. Toasts were made and returned. The German national anthem was sung along with other Nazi favorites such as "Horst-Wessel-Lied," in honor of a Berlin street brawler killed by Communists. The Nazi salute was on display everywhere. Even the führer sent a personal congratulatory note.

Fritz and Elisa were elated with all the attention and proud to have received a personal note from the führer. Fritz remembered a similar elation way back in 1936, when Herr Kuhn, the head of the German-American Bund, had arrived by ship. He marched through the streets of Berlin in the tree-lined historic Mitte district. What fun that was! Berliners were happy. They were taking pictures of their families with the banners and military men. There were parades and celebrations everywhere.

Now it was time for Fritz's parade, for his national pride. He was marching with Elisa on his arm. The pictures, banners, and celebration exhilarated him.

Albert and Freda's upcoming wedding would be much different, in comparison. Their wedding would be held in the chapel at Heidelberg University in April 1938. This location was very appropriate, seeing as Rolf had been on the faculty for so many years. The glamour of the venue was somewhat dimmed due to his earlier demotion, but it still felt like home. Albert arranged for free airfare to Heidelberg for the wedding party and guests. He also arranged a honeymoon in Paris.

The wedding was well attended by Freda's family members as well as Rolf's faculty friends. Albert and Freda agreed it was best that Fritz and Elisa not attend.

It was a short but beautiful ceremony presided over by the Reverend Dr. Leo Franke, a Lutheran minister in the theology department. Freda looked gorgeous, proudly wearing her mother's white-lace wedding gown with a short train. Albert sported a simple, dark suit. "So I don't upstage the bride," he joked.

After the ceremony, the group was treated to a light brunch, then the bride and groom were off to Paris by car. Freda snuggled close to Albert, and he draped his right arm over her shoulder.

She's maturing, he thought. *She no longer finds it necessary to always debate with me. We will definitely be a happy family.*

Then he remembered the promise he had made to Rolf to protect Freda at all cost. The risks of living in Germany seemed to be growing every day. He didn't want to worry Freda at this time, but he knew they would need to agree on a course of action soon.

Of course, that decision could certainly wait until after the honeymoon.

The Nazi Party encouraged large families, so it didn't take long for Elisa to become pregnant after their own honeymoon. But Fritz had business to attend. The year 1938 would be very good for him.

Work continued on the transatlantic flight as well as the Antarctic expedition planned for later that year. A great deal of research had to be done on wind levels, weather station information, and a host of other support services. Aircraft had to be selected and modified, and the crew had to be trained in a variety of ways not normally covered by continental flying.

Fritz was heavily involved in the crew training as well as the aircraft selection and modification. His extensive experience with multiengine

German planes and his formal aeronautical training gave him confidence as he made calculations for his flight to New York. Fritz was gaining more and more familiarity with the Fw 200. He liked being responsible for his own destiny. In addition, he insisted he was the only one who could properly lay out the navigation route to New York. He spent many nights hunched over charts and weather reports.

Fritz reveled in thoughts of looking into Americans' eyes and flaunting the success and expertise of his German people. He no longer considered the United States his home. This was his small payback for the murderous Treaty of Versailles.

Fritz was sad to hear that anti-German sentiments were growing in America. He did not understand the overall fear that Germany would start a world war. He believed that Germany was merely strengthening its forces to protect itself and Europe from the Communists.

While Fritz was preparing for the flight, Elisa delivered twin boys in July, a month early. Fritz named the eldest Adolf Petra. The middle name was a small concession to Elisa and her father. The younger twin was named Otto, in honor of Fritz's father. Now he had more news to share with his family when he arrived in the United States.

Fritz was as elated as Elisa was with the two boys. He could not wait for them to grow old enough to join the Hitler Youth movement. Elisa settled into a comfortable hausfrau position while Fritz worked many long hours.

Albert and Freda were also happy. There were no children in sight, as yet. They wanted to develop their relationship as one of mutual respect and admiration rather than concentrate on the romance. They also had a growing concern for their future in Germany. They wanted to be sure they could move quickly, if necessary.

Freda worked with social services to assist orphaned children. In some cases, the parents had died. In others, the parents had merely "disappeared." She was active in fundraisers to help with shelter, food, and clothing. In addition, she worked to provide the small necessities of life—soap, tooth-paste, books, and toys—for the children.

Much to Albert's surprise, he found Freda writing in a journal one morning.

"I want to document our life together," she explained. "We have been through so much, but there is so much adventure to come."

She forbade Albert from ever reading the entries. He respected her enough to resist the temptation.

Albert helped Freda with her fundraising when he wasn't working on the proposed air route from South Africa to Santiago, Chile. The führer wanted that operational by early 1939. With his experience, Albert was working on many of the same calculations as his brother was working on for the Berlin to New York route.

Despite their continued work with Deutsche Luft Hansa, the brothers did not see each other often. In fact, since Fritz's wedding, Albert tended to avoid his brother. He was concerned with Fritz's extremism. It was as if some alternate force had taken over Fritz. Yet Fritz was his brother, so Albert tried to be cordial. Fritz, on the other hand, could not understand his brother's lack of interest in becoming an officer in the Luftwaffe and the Nazi Party.

In August 1938, Fritz climbed into the cockpit of a heavily modified Focke-Wulf Fw 200 at the Berlin Tempelhof Airport and lifted off for Floyd Bennett Field in New York City. The flight lasted twenty-four hours and fif-ty-six minutes. During the flight, Fritz looked forward to seeing his parents and oldest brother.

When Fritz landed, he was quickly processed through immigration. Then he saw his American family waiting in the arrival lounge.

Otto looked old and tired. He had lost the fire in his eyes that Fritz remembered. He was stooped, as if the trials of being a German living in America rested heavily on his shoulders. He appeared beaten down. He was only fifty-six but looked seventy.

He was less enthusiastic about politics in general and European affairs specifically. He had spent some time in jail for his bund activities, and the militant anti-Nazi climate in America had taken years off his life. Gangsters, as they were called, systematically beat anyone in Detroit who was pro-Nazi. There were rumors that the FBI actually promoted this activity. Fritz saw this as a mirror to what the Brown Shirts were doing in Germany to anyone who was anti-Nazi. He felt it strangely hypocritical.

Johann also had a hard story. He had lost his job at Ford Motor Company merely due to Otto's bund affiliations. He had been subjected to intense interrogation by the FBI. Agents nearly destroyed his house in Detroit as they searched for "evidence." Looters did even more damage afterward. Thankfully, Johann landed a great opportunity to build an airport, and he had just recently been hired back at Ford. Johann may have repaired his reputation and career, but still, the whole experience had been stressful.

Fritz sympathized with his American family yet felt smug about his decision to immigrate to Germany. He had a new wife, two fine children, and a great job with a substantial income. His American family had tried to live the American dream. They had been loyal to the country and had been treated badly.

Fritz tried to set these thoughts aside and enjoy his time with his family. He flagged down a taxi, and they left for the famous Waldorf Astoria for a grand dinner, compliments of Deutsche Luft Hansa. It was the best meal his family had seen in many years.

Fritz took this opportunity to give Otto and Emma pictures of Elisa and the twins. He also brought a picture of Albert and Freda at their wedding. Emma could not stop the tears as she clutched the pictures to her chest, realizing she would never be a part of this family so far away.

Johann was especially pleased to see his younger brother, but he chose not to discuss the reports of continued German aggressions. He also didn't mention he'd be building bombers at the Ford Motor Company. He knew Fritz was a Nazi Party member. The Nazi Party was now the only legal party in Germany, physically oppressing anyone who dared to oppose them—Social Democrats, Communists, or conservatives.

Johann had started attending sessions with the local Communist Party. They seemed to be the only counterweight to the Nazis. They had tried and, unfortunately, failed in the Spanish Civil War, but at least they had attempted to stop the forces of fascism.

He had even considered going over to Spain to volunteer with the Abraham Lincoln Brigade. However, Ann had talked him out of fighting for the sake of their children. The brigade took heavy casualties. The US government did not support the volunteers, and it was rumored that the government encouraged harassment of the returning members, not unlike the harassment of the pro-Nazi activists. Apparently, any action deemed in support of the Communists aroused the same fears as did actions in support of the Nazis. Johann knew he could not tell any of this to Fritz or Otto. They both believed that the Communists were the real threat.

After dinner and a few hours of visiting, Fritz escorted his family to Grand Central Terminal to catch a train back to Detroit. Then he returned to his hotel room to rest. Tomorrow he would fly the return leg back to his true family.

The next morning, Fritz climbed back in the cockpit for the return to Berlin. He was well rested and prepared for the long day of flying. The aircraft performed beautifully. Due to the prevailing winds, he reached Berlin in only nineteen hours and forty-seven minutes. What an achievement!

As the months passed, Albert continued his calculations for the South Atlantic crossing routes and the equipment that would be required. In April 1939, Deutsche Luft Hansa announced a scheduled flight from Johannesburg, South Africa, to Santiago, Chile. The Fw 200 aircraft was used again with its extended fuel tanks. Refueling in Rio de Janeiro, as Albert recommended, was ideal.

Albert had the pleasure of being named the captain of that first flight. His hard work had paid off. He would fly from Berlin to South Africa, with a short stop in Madrid. After connecting with Deutsche Luft Hansa's South American partners, Syndicato Condor of Brazil and SCADTA of Columbia, he would head to Rio. This route was significant due to the number of

German families in Argentina and Brazil. The preparations for the flight were superb. The plane ran flawlessly, cruising at over nine thousand feet. Germany had one more aeronautical triumph.

After his return, Albert and Freda celebrated the birth of their daughter. They named her Katrina. Now with the additional responsibility for his growing family, Albert quietly considered this South African route as a possible escape from Germany.

It was becoming abundantly clear that war could break out at any time. With the German occupation of Czechoslovakia, the Western powers would not believe Herr Hitler again. England and France began to increase mobilization. In fact, Great Britain had been strengthening its air force since 1935. This had forced Hitler to reveal that he had created an air force, a violation of the Treaty of Versailles.

Albert had never believed Hitler was in accordance with the treaty. He knew the significance of air power. He had seen the new planes coming into the Tempelhof airfield. The sleek, deadly Me 109s had been the terror of the Condor Legion in the Spanish Civil War.

The newly modified Fw 200 was now being converted to wartime use by strengthening the wings and fuselage to carry bomb loads. Defensive machine guns were also being added to the front, aft, and dorsal sides of the aircraft. Even with these modifications, the Fw 200's fuselage often failed with this additional weight. The Junkers Ju87, known as the Stuka dive bomber, the Junkers Ju88, and the Heinkel He 111 were all powerful war planes used in the Spanish Civil War. They were now being refitted for another war.

Albert learned from a friend in the air ministry that Germany possessed over 7,350 aircraft. Specifically, the Luftwaffe would have nearly 4,000 modern combat aircraft—more than any Western country. Albert knew the only reason for this many aircraft was war. With war imminent, Albert was concerned about being drafted into the Luftwaffe. He did not want to drop bombs on cities, with their civilian populations.

He would get his family out before the war came. He had a plan, and it looked good. Now all he had to do was make it work—and work soon.

15.

ESPITE THE GROWING DANGER OF WAR, Albert tried to make
the most of life. He loved his free time with Freda and Katrina.
They spent time visiting Rolf and Margarette, who adored
their new granddaughter.

They also visited with Ruth and Petra Petter and their son, Karl, on
many occasions. Although Fritz and Elisa lived nearby, Ruth and Petra had
not seen the couple since the wedding "abomination," as Ruth called it. It
seemed Elisa kept busy with the twins, and Fritz was always away flying. The
Petters learned about the twins through Albert and Freda, but they never
received an announcement or a picture of their new grandsons. Without a
connection to their own grandchildren, Ruth and Petra delighted in spoiling
Albert and Freda's bubbly Katrina.

Albert and Freda also loved to take Katrina on picnics to the parks
in Berlin. Albert insisted on introducing her to the zoo. She cheerfully
oohed and aahed as he carried her from one furry display to the next. Her
dark-brown ringlet curls bounced around her face, and her bright-blue eyes
reflected her energy.

"She tires me out," Albert said with happy exasperation. "I don't know
how you do it day in and day out."

"Well, you don't see much of her with all your flying around Europe
and South America," joked Freda. "If you were here, you would figure out a
way to deal with it, my darling."

"Well, it's a living," sighed Albert as he bounced Katrina on his knee. "Anyways, it provides us with some options."

"What options are you talking about?" asked Freda.

Albert glanced over his shoulder for anyone who might overhear the conversation.

"Darling, things are changing rapidly." He rocked Katrina and smiled as she snuggled into his arm for a nap. "Everything seems to be balancing on the head of a pin. Not only in Germany but all of Europe. If there is one small mistake, there will be war. It will be a war much more violent than the last one."

Albert looked into Freda's eyes. They glistened with understanding rather than fear.

"Freda, I'm not comfortable with some of your activities to raise funds for the Nazi opponents. Do you realize what could happen if someone exposed you? The whole family could be arrested by the Gestapo."

Freda frowned and shook her head. "Albert, I'm trying to help Germany and keep it from going over the edge. Maybe, just maybe, there are enough rational Germans to prevent that from happening!"

"My God, Freda. You're living in a dream world. We live in a police state, and there's no organized resistance to the Nazi regime."

"Yes, there is. I've made contact with so many people willing to stand up against the party. Some are army officers. Some even work in Abwehr, the military intelligence agency."

Albert stared at his wife in stunned silence. He was just realizing the extent of her involvement with the anti-Nazi movement. *She's playing Russian roulette with our family*, he thought. Some of her friends had been arrested by the Gestapo and then disappeared. Although Freda was never directly tied to any wrongdoing, Albert didn't know how long it would be until she was targeted too.

"Freda, I'm concerned for you, for Katrina, for your father—who continues to teach against Nordic superiority even after his demotion." He nearly woke Katrina with the force of his oration. "It would take just one student to complain, and he would be fired from the university or even arrested. Your mother could also be arrested. At their age, they wouldn't survive in a Nazi prison."

Albert stopped to consider his timing—was it too soon to share his plan? He then turned to Freda and took a deep breath.

"I've been working on a plan to escape Germany. Hopefully, we can all use it before we are pursued by the Gestapo."

Freda looked at him with surprised exasperation. "Don't you feel an obligation to stay and help Germany?"

"My obligation is to you and Katrina and your parents. That is an obligation I can and will do something about. I see now that it was a mistake to leave the United States. I can't live in a police state."

"Albert, I love you and love that you are so concerned for our whole family." A tear slid slowly down her cheek. "I've been watching the changes around us too. I didn't want to admit it, but I think you are right. We need to get our family out of harm's way. Let's get your plan organized."

Rolf Fromm was in the middle of a summer class at Heidelberg University when the classroom door opened and four uniformed Gestapo agents walked in with pistols in their hands.

"This class has ended," one of them announced to the students, never taking his eyes off Rolf. "Please gather your books and leave the room."

Rolf stood frozen in place with his arm still extended toward the blackboard, chalk gripped tightly in his fingers. The students quickly gathered their belongings and hurried from the room.

When the shuffling of feet had ceased, the man spoke again. "Professor Fromm, you will come with us immediately to Gestapo headquarters to answer for your traitorous actions."

The agents pointed their weapons at Rolf. Rolf put down the chalk and started to gather his books off the desk.

"You won't need any of your filthy propaganda," an agent snapped. "The Gestapo just needs to ask you a few questions."

They marched Rolf out to the staff car and drove him to headquarters. For the rest of the day and part of the evening, they questioned him as only the Gestapo dared to do.

Freda was alarmed when she heard about her father's arrest. She was appalled when she saw him after his release from Gestapo custody. Rolf's right eye was swollen shut, and his lip was cut deeply and drooped. He gazed past her with a one-eyed hollow stare. He winced with pain as he walked and carried his left arm at a strange angle.

The threat was now too great to ignore. Albert quickly arranged for Freda, Katrina, Rolf, and Margarette to take a "vacation" to Switzerland. Albert could get them tickets on one of his Deutsche Luft Hansa flights. From there, he planned to smuggle them to Madrid and finally South Africa, where they would be safe.

Keeping the real purpose of the trip secret, Freda told her parents this would be a nice chance for the family to visit a part of Europe they had never seen. Autumn in the Swiss Alps would be lovely. The getaway would give Rolf time to recover before he returned to his teaching duties.

Freda told her parents she'd handle all the tickets and the passports for the vacation. With her government connections, she obtained false passports for her mother and father from the anti-Nazi underground to get them past any Gestapo checkpoints.

Albert handled the financial plans. He moved all their savings into a Swiss bank account to ensure it would be available, no matter where they ended up starting their new life. He also remembered that the Fromms had an account as well.

In late August 1939, the family gathered at the airport for the flight. As the pilot, Albert attended to many details on the flight deck while the family settled in their seats. He came back briefly before takeoff to ensure everything was as expected.

Rolf and Margarette had buckled their seat belts. Though Rolf still looked weary from his experience with the Gestapo, he and Margarette chatted happily about all the wonderful things they planned to do in Switzerland. Katrina, sitting in Freda's lap, was taking in all the sights and sounds and entertaining the travelers around her. Freda met Albert's eyes with a proud and assured nod. All was well, and the plan was coming together.

Freda told her parents they would land in Zurich in a couple hours. They both settled back into their seats. After takeoff, the couple fell asleep. The flight experienced some slight turbulence going over the Alps, though it was nothing compared to the flutters in Freda's chest as she pondered their plan.

An hour into the flight, Rolf suddenly awoke with a gasp. His chest was tight, and he struggled to breathe.

Margarette reached over and caressed his face. "Rolf, what's wrong?"

Freda, though, wasted no time as she called for the stewardess. "Please help him!" she exclaimed, pointing at her father. "He can't breathe!"

The stewardess hurried down the aisle with oxygen. Rolf's breathing gradually recovered, but he remained pale and weak.

When the flight landed in Zurich, Rolf was removed first and rushed to an ambulance, with Margarette at his side. Freda, Katrina, and Albert also deplaned, with Albert turning the flight over to a replacement Deutsche Luft Hansa pilot so he could tend to his family.

"Go," Albert said to Freda. "You can still catch the ambulance before it leaves. I'll meet you at the hospital."

Albert watched the ambulance pull away with Rolf, Margarette, Freda, and Katrina. He would get a taxi and follow the family to the hospital. But then what? They would not be continuing on to Madrid. The plan was already starting to unravel. He fought his fears.

At the hospital, Margarette stayed by Rolf's side and held his hand gently. When Albert arrived, he walked into the waiting room to find Katrina and Freda. Grabbing her mother's hands, Katrina begged for attention. She wanted to investigate this new and interesting place.

Albert met with the doctor, who confirmed Rolf had a weak valve in his heart. The stress of the Gestapo treatment plus the change in oxygen levels during the flight had prompted a heart attack. Rolf was in stable condition but would not be able to fly for several days—and then only if oxygen were available for the extent of the flight.

Albert still needed to keep his promise to take care of Freda and Katrina. That meant the escape needed to be in two steps now. He called Deutsche

Luft Hansa and changed their reservations. He was assigned as copilot on the next day's flight to Madrid and South Africa. Freda and Katrina were confirmed as passengers.

Next, he headed to the bank and withdrew all his funds. Most of it would go to Freda, but he kept some aside so he could pay for Rolf's hospital treatment and a hotel for Margarette. Once his own family was settled, Albert would return for the Fromms. He also verified the amount in the Fromms' own bank account, in case something delayed the plan again.

The night in Zurich was not the pleasant vacation Albert had promised his mother-in-law. Margarette reluctantly left the hospital to share a hotel room with Albert and Freda. Only Katrina was oblivious to the crisis and slept soundly.

In the early morning, Freda woke from her listless sleep to find her mother standing near the window, looking into the quiet Swiss street.

"What are you doing, Mamma?" she asked.

"I couldn't sleep. I'm watching the flower vendor setting up his shop across the street. The blossoms are so lovely. There are so many kinds I don't even recognize. I just wanted to watch. I wanted . . ." Her voice wavered, and she put up her hand to wipe away a tear.

"Mamma, Daddy will be fine. The doctors say he will be well enough to travel in another few days," Freda said, trying to sound optimistic. She wrapped a robe around her shoulders and moved to the window to join her mother.

"Yes, I know, my darling," replied Margarette. She turned away from the window and faced her daughter forcefully. "But fly *where*?"

Freda reached out and clasped her mother's hand. "Mamma, I will tell you the truth now that we're out of Germany," she started. "Albert and I are afraid for the family. After the way the Gestapo treated Daddy, we knew we had to escape quickly. We could not risk having any part of our plan slip out."

"Freda, your father and I understood what was going on. Didn't you think we had also dreamed of escaping Germany?" Margarette shook her head, and an angry tear escaped again. "We tried to act nonchalant about this 'vacation,' but we knew it might be our last chance. Still, we love our home and the Germany we once knew. It's hard to leave your home for perhaps forever."

"Do you think that may have contributed to Daddy's heart attack?" Freda inquired.

Margarette pulled her hand from Freda's grasp and stared across the room. "I don't think it helped the situation, but there was nothing you did to cause the heart attack. If anything, the offer of this flight eased his stress." She sighed and tried to smile. "I know Albert wants to continue on with you and Katrina somewhere. I want you to go. I want you to be safe. We will follow as soon as we are able. Don't worry about us. You know we have substantial funds to last a long period of time."

Mother and daughter joined hands again and turned to watch the flower vendor arranging bouquets to sell to his early morning customers.

16.

ALBERT DROVE MARGARETTE TO THE HOSPITAL in the rental car later that morning. She wanted to take a taxi, but he insisted. Plus, he wanted to check on Rolf's condition before he left with Freda and Katrina.

As they said good-bye, he pressed 1,500 Swiss francs into Margarette's hand to cover her miscellaneous expenses. He knew Freda had confided in her mother about the escape plan.

"I will get Freda and Katrina settled. When I return, I'll arrange for you and Rolf to join them. I've prepaid the hotel for the week, and the hospital bills are covered too. This is just for any other incidentals that come up."

"Albert, you have been more like a son to us," Margarette said, patting his hand as they secretly held the money between them. "I will return this to you when we are back together in a few days."

Freda and Katrina were waiting at the hotel when Albert returned. Albert gave Freda the majority of the funds he had withdrawn from their account. He was glad he had saved so much of his salary. Freda had fed and dressed Katrina and packed their meager belongings for the flight to Madrid and on to Johannesburg, South Africa. They went to the airport in a taxi, boarded the aircraft without delay, and, after a preflight check, took off for Madrid.

Finally able to relax at the controls, Albert let out a sigh as the flight passed into French airspace.

"Was that a sigh of relief or trepidation?" asked his pilot.

"I'm just praying you'll stay healthy on this leg. I'm good with my Spanish for Madrid, but I'm still a little shaky on my French," Albert joked. "How about you take over for now, and I'll be right back?"

With a nod, the pilot resumed control, and Albert left the cockpit to check on his family.

"All is right with the world," declared Freda, bouncing Katrina. The little girl giggled when she saw her father walking down the aisle.

Albert took his daughter's face in his hand and had to agree. All was right with the world. They were heading for a new life, far from the grasp of Nazi Germany.

The flight plan called for fueling stops in Madrid and central Africa before reaching Johannesburg, where the family would stay in a hotel. The next morning, Freda and Katrina would go to the home of Dale and Angela Martin, her British friends. The Martins were aware of the plan and were tracking the European tensions on a wireless radio. With his wife and daughter safe, Albert would return to pilot the aircraft to South America on the final leg of his obligation. Once he returned to Johannesburg, they would work out a plan to rejoin with her parents.

Albert returned to the cockpit with a small smile. The escape plan was working. It had just taken its own unforeseen twist. With what they had already been through, there was nothing they couldn't handle.

After landing in Madrid, Albert went back to check on his family again. "Stay on board, Freda," he cautioned. "Just walk Katrina in the aisle. I have to stay with the aircraft during the refueling, and I don't want us separated."

When the fueling trucks pulled away, he kissed Freda, patted Katrina on the head, and resumed his position as copilot. The next leg of the trip would be long and would take them well into the night. Albert hoped he could sleep rather than stay awake, going over and over his plan in his head. It *had* to work. Just a few short days, and they would disappear. No one would know where the family had gone.

A final refueling stop midway across Africa merely heightened Albert's anxiety. When he went to check on Freda, he found Katrina sleeping quietly. Freda just kissed him and snuggled back under her cover.

"Wake us when we get there, darling." She smiled and closed her eyes, fighting her own case of nerves. She didn't want Albert to know she was apprehensive.

Finally, they landed in Johannesburg. A car was waiting, as planned, to take the flight crew as well as Freda and Katrina to a hotel. They would have breakfast together the next morning before he headed off on the crossing to Rio de Janeiro. It would be one of his last trips for Deutsche Luft Hansa, although he had not told his employer.

In the morning, Albert woke both Freda and Katrina with a kiss.

"The weather looks great for the ocean crossing," he exclaimed over breakfast. "I might even make it in record time!"

Katrina clapped her hands wildly, though not understanding what the excitement was about.

Albert pressed an envelope into his wife's hand. "I don't want to travel with this much cash. Keep it with the bankbook and the number for your parents' account." Then he put a small envelope in his uniform jacket pocket with his wallet. "I kept a bit for essentials, but I won't need much. Will you and Katrina be all right staying with the Martins?"

"We will be fine, my darling." Freda reached over to straighten his identification pin on his jacket, then she patted him lovingly on the chest. "I will make sure Deutsche Luft Hansa has the Martins' address."

"See you in a couple of days," he said with a smile. "I love you so much, Freda. This will work out just right. You wait and see."

Freda wet her lips and gave Albert a long kiss. She smiled through her tears.

"I'll miss you until you walk back through the door, Albert Schmidt."

Albert was ready to go the next morning. He was assigned as the pilot on this leg. A slight delay for a routine engine repair increased his anxiety. It was the last day in August, and he was feeling the full stress of his plan.

"Deutsche Luft Hansa Seven-Zero-Three, requesting departure, runway two-two," Albert announced on the radio.

The sooner I finish this flight, the sooner I'll be back with Freda, was his mantra.

"Deutsche Luft Hansa Seven-Zero-Three, you are cleared for takeoff on runway two-two," came the reply from the tower.

Now he was on his way. As Freda had said, all was right with the world.

The Fw 200 engines roared as the craft headed down the runway, picking up speed. It wobbled under the weight of the extra fuel tanks and lifted off the ground like an overweight albatross.

"I'll never get used to that," his copilot declared. "The military reinforcements make this bird really awkward when we take off with a full fuel load." He put down the checklist and resumed his position at the navigation table.

"You and me both!" exclaimed Albert.

Secretly, he loved the feeling of controlling the power it took to get this heavy bird off the ground, but he didn't like the wobble. He knew it caused stress to the wings and engines.

As they flew westbound, the sun chased them across the sky. Albert could see tiny waves in the ocean below, although he knew they were much larger in reality. Occasionally he could make out a ship laboring below them before he overtook it.

This is definitely the way to travel. Albert took off his jacket and hung it behind him in the cockpit.

As the hours passed, Albert and the copilot took breaks for quick catnaps. The sun finally caught them, and the ocean disappeared into the darkness.

"Looks like we're right on schedule, Captain," the copilot announced. "We should be landing in about an hour. You need a break?"

"Sure. Why don't you take over, and I'll stretch my legs a bit. I'll be back in about ten minutes."

But just as Albert unbuckled his seat belt and stood up, the aircraft shuddered. He sat back down with a start. "What was that?"

"Nothing showing up on the instruments. Maybe just an air pocket," the copilot reported.

Again the aircraft shuddered. Albert buckled back in and grabbed the radio.

"Deutsche Luft Hansa Seven-Zero-Three to Rio tower. Deutsche Luft Hansa Seven-Zero-Three to Rio tower. We are experiencing some unexpected turbulence. Is there any issue identified near our coordinates?"

"Deutsche Luft Hansa Seven-Zero-Three, this is Rio tower," crackled the reply. "There is a storm east of you but nothing in your immediate vicinity. Do you want to declare an emergency?"

Albert looked at his copilot, who shrugged. "Deutsche Luft Hansa Seven-Zero-Three. Not at this time, Rio. We'll keep you apprised. Deutsche Luft Hansa Seven-Zero-Three out."

Albert continued to scan the instruments for an explanation. Maybe it was just an air pocket, as the copilot guessed.

This plane is like a flying boxcar and may react differently in odd winds, Albert reasoned to himself.

But then the copilot cranked his head and looked quickly out his side window. Spinning back toward Albert, he announced, "We have a fire in engine two, Captain!"

"We're close enough to make it in on three engines. Shut it down!" Albert quickly turned back to the radio. "Deutsche Luft Hansa Seven-Zero-Three to Rio tower. Deutsche Luft Hansa Seven-Zero-Three to Rio tower. We are declaring an emergency. We have a fire in engine two and are shutting it down midflight. Please clear airspace and provide coordinates for an immediate landing."

"Roger that, Deutsche Luft Hansa Seven-Zero-Three," squawked the response. "Is the fire still active, or do you need fire suppression on landing?"

The only response was radio static.

"Deutsche Luft Hansa Seven-Zero-Three, do you copy? What is your status? Deutsche Luft Hansa Seven-Zero-Three?"

No response.

17.

A T NOON ON SEPTEMBER 1, a uniformed Deutsche Luft Hansa representative knocked on the Martins' door. Freda had just fed Katrina and put her down for a nap. Dale and Angela were out shopping for groceries with plans for a gala feast when Albert soon returned.

Freda opened the door. Her face went from confusion to fear when she saw the uniform.

"Madam, may I step inside and talk?"

"The Martins are out shopping. I'm just a guest," she stammered, though knowing well he was there to see her.

"Yes, madam. I'm from Deutsche Luft Hansa. Your husband, Albert, left us this address in case we needed to reach you." The man paused. "I need to inform you that your husband's aircraft never reached Rio de Janeiro. A sudden storm delayed the air search. However, recent search attempts have revealed no sign of the aircraft. We have not found any wreckage or survivors, but in the extreme weather conditions, any wreckage might have been widely scattered." He paused again. "I am so terribly sorry to have to tell you this."

Freda felt her legs grow weak. She reached for a nearby chair and sat down with her head in her hands. Tears did not come. She could not believe what this man had just told her. All was *not* right with the world.

"How could this happen?" she gasped.

"We don't know for sure," the uniformed man stated. "They reported an engine fire one hour from Rio, then the radio went dead. I'm so sorry for your loss. Madam, I can make arrangements for you and your child to return to Germany as soon as possible."

Freda felt her panic rise. She shook her head. "No. Thank you. I'm with friends here. I need time to decide what I'll do next."

"Again, madam, I'm sorry for your loss. Please call us if you need any assistance." With that, the man put his card on the table, walked out the door, and quietly closed it behind him.

Finally alone, Freda went to the living room and turned on the wireless radio, trying to take her mind off the tragedy her life had become. The announcer's voice sounded pinched and ominous.

"Today, September 1, 1939, Nazi forces invaded Poland," he announced. "In response, Great Britain has declared war on Nazi Germany."

Freda gasped again. Now she could no longer control the tears. They washed down her face. Albert had managed to get their family out of Germany just in time. Freda and Katrina were in a British Commonwealth country, safe from the Nazis. Freda's parents were in a neutral country.

However, as a German, Freda could now be considered an enemy alien to the British. Albert had left her with the financial means to take care of herself and Katrina, but the South African government might have something to say if they found out about the money.

Freda dried her eyes and straightened her dress. She could hear Katrina stirring. She needed to take care of her daughter.

When Dale and Angela returned, Freda told them the news and asked them to watch Katrina. She grabbed her coat and purse and headed to the taxi stand. She had a plan.

"Government House, please," she told the driver. She settled back in the seat for the short ride.

Once at the Government House, she found the information desk and requested a meeting with the British ambassador. The clerk looked at her dismissively.

"The ambassador is quite busy at the moment."

"I am Freda Schmidt," Freda announced in a clear, strong voice. "I have important information regarding the military plans of Nazi Germany. I need to speak with the ambassador immediately."

The stunned clerk slid off his chair and hurried down the hall. At the last door on the left, he knocked, waited, then went in. Several minutes later, he returned and ushered Freda down the hall to the same door.

"Ambassador Holland, Miss Freda Schmidt to see you."

"That's *Mrs.* Freda Schmidt," she corrected.

Freda arrived in London on September 15, 1939, holding Katrina's hand with trepidation. British intelligence agents met them and welcomed them to what would become their new homeland.

The agents were impressed as Freda described her escape from Germany and shared details identifying key members of the anti-Nazi underground, including some people working inside the German military intelligence. This woman would certainly be a useful operative. She had the right contacts, critical war information, and a resolve they could barely contain.

Indeed, Freda was determined. Her daughter was now her life. She needed to make the world safe from the Nazis so her daughter and all the children in the world could know freedom, laughter, music, and poetry. That was her mission. Freda was now fully engaged in the war effort. She owed that to the memory of her husband.

To be effective, she would need to change her identity and start a new life. She also needed to help her parents flee Zurich and disappear.

— GERMANY, 1937 —

18.

I N THE LATE SPRING OF 1937, PLANS WERE ALREADY in development for war. A meeting was called at the reichsmarschall's office in Berlin. The meeting would detail a very special project. It would be strategically and politically significant, requiring the utmost in training and planning. The agenda for the meeting was top secret and known only to Luftwaffe reichsmarschall Hermann Göring.

Göring was a man who needed to sit on either an extra-large chair or a sofa. He was huge, a mere memory of the sleek, thin fighter pilot who had commanded the great German ace Manfred von Richthofen (aka the Red Baron). Göring was a very demanding man, and you did everything you could to please him.

This was an unusual meeting with unusual people. Waiting outside the office for the meeting were three men, each with several aides in attendance.

Admiral Wilhelm Canaris, chief of Abwehr military intelligence, was the oldest of the group. He was a shrewd spymaster who struggled with contradictions as he controlled the Abwehr. He secretly protected and motivated the opposition members who were eager to fight against Hitler even while he openly hunted them as conspirators.

General Robert Ritter von Greim was director of the Luftwaffe department of research. Slightly younger than Canaris, von Greim was a decorated World War I fighter pilot now tasked by Göring to build the German air force. He stood rigid with an obvious military bearing.

Dr. Hans Kammler was councilor of the interior ministry and a rising civil engineer in the Schutzstaffel, the SS—the Nazi Party's "protective echelon" corps. The youngest of the group and an ardent SS member, he stared narrow-eyed at the others, contemplating his position.

The group approached the waiting area near the reichsmarschall's office. It was huge, bright, and ornamental. Paintings, tapestries, and antique vases encircled a Nazi flag. Göring's aide greeted them, and they responded with a *"Heil, Hitler."* Opening the door, the aide announced the new arrivals.

Canaris, von Greim, and Kammler marched into the office, leaving their aides in the waiting room. They saw Göring already in a discussion with Heinrich Himmler, the head of the SS as well as the Gestapo. While Göring was a man you always wanted to please, Himmler was a man you never wanted to fail. Failure was often fatal.

Göring offered *"Heil, Hitler."* Everyone in the new group quickly clicked their heels and returned the salute.

"Gentlemen, please take your seats. We have some very important issues to discuss," Göring stated.

They all sat around the table. Göring led off the discussion by nodding to Himmler.

"The reichsführer and I have had discussions with the führer on important strategic issues. We need input from all of you. This information is to be considered the most secret. No information about this discussion will be shared with anyone outside this room. Do you understand?"

All the attendees nodded in agreement.

Göring met eyes with Himmler, then he continued to detail the strategy. "Gentlemen, each of you here have expertise that will be needed for this project to go forward. The situation in Europe is growing tenser each and every day. Following the Anschluss and the targeted annexation of Czechoslovakia, Germany finds itself more and more at risk from potential adversaries. Our ground, sea, and air strength is growing daily. We believe these forces are—or will shortly be—able to dispel or deter our enemies on the European continent. Even the Russians are weak with the purges to their officer corps.

"But we must assume that in the not-too-distant future, we will be forced to defend ourselves by all means at our disposal. We must avoid the problem of the Great War, when new, inexhaustible resources were brought to bear against us before we had completed our victory. We must have a plan in place to neutralize the greatest threat that could affect us."

There was a stirring among the group as they glanced at one another, wondering where this discussion was headed.

Himmler interrupted their thoughts. "Who do you think is the greatest possible threat?" he asked them.

The individuals looked at one another again and at Göring. They mumbled responses of "France?" "Great Britain?" "Russia?"

"No!" Göring and Himmler both shouted. "The United States!"

Göring continued. "Until we can consolidate our victory in Europe, we need an effective plan to thoroughly disrupt America's ability to organize and launch an attack on us. The plan must be powerful, hitting the most critical points of America's war potential. This plan must be put in place quickly so it can be immediately implemented when hostilities begin. It must also be put in place with stealth, as we do not possess aircraft capable of reaching the United States with a meaningful bomb load from any point in Europe."

Göring folded his hands across his ample belly. "Gentlemen, this is your task. You must devise a plan that can be operational in no more than six months. You will work with Dr. Kammler on your recommendations. You will meet on a weekly basis. Dr. Kammler is aware of all the special resources and weapons we are developing so that these can be integrated into the plan. Intelligence from the German-American Bund members and their liaisons in the United States will need to be evaluated and prioritized. You will develop an attack plan and define the resources we need to secure for the attack. We will present your plan in one month." Göring settled back in his cushioned chair. "Are there any questions?"

The "volunteers" dared not meet his gaze nor exchange any look that might indicate indecision. It was now clear that war was expected, and it could include the United States.

When the meeting with Göring and Himmler ended, Canaris left the room and walked down to a small conference area outside the office. He sat, leaned back in his chair, and thought about the discussion.

So the führer, Göring, and Himmler knew there would be a war soon. They wanted it to be a world war! *Have they forgotten so soon the result of the Great War—the utter destruction of the German nation?* Canaris thought.

This plan he and the others were to work on seemed utterly impossible, given with the size of America. The United States had industries on the East Coast, West Coast, Gulf Coast, and in the Midwest. The area was about the size of continental Europe.

How can we anticipate where to strike?

Canaris sighed in resignation. He realized Germany had to do something to at least delay America's production capacity; otherwise, that manufacturing potential would destroy Germany. The Americans could clearly produce more than razor blades with all their steel output.

As the other team members came out of Göring's office, Canaris invited them to join him in his office to begin their discussion. Each man dismissed his aides to handle important issues and reconvened in Canaris's office one hour later.

In Canaris's office, Kammler and von Greim drew chairs up close to Canaris. Von Greim started the discussion.

"Canaris, how do you want to proceed?"

Canaris took a deep breath. "We have a tight timeline, and we can't fail the führer or the reichsmarschall."

To himself, he added, *You Nazi sycophants don't have a clue how difficult this will be—if it can even be done. However, there is no way I will say that out loud!*

"Gentlemen," he continued, "we can each bring specialties to this project. Due to the secret nature of this topic, I feel the security of my office here in the Abwehr headquarters would provide the best privacy. Agreed?"

Von Greim and Kammler nodded.

"Does anyone have any specific plans in mind at this time?" Canaris posed.

Von Greim raised his eyebrows, and Kammler studied the wood grain in the table. The question was left unanswered.

"Well, then, I suggest we take a few days and pull together lists of weapons, aircraft, and available targets from our own perspectives." Canaris checked his calendar. "We can meet back here Friday afternoon to discuss the details we have discovered and begin formulating a plan."

Canaris was a master at keeping one step ahead of the competition, namely Himmler and the SS. He would try to control this plan so Germany would be protected but not sacrificed.

The next week, Canaris welcomed von Greim and Kammler back to his office. Canaris led off the discussion.

"America is a huge country. It would be impossible to attack the entire country with our present resources. Yet we may be able to attack all parts of it."

Von Greim and Kammler exchanged a quick glance, then nodded their agreement. Canaris offered the men cigars from the rosewood humidor on his teak desk. When they both declined, he withdrew a cigar, snipped the end carefully, then continued.

"I tasked my agents in America to provide information about targets of present and likely future military potential. They do not know our purpose. They are merely gathering information. It will take time for complete information to arrive from my agents. However, initial reports show there is currently very little war production in the United States. There is some ship-building, but no major aircraft production. There is also some heavy-gun production, but only as needed to supply the small American air force, army, and some naval ships. America's army ranks about twenty-sixth in the world, and they are still using equipment from the Great War."

Canaris paused for effect and lit the cigar with his gold lighter. "I have tasked my agents with finding a choke point, an important transportation route for raw material shipments. Damaging or destroying such a choke point would delay American war production and perhaps buy the Reich six months or more to establish dominance in Europe and prevent an American intervention."

"What do you have in mind?" asked Kammler, interested in the direction this discussion was heading.

"I'm trying to identify oil fields, refineries, ore supplies, coal mines, that sort of thing. In addition, I have asked my agents to identify industrial sites the Americans would quickly convert to war-material production once war is declared. I'm considering car manufacturing plants and the such. In addition to targeting the choke point, we could also conduct a combination of attacks of these various facilities to maximize the effect. Our best chance to conduct the attack is before war is declared—before those key sites could be reinforced."

Canaris paused. He inhaled a great amount of the fragrant smoke and carefully blew smoke rings at the ceiling.

"What do you think, gentlemen?"

Von Greim spoke up first. "From the Luftwaffe standpoint, we do not have an aircraft that could presently reach America with a significant payload to attack the choke point or any facilities. The transatlantic flight limits the weight of any armament. It would result in only a pinprick on the American war machine. We would have to come up with another way to approach this."

Kammler nodded. "I agree with the general. We do have weapons in production that could do tremendous damage, but we don't yet have the range to reach America. For your ears only, we are developing a small weapon of amazing destructive power. Furthermore, we have a delivery device of a new invention called the television. Dr. Manfred von Ardenne demonstrated this TV technology, as it is called, in Bonn in 1931. Using the TV technology, we can adapt it to control either the Henschel Hs 293 glide bomb, which has a range of up to sixteen kilometers, or the Ruhrstahl SD 1400, called the Fritz X, which is a radio-controlled bomb for heavily armed targets. Both now could carry at least three hundred and nineteen kilos of explosives."

Canaris forgot all about his cigar until ash fell from the end onto his desktop. Brushing it quickly aside, he said, "Please continue, Doctor!"

"We would need an aircraft to handle the launch weight of up to fifteen hundred and seventy-two kilos," Kammler said. "About one-third of the bomb's weight is in the explosives. However, if we could design a lighter, more powerful explosive, we could obviously cut the total payload while increasing the destructive power."

"I'm afraid the warhead you describe would still not be enough to destroy a major target," interjected von Greim. "We would either need multiple weapons or a tremendous increase in explosive power. Furthermore, we would have to sneak a capable aircraft into the US, hide it, and load it for the mission. Maybe an agent could purchase or 'procure' an aircraft from the Americans. If so, it would obviously need significant modifications and a crew familiar with American aircraft designs."

"Do the Americans have any aircraft capable of handling this payload?" asked Canaris.

"They do have aircraft capable of carrying at least one of the weapons Doctor Kammler described," explained the general. "The Boeing B-17 Flying Fortress can carry 5,806 kilos—roughly 12,800 pounds to the America measurement system. The new Consolidated B-24 Liberator is also a possibility."

The silence in the room was palpable as they all contemplated the plan.

"Deutsche Luft Hansa is testing a nonstop trip from Berlin to New York with the Fw 200 Condor," von Greim continued. "They have already added extended fuel tanks, so that may also be a possibility. In addition, these aircraft can be disassembled, transported to a neutral location, and reassembled for a later attack."

With nods around the table, the meeting adjourned.

The following week, the three met again to draw up an action plan heavily dependent on the special weapons Dr. Kammler proposed.

"Gentlemen," Canaris said, "based on Dr. Kammler's information, do we agree we should target several key areas in America for attack at the onset of hostilities?"

Dr. Kammler and General von Greim both nodded. "*Ja, ja*. We agree," they chorused.

"Dr. Kammler, what is the timing of the new explosive?"

"My scientists report that we have discovered a new and powerful explosive that will allow us to detonate material very effectively without the huge size of a conventional bomb," Kammler explained. "The material is called red mercury. It works by compressing a core of radioactive material. We have conducted several tests already. The explosion equals the power of one thousand of our present bombs. In addition, the size of the material allows a much lighter bomb that is easier to deploy. We could have thirty of these available in six months."

Von Greim smiled at the revelation. "This provides more options for weapon delivery. Our Henschel glide bombs could carry the lighter payload, if that is the delivery system."

"Great!" Canaris beamed. "I can report that we have feedback on several high-profile targets that would clearly impact defensive production in America. Several dams, locks, and industrial sites are possible targets. Even if they are not currently used for military production, my agents have indicated they would be rapidly converted in case of war."

"Where are they located?" asked Kammler.

"Many of them are located in the eastern half of the country. So far, we have identified Aluminum Company of America in Massena, New York; Wright Aeronautical in Paterson, New Jersey; and Curtiss Wright with locations in Beaver, Pennsylvania, and Caldwell, New Jersey. Three companies—Colt's Manufacturing, Pratt and Whitney, and Hamilton Standard—are located in East Hartford, Connecticut. And finally, both Chrysler Corporation and Ford Motor Company are located in Detroit, Michigan."

Von Greim and Kammler nodded at the impressive list of companies Canaris had detailed.

"There is one more site I would like to add to the list, though at a later date," Canaris continued.

Von Greim and Kammler both leaned forward in their chairs. Their puzzled expressions could not hide their confusion.

"In fact, this may be the best target," Canaris claimed. "Its destruction would stall wartime production in America for a good six months. When I receive some final data from one of my most trusted operatives, I will reveal it to you.

"Before we select our site, however, we need to continue our work on the action plan to present to Göring and Himmler. It will take six months to get the bombs ready. Then we need to arrange transport for the explosives, the delivery mechanism, and the personnel. I have already anticipated some of these needs. I have activated a channel to get material covertly into America by shipping freight through some of our own companies. We are in the process of identifying and procuring locations for storage and retrofitting, if needed."

"Good work," praised von Greim, though still pondering the mysterious addition to the list. "Any early work will expedite our meeting with Göring and Himmler and perhaps increase the odds of receiving their approval. I have been working on the delivery method and have identified pilots who could deliver the bombs when the time comes."

The three men had accomplished much in the few weeks, but much was left to do. They would present this plan to Göring and Himmler, hoping for approval. The six-month schedule looked unreasonable, but Canaris was not one to ruffle Nazi leadership.

He was a master of deception and had dodged, sidestepped, and countered Nazi impatience by always having an alternative plan. He would do the same in this case and pull the proverbial rabbit out of his hat. His own plan was already in development.

19.

OR TWO MORE WEEKS, Canaris, von Greim, and Kammler met often to work on the details of the attack on America. Kammler was not pleased to admit that some of the "wonder weapons" he initially proposed would not be ready within the six-month window.

"I am sorry, gentlemen," he said reluctantly. "Our scientists have not made enough progress on the red mercury bombs. The test bombs have not behaved the way we initially expected. We will have some, but not more than three or four, ready for our timeline."

Canaris sneered. "You mean *your* scientists, Dr. Kammler," he clarified.

"*Ja,*" Kammler agreed, bowing his head. He knew he could end up being the sacrificial lamb on this Nazi altar.

"Gentlemen, we are required to report back to Göring and Himmler next week," Canaris reminded his team. "We need to be realistic as to what can be done and the tools that will truly be available. We need a positive, workable, and significant plan—reality, not fantasy."

He paused for effect.

"Thankfully, I anticipated this worst-case scenario of our other plans failing. I have moved ahead with an operation structured to give us a high degree of success."

Both von Greim and Dr. Kammler seemed greatly relieved that at least some progress was being made. They knew they were beaten, so they merely nodded their consent.

Canaris had their full attention. He was ready to reveal his secret plan. "This is what I have initiated: I ordered the construction of an air base in a wilderness area in America. It is a close flying distance from many of the critical defense targets we have already discussed. Personnel are already working to build the base, which will include a long, all-weather runway; storage facilities for aircraft; and a weapons bunker that will be extremely well camouflaged and guarded."

Von Greim and Kammler exchanged a glance, knowing Canaris had outsmarted them.

"I propose we use the attack weapons that we already have at our disposal," Canaris continued. "If additional weapons are developed and effectively tested, they can be an added bonus at a later time."

Von Greim recovered his composure. "What type of currently available weapons would you suggest we supply to this base?"

"We should send over at least two Fw 200 aircraft, modified to look like Swissair or another nation's commercial aircraft. We could ship them over in pieces and assemble them, then fly them into the base later this year. We'll have room for three at the base," Canaris boasted, now taunting his audience.

"If the nonstop transatlantic flight succeeds, as expected, it should not be suspicious if additional Fw 200s fly to the United States to transport cargo. That leaves you to determine the most accurate weapons to use with these aircraft."

"We will need some accurate yet powerful weapons, right, Dr. Kammler?" von Greim stated.

"That is a certainty," agreed Kammler. "We do have a new bomb that has been successfully tested. It's called a fuel-air bomb. It works on a two-part principle. First, a container explodes at about three hundred meters above ground level, dispensing a special cloud of dust particles. The second container, filled with fuel oil, explodes a few seconds later, igniting the dust particles. The reaction is like a mine explosion with a large impact area."

Canaris and Von Greim exchanged victorious grins and urged Kammler to continue.

"Our tests with a small bomb on an airfield resulted in damage over a twelve-kilometer area."

The grins faded to shock.

"My God!" exclaimed von Greim. "How large was the bomb?"

"It was only two hundred kilos." Kammler sat back, proud he had finally gotten the upper hand in the discussion. "Once we drop one of these bombs, we could move in with a conventional bombing strike and push the destruction to an even greater depth."

Von Greim was sitting on the edge of his chair. "We could hammer the target with a conventional PC 1400 armor-piercing bomb with a four-teen-hundred-kilogram explosive charge. We have a new and improved explosive that can be placed in the bombs. The newly modified Fw 200 with its extra fuel can easily carry three of these conventional bombs for several hundred miles."

"This is really starting to take shape," exclaimed Canaris. "Flying from the secret base, the Fw 200 would not need additional armaments or extra fuel. In fact, if the targets are nearby, the Fw 200 could easily carry the fuel-air bomb and two conventional bombs, making the attack in one pass."

"Excellent!" said von Greim. "I suggest we send at least twelve of the fourteen-hundred-kilogram bombs and six fuel-air bombs to your secret base as soon as possible. This would allow us to attack up to six critical targets."

"If time permits," Canaris suggested, "we could also ship over some thirty-eight-hundred-kilogram large hollow-charge warheads. Those can be packed into an American Curtiss-Wright CW-20 or a Douglas DC-3. We will have one of each at the base, disguised as part of an airfreight company. If we included the remote guidance systems we have developed to fly those planes, it would give us a flying bomb to destroy what I think is the key target."

Von Greim and Kammler exchanged a surprised look and locked on Canaris with expectation.

"Key target?" asked von Greim. "What is your key target, Admiral?"

Canaris slowly rose to his feet. He removed a United States map from his briefcase and ceremoniously unfolded it across the table.

"Here, gentlemen," he said, pointing to a red dot near the center of the map. "The boat locks at Sault Ste. Marie, Michigan."

He let the surprise register. He definitely had their attention now.

"This target is the most critical, since ninety-two percent of all United States iron ore traverses through that lock during the seven or eight months of the year that their Great Lakes are ice-free. The area is unguarded. Both Canada and the United States are convinced no enemy plane could possibly penetrate their borders that far without being detected. What they don't know is that this target is a mere one hundred and seventy-five miles from our new base."

Kammler licked his lips in nervous anticipation.

"The ore that goes through that point," Canaris explained, "feeds the steel mills farther south in the states of Michigan, Ohio, Indiana, Pennsylvania, Illinois, and Wisconsin." He exaggerated the importance by forcefully pointing to each state on the map as he named it. "If we can destroy or even severely damage the locks early in the shipping season, it would take them at least six months to make repairs. If the attack happened in the summer, that would effectively make the impact a full year, since the ice forming on the massive Great Lakes would lock them out for another five months."

"Wouldn't they just find a different way to get the ore where it is needed?" asked von Greim, not wanting to miss a critical flaw.

Canaris had anticipated this question. "The American railroad system cannot move the amount of ore needed to recover. The ships move over ninety million tons each season. They will need much more if war is declared. They would need thousands of railcars to make up that volume, but they don't have that many available. And they couldn't build more railcars without the steel."

Kammler stood, smiled, and saluted the admiral. "Sir, this is truly a can't-lose proposition."

Von Greim, though, was the eternal pessimist. "I see the lock lies between the United States and Canada. The only problem would be if the two countries joined forces and decided to fortify the site before hostilities began."

"That would make it more difficult, for sure," Canaris replied dismissively, "but not impossible. Shall we formalize this plan to present to Göring and Himmler?"

Von Greim and Kammler nodded in agreement.

The team of Canaris, Kammler, and von Greim met with Reichsmarschall Göring and Reichsführer Himmler later that week.

"We have a plan we believe will bring American war production to its knees for six months to a year," presented Canaris proudly. He continued to explain how the airport was already being built under the guise of a mining support operation.

"No one suspects its true use," Canaris bragged. "In fact, my agent John Rogers has been praised by men such as Edsel Ford for his forward thinking. Mr. Ford unwittingly also recommended a very good engineer who has been indispensable in completing the airport on our tight deadline."

Canaris next gloated about the decision to name the locks at Sault Ste. Marie as the key target, even though other targets had also been identified. He was about to expound on the planes already on-site and the bomb cargo they had already sent on its way, when Göring halted the presentation, slamming his palm loudly on the tabletop.

"Admiral," Göring spoke with careful emphasis, "your *assignment* was to provide a plan that we could review with Herr Hitler and the leaders of the Reich." His glare circled the table, making each man squirm in turn. "You have apparently taken it upon yourselves to not only *design* a plan but *implement* it as well."

Himmler also glared at the team members as they slid down in their chairs, trying unsuccessfully to stay out of range.

"Herr Hitler is the one who controls the purse strings for expenditures such as this!" he shouted. "He has the last say on how many sites we will target or which ones are 'key' when we are in a war."

Canaris felt his legs begin to weaken. He realized he had made a serious error in going so far as to reveal details of the base construction in progress. He should have presented it all as a "plan," keeping the implementation secret. He took a slow, deep breath to steady his nerves.

"I'm sure you understand where your team overstepped its bounds, don't you, Admiral?" accused Himmler with a sneer.

"Yes, Herr Himmler," stammered Canaris.

The noise of the traffic on the streets below was the only thing audible in the room. Himmler and Göring allowed the silence to continue.

"However," Göring finally interjected, "the plan is a good one. I agree that its success is likely, as long as no one outside this room finds out about the plan. You will wait for the führer's approval before taking this any further, *ja?*"

Von Greim, Kammler, and Canaris all nodded their full agreement.

"We shall take the plan to the führer," Göring announced.

The meeting ended. A safe distance from the room, von Greim and Kammler congratulated Canaris on his excellent presentation.

Canaris accepted the praise, but inside his mind reeled. What would happen when Göring and Himmler would present the plan to the führer? The project was too far along to cancel if the führer did object. The aircraft were already in place or on their way to the airport. Many of the munitions were also either in shipment or already stored in the nearby mine. Plus, too many people in the United States were aware of the airport's existence—if it were abandoned now, it would raise alarm. People might suspect it was more than just a new airport in the wilderness.

If Hitler approved the plan, Canaris knew Göring and Himmler would claim it as their own. If Hitler did not approve it, however, Göring and Himmler—as well as Kammler and von Greim—would find a way to place Canaris directly on the hook by himself. Perhaps it would be a meat hook.

Canaris started to plan his own escape.

The next week, Göring and Himmler presented the plan to the führer. He listened with rapt attention. Himmler had never seen him so intent.

When the presentation was over, the silence was palpable. Hitler's eyes narrowed, and his thin lips actually disappeared under cover of his little square mustache. Finally, he broke the silence.

"Do we have pilots identified and trained to fly these missions?"

"Yes, Mein Führer." Göring was happy to answer this simple question. "We have several available, but there are two outstanding pilots with the multiengine aircraft experience we require. We will get them to the base before the mission needs to be launched."

"Will the base be ready early in 1939?"

"Yes, Mein Führer. We could begin shipping the required equipment immediately. However, we need to be careful not to raise suspicions by flying in too many aircraft in a short period. We will easily be ready by then."

"Excellent," replied Hitler. "In any case, you will wait for my signal before the attack is initiated. It will need to be ready by early 1939, when I plan to annex Czechoslovakia. The Allies could declare war on us at that time, as it will be a violation of the Munich Agreement."

With that, preparations continued with high intensity.

— VIETNAM, 1968 —

20.

BILL O'BRIEN WAS REALLY LOSING WEIGHT. After more than seven months in the jungle, he had dropped from a solid 190 pounds to just 165. His green jungle fatigues were as bleached out as his hair. His face looked like weathered leather.

On a good note, his actions on his first patrol won him praise from the ARVN and American forces as well as a Bronze Star for valor and a Purple Heart. His second patrol awarded him a Silver Star.

However, Bill still found himself in the field working as a forward observer. *That's what you get for being good at something*, he thought to himself. He tucked away the medals. No use for those here.

Occasionally, he received letters from college friends detailing their jobs and latest escapades. They always ended with "Wish you were here, but give 'em hell for us!" Some of his old friends were now protestors.

Barbara finally sent him a letter in response to the multiple letters he had sent her. She was still against the war. She had moved further in her relationship with Robert, her new significant other, though they had not married. Bill wondered if she was as unwilling to commit to Robert as she had been to him. Still, it was nice to receive a letter from her. Any letter was welcome.

Bill had been in the field on and off for months. The pattern of activity was picking up. He would be out on an ops mission for a week or so, then have three or more days back at the firebase to rest and recuperate.

In the field, he slept on the cold ground and ate C rations from the Korean War. The ham-and-something-questionable and the chicken-and-lima-beans were both green with preservatives. He'd eaten so many shades of green that he was even crapping green. He figured the rations had a shelf life of fifty years or more. He never liked to eat in the dark for fear the food would actually glow and give away his location.

Bill always looked forward to his opportunities to work with the Montagnards, or the 'Yards, as they were known. These were the hill people of the Central Highlands of Vietnam and ethnically different from the Vietnamese. They hated the Communists and had a general dislike for the Vietnamese majority. The 'Yards worked with US Army Green Berets and Rangers. They often were just children—but fierce fighters. The US provided them with dehydrated field rations that were greatly superior to the standard C rations. Bill liked to swap items from his ration pack to get some diversity in his food.

Life was a bit better back at the firebase. Meals weren't great, but at least they were real. (The cooks tried hard, but they could still nearly ruin perfectly edible food.)

Bill's tasks were light on the base. Occasionally he was assigned as officer of the day, which required checking guard positions at night. He was even able to get back to the rear headquarters, where they served mixed drinks at the officers' club.

On his days off, he could sleep late, drink some warm green beer (which tasted better than the heavily chlorinated water), and relax. Occasionally, he would wander over to the supply depot when a delivery came. That was more to see if the shipping priority was still true with limited space.

Yep, the priority shipping sequence was still ammunition, ice, and then beer.

The troops were nearly in mutiny when an enemy mortar managed to hit the shed storing the beer. It resulted in a ten-foot-high plume of green foam. It held its form for several minutes, like a Saint Patrick's Day marshmallow man.

One of the odd facts in Vietnam was that once a base was established, it took the rats from the jungle about a week to find the new location and invade it. Bill had to share his bunk with an occasional invader, though it beat sleeping on the ground.

While Bill couldn't avoid the rats, he did meet some interesting characters during his time on the firebase. One character was an officer in the FDC who tracked his rat kills on a piece of plywood. He set up a route he called the Ho Chi Minh Rat Trail. He set traps at various points on the firebase. However, his traps were special. They were baited with cheese and had a blasting cap installed. Once the rat grabbed the cheese, the cap exploded, killing the rat. He monitored the "trail" and kept a kill tally.

Another interesting character was a cook who made good use of the rations by making "special" brownies. Bill was warned about the secret ingredient. But one naive officer imbibed several of these brownies, even after warnings from several enlisted men. He was found the next day in his bunk with a marijuana-induced headache and little recollection of what he had done the night before.

The newbies were always a source of good humor and sometimes sheer fright. Bill was visiting a local firebase when a newly arrived second lieutenant ordered an experienced gunnery sergeant and his crew to practice a direct-fire exercise with their 8-inch howitzer. Direct fire aims the artillery piece into the perimeter of the firebase to stop attacking ground troops. A protective barrier of sandbags and dirt surrounded the weapon. The new lieutenant overruled the gunnery sergeant on the gun elevation required to clear the barrier. Despite protests from the gun crew, the new officer insisted the gun be fired.

The crew, gunnery sergeant, and Bill hit the ground. The shell barely cleared the top of the surrounding barrier, destroyed a boulder two hundred yards away, and sent a large chunk of shell casing flying over the prone men. The casing embedded in the unit's mailbox, where the stunned lieutenant was standing. The impaled mailbox rolled at his feet with an eighteen-inch hole. The lieutenant's face flushed green. Bill never saw that officer again.

Bill liked to keep track of another gunnery sergeant whose rank went up and down like an elevator. One day you would see him as an E-5 sergeant; the next he would be a private. Apparently, he liked to drink and got into fights when he went back to the rear. One time it took seven members of the military police to arrest him after he destroyed a noncommissioned officers' club. The man was like a teddy bear when he was sober, though.

Toward the end of his tenth month in Vietnam, Bill was assigned to a major operation near the Cambodian border, about thirty kilometers from the base. This would be a combined operation with elements of the Fourth Infantry Division and an ARVN battalion. This operation would be large, with four hundred men ferrying out on helicopters for a ten-day search-and-destroy mission.

Because of the size of the operation, it would require over sixty helicopter lifts to move all the forces to the landing zone. With only fifteen helicopters available for the transport, the troops would be landed in groups, which meant only a small portion of the force would be on the ground initially.

At dawn on the first day of the mission, Bill and William Spiritlight Norman, his RTO, boarded a helicopter with ARVN troops. Norman came from a proud Cherokee family in Oklahoma. His ancestors had served in the American army since World War I. Norman was an eighteen-year-old specialist fourth class. He was an excellent radio operator, and Bill found him indispensable.

Bill's slick was in the first wave to land. As usual, the prelanding bombardment commenced. Guns from several firebases fired to put a steel curtain around the landing zone. Bill and Norman hit the ground, running for cover.

By the time roughly 160 troops were on the ground, the group was pinned down by concentrated enemy fire from machine guns, 81mm mortars, and RPGs. The fire was coming from three directions. The enemy was well dug in and firing from bunkers that had not been destroyed in the artillery fire. Two of the ten choppers were hit by RPGs, crashing just after the troops jumped eight feet to the ground. The landing zone was now effectively closed. The remaining choppers broke contact and returned to base.

Intelligence for the mission had predicted only sporadic resistance at landing. Judging by the intensity of the fire, however, it looked as though the troops had been dropped in the middle of a North Vietnamese regiment of over one thousand men on their own search-and-destroy mission.

The troops dug in as fast as they could in the area just beyond the landing zone. The downed helicopters were exploding and burning furiously. Most of those helicopter crew members had not survived the crashes and lay scattered around the burning crafts.

The major with the ARVN troops crawled over to Bill and asked for added artillery support. Bill called the firebase to request close-in fire support and airbursts over the enemy positions that were only three to four hundred yards away. This was to be the most "danger close" support Bill had ever called.

The first rounds came from the 105s at Firebase Bertha. The 8-inch shells from Firebase Thunder followed. Shrapnel from the airbursts whizzed overhead, and an occasional scream was heard when some found a target. Bill could not tell who had been hit.

The enemy fire subsided somewhat, and it looked as though reinforcements might be able to land. At that moment, Bill heard a bugle blow. A long line of green-clad North Vietnamese regulars came running out of the jungle with fixed bayonets, firing their AK-47s and RPGs.

The ARVN line held for a few minutes. A large number of the North Vietnamese fell to the return fire of the M16s and M60 machine guns. But then, suddenly, the ARVN troops broke ranks and ran into the jungle, leaving Bill, Norman, and a platoon of Fourth Division troops alone.

Bill continued to call in the artillery closer and closer until the shells were chewing up the North Vietnamese lines. The shrapnel continued to strike all around Bill and Norman. Dirt and vegetation had so darkened the scene that day seemed to turn to night. When one shell landed, Bill could feel the heat and pressure of the explosion and feel hot metal on his arms and face. He was sure he would soon be blown to bits and die in this godforsaken country.

The next shell hit so close that Bill barely registered the whine of the shell's approach before he blacked out.

Slowly, the foggy haze cleared. Bill opened his eyes and found himself at the bottom of a foxhole with Norman lying on top of him. Sometime during the battle, Norman had pulled his unconscious lieutenant into the foxhole and covered him.

Slowly, Bill struggled to sit up. He was able to check their wounds. Norman had received bayonet wounds for his trouble and was bleeding profusely, but he was still alive. Bill had several pieces of shrapnel in his arm, head, and chest and was bleeding steadily.

He poked his head up carefully and saw that the immediate battlefield was quiet—eerily so. The enemy was gone.

Bill bandaged their wounds as well as he could. He searched for his personal M16 and found it smashed nearby. He had his sidearm in its holster, and Norman clutched an AK-47 in his bloody grip. Norman had no love for that "damn plastic M16."

Smoke floated from the shell craters and the smoldering wreckage of the two helicopters. The massive craters attested to the damage of the artillery Bill had called in. The coppery smell of death was all around.

There were dead men everywhere—mostly American and ARVN. Bill could see the trail of dead ARVN soldiers in the jungle, where they had run. There were helmets, broken rifles, and backpacks tossed like so many toys. Body parts—friends' and foes'—were scattered from the shelling. Bill estimated nearly one hundred bodies lying in all directions. They were stripped of their weapons, gear, supplies, and clothing. It was truly a sad and depressing sight.

Bill and his RTO had survived due to the stubborn fighting of the American unit. The platoon had held but had many dead and wounded.

The unit leader, Lieutenant John Michaels of Long Beach, California, was also wounded. He had already distinguished himself in the defense of a firebase Bill had visited. That day, John had charged into the open and led his men to defend the firebase just as it was about to be overrun. He was a friend, and Bill was doubly grateful that John had been with them on this mission and that he had survived.

Bill heard the helicopters again. This time, it was four Cobra gunships with rockets and 20mm Gatling guns just ahead of a dozen Hueys. The gunships raked the surrounding tree line, causing Bill to roll back into the foxhole and cover Norman as best he could.

Finally, the Hueys landed. Two American generals and an ARVN general stepped out. They placed their hands on their hips, slapped one another on the back, and seemed to be pleased with what they were seeing.

After a few minutes, medics came to the foxhole where Bill huddled over his wounded RTO. The medics were surprised to find the two still alive. The medics quickly placed the two men on stretchers and moved them to a medevac chopper.

Before the chopper could lift off, the American general came over to congratulate Bill and Norman on a great victory. He said the enemy body count—an estimated five hundred—was more than the Americans and ARVN had lost to enemy fire. Bill looked around, wondering where the "estimated five hundred" bodies were. The only uniforms he could distinguish were dead ARVN and American troops.

The ARVN general said the gunships and medevacs would have arrived earlier, but they were delayed because they had to protect some dignitaries on board.

"The landing zone was too hot," he explained. "We flew the dignitaries to safety first, then returned as soon as we could."

Bill was tired and weak from blood loss, but he still could not believe that anyone could be so callous with the lives of their own troops.

"Well, you're here now," Bill growled. "So get us the hell out of here!"

The medics worked quickly to stabilize and move the other wounded to the evacuation point.

Bill's ride on the medevac lasted about twenty minutes. He was hurting even with the morphine the medics had administered, but at least his bleeding had slowed.

The air was cool. Vietnam was hot and muggy on the ground but cool—actually cold—in the air. The change made Bill shiver even more. Norman lay quietly next to him. Bill couldn't tell if he were alive or dead, but he was covered in blood from bayonet wounds. Bill tried to talk to Norman but got no reply.

Most of the other wounded on the medevac were ARVN troops. Some were sitting up. Some were moaning or weeping and holding on to blood-soaked battle dressings. The copter's rotors and the wind flushing in from the open door muffled the sounds and created a white noise.

The copter's deck was hard, even on a stretcher. But this would probably be the least painful part of Bill's experience. He knew what he had to look forward to at the MASH unit in Pleiku.

The medevac dropped down quietly to the helipad, where medics grabbed the stretchers or helped the walking wounded off the copter. Bill spied the sea of blood on the floor of the helicopter as he was lifted to a waiting ambulance. As the last man was removed, troops threw buckets of water across the deck to wash the blood out while it was still fresh.

Bill also saw one of the medics gently lay a poncho over Norman's face and direct others to move his stretcher to the side with a group of other covered bodies.

Will Norman was dead. He had saved Bill's life the night before. Bill dropped his head to his chest and unashamedly let the tears course down his cheeks. The tears were not only for Norman and his family but also for the rest of the young men lost in this senseless war. Norman was only one of thousands of Americans to die in Vietnam that year.

The ambulance door closed with a solid thump, briefly interrupting Bill's thoughts. The vehicle jarred across the tarmac to the hospital building.

Bill was lifted from the ambulance and carried into a triage area. A doctor and nurse worked feverishly to evaluate the wounded and determine which ones to treat first. The doctor bent over Bill and exchanged a quick glance with the nurse. He cocked his head quickly toward the hall leading to the operating theater. Bill was obviously in the first wave.

Bill awoke from surgery with a huge case of gas. He felt like an inflated party balloon. Finally, he was able to relieve himself and got some comfort.

He looked around groggily. During surgery, Bill remembered feeling as though he were floating. He had been outside his body looking down, watching the doctor and nurses work efficiently to repair the damage to the body Bill was no longer a part of. It must have been the near-death experience he had heard about. But now he just needed to get back to reality.

Bill was in a hospital ward with other soldiers. Some were American, some ARVN. Some had been through surgery. Many still needed to be stabilized before their operations. He noticed the other men watching him as he checked out his wounds. The open wounds had been packed with gauze to encourage healing.

Lieutenant Susan Johnson came by to check on Bill as the fog of surgery was starting to lift. Her job was not to coddle patients but to get them up on their feet right away. She was an army nurse and would take no disobedience from her patients. Bill learned to enjoy her efficiency as well as her droll sense of humor.

She explained what she expected him to do. "Lieutenant, you are my favorite patient today—but it's still early, so get moving on your recovery," she ordered. "This is not a rest camp." She softened the message with a wink of her blue eyes and a firm but warm smile.

Lieutenant Johnson enlightened Bill that his wounds needed debridement to scrape away the dead tissue caused by the high-velocity-projectile impact. There would be limited pain medication.

For the next week, at least daily, the dead and dying flesh was scraped away. It was excruciating, but it made room for healthy tissue to grow and replace it. Despite how lovely Lieutenant Johnson was, Bill started to regret hearing her heels clipping on the floor toward his bed. He was already dreaming of the day he could rejoin his unit.

After a few days, he was well enough to leave and make room for other patients. His wounds had healed somewhat and were closed up with stitches he was told to be careful not to break open. Bill was elated to be out of the hospital, although he would miss the gentle touch of Lieutenant Johnson. He had not been touched so tenderly in many months.

Bill got new jungle fatigues and reported to the battalion headquarters. The battalion first sergeant announced him to the battalion commander, Lieutenant Colonel John Davis. Rather fatherly, Davis was a square-jawed banty rooster of a man. He was known as Red Leg Davis and was a career artilleryman. Colonel Davis was also known to be a very kind man and a good leader. He was on his third tour of Vietnam.

The warmth of the colonel's welcome surprised Bill. "Lieutenant, I would like to reassign you to the battalion headquarters, if you so choose. You can recover and then have your R and R whenever you want it."

Bill was surprised. This was the first time he had been offered a choice in the months he had been in Vietnam.

"Sir, I would like to go back to my battery and recover before my R and R. I think I can be of more help at the battery than at battalion headquarters."

"It's your choice, Lieutenant O'Brien," Davis responded. "I respect your decision."

Bill was assigned to go back to the battery the next day. The resupply chopper left that morning with Bill straddling the typical supplies—ammunition, ice, and beer. Bill noted with enthusiasm that this shipment also included mail and food, although the reality of the "food" likely differed from his expectation of it.

A group of new enlisted replacements were also on board, glancing around and looking out the small windows with wide-eyed curiosity. Knowing what he did about their future, Bill could not meet their eyes.

The firebase was too small to accommodate a regular helicopter landing area. The chopper landed outside the firebase perimeter fence. As it was unloaded, Bill walked through the barbed wire gate and reported to the battery commander, Captain William George Washington Hanson. The captain was a tall black West Point–trained officer. He tried to run the battery as if it were a tight ship in the navy. However, he conceded, it *was* the army and they *were* entrenched in a dusty, muddy little firebase thirty miles from the Ho Chi Minh Trail, so he was a bit more forgiving.

"So, O'Brien, they didn't kill you yet!" the captain greeted Bill. "Sorry about Specialist Norman. I liked and respected him a great deal. A real professional."

"Specialist William Spiritlight Norman was not only a professional," responded Bill, "he was a hero. He saved my life at the cost of his own. I would like to recommend him for a posthumous Silver Star."

Captain Hanson met Bill's eyes and carefully assessed his sincerity. With a stern nod, he reached in his desk drawer to start the paperwork.

"Sir," Bill continued, "I spoke to Lieutenant Colonel Davis at battalion headquarters regarding my next assignment. I told him I would like to return to the firebase and help out as much as possible while my wounds heal." He lifted his bandaged arm like a wing. "He said I could hold off on my R and R until I recovered a bit more."

"Lieutenant, you will be of great assistance as my executive officer," Hanson responded. "I've got a new second lieutenant in the fire direction center who could use your advice. There's a bunk there in the FDC for you, and your gear is already stowed on your bunk."

"Thank you, Captain."

Bill saluted and walked out of the captain's office, then he turned to look at the structure. Four rows of sandbags were piled to reinforce the walls of the metal shipping container housing the commanding officer's office. The captain had eight layers of sandbags around his sleeping area. The idea was that it would protect him from a 140mm rocket. Of course, no one really knew for sure. The theory had not yet been tested.

Bill looked over Firebase Thunder. For months, he had been in and out of this place, between stints in the field and assignments at other firebases. *I really never noticed its "intrinsic beauty,"* he thought. He snorted and shook his head sadly. *Beauty like a slum for a pack of jungle rats.*

As he wandered around the base getting reacquainted, he felt the stark difference between the firebase and the jungle. The jungle was hot, steamy, and unforgiving. You slept on the cold, hard ground, hoping you didn't wake up with a snake for a bed partner. Dinner was reheated or cold C rations—a new definition of leftovers. In addition to the North Vietnamese Army and the Vietcong forces, there were deadly snakes (one-steppers and two-steppers—meaning, the number of steps you'd take before you'd fall flat dead), booby traps, rivers with leeches, and all kinds of bugs. Some of the bugs were so big that they made you think you had been hit by a bullet when they bounced off your helmet.

On the other hand, the jungle was also alive and green. It was a green so bright that it burned your eyes. The birds, monkeys, water buffalo, boars, and tigers created a cacophony that echoed around the hills. Walking in the jungle was a hard slog, but there was life all around you.

The firebase was just the opposite. The only certain green in sight was olive drab army vehicles and uniforms and the warm green beer from the PX. The firebase was designed to deliver strikes on a moment's notice to an area forty miles in diameter. It was a small bare strip of brown and red dirt with artillery pieces, support vehicles, and men covered with dirt like camouflage. A smattering of sandbagged huts buried in the ground housed 150 personnel.

In the dry season, the dust was six inches deep and would get into everything. Everyone's uniforms, hair, and skin were stained reddish-brown. Even sweat was a reddish-brown rivulet as it ran down their faces and arms. In the mess hall, you had to cover your plate whenever the guns fired. If you weren't fast enough, the concussion would sift a layer of red dust over your food like paprika, but without the flavor.

In the monsoon season, the dust turned to ankle-deep mud. Soldiers slipped in the water pools, and the mud sucked boots right off their feet. When it rained, everything was damp and clammy. Drying boots overnight was a necessity but also an invitation to an intruder. Spiders and snakes were looking for places to get warm and dry at night too.

Still, the men of the firebase found some entertainment. They would play a version of volleyball called "jungle ball," where there were no rules. That often resulted in tackling and fights.

Bill settled into the fire direction center, which was buried fifteen feet in the ground. It had a plentiful number of sandbags as overhead cover. This was the nerve center for the battery. Two cement ramps led down to the FDC. One ramp was covered with chain-link fence to stop the enemy from throwing in satchel charges, which were packaged explosives designed to destroy the bunker.

Six enlisted men and one officer staffed the FDC. They were housed in the center in various bunks with a floor of six-by-six timbers treated with diesel fuel. The fuel was rumored to keep burrowing cobras from coming up through the floor at night.

The FDC received requests for artillery support. The fire missions were plotted on maps with grids to direct the firing direction. An analog computer was programmed with details to provide the appropriate elevation and powder charges needed to hit the target. Phone lines were connected to the guard bunkers and to the four heavy guns to transmit the fire coordinates.

The FDC team was well educated. Most of them were college graduates. Generally, an officer and a noncommissioned officer were also a part of the team. Bill would help here as officer of the day, if needed.

The firebase was only about three hundred yards across. The two 8-inch howitzers and two 175mm guns occupied the majority of the space. Around those weapons was a heavy earthen and wooden beam wall about six feet high. Each piece was self-propelled so it could be moved around, as needed. Reinforced bunkers stood near each gun to provide living quarters for the gun crews.

Several hundred 8-inch and 175mm shells were kept in the ammunition storage bunker. Bill wondered about the wisdom of storing all the ammo together. He estimated there were almost forty tons of explosives in those shells. If just one lucky enemy shell hit, it would all be over. Instead of a small hilltop, there would be a large crater.

Four large guard bunkers were placed around the perimeter, and each had .50-caliber machine guns on permanent mounts. They were manned each night. Three twin 40mm track vehicles stood near the bunkers. These bunkers belonged to another unit and were assigned to support the base. Smaller bunkers were also scattered around the compound to provide immediate cover, if required.

A lot of stuff in a small area, Bill thought. *It would be hard to miss if the enemy found the range.*

After spending the next week doing routine chores, Bill finally got sign-off for his request for R and R. At one time, he had dreamed of going to Hawaii, where he could meet Barbara for a few days. But since she had moved on from their relationship, he now opted for Sydney, Australia.

Bill decked himself out in his best uniform and grabbed the first flight to Pleiku. From there, he flew to Saigon's Tan Son Nhut Air Base, where he changed into civvies for his military travel to Australia.

21.

AS HE DEPLANED AT 6:00 A.M. IN SYDNEY, Bill felt a strange apprehension. The hair on the back of his neck stood up as if expecting an attack, but the surroundings were serene. As he walked out of the terminal, he could smell sweet ocean salt instead of sweat and jungle mold. The coming and going of jets mixed occasionally with soothing music through overhead speakers. If he strained his ears, he could hear the wind in the palm trees.

Traffic was light at this hour. Bill took a cab to the service center in Sydney. His hotel was already assigned, and the receptionist at the service center provided instructions.

As he headed out on the street, the cockatiels peeked at him and squawked a greeting through the green branches of the palm trees. This was a different green. One he had almost forgotten. Here there were bright shades of green and other colors—so many colors of plants and flowers and fabrics and lights. The aching beauty caused his eyes to water.

Bill started taking in the details around him. No dirt, no sandbags. Even though there was no blowing dust here, his eyes still blinked out of habit. He licked his lips and was surprised that there was no sand grating his teeth.

Throngs of friendly people were heading to work or opening shops with all types of merchandise in the windows. He even met an exotic dancer walking the streets with a boa constrictor draped around her neck.

She was probably a leftover from an overnight party. He wondered when the snake had last eaten. Instinctively, he gave the woman and her pet a wide berth.

As if the streets weren't enough, Bill felt transported to another planet as he entered his small hotel room. The air flowing through the open window was fresh. The bed had clean sheets. Hell, there was a *bed*! He had his own bathroom with a flushing toilet and a tub, where he could lounge in clean, hot water until his skin wrinkled like a prune.

He dropped his gear bag and gazed out the window. The proprietor of a local deli had just opened the shop door. The aroma of fresh-baked bread assaulted his nostrils. Bill grabbed the city map he had received at the service center, then galloped down the stairs and out onto the sidewalk like a puppy let off its leash. He dodged cars and trotted to the deli, stopping at the door just to take in all the offerings in the window. They sold bread, cheese, coffee, tea, and pastries. Inside were small metal tables with white linen tablecloths.

"Mornin', mate," the proprietor greeted him. "What kin I git ya?"

Bill's eyes settled on the glorious French rolls and cheddar cheese. "One of the rolls and some cheese. Maybe a half pound of your cheddar. And coffee—yeah, black coffee!"

"Just in from the war?"

"It shows, huh?" Bill asked.

"Always tell by the tan. Yep, I kin spot 'em every time. Welcome to 'stralia, mate! My name's Dalton. Grab a table, an' I'll bring her out ta ya."

Bill found a little table next to the window. With his back to the wall, he sat and watched the passing traffic as he waited for his breakfast. He wasn't used to being served. No olive drab metal mess kit with sand-encrusted utensils.

He glanced around the room at the little floral pictures hanging on the walls. Other than the hospital, this was the first time in over ten months that he had been in a room with a true ceiling.

Ten months, he thought. *Seems more like ten years!*

"Here ya go," the proprietor said, breaking into Bill's reverie.

Bill forced himself to eat small bites, enjoying the crisp but chewy texture of the crusty bread. He savored the smooth yet sharp tang of the cheese and the warmth and depth of the rich black coffee. He was in another world, and it was amazing. Now he just needed to work up the courage to go out and see the sights.

"A warm-up on that coffee, mate?"

Dalton's question seemed like a gunshot in the quiet room. Bill jumped.

"Sorry, mate. Didn't mean to startle ya."

"No problem, Dalton. I was just kind of lost in thought. But sure, I'll take a warm-up. It's great to have time for seconds of anything!"

Bill smoothed the map out on the table and studied it while he finished his coffee. It was nearly eleven already. *Time for a little recon*, he ordered himself. He saw a park marked on the map and noted it was just around the corner. He decided that was a perfect place to start.

Bill paid for breakfast before heading to the door. "Thanks for breakfast, Dalton," he called as he apprehensively stepped out.

Traffic had picked up, and noise came from all directions. Bill flinched at the din surrounding him. He made his way quickly to the park, hoping for quiet.

The park turned out to have a fabulous view of Sydney Harbour. Waves pounded the shores with white surf. Flowers were everywhere in geometric gardens. Once again, the colors were almost overwhelming.

Bill relaxed a bit as the sidewalk led him beneath the cover of palm trees. But then the sidewalk suddenly emerged from the trees and angled across a wide area of open grass leading to a large fountain in the center of the park.

Bill stopped abruptly, causing a biker to veer onto the grass to avoid him.

"Hey, what's yer gripe, mate?" the biker barked as he righted himself.

Bill was frozen, unable to take a step. In the last months, he had learned that survival meant staying under cover, watching your back, listening for anything out of the ordinary, trying to determine the next threat. He had become a creature of the shadows. Try as he might, he could not make himself walk across the open space to the fountain.

Maybe this is good enough for day one, Bill thought.

He turned on his heel and headed back toward his hotel. Across from the deli, he met two Australian servicemen who had spent time in Vietnam. They invited him to join them for a pint at the local pub. After hoisting a few glasses, they shared some of their experiences. It was obvious that these happy-go-lucky office boys had never been to the front lines.

Bill decided it was time to part ways with the Aussie servicemen and head back to his room. The snake lady made another appearance, wandering the streets and looking for customers. On his way, Bill stopped at the Tobacco and Book Emporium. He selected a fine cigar, a large decadent Toblerone chocolate bar, a *World Travel* magazine, and a Zane Grey novel. Between college and his time in the service, it seemed like years since he had read for pleasure. The other purchases were self-explanatory.

Bill soaked in the tub the rest of the afternoon. He was careful not to allow the cigar ash to drop in the water. The water turned red and left a huge ring around the tub that would challenge the most aggressive cleaning product—it would have made an impressive "before and after" television commercial. He nibbled the chocolate like a mouse, trying to make it last. The pages of the magazine were beginning to curl from the moisture when he finally decided it was time to emerge.

The hotel had a small restaurant that was open only for dinner. Bill donned his civilian clothes and wandered down to check it out.

"Let me seat you at one of our best tables near the window," the maître d' offered.

Bill shook his head. "No, thank you," he said. "I'd be happy with that table instead." He pointed to a spot in the corner, where he could sit with his back to the wall. "I just want to watch people," he explained to the confused waiter.

Force of habit, he admonished himself. At Dalton's deli and now here, he needed his back to a wall. In Vietnam, you never had your back to a door, in case someone were to come in with a bomb or start shooting up the place.

Bill slathered the thick slab of beef with steak sauce and dipped the french fries in ketchup. *Probably don't need either*, he thought. Again, it was force of habit. Army food always needed some kind of sauce.

He treated himself to a delicate éclair and coffee for dessert. Rubbing his stomach in appreciation, he headed back to his room for a much-needed night's sleep.

Bill woke with a start. An engine rumbled nearby, and a light flashed off the ceiling. He rolled over and fell to the floor in an instinctive and conditioned response to the noise and lights.

"Where the hell am I?" he grunted.

Thoughts streamed through his head of falling asleep in the field, of enemy vehicles rumbling up for a sneak attack, of gunfire.

Then he realized where he was and—more importantly—that he was safe. He sat up and wiped the sweat off his brow. Down on the street below, an early-delivery driver slammed the truck door, shut off the flashers, and drove off. It was just 6:00 a.m.

Seeing as he was wide-awake already, it was time to start day two of his week in Sydney. He checked out the window. Dalton was just opening up. Bill dressed and headed to the deli for a quick breakfast.

Back on the street, he found his way to the service center to see what activities might be of interest. On the bulletin board, he read several postings from local families inviting servicemen and servicewomen to come for dinner at their homes. He jumped at the chance to meet a local family and get a free meal in the deal. With a quick phone call, he arranged for dinner that evening. The family would pick him up at his hotel at 5:00 p.m.

Bill spent the rest of his day wandering the streets around the harbor. He was slowly becoming more accustomed to the hubbub of people on all sides. Although car horns and squealing brakes made him flinch, he no longer dove for cover.

Phil and Jean Yeats picked him up as scheduled and drove quickly through the busy streets to a small, neat house in the suburbs. They were a middle-aged couple.

Phil was tall and slender with graying hair. When he shook hands with Bill, his fingers felt strong and flexible, like a pianist's. Phil had worked as a chemical engineer in a uranium mine.

Jean reminded Bill of Julia Child—both in her physical appearance and her interest in cooking. She had been an army nurse in World War II. She proudly announced that she was a direct descendant of the original penal colony inhabitants.

Jean kept up a constant chatter, telling him about Sydney and about their two daughters—both off to school unfortunately, as Bill no doubt would have liked to meet them. She asked him questions about himself but never pried if he hesitated.

Phil raised orchids in a small garden shed out back. "The more exotic, the better," he boasted, puffing out his chest. These were plants like Bill had never seen. Some stood tall in pots on delicate stems; others were vines that draped overhead in a glorious combination of colors and scents.

Once stuffed with English pot roast and mashed potatoes, Bill thanked the couple for their kindness. While Jean started the dishes, Phil grabbed his car keys to bring Bill back to the hotel.

"Can you join us another night before you go back?" Jean hollered from the kitchen.

Bill took in her warm smile and agreed to a second visit later in the week. He had made a long-term friendship.

As he walked the streets of Sydney the next day, Bill contemplated his luck at choosing Australia for his R and R. The clean shops and friendly people were a direct contrast to Vietnam. He looked forward to his next dinner with Phil and Jean.

He also thought about what he would return to when his R and R was over. It was so easy to adjust to Sydney. How would he readjust when he had to return to the jungle and the stench of war?

On his last day in Sydney, Bill forced himself to walk through the park to the fountain. In reality, he stuck as close as possible to the tree line for as long as he could. But the fact that he got to the fountain nevertheless seemed a major success.

On reflection, he realized that his inability to even walk through a park was a harbinger of issues he might face when he finally went home—assuming he survived Vietnam. Would he ever see this type of civilization again?

22.

BILL RETURNED FROM HIS R AND R and gradually found his way back to the firebase. He was now the official battery executive officer and second-in-command. Captain Hanson had been rotated back stateside, where he was reassigned to the Pentagon.

The new commander was Captain Ross Jones, who had graduated from officer candidate school. He was new to Vietnam and had not yet seen combat. Bill was now the only officer with combat experience at the firebase.

A new role for the battery was now being established. Preparations were in place to be able to split the battery up on occasion, with two of the four artillery pieces moving closer to the Cambodian border for support of various activities. They weren't supposed to be going into—or firing into—Cambodia yet, but it looked as though they would be soon.

The firebase was still fairly quiet several weeks after Bill's return. There were a few fire missions each week, but no serious ground or mortar attacks on the base. He appreciated the relative calm, but intelligence reports indicated an enemy buildup. It was hard for Bill to convince the new commander of the imminent danger to the unit—until one evening.

It was only 6:00 p.m. The jungle birds suddenly became eerily silent. The solitude was broken when 81mm mortars rained down on the base.

The attack lasted nearly an hour. Fortunately, the only casualty was a bunker of beer. Bill had to smile when he once again saw the geyser of green foam burst into the air.

Thar she blows, he thought. Remembering the warm, tasty Australian brew, he licked his lips. He tasted only the return of dust and sand.

Enemy forces were on the move in the area. The next day, the firebase received orders to split the battery. They moved an 8-inch and a 175mm gun closer to the Cambodian border. The splitting of the battery also meant moving half of the personnel, leaving the firebase with only seventy-five men for full operations. Captain Jones would lead the Cambodian support unit while Bill commanded the base camp. When the move was completed, Bill redeployed the remaining guns around the firebase.

At dawn the next day, the North Vietnamese attacked the base. More than two hundred mortar rounds rained down on the guard bunkers and the remaining artillery pieces. Both guns were destroyed, and men were seriously wounded in the bunkers. Bill had to use his belt to apply a tourniquet on one soldier's leg that had been blown off below the knee.

Time slowed for Bill. His experience and training now allowed him to suppress his personal fear and focus on making the appropriate decisions to protect the base.

The FDC was the target of satchel charges thrown by the sappers. It survived only due to a determined defensive effort by the FDC personnel, who killed five sappers at the mouth of the bunker. Fortunately, the satchel charges placed in the ammunition bunkers failed to explode.

Firefights broke out all over the base. The gun crews fought from their protective bunkers. The main power to the radio and antenna was knocked out. Bill managed to use the remaining generator and auxiliary radio to call battalion headquarters for gunship support in and around the perimeter. He was assured that gunships and medevacs were coming—but he'd heard that before. He established direct contact with the gunships to direct them to repel the attack. Once he determined the area was safe for evacuation of the wounded, he directed the medevacs to the landing zone.

The enemy occupied one end of the mess hall; the Americans the other. The North Vietnamese shot a medic and left him wounded just out of reach in hopes his cries for help would draw out the defenders. Bill knew the ploy. He could not allow his men to be drawn into the open. Although he knew the medic personally, he also knew he had to sacrifice him to save others.

Bill wiped the sweat and stray tears from his eyes. He rallied a group of his men and rushed the North Vietnamese in the mess hall. Ten North Vietnamese troops were killed, but not before Bill caught an AK-47 round in his shoulder and a large grenade fragment in his leg. The impact spun him around and threw him to the ground. He didn't know the seriousness of his own wounds, but he knew he had to get up quickly and maintain control of the troops.

Just then, the Cobra gunships rose up out of the trees like the snakes after which they were aptly named. They strafed the perimeter and either killed or drove off the remaining North Vietnamese soldiers.

Bill placed an emergency bandage on his wounds. As the enemy pulled back, the medevac choppers dropped into the cleared area, and triage began. Despite the enemy pullback, green tracers from their heavy machine guns still reached out toward the medevacs, though none of them hit the helicopters with the wounded.

Bill was painfully aware of the debridement process awaiting him once he reached the hospital. He was in no hurry. He opted to stay in command at the firebase until the situation was stabilized and secure. He set up headquarters in the FDC and waited out the last few hours until daybreak.

Reinforcements arrived at dawn. Bill took the last medevac out after turning over command to Captain Dave Saunders. The plan was to reunite the battery under Captain Jones as quickly as possible.

The battle for the firebase had cost the North Vietnamese at least fifty dead. Blood trails leading off into the jungle spoke of many more wounded. A dead Chinese officer was found outside the base perimeter along with a North Vietnamese flag.

For the American battery, only the medic who had been left as bait had died during the assault. But they still suffered thirty casualties. Some, like Bill, had simple through-and-through wounds. Others had more serious wounds, such as those who lost limbs from satchel charges.

Bill once again cheated death and once again headed to the hospital. He knew he would not be the first served this time around. However, he secretly hoped Lieutenant Susan Johnson was still in charge.

The ceiling came into focus as Bill regained consciousness following surgery to remove the shrapnel from his leg and repair his shoulder. He turned his head slowly, and Lieutenant Johnson came into view as she checked the patient in the bed next to him.

Déjà vu, he thought.

She turned and saw that he was awake. "Welcome back. We have to quit meeting like this!" she joked.

"Actually, I'd like to see you more often," he responded, "just not necessarily this way."

Susan leaned over his bed, checked his IV, then placed her hand on his forehead to check his temperature.

There's that touch again. He sighed and drifted back to sleep.

Susan stretched her back, pushed her blond hair more tightly under her cap, and smiled at her sleeping charge. *He's special*, she thought. *I'd like to see him more often too—but outside the hospital, as he said.*

The battery's first sergeant, Paul Ramon, came by to see the men the next day. He had tears in his eyes as he scanned the sea of beds holding his friends. He had been assigned to the other half of the battery and was out of harm's way when the attack happened.

Major Donovan, the battalion executive officer, also came by to give everyone a pep talk.

"Good work, men," he praised. "Your country is proud of you!"

What a piece of shit, fumed Bill silently. *The "country" doesn't even know what happened last night and probably doesn't care.*

The protests against the war were booming (no pun intended), while the news from home boasted increased sales in weaponry and aircraft exports. Politicians and armchair soldiers were using the war for propaganda to pump up their latest reelection or promotional bid.

It's the poor, dumb bastards fighting over here who really pay the price! Bill thought.

During his time in the hospital, Bill knew the drill: up early each day, make your bed, go through the debridement procedure, repeat the next day.

Those most seriously wounded were isolated in a separate ward. Their condition was never mentioned.

During his seven days of hospital routine, Bill had plenty of time to reflect on the battle. He was aware that they had survived the onslaught of a superior enemy. The impact of his own injuries and the injuries of those around him—as well as the loss of the medic—began to weigh on him. He didn't know how much more of this he could take. He had been so close to death so many times already. He turned his head to the wall and closed his eyes. At least he had clean sheets again.

Of the soldiers who had been under his brief command, he never did know how many later died of their wounds. Even if they survived, the memory of the battle would haunt them the rest of their lives, as it would Bill.

Bill was released with a souvenir cane to aid his walking. He returned to the firebase and found that his first task was to gather his thoughts and write a letter to the family of the medic who had been killed—murdered—during the attack. This was a man who had helped so many during his time on the base. Bill fought to reconcile what he knew about the medic's horrible death with what he could truly tell the family.

Bill had been wounded several times. That meant he actually was given some choices. He could stay at the firebase, return to the rear battalion headquarters, or go home. Because he was still recovering, he was not able to perform combat duties, so he had some time to weigh his options.

He was getting sick of the rear echelon's bullshit. There was incredible juxtaposition of the front and rear areas. He didn't want to be someplace where it was important to spit-shine your boots and starch your uniform. Hell, his boots were so ragged they looked brown instead of black, and he hadn't worn a starched uniform since he got to Vietnam. In fact, some of his uniforms smelled moldy from being stored underground in his duffel bag. In the rear battalion, the soldiers were actually required to clean the sand around the barracks. They spent their days picking up cigarette butts and raking the sand in a regimented pattern.

My God, Bill thought. *A regulated sand-raking pattern? This is a war zone!*

Bill also loathed the cesspool environment of the firebase, but he felt a fierce loyalty to his brothers-in-arms. If he stayed, maybe he could teach some of the newbies how to stay alive. But would it matter? They just kept coming. When someone was killed or rotated to the rear or sent home, someone else just replaced him. The rules never changed. The effort never changed. The soldiers just wore new faces.

Bill was still contemplating his options when Major Donovan called the FDC on the secure radio channel one late afternoon. He had received information that the firebase should expect an attack by an enemy regiment the next night.

"There's little help that can be provided due to other ongoing operations, but at least you have a day's notice," he said. "Do your best to honor the country, the army, and the battalion in the battle."

Bill and the others in the FDC exchanged glances of disbelief. It felt as though they had just received a death sentence with a "pip-pip, chins up" at the end.

The group spent the next day gathering and doling out ammunition and preparing defensive positions. All the while, the officers tried to keep the troops on an even keel. They sat in their bunkers all night, waiting for hell to rain down.

The next day dawned, and nothing had happened. Bill was furious that the major had called them on a false alarm.

I'd shoot that bastard myself, right now, if he walked in here! Bill thought to himself. He was sure he was not alone in that sentiment.

That was when he decided the whole situation was going nowhere. He was tired of trying to explain why they kept fighting for the same little parcel of land in the middle of a godforsaken country. He wanted out—now.

Bill flew back to Pleiku the next day to talk to Lieutenant Colonel Davis and the battalion personnel officer. He was ready to return home on the next Freedom Bird.

But then Davis presented a new option: a three-month training assignment at the I Field Force headquarters in Nha Trang. Davis knew Bill would be perfect for the position. Bill had been awarded a Silver Star, Bronze Star, and three Purple Hearts. His battery and battalion commander had given him glowing assessments.

Despite his original plans, Bill decided to take the training assignment. This would increase his time in-country but also increase his pay grade. This option also gave him a leg up on choice assignments for the rest of his time in the stateside army. With this assignment, he would receive a promotion to first lieutenant and be required to perform light training duties. The good news was, there would be clean beds, good food, and no combat assignments.

Besides, what did he have to rush home to? A job? A girl? Family? No, he had nothing to make him want to hurry home.

Monday through Friday, Bill was assigned to work half days, followed by an hour in rehabilitation to aid his recovery. His afternoons were spent on the beach or in other facilities without restriction.

Once his three months as a training officer concluded, Bill was again authorized to return home on the next Freedom Bird, if he wished.

This time, he took the offer.

As Bill waited with the other returning veterans on the tarmac, the newly arriving troops exited the plane with startled expressions when that first wave of jungle odor and acrid burning feces hit their nostrils.

Bill remembered his first day. *They have no fucking idea what's really going to happen*, he thought to himself.

These were the replacements. Some of them replaced those who were leaving. Some replaced those who had been killed. It was rumored that each man's fate would be the same as the one he replaced. Bill wondered about the soldier he had replaced—and the soldier who was replacing him now.

Walking across the open tarmac to the running Boeing 707's loading ramp nearly caused him to have a meltdown. It was open—no cover in sight—and they were still in-country. He was glad he was an officer and was the first on. He didn't want to stand in line, waiting to get picked off.

Bill limped up the ramp. He moved to his seat, tossed his cane into the overhead bin, and pulled out a small hip flask of brandy. He took a long, satisfying draw. The cabin attendant shot him a look of disapproval. Alcohol was not allowed during the flight. He saluted her with the flask and a wry smile, then drained the burning golden liquid down his throat.

He sat down and closed his eyes. *Tell it to the families of the soldiers lying in the sea of metal caskets on the tarmac*, he chided quietly.

The airplane door swung and closed with a bang. He was startled from his seat.

A fitting end to this period of my life, he growled to himself—even though he realized this wasn't truly the end. Leaving all this behind would not be as easy as just flying home.

The plane taxied and increased speed quickly. They moved immediately to the runway and with full power shot down the runway and out over the South China Sea to avoid potential enemy fire.

In twenty-four hours, they would be in San Francisco. That was where Bill's next struggle would begin. He still had a year to serve as first lieutenant stateside before he could really go home—wherever that would be and whatever that might entail.

They made refueling stops in the Philippines, Guam, and Hawaii. There was no time to do any sightseeing, though. They were not even allowed to get off the aircraft. Bill had a lot of time with his thoughts on this return trip. He preferred thinking to taking the sleeping pills the flight attendants offered.

Bill reflected on the fact that he had been in Vietnam for more than a year. Other than the short R and R in Sydney, it had been pure chaos. It felt like a lifetime.

He had spent long, back-to-back days without any sleep. Sometimes he stayed awake for thirty-six out of forty-eight hours, watching for attacks or monitoring the radio. In other cases, he was out in the field for a week, not sleeping more than an hour or so each day. Time stretched and distorted. Days seemed like weeks. Weeks seemed like months. And months seemed like years.

He turned his gaze to the window, where the night was as black as the jungle, save for the full moon that lit an impossibly narrow path on the open ocean below.

Bill saw his reflection in the dark window. He had changed so much. For one, he had never recovered his thirty-pound weight loss. *That's a hell of a price for a weight-loss program!* He still walked with a limp, but the doctor predicted it would improve with another thirty days of rehab. Until then, he would still need his cane. He felt some pain occasionally, but it was not severe. Still, he had spent time in the base hospital for battle wounds and would carry scars for the rest of his life.

As he drifted in and out of sleep, Bill relived his experiences. Before he left home, he had endured a full series of shots to protect him from all sorts of unknowns, including the plague. The week after his arrival, he spent more time in the head than on duty. Diarrhea was his true introduction to Vietnam. During that first month of misery, his body adjusted slowly to the heat and humidity, not to mention the bugs—and the dirt. Dirt everywhere! Even the water tasted foul from the chlorine. He did what he was told. It didn't seem to matter.

He had been careful to take his weekly malaria pill, choking down the huge capsule along with the daily doses. Now he found out he would still need to take some of these once he got back to the States. Thanks! Despite all the preventative actions, he managed to contract a fever of 103. Typhus from rat feces, the medic told him—just sweat it out. God, what a hellhole!

He was sure the C rations had cured him of eating ham and lima beans for the rest of his life. Why was that the only available ration when the temperature soared over 100 degrees? Damn!

Checking his reflection again, Bill noted the great tan. His hair and mustache were bleached nearly white from the sun. He felt as if he had spent the year in a food dehydrator.

He tallied his other changes. His drinking habits had shifted from an occasional beer to hard liquor. The ability to get a mixed drink in-country was one of the few privileges he enjoyed as a lieutenant. Oh, and he had been the first to limp on the plane heading home and would be one of the first to deplane when they touched down in good old California. There was a plus to write home about.

Yeah, write home. Rudolph was the only one left at home. Bill had written occasionally, but he didn't feel he could share his experiences with

Rudolph as he might have done with his own father. Barbara's letters came so infrequently that he was sure she had little interest in writing to him.

Move on, O'Brien. Move on, he chided himself.

Only, it was difficult for him to move on from anything. He was callous. He was cold and frank in his comments. He was quicker to anger, and his language was more colorful.

Whenever he walked, he instinctively searched the ground for trip wires or booby traps. He had become accustomed to sizing up his environment quickly—deciding where he could safely walk, whom he could talk to, what he could eat or drink in any given scenario. He still needed to keep his back to a wall in a restaurant or bar. He figured that wouldn't change for a while.

It felt as though a substantial portion of his character had been ripped away and replaced by . . . what? He didn't know the answer.

Bill closed his eyes briefly but then was startled awake by a loud crash. A stewardess had dropped a tray in the galley just in front of his seat.

"Sorry," she said, sheepishly peeking around the pulled curtain and smiling like the Cheshire cat at Bill.

"You dumb bitch! What the hell are you doing?" he swore at her.

She looked apologetic, but it didn't matter. If he had not been buckled into his seat, he would have either been on the floor, behind the seat, or even at her throat in an instant. These were instincts honed by combat. Those instincts had saved his life many times. He may have received multiple wounds, but he was still alive.

Bill wondered what his father would have thought of all this. What internal wounds did his father bring back from the war? His dad had been involved in aerial combat for three years and under constant stress on his combat missions. Bill, in contrast, had spent only fourteen months in Vietnam.

Am I too sensitive? he wondered.

Then again, Bill had heard from a company clerk that the casualty rates in Vietnam were much higher than in World War II. The clerk said that one in ten Americans serving in Vietnam were wounded or killed. Bill knew the weight of that statistic was even more significant because most of the casualties fell on a very small part of the entire force in Vietnam: the "ground pounders."

He glanced out the window again at the eternal blackness. At least his dad had something to bring home. They had won the war. His dad won. They all won. They came back to parades and flag-waving. What was Bill bringing home? There would be no parades for him. There would be no "Welcome Home." He knew that for a fact.

Bill leaned his head against the seat. In less than a day, he would be back in a society that was little touched by the war. The people in America were light-years away from the dirt, the heat, the violence, the terror, and the death in Vietnam. The protestors had no clue what was happening over there. Neither did the general population. He sighed heavily.

Bill was bringing back the only thing that really mattered to him. He was bringing back himself. He might have a permanent limp, but he was determined to get on with his life. The rah-rah attitudes, the screams of protestors, the flag-waving or flag-burning—it was all a bunch of crap. He had killed or helped kill or seen killed so many hundreds of people, American and Vietnamese. There was no glamour or chest-pounding pride in all of this. The goals and reasons for the war were even less clear now than when he had arrived in Vietnam more than a year ago.

He would have to make do with what he was sure of—himself.

— CALIFORNIA, 1969 —

23.

THE LONG FLIGHT FINALLY ARRIVED at Travis Air Force Base in Oakland, California. Bill and the other officers left the plane first. Bill walked slowly with his cane. They were directed to the buses headed to the Oakland Army Base.

At the base, they were required to turn in all their gear and get new orders while the gear was searched. Soldiers were well known for smuggling a variety of strange and exotic things, from trinkets to arms and ammunition. Bill knew the security teams made a good effort, but they didn't catch everything. Occasionally, snakes and spiders hitched a ride stateside—either voluntarily or as pets. Bill hoped the searchers would find some live, natural contraband in his gear. It would probably be the searchers' only real taste of the war.

With his orders in hand, Bill moved to the cashier to trade in his Vietnam scrip for US currency. Finally, he repacked his duffel bag and awaited transport. He hoped he'd have a chance to clean up before he went to the hospital to have his leg wound evaluated.

While waiting for transport, he reviewed his orders. He was being given a thirty-day leave, but he still had one year to serve as an officer. After his leave, he was to report to Fort Sam Houston near San Antonio, Texas, for thirty days of rehabilitation on his leg. They obviously didn't trust him to do it on his own. Once he was deemed sufficiently recovered—or after thirty days, whichever came first—he would report to Fort Sill, where he had received his officer's training. There he would be in charge of an artillery training battery.

Bill stood in the long line. Once again, he was getting nowhere fast. He blew out his frustration through pursed lips. He set his papers down and looked around to see what was holding up the line for the transport.

"What's your problem, soldier?" he heard a voice chide him from behind.

Bill spun around and raised his cane, ready for a confrontation. His face went from flushed anger to joy when he saw his tormentor was his old friend from Fort Sill.

"Dale Patterson. What a sight for sore eyes!" Bill fought back the emotion of seeing his friend again. He noted a cane in Dale's hand as well. "Lieutenant, what have you been doing, other than not ducking at the right time?"

"After we left Fort Sill, I was assigned to the First Cavalry near Saigon. Can't say I was really on a firebase because we moved more often than a herd of deer being chased by wolves."

Bill grinned. He knew that was a reference to Dale's upbringing in the Upper Peninsula of Michigan.

He also knew there was little distinction between "on the firebase" and "in the bush" for the First Cavalry. They had suffered multiple attacks on their firebases, surviving only by using 105mm direct-fire shells called beehive rounds. The shells were loaded with steel darts and were fired directly into the attacking enemy troops, not unlike the old cannons from the Civil War.

Bill's grin faded to a knowing nod. His own experience could have been much worse.

The friends compared their orders and found they were both headed to the same base hospital for a checkup, then leave.

"You headed home to Minneapolis?" Dale asked.

"Nope. Not a damn thing left for me there. Not sure what I'll do for a whole fucking month."

"I'm looking forward to seeing my family in Lansing," Dale responded sheepishly. "My family wants to roll out the red carpet for a couple of days.

Then I'm planning on a couple of weeks at our camp in the Upper Peninsula. No hunting, no shooting, no explosions. Maybe I'll dangle a line in a trout stream or take a boat out on Lake Superior."

"Sounds like heaven after the hell we've been through," Bill responded with a tinge of jealousy.

"Why don't you come with me? Even *you* can catch trout in the Huron River."

"Seriously?"

"Yeah. I'll teach you how to catch trout and cook some decent meals."

Bill remembered Dale bragging about his culinary expertise. "Sounds like you have a roommate!"

The friends agreed to get orders to fly to Lansing to start their leave. They would meet at the San Francisco airport and fly out together. Bill felt lighter, more hopeful, as he went through processing, gathered his back pay, and shopped for civilian clothes at the base PX. He was looking forward to trying his hand at trout fishing. More importantly, he was looking forward to a return to normalcy.

The doctor at the base hospital quickly examined Bill's leg wound and decided he was cleared for his leave. The doctor also told Bill it would be important to talk about his war experiences with a family member or friend.

"Don't bottle it up," the doctor warned.

Who better to talk to than Dale Patterson? Bill thought.

Bill was eager to head to the San Francisco airport and start this "vacation." Just as he headed out the door of the base hospital, the officer of the day spoke to him in an authoritative voice, stopping him in his tracks.

"Change into your civvies, soldier. There are war protestors at the airport. You want to look like a normal tourist coming back from a lovely vacation in Hawaii."

As Bill changed his clothes, he looked at the hard, tanned face in the mirror. *You can change the clothes, but you can't hide the jungle,* he thought. Even after taking a shower, he could still feel the grit of the jungle on his skin, in his teeth, in the hard creases that had formed around his eyes. It would be months before the dirt of Vietnam would be gone from his body.

Oh yeah—and the eyes. The thousand-yard stare. His eyes held an apparent look of fatigue when, in reality, they were like laser beams, searching and not missing a detail with the intensity of their focus.

Leaving the PX, Bill donned his newly purchased San Francisco Giants cap and sunglasses. Talk about ironic—his first purchases in America were for a disguise. He hurried out to the taxi stand and found Dale dressed in a floral Hawaiian shirt and straw hat. He was in disguise too. Unfortunately, they couldn't cover their canes and olive drab duffel bags standing like sloppy recruits next to them on the curb.

They shared a cab to the airport. Bill was starting to feel a bit elated at being stateside. The colors and sounds were reminiscent of Sydney. The heat and humidity were still present but not oppressive. The billboards along the highway hawked their products in English. He didn't realize how much he really had missed the good ol' US of A!

As the cab pulled up to the curb at the airport, Bill heard chanting and whistles. He slipped out of the cab's protective shell with his cane and duffel bag in tow and saw the source of the noise. A solid picket line of war protestors blocked the sidewalk. They carried signs that said "Murderers!" and waved torn American flags strung upside down on a staff.

One of the protestors jumped in front of an officer heading into the airport. On the officer's uniform, a Silver Star glinted, just visible under the sling supporting his arm. The officer ducked his head and dodged just in time to avoid a wad of spit from the protestor. He just shook his head sadly and quickly continued into the airport.

The same protestor saw Bill's duffel bag and cane and rushed at him. He apparently liked attacking the walking wounded. Bill was not feeling so accommodating, however. He dropped his duffel and balanced on his cane with his left hand. He grabbed the young agitator's long hair and spun him into a choke hold. As he felt the protestor's legs giving out, he released his hold and dropped him with a quick right jab.

The protestor fell to his knees. "This is bogus, man! Shit—you broke my nose!"

"Stay down, you son of a bitch," growled Bill, "or I'll break your fuckin' neck."

The line of protestors moved in quickly to rescue their injured pal, but as they turned toward Bill to object, they saw his nearly psychotic glare. Grabbing their cohort, they quickly moved away from the cabs that were disgorging more soldiers into the void.

"Let's go," suggested Dale. He raised his eyebrows at Bill, hoping to head off any other altercations. "We've got a plane to catch."

A San Francisco police officer had watched the whole encounter. As Bill and Dale moved toward the door, he saluted them.

"Thanks, fellas. I was in the Hundred and Seventy-Third Airborne in 'Nam. I've been dying to do that to one of those punks for weeks! Welcome home."

Walking over to the group of protestors, he placed the bloody-nosed longhair in handcuffs. "You're under arrest for assault and battery and for spitting on a uniformed soldier."

Bill and Dale melted into the crowd, checked their duffels at the Northwest Airlines counter, and headed for the bar to await their flight.

"Dale, where are you headed after our fishing excursion?" asked Bill, sipping his first Jameson from a glass in weeks.

Dale wiped the beer foam off his neatly trimmed mustache and grimaced. "I have relatives scattered like proverbial Trolls all over the Michigan 'mitten,' so I may not be able to stay in one place very long."

"What do you mean, Trolls?"

"Michigan is in two pieces," explained Dale. "Those who live above the bridge—that's the Mackinaw Bridge—are called Yoopers, for the UP, or Upper Peninsula. Those who live 'under the bridge,' or in the Lower Peninsula, are called Trolls." He shrugged, and they both laughed.

"Where to after visiting everyone in Michigan, then?" Bill asked.

"My orders are for Europe. What about you?"

"I'm San Antonio bound for thirty days rehab, then to Fort Sill's artillery training base."

Dale cocked his head to one side. "I think my dad knows a three-star general at Lackland Air Force Base in San Antonio. Maybe Dad could call and make some introductions for you in ol' San Anton' so you'd get the red-carpet treatment."

Bill squirmed on the barstool. He was not used to getting the red-carpet treatment anywhere.

"Hey, there's our flight call," Dale said. "Bottoms up!"

They slid off the barstools in tandem and limped to the loading gate with only the support of their canes and each other.

The flight to Lansing gave the two lieutenants a chance to get reacquainted. Whereas Bill had lost his entire family in the plane crash before he graduated from high school, Dale was raised with a silver spoon in his mouth. He didn't brag about it; it was just a fact.

"My family's estate is just outside Lansing. In fact, depending on the runway they use when we come in, we may be able to see it from the air."

"Estate?"

"Yeah, I guess. My dad has done very well for the family. He's a prolific inventor. He has maybe twenty patents to his name. He's developed and sold electronic components to Ford, GM, and the US government. He's made millions on those patents. I'm really proud of him."

Dale paused and stared out the window, lost in thought, then he continued.

"His job was deemed too important to the war effort in World War II, so he never saw combat. He offered to get me an exemption from the service, but I felt I had an obligation to follow in my grandfather's footsteps. He fought in World War I. I wish now that I had taken the offer of the exemption. The Vietnam War is like no other war in this country's history, and I don't think it'll have any beneficial results."

"Huh. I never really considered the exemption racket either—not that it would have mattered," Bill replied. "I was just another dumb peckerhead ready to be drafted. That was why I went through army ROTC. It kind of gives new meaning to the phrase 'when your number comes up.' "

Dale glanced at Bill, and they both laughed at the irony.

Hours later, the plane began to bank and line up for its approach. Dale leaned over and pointed out the window. "There's the home spread." His tone was a combination of nostalgia and pride.

Bill looked out the window to see several hundred acres of pastureland neatly separated and lined with bright white fences. Cattle and horses grazed in the pastures, and a tree-lined driveway led up to a three-story mansion on a hill slightly separated from four barn structures.

Dale continued the guided tour. "The barn on the left is for cattle milking; next is the calving barn. On the other side of the house is the horse barn and indoor riding arena."

"Good God!" exclaimed Bill.

Dale laughed at Bill's response.

As their flight passed east of the estate, Bill could look back and see the Olympic-sized swimming pool and tennis courts at the rear of the house. Dale sat back and tightened his seat belt for landing. Bill tightened his belt as well and cranked his neck around to get a last glimpse at the estate. He was looking forward to seeing the inside of that place and meeting Dale's family.

After they grabbed their duffels from the luggage return, Dale took the lead through the airport to the taxi stand. Tossing their duffels in the taxi's trunk, they climbed in, and Dale directed the driver to the estate.

Jack Patterson had indeed done well for the family. The trip up the driveway reminded Bill of the Southern mansion Tara in *Gone with the Wind*. The butler opened the front door and announced their arrival.

Jack and Mary Patterson came out of the sun-room and engulfed their son in hugs.

Mary gushed excitedly. "It's so great to have you home, my dear boy! How are you feeling? Does your leg hurt badly?"

"Mom, Dad—I'm fine." Dale laughed and disengaged from his mother's embrace.

Jack was a bear of a man and towered over his son while he eyed Bill.

"I want you to meet a fellow officer and good friend, Lieutenant William O'Brien from Minneapolis. Bill doesn't have any family, so I invited him to come home with me and head up to the UP for a little fishing."

Mary grabbed Bill's hand and pumped it warmly. She was only slightly shorter than her husband. She swept her blond hair behind one ear.

"Bill, it's so good to meet you. I'm glad you came to stay with us." Her sparkling blue eyes darted to his cane. "Are you okay?"

Bill knew that question could be answered in a lot of different ways. "Yes—thank you, Mrs. Patterson. Nothing a few weeks in rehab won't resolve."

"Let's go sit in the sun-room until dinner is ready," suggested Mary. "The roses in the back are just gorgeous right now."

Mary led them to the sun-room with the grace of a dancer. Bill's eyes darted around at all the opulence. The Pattersons had money, for sure. But they were really down-to-earth people. His trepidation began to ease.

"Dad, is the Huron Mountain camp available?" asked Dale. "I thought Bill and I would head up there for a couple of weeks and do a little fishing."

"Sure thing," Jack replied. "We had a little wind damage when a big storm went through last month, but that's all cleaned up. Henry's place got hit the hardest, so we've been helping him cut up trees and clear roads." Turning to Bill, he explained, "Our camp borders on property owned by the Ford family."

"My parents knew Edsel Ford quite well," said Bill. "In fact, my father flew airfreight for the Ford Motor Company in the early 1960s. He had his own business: M. O. Airfreight."

The elder Patterson was pleasantly surprised. "What's your father's name?"

"Michael. Michael O'Brien. Unfortunately, he and the rest of my family were killed in a plane crash in Colorado several years ago."

"Oh my God!" exclaimed Jack. He walked over to where Bill was perched on the love seat. "I worked for Ford in Detroit at that time. I knew your dad. I remember the accident. The Fords were vehement that the company be represented at the funeral. As I remember, he sent his vice president, Johann Schmidt."

With that, Jack wrapped his arms around Bill's shoulders, engulfing him in a bear hug. Finally releasing his hold, he patted Bill on the shoulder one last time.

"How about we get you boys settled upstairs? That'll give you a chance to clean up after your long flight. Dinner should be called in just a few minutes, and we can talk more then."

"Great idea, honey," Mary agreed. "I assume you boys are hungry."

Dale and Bill looked at each other and grinned. "Starving!" they said in unison.

Dinner was served at a long linen-covered table under a crystal chandelier. Bill had never seen such a marvelous spread. They started with hot tomato basil soup and a fresh green salad topped with tomato, broccoli, carrots, and walnuts, all drizzled with a sweet honey mustard dressing.

"The vegetables are all from our own garden," Mary announced.

Bill truly appreciated fresh garden produce. His thoughts went to the one-acre garden he used to weed back at the family farm when he was growing up. He would no sooner finish making one weeding pass when he had to start over again.

The main course was roast beef, mashed potatoes with gravy, and fresh snap peas. Second helpings were encouraged, and both boys took advantage of the offer. For dessert, they each had a large slab of apple pie with ice cream and coffee.

Bill pushed himself back a couple of inches from the table and instinctively patted his stomach. "I haven't had a meal like that in years. Maybe ever! Thank you so much."

Mary laughed. "I'm glad you enjoyed it. Hope you saved room for a couple more days of eating like that."

Bill just grinned in response.

"Let's head to the smoking room, boys," suggested Jack, wiping his mouth with his napkin and pushing his chair back.

"You boys go ahead," Mary encouraged. "I'm not fond of smoke, and I have a couple of things to attend to." She squeezed both boys lovingly on the shoulder as she headed out of the room. "It's really great to see you both home safe."

Once inside the smoking room, Jack closed the door, turned on the requisite fan, and offered cigars from the humidor. He lit each man's cigar in turn and took a deep draw on his own Cuban.

"How about an after-dinner brandy?"

Bill quietly puffed his cigar and stared out the window at the rose garden surrounding the nearby swimming pool. In the distance, the setting sun tinted the sky in shades of purple.

"Sure. I'd like that, sir," he responded, turning back to Jack.

"No need for the 'sir' here, Bill." Jack handed the two boys snifters of golden cognac, then went back to gather his own glass and cigar. "Have a seat, boys."

They all found comfortable leather recliners and then followed Bill's gaze, watching the sun finally dip beyond the horizon. Bill noticed that the room was lit by automatic sensor lights that adjusted the interior illumination as the sun set.

Jack blew a smoke ring and looked at the two young men sitting quietly, surrounded by the warmth and security of the mansion. He knew the two had a special bond from the war that he could never truly understand, but he needed to ask.

"What was it really like over there? Is war worth it?"

Dale and Bill met eyes. Dale shrugged.

"It changes people," Bill started to explain. "It's a war without a front line. You can be killed just as easily sitting in a café in Saigon as in the jungle on a mission. It's a war where our troops take and retake the same ground over and over again with the cost of so many good men. The climate is hostile—too hot and dry or too hot and wet. Even the animals seem to be hostile to us. But worse, there seems to be no strategy to win.

"We have over five hundred thousand troops in Vietnam, but we have only a small number of combat troops, probably less than fifty thousand. The enemy always outnumbered us. Only our mobility with helicopters and our ability to use artillery and aircraft allowed us to offset the advantage the enemy has in numbers."

Dale picked up the conversation. "There is so much death and destruction and so little observable result. Someone, somehow, will have to answer for it either in this world or the next."

Jack took another drag on his cigar and stared at the darkened window.

"Bill, you said you're headed to San Antonio after you guys get back from your two weeks at the camp. I'd like to make a call to my friend General Wallace Abrams, who's stationed at Lackland Air Force Base. He flew with your dad in the war, actually. I'm sure he would love to meet you and give you a grand tour of the area."

Bill grinned and nodded his appreciation.

24.

TWO DAYS LATER, THE BOYS PACKED THEIR GEAR after lunch and headed back to the Lansing airport. Tim, the family pilot, would take them to Marquette. The plane was already checked out, fueled, and ready for them on the charter tarmac.

"So glad to meet you, Bill." Tim's gaze was as warm and welcoming as his handclasp. "I hope you can relax and enjoy your time in the woods. It's always rejuvenating for me—and you guys have been through so much. If you're ready, let's head for Marquette. I have a car waiting for you to drive up to the camp."

The Beechcraft was a bit more cramped than the DC-10 from San Francisco, but Bill started to think cramped was okay as long as you were cramped with people you enjoyed. An hour and a half later, Tim pointed at the headset hanging in front of Bill and motioned for him to put them on. Dale already had his on.

"Check out the Soo Locks from up here," Tim said as he banked the plane so they had a better view out the right side. "See all those ore boats lined up? They go through the locks—one upriver, one down—almost non-stop at some times in the day. If it weren't for that lock, we wouldn't be shipping anything by boat down to the South."

Almost on cue, one of the locks began releasing water. Bill could see the rush of water creating rapids outside the dam gate.

"Wow," he said. "I heard about this when I was in school, but I've never seen it. Sure didn't expect to see it from above!"

Tim landed at the Marquette airport and taxied to the charter terminal, where a beige Ford wagon waited.

"There are your wheels for the next couple of weeks. Dale, your dad gave me this credit card in your name for gas, boat rentals, meals, or whatever you need to pick up."

As they drove out of the airport, Dale was quiet. Bill didn't interrupt the silence. He was overwhelmed by the Patterson family's generosity. Heading out of Marquette, Dale pulled the car into Pat's Foods.

"Let's go grocery shopping," he announced, grabbing his cane. "Get your own cart and load it with whatever you want."

Bill's thoughts drifted briefly to the TV game shows: "You have won a free shopping spree at SuperValu!" When he came back to earth, he saw his friend at the meat counter, loading up on T-bones and porterhouse steaks, pork chops, and chicken breasts. They would definitely not starve.

Bill knew what went with meat—*real* baked potatoes, smothered in butter. Or maybe mashed potatoes and gravy. Standing in the produce aisle, he was suddenly stymied by the selection. What kind of potato makes a good baked potato?

Dale came up behind and banged into Bill's cart. "Come on, Lieutenant, make a decision! If I'm cooking, I want Idaho bakers. If you're cooking, you probably just want a box of potato flakes."

Bill grinned at his friend. "Idaho bakers it is, Ms. Julia Child!"

Loading the food, beer, liquor, and a generous pack of toilet paper into the car, they headed northwest up the shoreline, then turned onto what Dale called Blind 35.

They opened the windows and sucked in deep breaths of the fresh air, trying to purge their lungs of nearly a year of fungus and diesel fuel. The sun was starting to set. The clear sky glowed with fabulous red and gold light that shone through the trees.

"The last time I saw a sky that color, I was ducking for cover," Dale noted.

"Yeah, but the smoke and choking fumes are missing here," noted Bill. Then he added, "Thank God!"

As the skies darkened, Bill felt his eyes sharpen. He could pick out deer darting to cover in the trees. Occasionally, the headlights lit up the eyes of a bear or coyote slipping through the grasses in the ditch. There were no human enemies hiding to harm them. This was a different kind of wildlife, and he could already feel the relaxing effects of Michigan's Upper Peninsula.

As they passed by the Huron Mountain Club's perimeter, Dale explained its history.

"The Huron Mountain Club is about six miles west of Big Bay, Michigan, and protected by a gate and security guard. Although there's a dining area where members can enjoy meals, the acreage is separated into multiple lots with individual owners. The owners pay membership dues for access to the private grounds and build their own version of paradise."

Bill caught glimpses of some of the homes through the trees. Some camps were sprawling, yet unassuming, single-story homes. Others had two or three levels with wraparound decks.

"Only fifty members were allowed when the club was formed," Dale continued. "They were the aristocracy of America, such as Cyrus McCormick, of International Harvester fame, and Frederick Miller, owner of Miller Brewing Company. Henry Ford applied for membership rather late in the game and was denied, seeing as they had already reached their limit. Ford later purchased thousands of acres of land just west of the club property and built his own home. It's now been handed down to his grandson, Henry. We bought our property from Edsel Ford and built our camp on the west side of the acreage adjoining the Ford property."

The Patterson camp was a two-story log construction standing at the top of a long drive. It was not the largest structure they had seen on the drive, but it was impressive and inviting. Bill raised his eyebrows at the thought that any one of these buildings was bigger than the homes he had grown up in.

Bill thought back to his conversation with Jack about his father. He glanced skyward.

Dad, there are a lot of people here who were glad to have known you and who have fond memories of you. That's quite a legacy. I sure hope you had the opportunity to see the beauty here in the Huron Mountains.

They unloaded the car, packed the refrigerator, and settled in. Dale cracked open two beers, passed one to Bill, then started grilling two porterhouse steaks while preparing the Idahos for baking.

"Think you can make a tossed salad for us, rookie?"

Bill pulled the salad fixings out of the refrigerator and started work while he sipped his beer. He was still pondering all the strange connections that were falling into place for him, thanks to his father's friends. Once he served his time in the military, he hoped these contacts would provide some job opportunities.

In addition, he was still trying to determine how to make a move on his uncle Sean and reclaim his inheritance. With all the glowing compliments he had heard of his father, he couldn't believe his father had entrusted the family and all their savings to Sean. That was a personal mystery he needed to resolve.

But for now, he would enjoy fishing in the Huron River and do as much hiking on the Lake Superior shore as the two gimps could stand. This was the kind of rehab he needed.

The opportunity to spend time with a fellow Vietnam vet allowed Bill and Dale a chance to talk and mentally decompress as well as physically heal. Talking about their fears, the shock of seeing friends die, and the overall waste of war allowed them to start putting the war behind them. Dale's cooking also helped offset some of the Vietnam weight-loss program for Bill.

The visit ended much too quickly. After two weeks, Dale and Bill headed back to Marquette, where Tim waited to fly them to Lansing. Jack and Mary warmly greeted them when they finally arrived at the estate.

"Welcome home," Jack said with a smile to both men. "Bill, you're welcome to stay the rest of your leave with us here in Lansing. I talked to General Abrams, and he said to just let him know whenever you would be in San Antonio. He's looking forward to meeting you again."

Again? Bill thought. *I don't remember ever meeting General Abrams before.* He just shook the thought from his head and smiled at Jack.

Mary stood by Jack's side, smiling her agreement. "Yes, Bill. I do hope you stay. In fact, I've planned an intimate 'welcome home' reception for the two of you with several of our friends." She cocked her head at Bill with a gleam in her eye. "There will be some single women there too."

Bill nodded to Mary. "I appreciate the invitation, but I don't want to overstay my welcome. I'd be happy to stay for the reception, but then I better head out. I want to respect the general's time. If I get to San Antonio early, it will give him more options to schedule time with me." Bill looked at Jack. "Thank you again, sir, for arranging this for me."

"Remember what I said about that 'sir' stuff around here," joked Jack. "You can save that for the general. Whenever you want to head out, just let me know, and we'll get your flight to Texas arranged."

"I really can't thank you all enough for taking me in like family."

"You are family to us, and you are always welcome," Mary interjected. "You've been family ever since you and Dale met at Fort Sill. He mentioned you in so many letters."

"Nothing bad, I hope," Bill said glancing at Dale with a smile.

Preparations for the reception began in full swing. Jack and Mary Patterson were not going to miss the opportunity to welcome Dale and Bill back home. Dale looked at the guest list and saw several women he was eager to be reacquainted with. He definitely wanted to see Sara Williamson again. She was the daughter of his parents' good friends.

Apparently, the invitation to the Williamson family had fallen to Sara, seeing as she was the only one who happened to be available. She was willing to attend but was not enthusiastic.

Sara was several years older than both Dale and Bill. As a teen, Dale had always wanted to date her, but she only ever saw him as a younger brother. Dale hadn't seen her in years and didn't know where life had taken her, but he was eager to see her again and introduce her to his friend.

"Wait until you meet Sara," Dale told Bill. "She's the most intelligent person I've ever met. She comes from a family of doctors. As a bonus, she's also unbelievably attractive." He nudged Bill in the ribs.

Bill took this all in. He was a penniless soldier with no place to call home. This Sara seemed way out of his league. Still, he would enjoy meeting her. It was always great to meet an intelligent and beautiful woman.

25.

T WO DAYS LATER, DALE AND BILL DONNED their full dress uniforms for the dinner. Bill wore his uniform out of necessity—he
had no civilian clothes appropriate for the formal affair. Dale,
then, wore his uniform just so Bill wouldn't be embarrassed.

As the guests arrived, they formed a receiving line so Jack and Mary
could introduce Dale and Bill to everyone. Mary emphasized the unmarried
status of the young women in the line as they passed through with their parents. The girls were college students. They were polite but hesitant to meet
the soldiers and did not engage with them.

Dale noticed Sara at the end of the line by herself. The other guests
were dispersing to the dinner table by the time she finally made it up to Dale.
He nodded to his mother so she could feel free to attend to her guests, then
he turned to reintroduce himself to Sara.

"Sara, you look great tonight!" he said with a smile.

Much to his chagrin, she looked at him as a sister would her younger brother.

"You look wonderful too. Welcome home." She noticed the cane in his
left hand. "I hope you're all right."

"Yes, thank you. Nothing that won't heal with time."

Bill was just finishing up his greeting with another guest when Dale
tapped him on the shoulder to get his attention. Then Dale turned back to Sara.

"Sara Williamson, I'd like to introduce you to a very good friend of
mine, Lieutenant William O'Brien."

Bill looked up and met Sara's eyes. She was the most beautiful woman he had ever seen. Her smile. Her soft, long bright-red hair. Her expressive deep-green eyes.

Suddenly, there seemed to be no one else in the room. He was captivated—and so was she. In that instant, something extraordinary happened that neither one could explain.

"William, it's so good to meet you."

She clasped his hand warmly in both of hers. Bill was startled by the softness of her caress.

"Will you sit next to me at dinner?" she asked, his hand still in hers. "I believe it's time to find our seats."

"Yes, Miss Williamson. It would be my honor. Thank you." He fumbled with his cane.

"No, William—it's my pleasure!" She smiled. "Take my hand, and we can find a seat at the table."

Bill allowed Sara to lead the way to the table, leaving Dale standing there, stunned. He had never seen or heard Sara act that way before. In fact, he had never seen anything like that before. Bill and Sara had instantly connected. Dale was happy for Bill to finally have something good happening for him.

As for Bill, he still wasn't sure what had happened. Whatever it was, it was wonderful. Finally seated together at the table, Bill tried to make small talk, but few words came out. He knew his mumbling made no sense.

Sara just looked at him and smiled. "You can relax. I can tell you right now that we'll be spending quite a bit of time together in the next few days. The words will come easier then!"

The waiter appeared just then and poured wine for them. Once he moved on, Sara leaned over and whispered to Bill.

"Besides, William, I want you to walk with me outside after dinner, so we can be alone."

"You can call me Bill," he managed to respond.

The dinner was magnificent, but Bill couldn't concentrate on the food. He couldn't believe someone like Sara was interested in him. Something magical had happened.

Sara felt the magic too. When they first locked eyes, she had been totally absorbed—almost as if she were in a trance. It surprised her, rocked her, yet totally satisfied her. It touched her to her very core.

She saw how his eyes danced when he smiled at her. She could almost see into his soul. She loved his innocent and radiant smile. He was ruggedly attractive and strong, but she sensed a great kindness and compassion in him as well as modesty. Warmth just radiated from him. She knew that was very unusual in combat veterans.

Sara knew the meaning of each of the medals he wore—valor, courage, and three stars on his Purple Heart for wounds received in combat. He was indeed a very brave and honorable man, one she wanted and needed to know more about.

His presence filled a void that had been inside her since her husband had died in Vietnam. She knew this man would be special to her, so very special. She would do whatever it took to be with him.

As the dinner ended, Sara carefully patted her lips with her napkin, then folded it next to her plate. "Bill, why don't we let the Pattersons know we're going for a walk?"

Bill nodded quickly. He gathered his cane, stood, and held Sara's chair as she also rose. He headed over to Jack and Mary. "Thank you for the wonderful dinner reception." Next, he nodded to the rest of the guests. Taking Sara's hand, he announced, "I think we'll take a walk and try to wear off some of those calories."

Jack and Mary smiled at the prospect of a budding romance between Bill and the daughter of one of their closest friends. They had always loved Sara as one of their own, and they thought the world of Bill.

Bill retrieved Sara's coat and his own. They walked out into the still, brisk spring evening. Sara reached down and took Bill's hand, swinging it as they walked in silence. She smiled to herself—she knew Bill was still tongue-tied.

Indeed, he was. He had been away from women for so long that he was having trouble thinking of what and how to say anything. Even though he knew there was something special between him and Sara, he was very nervous.

After a few steps, Sara stopped. "Bill, I'm going to do something that should help you understand how I feel right now."

She put her arms around him and kissed him. It wasn't just a quick peck on the lips. It was a long, glorious kiss. For a moment, he was stunned, as if a lightning bolt had gone down his spine. Then he embraced her tightly with both arms, trying to keep his cane out of the way as he softly returned her kiss. As their lips finally parted, he moved to kiss her softly on her neck.

Her eyes closed, and she smiled. "That was a nice communication, don't you think?"

"That was amazing!" Bill admitted sheepishly, suddenly finding his words.

Sara laughed. "Oh, so you're finally not tongue-tied? Do I have to kiss you every time I want you to talk?"

"I wouldn't mind, but you might end up with chapped lips," he responded with a laugh.

That confirmed to Sara that Bill had a wry sense of humor despite what he had endured. Every time he spoke, she loved him more. Yes, *loved* him.

Sara put her head on his shoulder. She felt such contentment with him. She was not some young schoolgirl on her first romance. No, she had a lot of experience. And the only time she had felt this before was with her husband. She was glad she had found another brave soldier.

"Bill, I'm in love with you. I knew it as soon as I saw you tonight. I can't explain it, but I am. How about you?"

"I love you too," Bill responded instantly. Then he paused. "But I don't have a lot of positive experience with love. My college sweetheart left me before I went to Vietnam. And honestly, I'm not the greatest catch in the world. I'm sure you can have your choice of any man. I can't believe how lucky I am to be with you right now. Are you sure you didn't have too much to drink tonight?" he asked with a wink. Then he turned serious again as he held her close. "I know I want to be with you, if you want to be with me. There is nothing that would please me more."

Sara looked up at Bill and beamed that smile. Oh yes, she wanted to be with him. The more she knew about him, the more she wanted him. Her first impressions had been spot-on.

They walked back toward the Patterson home, arm in arm.

Dale saw them come in the door. "Thought you two got lost. I was going to rally the search team," he joked.

Bill and Sara blushed. Then Bill surprised Sara by pulling her to him and kissing her in front of all the guests. Dale started a round of applause. Everyone knew something amazing had happened that night.

Before long, guests began departing for home. Bill reluctantly escorted Sara to her car. With each step, reality sunk in a little more. Love at first sight was wonderful, but could they sustain it?

Like most in her family, Sara was a doctor. She told Bill she had recently been promoted to head of the pediatrics department at Boston Children's Hospital, an impressive position for a woman to hold. The hospital was deemed the best pediatric hospital in the country. Sara would soon return to Boston, while he would leave for Texas. Bill knew a long-distance romance could be a problem. He wondered if the glamour would wear off for Sara once she assumed her new position.

Sara sensed his concern as they reached her car. "Bill, I've been around the block. I'm not some naive, emotionally challenged schoolgirl who would fall for any man's line. I was married to a wonderful man, but I lost him in the war. It hurt me deeply, but now is the right time to move on with my life. I know you are the real deal. No one is going to pull me away from you. I know we're going our separate ways for a while, but we can make this work. You'll see me a whole lot more than you think."

She put her hand against the car door to keep him from opening it.

"For now, I want us to make the most of our time together for the final days of your leave. I'll pick you up tomorrow morning at nine. We'll spend the day together. We'll spend every day together until you leave for Texas."

"Yes, ma'am," was all Bill could say.

He leaned down and gave her a long farewell kiss, then held the car door for her. As she drove off into the night, she honked the horn.

My God, how I love her! he thought. It was his first warm, human feeling since college. He didn't want it to end. He stood in the dark for a long time gazing at the end of the driveway, where her taillights had disappeared in the night.

When Bill got back to the house, Mary met him at the door. "William, that was one of the most beautiful sights I've ever seen. I could tell from your first few seconds that you and Sara would connect. When you two locked eyes, it was like an explosion. The whole room just stopped and looked at you both. It couldn't have happened to a nicer couple."

Dale slipped in behind his mother like a Cheshire cat. He couldn't restrain himself. "You, my friend, have a hell of a lot of mojo! Seriously, though, I couldn't be happier for you both. You both deserve it."

Mary placed her hand on Bill's shoulder. "You know, I have something for you," she said thoughtfully. "Something you'll probably need soon. Come with me."

Dale just grinned as Mary led Bill upstairs.

The next morning, Sara was right on time. She drove them down I-96 from Lansing to the Detroit and Dearborn area to show him her old haunts. She pulled up to the house where she was raised in Dearborn, not far from the Ford family homes. Bill noted it was a lovely large house, clearly reflecting the upper class.

"My parents still live here," she said. "In fact, since they couldn't make the reception, I'd like to introduce you today, if that's okay. They're not home yet, but I know they'll be back shortly."

"I'd love to meet them," Bill replied. "Tell me more about your family."

"My father and mother met and married just before World War II. He was a surgeon at the Henry Ford Hospital in Detroit, and my mother was a nurse. Dad spent time in France as an army doctor, and my mother was an army nurse, so they understand sacrifice and war. Now my father is chief of staff at the hospital. In fact, I was born there."

Bill smiled. "I was born in that hospital too. We've had something in common since we were born!"

Sara laughed and nodded in agreement. She was so beautiful when she laughed—Bill just had to lean over to kiss her.

"Okay, Bill, we'll never get through my story if you keep distracting me! Now, where was I?"

Bill laughed at her and said, "Your family, my dear. Your family."

Sara poked him in the ribs and continued. "I have two brothers—both doctors. One is in the army at Walter Reed. The other is in private practice in Chicago."

"You have a huge medical tradition," Bill acknowledged, suddenly feeling overwhelmed. "How do you think I fit into all this? Don't your parents want you to marry a doctor, who can provide for you?"

Before the words were out of his mouth, Bill knew he should have phrased that better. Sara was a department head at Boston Children's Hospital—as if she needed someone to provide for her. He clenched his teeth, knowing what her reaction would be.

Sara spun in the seat with fire in her eyes. She relaxed a bit when she saw Bill's chastened face, knowing he had not meant it as it sounded. Then she understood what he actually meant—he was worried he wouldn't be "good enough" in her parents' eyes. She appreciated his honesty.

"Bill, my parents love me and want me to be happy. I've known medical people all my life. They are no better than anyone else. What matters is what any of us have inside, what we value, how we live, and who we truly are. My parents had to work hard and sacrifice for what they have, but they realize their love is the most important thing. Love is life itself! Most good doctors know that, and my parents and I know that. So that's how you fit in with me. My love for you is life to me."

Bill was stunned by Sara's beautiful statement. He paused, trying to formulate a response.

"I can't even come close to expressing my love for you in the way you just have. But I offer you all I have and will ever have. I will always want to be with you, to love you and support you where I can. I will always respect you in all things."

Bill reached into his pocket and pulled out a small box. Sara smiled but found herself tongue-tied.

That's a first, Bill thought to himself.

Sara opened the box to reveal a beautiful, simple gold engagement ring. Mary had offered Bill her old engagement ring the night before. She knew

Bill wouldn't have time to shop for a ring before his leave was up, yet she could tell he would need one very soon.

And now the time was right. Bill felt the same strange magic overcome him as the night before. Something was moving him, and it was wonderful.

"Sara, if I can be so bold—I want you to be my wife. I'm sorry I haven't had the opportunity to purchase a ring, but until I do, please accept this ring Mrs. Patterson was gracious enough to loan me. In a way, it reflects love from one great family to another. Will you accept this ring and me as your husband?"

Sara started to cry. Bill had a fleeting thought that she might reject him. Then she threw her arms around his neck.

"Yes, Bill! I do accept your proposal. I love you!" she exclaimed as she smothered him with a kiss.

"Why don't you try it on? I hope it fits."

He took the ring out of the box and placed it on her finger. It fit perfectly.

"Bill, I will always honor, love, and respect you. I am proud to accept your proposal."

They sat in the car, entwined in each other's arms, and let the whirlwind of emotions roll over them. Less than twenty-four hours ago, they didn't know the other existed. Now, they were engaged.

Sara broke the reverie. "Okay, Lieutenant—time to face the parents. I see them pulling up."

Bill grinned and stepped out of the car. He hobbled to her side to hold the door, then walked arm in arm to the house.

"Mom, Dad," Sara started, "this is Lieutenant William O'Brien. I met him at the Pattersons' reception, and I'm happy to tell you we are now engaged! Bill, this is my mom and dad, Walter and Elizabeth Williamson."

"Please, call us Walt and Lizzy," Sara's mother clarified as she warmly took Bill's hand. "And we couldn't be happier for you! Mary called me last night to tell me all about the party. She said you two seemed to hit it off."

"Hit it off?" Walt laughed. "I think she described it a little more clearly than that!"

The Williamsons were thrilled with Sara's decision, no matter how swift. They could see the sparkling light in her eyes that had been missing for so long. They knew she had been consumed by an emotional darkness after her husband's death. This was truly a blessing.

"Let's head into the porch and get to know one another," offered Walt, leading the way.

Sara's parents embraced Bill with their kindness. He saw where Sara got her wonderful qualities. Walt and Lizzy were impressed by Bill's strength and focus. He talked briefly about his time in Vietnam, his friendship with Dale, and his plan to get his father's business back. And, of course, his love for Sara.

The afternoon turned to early evening quickly. Bill and Sara opted out of dinner so they could head back to Lansing for the night. With over an hour of driving ahead, it would be late before they got back to the Pattersons'.

After their good-byes, Bill and Sara were on their way. The drive back seemed shorter somehow.

"I'd liked to take you up to our camp on the shore of Lake Michigan tomorrow," Sara said. "That's where I want the wedding to be held."

Bill glanced at her quickly. *Wow, she's already got the wedding plans in motion!*

Before long, Sara drove up the curving driveway to the front of the Pattersons' estate. Bill slid over on the seat, then embraced and softly kissed his fiancée.

"How about we go to a jewelry store first thing tomorrow so you can pick out a proper engagement ring just for you?"

"No need, Bill," Sara explained. "While you and Dad were sharing war stories earlier, I called Mary and asked if we could keep the ring. A store-bought ring would never have the same value to me. She said she would be thrilled to provide this gift to us."

Bill just laughed. Once again, Sara was one step ahead. After one more kiss good-bye, Bill headed inside.

Mary, Jack, and Dale were enjoying dessert at the table as he walked in. They greeted him with broad smiles.

"Way to go!" Dale exclaimed, clapping Bill on the back.

"Yes, congratulations, William!" Jack said, standing to shake Bill's hand.

"We were so pleased when Sara called Mary this afternoon and told her about the engagement. I hope you both will be very happy together. I have never seen a more perfect couple."

"Mr. Patterson, I have to believe you and your lovely wife were equally as stunning when you married," Bill responded. "If we can be anywhere near as happy as you are after your long marriage, it would be a blessing."

Mary pushed in between the two men and hugged Bill. "You're just like another son to us!"

Bill had trouble sleeping that night. He knew he loved Sara intensely—but he kept recounting all the ways he could lose her. They had such little time together left. He would head for Texas the day after tomorrow. Who knew when he would be with her again? Then again, he realized Sara had been through a long-distance romance with her husband in Vietnam, before he was killed.

Just thinking about her husband made Bill pause. He knew he needed to broach that subject tomorrow. He wanted to be sure she wasn't moving too fast after her husband's death. Bill didn't want her to be hurt by making a wrong decision.

The night passed slowly as he tossed and turned.

After breakfast, Sara arrived right on time. Jack invited her in for a cup of coffee and a little congratulatory conversation before Sara and Bill headed out.

The drive to the Williamsons' camp was a bit farther than yesterday's tour. As they drove off, Bill glanced at Sara and the ring glistening on her finger. He wondered silently if she had any misgivings.

"Are you sure you don't want to stop and pick out a ring?" Bill asked again. "You're letting me off pretty cheap."

"Nope. Mary is happy. I'm happy. You're off the hook. Well, sort of." The glint in Sara's eyes ensured there was more to that thought. "You can splurge on the wedding ring," she continued. "Besides, I expect you to pay in other ways today!"

Bill didn't have to be told what that meant.

Sara pulled up the long drive in front of a log home. Bill could hear the waves crashing on the shore on the other side of the house. For a brief moment, he stood gawking at the beautiful setting.

But then Sara grabbed him by the hand and led him into the house, toward the master bedroom. Before they reached the door, Bill stopped her. He dropped his cane on the floor and scooped her up in his arms. Much to her surprise, he carried her into the bedroom, nudged the door shut with his elbow, and gently laid her on the bed.

Sara smiled up at Bill as he slowly stroked her silky, soft red hair and began to kiss her forehead, then her ear, and finally her neck.

"Down payment time, little lady," he whispered.

She ran her fingers through his hair and helped him remove his shirt and loosen his belt. She ran her fingers over his bare chest, tracing some of his war wounds.

He carefully unbuttoned her blouse, slipped it off her shoulders, and unhooked her bra. She shrugged the clothing to the floor while he continued to kiss her neck and breasts. She inhaled deeply and rolled off the bed to remove her skirt and panties.

She was back on him quickly. He slid his hand to her crotch and rubbed her rhythmically, increasing the depth of her breathing. As she rolled to her back and moaned softly, he slipped off his pants and underwear and tossed them in the corner. She beamed a glorious smile and moved her legs apart for him.

He kissed her and entered her for the first time. They lost track of time, simply enjoying each other until exhaustion took over.

As they lay side by side, Bill decided he needed to finally discuss what had kept him awake most of the night. "Sara, I keep thinking about your husband. I'm so sorry for your loss. I need to make sure we aren't rushing ahead in this relationship."

Sara rolled on top of him and stared directly into his eyes. "Bill, do you think I'm rushing into this?"

Bill smiled at the intensity of her stare. He knew she did not expect an answer.

With Sara there on top of him, this time she could have the upper hand. He would just enjoy the full love of his fiancée.

Finally, they were totally spent once again.

"I can't believe how amazing you are, Sara—and not just the sex," Bill added with a laugh. "You are amazing in everything you do."

"Well, you're amazing too, and I also mean the sex!" Sara admitted. "I wasn't sure how you would respond, seeing as you've spent over a year in the jungle. But my God, I've never been so turned on like that." She flopped back in the bed. "I'm actually groggy—nearly drunk!"

Once again, the day ended too quickly. Bill knew he needed to get back and pack up for his flight the next morning. He didn't want this time to end, and he knew Sara felt the same.

At first, Sara couldn't remember the route back to the Pattersons. She took a few wrong turns before remembering her way, adding to the drive time.

"You're probably just trying to delay the inevitable," Bill teased. "But I truly don't mind."

They both were quiet during the drive. Sara started to plan a surprise for Bill. She knew he was heading to Fort Sill after his time at Fort Sam Houston. Then when his service was up, she knew he would be going back to Minneapolis to recover his father's business. She decided right then and there she would apply for a position with the University of Minnesota hospital system. By the time he'd finish his active duty obligation, she would already be in the Twin Cities, settled in waiting for him.

26.

BILL LEFT ON A FLIGHT TO SAN ANTONIO the next morning. He couldn't believe how wonderful the last three days had been. He never thought he could love someone as much as he loved Sara—and so immediately. It was still hard to grasp. They would be separated briefly as he finished his time with the army, but he was sure their deep affection would provide a solid future together. He was happier than he had ever been.

He had contacted the hospital at Fort Sam Houston and was cleared to check in early and start his rehab on an outpatient basis. Finding his room in the officers' barracks, he dumped his duffel contents on the bed. Time to get organized. He would be there for a month, so it was worth unpacking.

He heard a knock on the door as a nurse walked in with his chart in her hand. She looked at him carefully, then she broke into a smile. Reading from the chart, she said, "Lieutenant William O'Brien. We've met before."

Her name badge gave her away—but so did her deep blue eyes and bright smile. Bill returned the smile. This was a friendly face he recognized.

"Lieutenant Susan Johnson! The last time I saw you, I was in the hospital in Pleiku."

"That's right, soldier." She pointed mockingly to the folded sheets still sitting at the end of the bed under his pile of clothes. "I see you still need some training on how to make your bed."

"Yeah, you know us walking wounded—we just never learn." He winked. "I'm really glad to see you under better circumstances."

"Lieutenant O'Brien, you are much more coherent than the last time I saw you. I can honestly say, I'm glad to see you here too."

Bill let out a sigh. "How about we dispense with the 'Lieutenant' stuff, and you just call me Bill?"

"Sorry. I think we need to maintain the Lieutenants when we're on duty. But off duty, that would be fine."

Bill jumped at the opening. "Okay. Maybe we could have dinner tonight in the officers' mess or the restaurant of your choice off-base. My treat as a thank-you for taking care of me all those times. It'd be great to catch up. I can wow you with some of my fishing stories from Michigan's Upper Peninsula."

Susan smiled. "I would really like that. I'm an avid fisher myself. My dad taught me, and he insisted I bait my own hooks. By the way, I have a late afternoon meeting, so I'll be in my dress uniform, not fishing duds. I'll meet you at six in the hospital lobby . . . Bill."

With that, she turned on her heel and headed down the hall.

Bill unpacked and ironed his dress uniform just to make sure it was crisp for the night's outing. He carefully pinned on his medals. This was only the second time he would be in a dress uniform stateside. The medals were customary.

They met in the lobby at the appointed time and walked together to the officers' club. Bill couldn't help but notice how great Susan looked in her dress uniform, her blond hair tucked neatly up and under her cap. In her own way, she was a very attractive woman, but he was happy with his commitment to Sara.

Bill also couldn't help but notice how Susan returned the glance, sizing him up in his dress uniform with his medals.

"How did your meeting go today?" Bill asked as he carefully placed his cane to climb the steps to the officers' club.

"Fine. It was a routine but must-attend staff meeting," she responded.

Bill hesitated for a moment, not sure how to keep the conversation going. He had been so happy and surprised to see a familiar face that he had suggested this dinner on a whim. *But what do we have in common, other than Vietnam and my time in the hospital?* he asked himself. *I know nothing about her! It's not like we're old friends.*

He sorted through some topics and finally had his opener. "Tell me about your family, Susan. What made you sign up for the army?"

"I was raised on a small farm outside Madison, Wisconsin," she started. "I'm the oldest of five kids. I wanted to go into nursing, and caring for my siblings gave me lots of practice. There wasn't a lot of money for college, so I requested money from a federal grant. That obligated me to serve in the military as a nurse. Little did I know the 'Vietnam conflict' would become a war."

Bill smiled as he remembered having that same feeling.

"My grandparents emigrated from Sweden in the early 1900s and bought the farm property. My youngest brothers are still working the crops and livestock. When Grams and Gramps wanted to move to the senior-living facility in Madison, the family subdivided the acreage to provide homesteads for my mother and father, and my two oldest brothers and their families. It's nice to still have the family living close together."

"What happened to you after I got released?"

Susan paused and looked out the window, collecting her thoughts. "I was still at the MASH briefly after your release. The Vietcong attacked the base, and a mortar shell went through the roof of our ward. Many of my patients were either killed or wounded. The Vietcong nearly overran the hospital. Eventually, we were able to evacuate everyone, but I can still hear the screams of the patients when I try to sleep at night."

She reached up and tucked her hair back behind her ear. Bill saw a purple ribbon on her uniform blouse, just above her other ribbons.

She too had been wounded in action and awarded the Purple Heart, he thought. He could only imagine how terrible those screams had been for her, a nurse charged with saving all the wounded. In addition, she had trauma from her own wounds.

"I hear screams too," Bill admitted. "I can't seem to forget them either."

She just nodded and quickly changed the subject. They spent the rest of the evening avoiding Vietnam and exchanging stories of happier memories. He didn't ask anything too personal, and neither did she.

Bill was glad he had asked her to supper. Maybe they weren't old friends, but it was good to get to know each other.

After dinner, Bill and Susan said good-night and went their separate ways. Back in her room, Susan found herself reminiscing. Her first posting at Fort Sam was right after graduating from the University of Wisconsin. She was eager to start her two-week officer orientation program before she received her first posting from the army. Susan was a newly minted second lieutenant, and she was directed to the dormitory that housed all the new nurses.

As she was moving in, she met Brenda Johanson, a fellow nurse who had just arrived from Nebraska. They had a few free hours before dinner. They wandered down to the small lounge in the dorm, where several other new nurses had gathered, anxious for the orientation to begin the next day. They seemed to have a lot in common, sharing stories about their schools, families, and boyfriends.

The other new nurses seemed a bit inexperienced, a bit naive, to Susan. She had worked on the farm since she was ten years old. She could toss hay bales on a wagon, hand-milk the cows, and even wrestle her brothers to the ground when they teased her and called her Lima Bean. Susan was ready and willing to take on anything.

But she didn't see that attitude in the new nurses she was now meeting. For the most part, they had lived in large urban areas and were not accustomed to manual labor. She wondered how they would fare in the heat of battle.

Truly, she also wondered how she would fare.

"What's your background, Susan?" Brenda had broken into Susan's distant thoughts.

"I grew up on a Wisconsin dairy farm with four brothers I had to keep in line."

The other nurses laughed at their own memories of sibling rivalries.

"I was grateful for the aid I received from the government so I could go to nursing school. My mother didn't understand why I wanted a profession. She wanted me to marry a nice farmer and raise her grandchildren."

That comment brought a mixture of responses and knowing smiles, even from the urban girls. Maybe their mothers didn't expect them to marry farmers, but they didn't understand their daughters' desire for careers.

"Fortunately, my dear father prevailed. He saw times changing. He said he would be proud if I had a career."

She shared a secret with her sister nurses that night as well.

"I'm engaged to an air force fighter pilot. We plan to be married when we both complete our military responsibilities."

The nurses quickly gathered around to view Susan's simple gold engagement band.

"We haven't told our families yet. Larry's family is strict Catholic, and my family is Lutheran. There would be a lot more pressure on both of us if we announced our engagement. We don't care about the differences in religion, but right now, there's no need to raise concerns."

Again, there were knowing nods.

"Larry is a wonderful guy. He's really my Prince Charming. He was captain of the Wisconsin baseball team and a top student. We met at a dance when I was a junior, and I fell almost immediately in love with him. He was a senior and in the air force ROTC. Larry's family is from Milwaukee and owns various factories around the area. He will probably run some of them when he returns from Vietnam. We plan to have a great life together."

The mention of Vietnam took much of the joy out of the room. They would soon see for themselves what this conflict was all about.

After the two-week orientation, the nurses received their orders. They were all headed to Vietnam as replacement nurses for various MASH units. They had time for a thirty-day leave, and then their lives would change forever.

When Susan went home and told her family where she would be stationed, her mother was almost inconsolable.

"It's bad enough that you decided to be a nurse, and an army nurse besides. Now you're going to war. What is this country coming to?"

When her leave ended, Susan's parents hugged her and cried before she left for the Madison airport. Susan had not seen her father cry in many years.

"Don't worry—it's only a year," Susan announced bravely. "I'll be home before you know it."

She had an additional incentive for the year to go by quickly: she would marry Larry. She thought her parents would be so proud to have him as a son-in-law.

But in the end, the time in Vietnam would seem much longer than a year, and it would be much harder than Susan or any of the nurses expected. When she boarded the plane at Travis Air Force Base, Susan got a quick glimpse of the next twelve months. She was one of only two nurses on board.

The next twelve months would be an isolating and stressful time for the few nurses in the midst of chaos and horror. They would not escape the trauma of the war.

27.

hen Bill arrived at the Fort Sam Houston hospital for his first therapy session, he was surprised to find a note waiting for him from General Abrams:

William:

I am looking forward to meeting you again. Please call my aide at the number printed at the top of this memo, and he will arrange a time for us to meet.

—Wallace Abrams, LT General USAF

It was nice to have such a kind note waiting for him from such an important and busy man. Bill noticed the "again." This was the second time someone had said General Abrams would be meeting him "again." First Dale's father said it, and now the general himself. But Bill just didn't remember any such meeting.

Bill dialed the number for the general's aide. The call was answered on the first ring.

"Lieutenant General Abrams's office. Captain Smith speaking. How may I help you?"

Bill smiled. He could almost hear the salute coming over the line.

"Captain Smith, this is Lieutenant William O'Brien. I would like to arrange a time to meet with Lieutenant General Abrams at his convenience."

"Yes, Lieutenant. The general mentioned he wanted to meet with you as soon as possible. Would you be available at eleven hundred hours tomorrow?"

"That would be fine. I'll be there."

"Lieutenant O'Brien, the general also indicated he would like you to plan on having lunch with him, if you are available."

"That would be great," responded Bill, a bit surprised by the offer. "Please thank him for me."

"Yes. I will have a driver pick you up in front of the hospital at ten hundred hours to allow for drive time."

"Thank you, Captain. I'll be ready."

Bill put the phone back in its cradle and stared at the ceiling. *I can't believe a three-star general, responsible for the United States Southern Command, is so eager to see me*, he thought. *Not bad for a lowly first lieutenant.*

Bill spent the rest of the day gathering information about General Abrams. Everyone he talked to had a high opinion of the general: "Great leader," "Very brave and capable," "Tough, but fair," they said.

Bill went to the base library to research Abrams's service. He found he had served in World War II flying B-24s from Britain, then served in Korea flying B-29s. He had seen plenty of action and was heavily decorated, having been awarded a Distinguished Flying Cross, a Silver Star, a Bronze Star, and two Purple Hearts. Bill mused that all Abrams was missing was the Medal of Honor. And now he was slated for his fourth star and in line to become the commander of the United States Air Force.

Bill was still confused as to why the general was so intent on meeting him—meeting him "again," that is.

The next morning, at 10:00 a.m. sharp, an air force car pulled up to the door of the hospital. Although the general's office at Lackland Air Force Base was only about ten miles away, they had to traverse the length of San Antonio, and traffic was heavy. It was nearly forty-five minutes door to door. Bill sat back and enjoyed the luxurious ride.

Captain Smith, the general's aide, met him at the door. Bill was getting used to saluting, and he adjusted his cane appropriately.

After exchanging salutes, the captain said, "Glad to meet you, Lieutenant. General Abrams is very eager to see you again."

"Pleasure to meet you, Captain Smith. I look forward to meeting the general."

Bill wondered if Captain Smith noted that Bill didn't say "again." If Captain Smith did notice, he didn't acknowledge it.

"Please follow me to the general's office," the aide said.

Captain Smith paced himself carefully as he led Bill up two flights of stairs to a large office wing labeled Southern Command. Smith stopped and knocked. He then opened the door and announced, "General Abrams, Lieutenant William O'Brien is here to see you."

"Captain Smith, have him come right in!" a voiced boomed from inside the office.

Bill took a quick look around the massive office as Captain Smith ushered him in and closed the door behind him. Bill could hear the captain's footsteps echoing on the granite floor and down the steps as he returned to his post.

A large desk was positioned near the window, flanked by the American flag and the United States Air Force flag. But the desk chair was empty. Bill scanned around quickly, looking for the general. He snapped to a salute when he finally noticed the general lounging back in a chair behind an over-abundant mahogany table.

General Abrams responded with a broad smile. "William. Is it William or Bill?"

"Either, sir," Bill replied.

"Then William it is. Please come over to the table and have a chair. We have a lot of catching up to do."

"Catching up, sir . . ." Bill began. "I'm truly sorry, but I don't recall meeting you before."

Abrams gave a hearty laugh. "You were only four years old when I saw you last. I was visiting your dad and mom in Detroit while I was on leave from Korea."

Hearing this, Bill could vaguely remember a big, burly man coming for a visit. He was apparently a close friend of his dad's, and he had insisted on saluting Bill. With a smile, Bill remembered his own clumsy attempt at returning the salute.

Abrams noticed Bill's cane and then the Purple Heart ribbon on his chest. The medal had three stars, meaning three combat wounds. He also noted that Bill had ribbons for both a Silver Star and a Bronze Star. He was very proud of this young man and knew he had been through some terrible situations.

"I was not aware you had been wounded, William. How long is your rehab at Fort Sam?"

"Sir, I'm scheduled for thirty days, and then I should be done with the cane."

"Splendid. Let's get reacquainted," replied Abrams.

Bill settled into the other chair behind the mahogany table.

"William," the general continued, "I was terribly saddened to hear about the death of your family. That was one of only a few things in my life that have brought me to tears. Your mom and dad were like family to me, and of course so are you. I was terribly sorry that I couldn't attend your parents' funeral, but I was abroad on a classified mission at that time for President Kennedy. You remember all the turmoil during that period— the Bay of Pigs incident, the Cuban Missile Crisis. We came closer to total nuclear war than most people know. I just couldn't be there for you."

Abrams paused and glanced across the office to where the sun shone brightly through the window.

"I trained on B-24s with your dad in San Antonio and served with him in the same squadron in England. We flew twenty-five missions together and survived. He was an excellent pilot, a brave man, and a great friend."

As Abrams paused again, Bill interjected, "Dad never really talked about the war. He didn't keep any mementos. I know he was decorated at least once, but I never found any medals after his death."

"I'm not surprised." Abrams shook his head. "He saw so much death and destruction. He was deeply affected by the deaths and injuries of members of his squadron and of the innocent civilians in the cities he was helping the British destroy. That's one of the reasons we were so close.

"William, on your father's first mission in early 1943, his wingman was hit by antiaircraft fire. His plane went down, killing everyone on board. That was hard for your father to endure on his first mission, but he dealt with it. On at least three of his missions, he was wounded either by antiaircraft flak or German fighters. But each time, he managed to bring his plane and crew home safely. He was a damn fine pilot and leader.

"I heard him joke once that his plane was the first one off the Ford production line at Willow Run. For him, that made it extra special. It turned out to be a true story! Edsel Ford had personally seen to the production of that first aircraft. His son Henry Ford II made an effort to meet your dad later. The connection with that first aircraft endeared your father to the Ford family."

Bill had never heard these accounts of his father's war service. After what Bill himself had endured in Vietnam, he was getting a much different picture of his father. It made him even prouder to be the son of Michael William O'Brien.

"I owe my life to your father, William." Abrams sat up in the chair for emphasis and locked eyes with the rapt Lieutenant O'Brien. "On a mission in late 1943, a shot from a German fighter knocked out one of my engines and threatened the other engine on that side. I was rapidly losing airspeed and had to drop out of formation. That, of course, meant I also lost the protection of the squadron."

Bill bit the side of his lip and listened intently.

"As I lost altitude, I was a sitting duck. I was pretty sure I was a goner. Your dad was the flight leader—did you know he had been promoted to major?"

Bill's mouth dropped open in surprise, but no words came out.

"I'll take that as a no." Abrams smiled. "Well, your dad turned over the formation to his second officer, dropped his craft in between me and the German fighter, and maneuvered so his gunners could fight off the enemy until we were within reach of our fighter screen. Two of my crew died from the initial shell hit, and the other three were severely wounded. But none of us would have made it without your dad. He was awarded the Distinguished Flying Cross for that action."

Bill was stunned. "Dad never mentioned any of this! At most, he told me bits and pieces when I asked about the war, but never the full story. I've always hoped to someday meet someone who knew him, but I never expected this!"

Abrams laughed. "That's not all, William. I also knew your mother. Actually, I knew her quite well. We dated a bit when we were in London. I competed against your dad for her hand, actually. I guess she had better taste in men!"

Bill was once again surprised, and he joined the general in another laugh.

"William, do you know what your mother did in the war?"

"No. I know she was born in Germany and left before the war started, then she worked for the British. I don't know in what capacity."

"Your mother was an agent for the Special Operations Executive, SOE, organization. They were commando units established by Winston Churchill after the British were forced off the Continent in 1940. Churchill wanted to 'set Europe ablaze' using these agents. They were trained in hand-to-hand combat, weaponry, and demolition. In general, they were taught how to kill in stealth and then disappear."

Bill's eyes narrowed as he remembered his history classes describing the vital role these agents had played in the war effort for Britain. Bill had no idea any of the agents were women—much less his mother. "Your mother parachuted into Germany to gain intelligence information," Abrams continued. "She established many contacts with the anti-Hitler German military and even the Abwehr German intelligence service. She provided information that was critical for the Allies in preempting several German attacks. Some of the activities she was involved in are still classified."

Yet again, Bill's eyes were wide, his mouth agape. "Holy shit!" he exclaimed out loud. "My dad was a decorated war hero, and my mom was a secret agent?" He paused, then blushed at his outburst. "Sorry, sir. I just . . . I just had no idea!"

Abrams laughed at Bill's response. "I'm not done yet. She barely escaped the Gestapo on her last mission. Because of that, your mother came out of the field. She continued to use her skills at Bletchley Park, breaking codes from both Germany and the Soviet Union. At Bletchley Park, she worked with the OSS—the American equivalent of the SOE, and the precursor of the CIA. Your mother was incredibly skilled. She was decorated by the British government and awarded the George Cross, their second highest decoration. She remained in Britain until she met and married Michael."

Bill tried to take it all in. No wonder his mother hadn't disciplined him for defending his brother from that bully Henderson. He smiled as he reminisced. *Henderson's mother was probably lucky my mom didn't kick her ass!*

"William, I thought you should know the details of your parents' service. I know they would have been the last to brag to anyone about what they had been involved in."

Bill so wished that his parents were alive so he could ask them for more details about their adventurous lives. Or perhaps, like him, they would have preferred not to talk. They must have had many terribly bad memories, just as Bill had.

"Sir, thank you for sharing." Bill swallowed a lump in his throat. "Their loss has left a void that I still struggle to overcome, but this information makes the loss a bit easier to bear."

"There's more," Abrams said. "Your parents visited me here about a month before their deaths, just as I was scheduled to leave the country on the presidential mission. We signed power of attorney and guardianship papers for you children. They asked me to be executor in case anything happened to them. I put the papers in my safe deposit box.

"Many months later, I returned to San Antonio and finally heard about your parents' and siblings' deaths. Your uncle, Sean, had stepped in as your guardian and was exercising his power of attorney. I was concerned, but I felt that maybe he didn't know about the most recent papers your parents had signed with me. Besides, I had been in no position to personally oversee the situation, and I knew Rudolph was there to help you.

"By the time I realized what had happened, the farm was up for sale, you were living with Rudolph, and you had plans to go to college. I knew Rudolph in England. I trusted you would get strong support from him. I also knew you needed time to heal and adjust to your new circumstances. I decided to wait, stay in contact with Rudolph, and keep a close eye on Sean. I wanted to find out his intentions."

Bill's chest clenched. He felt the recurring rage rising against his uncle. "He took everything I had left. He spent my inheritance. And now he's sucking my dad's business dry. I vow that he will pay for what he has done if it is the last thing I ever do!"

Bill paused to catch his breath. He cleared his throat before he continued.

"Sir, what I mean is, my uncle apparently used his power of attorney to enrich himself. And now I find out he had no authority to do it!"

Abrams leaned forward, his eyes piercing the space between them. "William," he commanded, "you need to calm down and focus on what's important. Don't do something you'll regret later. I'm not convinced Sean is 'enriching' himself. I think he's just in over his head."

Bill felt his Irish temper cooling a bit. "Yes, sir. I'm sure you're right. I'll try not to take any misguided actions. But I will make him pay for his mistakes."

"I also knew Sean in Britain," Abrams responded. "He washed out of pilot training due to a lack of skill and some attitude issues. He ended up on the ground crew for the air group. Eventually, Sean was mysteriously sent back to the States before the rest of the unit. I could never find out why.

"I didn't really like him. He seemed jealous of your father. He was also outspoken about your father 'consorting' with a German woman. I know he didn't like your father marrying out of the Catholic faith. He was always difficult, but Michael always looked out for him, tried to help him. All of this is why Sean was never really a close part of your family. No doubt, there are other reasons, particularly from your mother's perspective. She was always a good judge of people. That's probably the reason she married your dad instead of me," Abrams said with a laugh.

"Both Rudolph and I felt—at least, initially—that Sean was trying to do his best for you after your parents died. Sean seemed slow but not necessarily dishonest. But I do want to help you get back as much of your inheritance as possible. When you're ready to act, you'll have a lot more assistance than you ever knew was possible."

Bill considered the general's comments. They stirred up memories, raised new questions he wished he could ask his parents—and confirmed his suspicions of his uncle.

"Sir, I remember several agitated discussions between Dad and Sean." Bill paused, unsure whether to continue. Finally, he did. "Was it possible that Sean sabotaged the plane?"

Abrams leaned back and softened his tone. "I had a concern about the crash too. Your parents were heading out to Colorado to visit Brigadier General Fred Schwartz, an old war buddy. Your dad called him Fast Freddie. I got in touch with Fred as soon as I returned from my mission. Your dad was just too good a pilot to have crashed into that mountain under normal circumstances. Something else must have caused it. Fred and I were able to arrange for the wreckage to be stored near the Air Force Academy. It's still there. When you're ready, I'll encourage the FAA crash investigators to tear it apart to answer your questions."

"I appreciate that, sir." Bill was amazed by the general's information. "When I'm ready, I'll let you know to proceed."

Abrams reached for an envelope on the credenza behind him. "This envelope contains the original power of attorney papers we signed. It also contains a few things your parents entrusted to me many years ago. They wanted their children to know their story, but not until you were ready. Now you are the only one left, and you should have these mementos. I've kept them in a safe deposit box here in San Antonio all these years."

Abrams produced a small box from the envelope and opened it for Bill to see.

"This box contains your parents' military medals. They would have wanted you to have them now that you know the story of their service."

Bill stared at the shiny reminders of their sacrifice. *They probably felt as proud of their decorations as I am of mine*, thought Bill. He reached across the table, closed the box, and slid it into his pocket.

"Thank you, sir."

"And finally . . ." Abrams cocked his head to the side as he pulled out an official-looking document from the envelope. "Your dad and I always talked about fishing in the Upper Peninsula of Michigan. Did you know your dad loved to trout fish? He wanted to get a bit of land and build a cabin up there for fishing and hunting. When your dad mentioned this to Henry Ford II, Ford gave your dad a really good deal on some land near the Huron Mountains.

"This is the deed for that hundred-and-twenty-acre parcel. It has two hundred feet of shoreline on Lake Superior and an A-frame log cabin your dad built when he was working for Ford out of Detroit. The camp is off the grid—no electricity, no phone—but it has a great view of the Huron Islands. My wife and I had a chance to stay with your folks there once, and it is truly a magical area.

"Your mother and father used it for a second honeymoon—even though they never had a first honeymoon due to the war. Then they got so busy with the business and family that they didn't have time to be away in such a remote area. They gave me the deed for safekeeping, and a neighbor has been maintaining the camp."

Bill smiled as he thought about the time he had just spent in that same area with Dale Patterson. They could be neighbors now. *Won't Dale just shit bricks!* Bill thought.

Then Bill thought he would make an offer of his own.

"Sir, I would like to return your kindness and invite you and your family to share that cabin retreat any time you want to."

Abrams closed his eyes and let loose with one of his belly laughs. Bill was warmed by this comfortable camaraderie.

"I'm not sure my wife would want an 'off-the-grid' vacation these days, but I would love to take a break up there once in a while and maybe drag my city-wise son along, if you would be so kind to let us visit."

"I would be honored, sir."

Abrams leaned back in his chair and folded his arms across his chest. "So, William, where do we go from here?"

Bill clasped his hands over the envelope with the power of attorney papers. "Sir, these are unbelievable treasures from my family. I can't begin to express my appreciation for you taking care of them for me. Now I need to review all that you've given me, pick the right time, and decide how to go after Uncle Sean. I will not let him get away with what he has done, but I don't want to make any missteps."

Abrams smiled warmly at the thoughtful young man across from him. "I have a couple of fairly influential friends who served with the judge advocate general's office for many years. They now have joined a law firm in

Minneapolis. When you give me the word, I'll ask them to do the case pro bono. They'll find an angle to wrestle the business and money away from Sean before he knows what hit him."

"Thank you, sir. No wonder my father entrusted you."

Abrams stood and extended his hand across the table before Bill could jump up and salute.

"I wasn't there to help you when you needed it, like how your father helped me. But that won't happen again. Call me when you want those legal contacts, and keep me apprised of your progress."

"I will, sir."

As Bill turned to leave, there was a knock on the door.

"Come," ordered Abrams.

Captain Smith opened the door and nodded.

"Captain Smith. Excellent." Abrams turned to Bill. "Looks like lunch is served."

Bill had all but forgotten about lunch, but his stomach growled a response.

28.

D AYS PASSED, AND BILL WAS IN HIS SECOND WEEK of his four-week rehab process. He enjoyed seeing Susan on a daily basis. With her smile and warmth, she was a wonderful bright light amid the drudgery of the rehab that could at times be quite painful and frustrating. She had a real gift in working with patients.

No doubt, many of her patients were silently in love with her. Bill couldn't blame them—she was a beautiful, caring woman. She confided in Bill that she had dated some other staff at the hospital, but she seemed serious only with an Australian physician named Zack Robinson. At least, she was serious with him for a while. She hinted to Bill that she was moving on from Zack.

Bill sometimes wondered why Susan confided in him about such personal things. Then again, they were growing closer due to their shared history in Vietnam. They often had coffee together and shared family stories—that is, she shared hers. Bill avoided talking about his family, especially now that General Abrams had given him so much new information to digest. His memories were just too painful at this point.

Bill was a good listener, and Susan needed that. Recalling her days on the farm in Wisconsin seemed to comfort her. When she talked about her family, she radiated such warmth and happiness that it briefly seemed to mask the pain she carried from the war. Bill had spent enough time in the Seventy-First Evacuation Hospital in Pleiku to know firsthand what the nurses experienced there. He knew what a nightmare it had been for this beautiful, kind, and loving woman.

Sometimes Bill wondered if Susan was attracted to him. She dropped little hints here and there. Then again, Bill hadn't told her about Sara. He hoped Susan could sense the unspoken message that he was committed to someone and that he just enjoyed Susan's company as a friend during his rehab.

That week, Bill received a call from Sara. Initially, he was so excited to hear her voice, but her tone and hesitation told him something was wrong.

"I'm flying out to San Antonio tomorrow," she said haltingly. "I'll come to the hospital. There's something I need to tell you."

Bill knew what Sara would tell him—the engagement was off. It was over. He knew, yet he hoped he was wrong. He hoped it was nothing more than some delay in the wedding plans.

He slept little that night. When Susan checked on him during the night shift, she gave him a concerned smile.

"Lieutenant, is everything all right? Do you want something to help you sleep?"

"No, I'm fine," he replied. He took a breath and decided to share a little more. "It's just that I'm meeting with a loved one tomorrow and I believe I'll get some very sad news. But I should be used to those things now. I've had so many losses." He tried to smile. "Thank you for asking. You're very kind."

Susan inwardly frowned, upset by this news. She assumed this loved one was his girlfriend. He had never directly mentioned a girlfriend, but it was easy to guess he was involved with someone. In fact, Bill's being committed to another woman was comforting to Susan. She wasn't ready to commit to anyone herself, so Bill made her feel safe. But now here he was, preparing himself for painful news.

Just what he needs—more pain, she thought.

She had watched Bill struggle through the painful rehab without complaint. Despite it all, he always had a smile for her. On multiple occasions, terrible nightmares awoke him in the night. During these times, she gladly walked the hospital hallways with him as he tried to reorient himself to his reality. She was amazed at his strength and courage. She had always hoped his girlfriend knew how lucky she was.

But Susan could tell that most of Bill's joy seemed gone now. Her heart ached for him.

The next afternoon, Sara arrived at the hospital. He met her at the reception area. Her red hair was clipped back from her face. Her green eyes were lit by the sunshine. At first she smiled, which gave him some temporary hope. She was just as stunning as he remembered. Maybe her message was not what he had thought after all.

But then her smile changed to a pained and somber look. The beautiful bright smile that he loved was now gone. Without her ever having to say a word, he knew the worst would happen. He had been right all along.

She spoke to him in a low, pleasant, firm voice, as one does when delivering bad news. It was the trained voice of a physician.

"Dear, can we go outside and sit in the sun?" she asked. "It's such a nice day."

"Certainly. There are some benches close to the hospital door."

He held her hand as they walked and then sat on the bench.

She had a hard time looking at him. She was terribly distraught as she searched for the words she knew would rip him apart emotionally.

Bill decided to speak first. "Sweetheart, I want to make this as easy as possible for you right now. I know what you're going to say—I know you're breaking our engagement. I can see how hard this is for you. I understand. Please don't be so sad. I was never good enough to be with you. I was happy to think so, but now I can face the truth. You are an amazing, intelligent, talented, and beautiful woman. It was wonderful to be with you for even the brief time we had together. I will always remember those days we had, especially that last day at your home on the lake. You gave me the first happiness

I've had in many years, and I thank you for that. You'll never understand how much our time meant to me after the hell in Vietnam. I do love you more than I could ever say or demonstrate, but that is often not enough. I'll always want the best for you and for you to be happy."

Sara stared at him in shock, then sighed. She cocked her head and smiled at him, but he could see the tears in her eyes. "My God, you sweet man! I do love you so! You are the most unique and caring man I've ever met. I so want to be with you, to always be with you."

The smile faded from her face, but the tears continued to brim.

"But yes, I am breaking our engagement. Not because I don't love you or want to be with you. After what you just said, I want to be with you more than ever, and it makes this news even harder to deal with."

She paused to gaze down at their hands still tightly together.

"But something has happened that I never expected: my husband has been found alive but very badly wounded. Apparently, he was in a hospital in the Philippines and had been misidentified. He's being sent to the VA hospital in Boston." She looked up at Bill now with her eyes pleading for understanding. "I can't abandon him. It's my duty as his wife to look after him. I can't abandon him as so many in this country are doing to our soldiers. I know he'll never be the same man I married. He's lost to me physically and emotionally. But now it means I'm losing you too."

Sara started to cry, so Bill slid over and embraced her for several minutes. He kissed her first on the forehead and then on the lips to calm her.

"I will always love you, wherever you are and whoever you're with," he said. "You are remarkable to support your husband this way. This just makes me love you even more. I not only love you but am so proud of you."

Bill didn't know how much time passed as they held each other in silence. Finally, Sara straightened.

"Bill, please know this is as hard as hearing my husband had been killed. I love you so much, but it's my duty to not abandon or divorce him. I have an obligation to stay. God, I'm so sorry. I know I'm making both of us suffer for this. But I'm most concerned about adding to your pain. You have been disappointed and abandoned by so many loved ones—you don't need this from me!"

She looked at her watch and sighed again.

"I know I just got here, but I have to catch my plane back to Boston. Know that I love you. I hope sometime you will find someone who will love you as I do right now. I'll write you and keep in touch, if that's all right with you. I will always care about your welfare. So . . ."

But Sara could not say good-bye. That word just hurt her too much. She looked so terribly sad. She quickly stood and began to weep as she walked away. She could not look back at Bill, who reached out to comfort her one last time.

He stood and watched her move off to her car and drive away. It was so reminiscent of that night in Minnesota—the last time he saw Barbara. Watching her leave him made him feel as if a limb had been ripped from his body.

Bill stood there, physically and mentally stunned. It seemed unreal, as if he would wake up and discover this was just a nightmare. But it was only too real.

Eventually, he must have turned and walked to the bench because he found himself sitting without even knowing how he got there. Tears welled. He placed his hands over his eyes in an attempt to slow the flow of tears. But it was no use. He cried for one of the few times since the death of his family.

Actually, this was so much worse than losing his family. He saw this as the death of the most wonderful future he could ever imagine—death just as sure as a fatal bullet wound. He had just lost someone who had meant more to him than anyone he had ever met or would probably ever meet. Sara lifted him into another dimension, where his fears and pains did not register. This loss he could never forget or accept. He feared it would shadow and affect him for as long as he lived.

His future seemed very bleak and hardly worthwhile now. What did he have to look forward to, to share, or to care about? It all seemed hopeless. The future would only bring more sorrow, disappointment, and struggle.

He realized it was a good thing he was not armed now. He worried that if he were armed, he would descend again into that dark place he had experienced in Vietnam. Death, at times, was a relief from the trauma, fear, and hopelessness, even death you administered to yourself.

Susan walked out the hospital door and noticed Bill sitting on the bench. She saw the hollow, dreadfully somber look she knew all too well. It was the look of those in the MASH unit who had seen too much to go on living. His loved one must have delivered him a terrible emotional blow, just as he'd predicted in their conversation the night before.

She knew she needed to intervene right now for his own safety. It was something she had desperately wanted to do for so many soldiers in Vietnam, but she couldn't due to the workload. It made her suffer to hear what had happened to those men.

Susan went over and sat next to him. "Lieutenant O'Brien, isn't it a lovely warm day?" she just commented. "It's great to be alive on days like these. These days remind me of being back on the farm. How about you?"

Instantly, Bill came out of his funk and smiled. Susan obviously knew what had happened, but she cared enough to help him without embarrassing him.

"Yes, Lieutenant, it is a lovely day for most people," he said. "But the rest of us just have to move on even when we don't want to. Thank you for stopping to talk. You'll never know what this means to me."

"Lieutenant O'Brien, can I buy you a cup of bad coffee in the canteen? I can't believe they make us pay for it!"

They both laughed.

"Lieutenant Johnson, you can buy me a cup of coffee anytime you want!"

On their way to the canteen, Bill stopped and looked at Susan.

"Lieutenant, I'll wager that for the last ten minutes, no one has told you that you are beautiful. So I will tell you: you are a very beautiful woman. I would also like to ask if you would do me the honor of having dinner tonight at an off-base restaurant, where we can wear our civilian clothes, and you can call me Bill, and I can call you Susan. I want to get to know you better, and perhaps you would like to know more about me—not that it's that interesting."

Susan stopped in her tracks and turned to face Bill. "Yes, Bill, I would like that. And you can call me Susan anytime you want. I think knowing more about you would be very interesting. As for knowing more about me, it's good that you're a great listener, because I talk a lot!" She laughed. "We have a couple of weeks before your rehab is over, so we'll have time to get well acquainted. Maybe even more than two weeks, if you'd like to continue seeing me even after rehab is done."

"I'd like that a lot. I won't be that far away at Fort Sill. Besides, I enjoy listening to you talk!"

She beamed as they headed into the hospital for their coffee. Her smile warmed him after the chill and sorrow Sara had left him with. It was like a warm sun rising after a cold rainy night. Susan was such a beautiful woman, so bright and caring. But also one who had suffered her own pain. Bill knew he had to be very careful with her. Hopefully she would let him help her face that pain.

As if a lightbulb had turned on, Bill suddenly realized he had been attracted to Susan ever since Vietnam. And despite his love for Sara, his attraction to Susan had grown during this time at Fort Sam. Perhaps it had been a premonition of Sara leaving him—some sort of "second sight." He had sensed Susan's growing interest, and he had looked for ways to be with her. He loved her company, and she seemed to love his.

Now he would not be constrained; he could see just how far that interest would go. He hoped it would go far. He hoped that perhaps with her, he would finally have some good fortune. He also wanted the same good fortune for her.

— GERMANY, 1939 —

29.

FRITZ SCHMIDT WAS NO LONGER FLYING for Deutsche Luft Hansa. Now he spent all his time training with the Luftwaffe, the German air force. He commanded the powerful Heinkel He 111 squadron stationed in eastern Prussia, about 150 kilometers from the border of Poland.

He was stationed outside Berlin, not far from where his family lived, but he rarely had a chance to go home. He was busy with either practice bombing missions or squadron paperwork. Fritz was proud of his promotion to oberstleutnant, a rank equivalent to lieutenant colonel in the US Army. This promotion came only a little over a year after he was commissioned from civilian flight captain to major in the Luftwaffe. Now Fritz commanded a squadron of twenty-four He 111s. He ensured that they were a sharp and professional unit at all times. Göring himself had reviewed the squadron and praised their performance.

Elisa was proud of her husband's promotion but not pleased that he spent much more time away from the family. He had been home only twice in the last four months.

"The squadron is on constant alert," he told her. "Poland is making overtures of war, and we're the first in line to defend Germany. I cannot believe the Poles would be so reckless as to think they can take on our air force. They're certainly no match for us."

Still, Elisa wished Fritz could be home more often. Time with the twin boys was precious. She watched them growing so quickly and realized how much Fritz was missing—and how much the boys were missing without his contact. She spent her days taking them to the Tiergarten park or the zoo, where there were other children with their mothers or nannies. Those contacts were the few adults in her life. She yearned for the companionship of artistic friends she had not seen for months.

On a rainy Thursday, Elisa asked a neighbor with a young boy to watch the twins while she did some shopping. The neighbors often helped each other by trading babysitting duties. The children loved to play together.

But Elisa had no plans for shopping. She wanted to surprise some of her old friends from the Prussian Academy of Arts. She had seen only a few of them since her marriage and was anxious to see how they were faring. She hoped they were as happy as she was with her children. She had grown concerned about her friends based on the reports in German newspapers and on the radio about the "authorities" eliminating certain elements from society. Plus, she could certainly use some cheering up. Her only chance to get out without the children was to attend political gatherings with Fritz, and even that was rare these days.

Elisa's first stop was Café Bistro, a small bakery and coffee shop owned by her friend Klaus. In the early and mid-1930s, his bistro had always been overflowing with artists, authors, and actors.

The streetcar was a bit delayed, and there were only two other riders. One was a well-dressed gentleman sitting near the front and wearing dark sunglasses. He clutched a cane tightly and listened blindly as she boarded. The other was an elderly woman sitting on the left side with her shopping basket. She turned her face away, toward the window, as Elisa walked down the aisle. Elisa took a seat near the back of the car and rode in silence, watching the city pass by.

After riding several miles, Elisa reached up and rang the bell. She exited the car with a lilt in her step. The bistro was just around the corner. She imagined the look of joy Klaus would give her when she walked in to order a cup of his special cardamom tea and a biscuit.

But when she turned the corner, she was confused. Although it had admittedly been a few years, she was sure this was the right block. She could make out "Bistro" on a faded sign, but where were the red-checkered curtains?

Where were the bright multicolored lights that always made her think of Christmas? One window was painted black, the other broken and partially covered with a piece of wood. The café front looked as though it had been vandalized. On the door was a hand-painted scrawl of JUDEN! The red paint had drizzled down the entire doorframe. It almost looked painted in blood.

Elisa was startled. *Klaus isn't Jewish!* she exclaimed to herself. Then she stopped and recalled that no one had really asked years ago. It simply wasn't important in her circles. People were people. *That's still true*, she reminded herself, taking another look at the sad little abandoned bistro.

A market was open across the street. Elisa checked for traffic and dashed across.

"Excuse me," she addressed the clerk arranging vegetables in baskets on the sidewalk. "Do you know where Klaus Menkine has gone?"

The shopkeeper looked at her in disgust. "The Gestapo cleared them out last year. Good riddance, if you ask me!"

Elisa shook her head in bewilderment and walked away. *What is happening in Germany that we would do this to good people?* she asked silently, though she would not dare voice that question. Perhaps her friend Greta Soliska could help Elisa connect with the old crowd. Greta was an acclaimed actress and had even performed in the Berlin ballet. She had the lovely blond hair and sharp cheekbones common to Elisa's own Volga German background. She could sweep into a room and command attention without ever uttering a word. Greta also spoke many different languages, which brought her offers from foreign film companies and gave her a chance to travel all over Europe. Elisa had been secretly jealous of Greta at Fritz's parties. However, she was proud to be in Greta's circle of close friends.

Elisa made her way to Greta's building. As she double-checked the address at the door, a stooped woman came slowly up the sidewalk with a small shopping bag of vegetables and bread. A purple floral headscarf was tied tightly over her ragged hair, and the gray knit shawl over her shoulders was unraveling on one end. The woman hesitated, squinted at Elisa, then slowly navigated the four steps to the front door.

Elisa held the door open for her and greeted her. "*Guten Tag.* Can I help you carry your bag?"

The woman looked up in terror and clutched the bag tightly to her chest. Seeing a dirty bandage on the poor woman's arm, Elisa felt even more pity for her. Then when she met the woman's squinted eyes, she noticed a glimmer of recognition.

"Greta?"

Elisa was shocked and grief-stricken at the same time. This pitiful creature in front of her was the same woman Elisa had partied with at Fritz's apartment only two years ago.

"Run away, Elisa," Greta implored. "Go away and never return. I cannot be seen talking to you."

"Greta, don't be silly. Let me help you."

Elisa took the shopping bag and offered her hand for support. At first Greta shook her head in humble refusal, but then she led the way to a first-floor room in the rear of the building. She fumbled with the key in the lock and finally opened the door.

Elisa remembered the parties she had attended at this two-story house. Greta always invited her fellow artists home after a production. The rooms had been bright and beautifully decorated. Greta and her housemate, Georgia, were excellent hostesses and even provided overnight accommodations for some of their friends who partied a bit too much.

Greta had closed up all the rooms except the back kitchen on the first floor. This had become a one-room apartment for her. Elisa put away the groceries, then joined her friend on the couch.

Greta was crying softly as she tugged off her scarf and shawl. "You cannot stay here. You cannot be seen with me."

Elisa shook her head defiantly. "You are my friend. I will not desert you now that I have found you again." She reached over and put her hand on her friend's shoulder. "Tell me what has happened."

Greta bowed her head. Reluctantly, she updated Elisa. "Five years ago, as you know, I received a fabulous offer to travel with a foreign production company. It was a Russian film company. We made films all over Europe—France, Italy, Germany, Poland, Russia. I also had a wonderful part in *Swan Lake* with the Russian ballet. Oh, Elisa, it was a marvelous time!"

Greta took a breath. Elisa could see her eyes glisten lightly with tears as she remembered those happier days.

"Shortly after that production ended last month, I returned home to Germany to be with Georgia. We were always so happy together. But the Gestapo must have watched us for some time. No doubt because of complaints from some of the local party members. When I returned, they arrested us both. The Gestapo beat us. They called us lesbians. They smashed everything in the rooms upstairs before they took us into custody. They tortured me, broke my arm, cut my hair—and raped me."

Elisa wrapped her arms around Greta's shoulder and gazed toward the window in shock. *How could anyone treat another human being this way?* She could think of nothing she could say to comfort her friend.

Greta straightened up and pushed away from Elisa's embrace. She swallowed hard and fought back the tears. "I was released just last week. I don't know what happened to Georgia. I just hope she was released." Greta's voice cracked. "I came back to the house, thinking she would return here as well when she was freed. I tried to clean and straighten the ruins, but it was overwhelming. There is just too much destruction upstairs."

Greta looked around the small room. "I decided to keep this back room as my new 'home' to stay out of sight and wait for Georgia. I really do love her, you know."

That comment opened the floodgates. Elisa draped her arm over her friend and held her close until her sobs abated.

"Did you report this activity to the police?" Elisa asked. "You did nothing wrong. They can't just walk in and destroy things."

"Oh, my God, Elisa," Greta responded. "What fairy tale world do you live in? The Gestapo can and will come into anyone's house, arrest anyone, for any reason. If you try to report them, you're probably talking to the same officials who ordered the attack in the first place. That's how people disappear."

Elisa blinked quickly to clear the tears forming as well as to gather her thoughts. *How could I have been so blind to this? Maybe she's right—I have been living in a fairy tale world! Does Fritz know any of this? Has he played a role?*

The two women spent the next hour discussing the fates of their old friends. Greta had contact with only four of their friends from the earlier years. She gave Elisa the address of one couple. The other two friends she had warned to get out of Germany after her release from the Gestapo. One had fled to London. The other went to stay with relatives in Canada.

"I had no idea this was happening . . ." Elisa admitted sadly.

Greta shook her head. "We were afraid to contact you when we saw your husband's rapid advancement in the ranks of the Nazi Party. He has many very influential friends. If you are seen here, it would go very bad for me and even for you."

Elisa left her friend just after noon, inconspicuously slipping out the door to avoid drawing attention to herself. She caught the streetcar to go visit the couple Greta had mentioned. As she gazed out the streetcar window, she noticed more and more shops boarded up with signs across their doors or a red Star of David haphazardly painted in bright red enamel.

What a fool I have been—truly living in a fairy tale world!

Elisa approached a three-story gray apartment building. She had been here on multiple occasions to visit her friends before she met Fritz. She walked up the two flights of stairs to the upper level and knocked loudly on the door in anticipation.

"Wilhelm? Brendan? It's Elisa. Are you home?"

She heard the rustle of quick footsteps. The mahogany door slipped open cautiously, and a man peered out at her.

"Elisa? You shouldn't be here. It is not safe."

The man opened the door quickly. In his right hand, he held a stick from a tree as a cane. He used it to gesture for her to enter.

"Wilhelm, are you all right? What is the cane for?" Elisa asked, afraid to hear the answer.

Wilhelm quickly shut the door and put his finger to his lips to shush her. "Why are you here? Your visit may bring the Gestapo. They closely monitor significant members of the Reich, such as your husband. You need to leave as soon as possible!"

Elisa pointed to the cane and awaited the explanation.

"My cane? I'm still recovering from a Gestapo beating last month. Someone complained about Brendan and me. We were arrested and taken to an 'adjustment camp' to teach us proper behavior."

"Adjustment camp?" asked Elisa as she moved to a chair near the couch, where Wilhelm had perched. "I don't understand."

"Yes. There were a lot of different people there—gays like Brendan and me. But also straight men and women. There were young and old too. There were all sorts who apparently needed 'corrective indoctrination,' as they put it."

Elisa gasped. She wanted to hug her friend and comfort him, but he sat bolt upright on the couch, gazing across at the facing wall as he told his story. He was in another world.

"They put Brendan and me into wire cages to teach us a lesson. They removed all our clothes and called us dogs."

Wilhelm stopped. His eyes still looked into the distance, unable to focus on anything in the room.

"One day, they pulled Brendan out of his cage and tied him to a post in the middle of the room. They whipped him until the blood ran in rivulets down his back. Then they took turns beating him with a board, calling him a 'fag,' all the while laughing. He died the next morning," Wilhelm said, his voice failing. "He was still tied to that post."

Wilhelm broke down. Elisa quickly moved to the couch and wrapped her arms gently around her friend. Several minutes later, he pulled away from her grasp. He stood and walked over to the window, though he did not pull the curtain back.

"Very early the next morning, they pulled me out of my cage and tossed some rags on the floor beside me. They told me to dress, threw me in a car, and drove me to the center of Berlin, where they dropped me on a street corner. They told me that if I had not properly learned my lesson, they would return, and I would suffer the same fate as 'the others.' I found this stick for a cane as I walked home." Wilhelm looked at the wood held tightly in his grasp. "It's really been my only support since I got here."

Elisa stood to hug her friend again, but Wilhelm held up his hand to stop her.

"You really cannot stay here, Elisa. Please don't come back. I've made arrangements to leave Germany as soon as possible."

"Where will you go?"

"It's best you don't know. I cannot risk your husband finding out." He shook his head and looked at her sadly. "You were a true friend to our whole group until you married that Nazi husband of yours. We are in danger in this new Germany. It is safer for you, and for us, if we do not have any further contact."

With that, he walked to the door and opened it cautiously, checking the corridor. Then he motioned for her to leave.

"It is time for you to go."

She kissed him briefly on the cheek as she passed through the door. "I'm sorrier than I can say. I never knew what was happening to you. I will miss all of you."

Elisa admonished herself as she quickly slipped out the door. *How could I have been so blind for so many years? How could Fritz not see what was happening?*

The closer she got to home, the angrier she became. With her eyes now truly open, she realized that the shops along the street had all been sterilized of their vitality—the vitality she had so loved in the past. She was ashamed to admit she had been too busy to notice how "city improvements" had replaced playbills with Nazi propaganda posters on windows and street corners. She had been living in a vacuum, attending political parties with Fritz as he was promoted through the Nazi culture. She had been raising her boys in this vacuum.

Elisa walked the final few blocks from the streetcar stop in deep thought. She realized she had been protected. The Gestapo went after her friends, but they would never touch the wife of a rising party symbol. Fritz was supposed to keep her in line and bring their sons into the Hitler Youth movement. She had once mentioned to Fritz that she didn't want her sons regimented when they became of age. But he dismissed her concerns, as he always did.

"You don't understand," he instructed her. "They won't become strong if you coddle them."

When Elisa finally got home, she was more depressed than ever. She picked up the boys from the neighbor's and brought them home. The twins prattled on about all the things they had done that day. Usually Elisa listened with rapt attention, delighting in how fast they were maturing each day.

Now, she was only afraid for her sons. The more they matured, the closer they were to indoctrination in the youth movement.

That evening, Elisa called her mother. They had not talked since before Elisa's wedding. Ruth was overjoyed. She invited Elisa to bring the boys for a visit the next day.

"Your father has a car and can pick you up for a wonderful reunion in the country," Ruth suggested.

Elisa readily agreed. A family reunion was definitely needed. When she put the boys to bed, she told them they would be off on a grand adventure the next day.

She did not truly know how grand it would be.

Petra arrived in a well-used Opel sedan. He hugged his daughter tentatively, then helped the boys into the back seat. Reaching into his pocket, he produced a small bar of chocolate for each boy, then looked at Elisa, expecting a complaint.

"Oh, Papa." Elisa smiled and gave him a proper hug, then ran around the car to the passenger seat before he had the opportunity to open her door.

The transition from the city to the countryside was mesmerizing. Elisa felt the tension and stress of her life begin to ease.

At last, they pulled up to the modest country house. "Welcome home, *Liebchen*," Petra said.

Ruth hurried out the door to meet them. She hugged her daughter tightly. "Elisa, my darling, I have missed you so much!"

Petra looked on in amusement as the twins clutched Elisa's hands to her sides, immobilizing her.

"Ruth, let the poor girl take off her coat so she can introduce us to the boys," he admonished, the grin still on his face.

"Oh, my stars—yes!"

Ruth broke her grip and bent down to greet the boys. Both quickly hid behind Elisa and peeked out at the strange woman.

"Mom, this is Otto," Elisa said as she pointed to the blond head on her right. Reaching behind her, she pulled the other child forward. "This is Adolf Petra. Boys, these are your grandparents."

The boys both held tightly to Elisa's coat as they shyly smiled at the elderly couple. Elisa noticed her father's twitch when she introduced her second son. She knew the name—his own name along with the führer's— would make him pause, but she was pleased that he had restrained from making a comment in front of the boy.

"Ruth, why don't you take the boys into the kitchen and see if you can find them some cookies and milk." Petra took his visitors' coats and gestured to Elisa to join him in the family room, where they could talk.

"Sit down, my dear. You look tired. How are things for you in Berlin?" he asked.

"We are fine, Papa."

Elisa sat down heavily on the familiar couch. She was pleased to see her parents had been able to move much of the family furniture and decor when they left Berlin.

"Fritz has just received another promotion, and he is working very hard," she said.

"He is a good provider for your family?"

Elisa noticed it was a question, rather than a statement.

"Yes, he provides everything we could possibly need." She toyed with the fringe on the hand-knit afghan covering the back of the couch. "Everything except him, that is."

"He's away a lot?"

"He's never home, Papa. I've seen him only twice in the last four months. The boys miss him dearly too."

Petra sat across from her in his leather chair and carefully considered his response. "He's an important man now. You can't expect him to take time off from his squadron to visit the family."

"I know, Papa, but I'm afraid," Elisa finally admitted. "I'm afraid for what Germany has become. I'm afraid for what Fritz has become. He's not the same man I married. And I'm afraid for my boys most of all."

"My dear, your mother and I have been concerned about you and the boys for some time." The leather squeaked as Petra moved to the edge of the chair. "Elisa, I have some sad news for you: your brother, Karl, has already disappeared. We don't know if the Gestapo arrested him or if he managed to escape to a neutral country. I'm afraid his anti-Nazi activity may have caught up with him. We can only hope he is safe. I still have contacts with many government officials who do not support the Nazi regime," Petra continued. "Ruth and I are fairly sheltered here in the country. I can help you find shelter or escape, if you ever get to the point where you feel it is needed."

Elisa was relieved by her parents' warm reception, but she hadn't ever considered a need to escape. *If Fritz knows about these atrocities and he does nothing to stop them, I cannot stay with him,* Elisa thought. *Protecting my sons from that barbarism is the only thing that matters.*

The boys enjoyed their stay in the country. They spent their time chasing the goats in the pasture while Elisa reconnected with her past—as well as thought about her future.

30.

A WEEK LATER, FRITZ WAS GIVEN A BRIEF LEAVE from his squadron. He decided to go home to visit his family. It was a gorgeous warm day at the end of August 1939. Elisa was pleased to see Fritz but was also determined to discuss the current state of Germany with him, along with her concerns for the welfare of the family.

Once the boys were put to bed, Elisa poured two snifters of brandy and sat in a rocking chair near her husband. He was comfortably settled in the overstuffed chair that had been her father's. His feet, still clad in boots, were propped on the ottoman.

"Would you like to remove your boots and get comfortable?" Elisa suggested.

"I'm fine, darling." Fritz shifted his foot, grinding dirt into the brocade.

"Fritz"—Elisa winced for the ottoman—"do you know what's been going on in Germany? Do you know about the abuses, the torture, the murders by members of the Nazi Party and the government you support?"

Fritz sat up straighter in his chair, stunned at his wife's accusatory tone. "Darling, you know we must protect our German state from influences both inside and outside our borders. That is the only way we will be safe!"

"Safe?" Elisa was angered by the party line Fritz expounded. "Your German state has terrorized, beaten, and killed friends of mine. They were artists, actors, and singers. They are wonderful and harmless people. Their only crime—if it is a crime—was trying to make the world a more beautiful place."

"Germany must purify itself," Fritz again quoted the party line. "We must remove the unclean elements—the Jews, the homosexuals, all the foreigners and the art and music they promote—if we are to survive!"

"Fritz, you're an American citizen. *You* are a foreigner," Elisa reminded him as she finished her brandy in one swallow. "Does that mean you should be cleansed out as well?" She rose from her chair and faced him in defiance.

Fritz slammed his glass down on the end table and rose to meet her. Without warning, he slapped her hard across the face.

"I am a German. I have sworn allegiance to this country. You better think hard about how to be a better German wife and raise our children properly." He pushed her away. "I'm going out."

"You Nazi bastard!" Elisa yelled as the door slammed shut. "I'll show you what a good German wife can do," she added under her breath, putting her hand to her cheek, where it still burned.

Elisa hurried to the window and watched as her husband retreated down the street, heading to a nearby bar. Racing upstairs, she pulled the suitcases out of the closet and stuffed them with clothes for herself and the boys. She called a cab, then hurried upstairs to roust the sleeping twins. As soon as the cab arrived, she hustled the sleepy-eyed boys out the front door.

Fritz arrived home late that night. He had spent his time trading stories with his old friends at the bar until well after midnight. He found an empty house and remembered the argument with Elisa. Grabbing the phone, he dialed Petra's number.

"I want to speak to Elisa immediately," he stated angrily.

"What?" Petra responded. "She's not here. We haven't seen her since before your wedding."

"I don't believe that for a minute!" Fritz snapped before slamming down the phone.

He paced across the room in a rage before the phone rang. He stormed back and picked it up, assuming it would be Elisa calling to apologize.

"Oberstleutnant Schmidt, this is the air wing adjutant, Captain Dietrich. You're ordered to report back to your squadron immediately! You're needed to run a mission first thing tomorrow."

Fritz packed his bag and called for his car. When the car pulled up, he walked right out, leaving the lights on and the door open.

That will teach her to walk out on me, he thought smugly.

Major General Ulrich Otto Kessler, commander of the Kampfgeschwader bomber wing, met with his unit commanders at his headquarters in the early-morning hours.

"Gentlemen, there has been an incursion by Polish forces across our borders," Kessler explained. "We will launch full air strikes at dawn on key Polish installations, including Warsaw."

Fritz was surprised. He had heard rumors of a Polish incursion, but they had always proven false. But now the Luftwaffe had been ordered to attack with its entire bomber group. That would entail over eight hundred He 111 aircraft as well as hundreds of Ju87 Stuka bombers, Me 109 fighters, and other support aircraft. Indeed, the attack could use over one thousand aircraft—something never done before.

Fritz was confident they were ready for such a strike, but he also knew this would start a true war. Britain and France had signed a defense pact with Poland, so they would also join the fighting. Russia had just signed a nonaggression pact with Germany this month, so he assumed they would not join in.

Fritz called in his squadron leaders and told them to ready all the aircraft and equipment.

"This is the real thing," he announced triumphantly. "It is a day historians will always remember."

When Fritz completed the squadron briefing, he took time to call home. He was sure Elisa would have returned by now, ready to apologize and be a proper German wife. He was ready to gloat.

There was no answer.

Fritz called Petra again, demanding to talk to Elisa. And once again, Petra told him they had not seen their daughter.

Exasperated, Fritz called a Gestapo contact. "My wife has taken our children and disappeared. I need you to find her and bring my family back to serve the party."

Word spread quickly throughout the Gestapo in Berlin. The officers devised a plan that would find Fritz's wayward wife and young boys. Secretly, though, they scoffed at the man who could lead a bomber squadron yet not even control his wife.

At 5:30 that morning, Fritz and his squadron joined thousands of other aircraft lifting off to crush Poland. In less than two hours, World War II had begun. The targeted Polish cities and towns were turned into rubble. The railroads and roadways were smoking tangles of metal and debris. There was no question about the efficiency of the Nazi war machine. No one had ever seen such power and total destruction in a war. The blitzkrieg—the "lightning war"—was appropriately named.

But soon Fritz would learn what war was truly like and what it would cost him.

Sitting by the picture window, Petra tried to read the newspaper. The wireless radio vibrated with reports of the brutal attack on the Polish towns and the German justification.

There was a hard knock on the front door. Petra answered it with the newspaper and his reading glasses still in his hand.

"We are here to find the wife and children of Oberstleutnant Fritz Schmidt," declared a uniformed Gestapo agent.

Three men burst through the open doorway, pushing Petra aside.

"We do not know where she is," Petra responded, startled at their abrupt entry into his home.

The shortest of the agents narrowed his piercing black eyes at Petra. Walking back to the doorway, he kicked the door shut, then slapped Petra before he could move away.

"Don't lie to us, Petra Petter!" he yelled. "You are on the list of anti-government activists. You are a traitor to the cause. You've only been safe because of your relationship to the wife of Oberstleutnant Schmidt."

The little man stroked his stubby brown beard. His smile revealed his tobacco-stained teeth as he continued.

"If you do not tell us where they are, we will take you to Gestapo head-quarters for further persuasion."

Ruth heard the noise and rushed out of the kitchen. "We don't know where Elisa is," she pleaded with the officers.

Turning toward the woman, the third agent quickly pulled out a club and thrust it hard into Petra's stomach. Unprepared for the blow, Petra collapsed to the floor. Ruth rushed forward to help her husband, but the agent backhanded her across the face, snapping her head back and sending her into the nearby wall.

"Take them to the car. We will get the truth out of them at headquarters."

The little man held the door open while his accomplices dragged the stunned couple out of their home. Lying on the back seat of the car, Petra and Ruth could hear furniture and china shattering while the wireless radio declared, "And the attack on Poland was a successful defense of the Fatherland. *Heil, Hitler!*"

Petra and Ruth Petter were never seen again. There were rumors that Petra died during the Gestapo interrogation. Other rumors surfaced that Ruth had been sent to a concentration camp.

Fritz was surprised when he heard of this outcome. He had only wanted to find his wife and children. He had not expected such a heavy-handed approach from the Gestapo. Now he was afraid he would not be able to control the Gestapo actions if the search continued for his family.

Fritz knew Elisa had contacts outside of Germany, but he had never paid attention to her stories about her friends. He had no clue where to start looking. Elisa had found her own way to disappear. Fritz's boys would never know him.

Elisa would see to that.

31.

THE YEAR 1939 WAS RAPIDLY COMING TO A CLOSE. Canaris had his hands full with "the plan," but all was not going smoothly. He reviewed the latest losses as he waited for his teammates, von Greim and Kammler, to arrive for a meeting.

The German army had great success in Poland, but the Poles held out longer and did more damage than projected. The German air force had eliminated the small Polish air force and pounded the Polish ground troops, railways, and supply ports. However, the Germans lost nearly three hundred aircraft to a variety of causes. An additional three hundred aircraft were irreparably damaged and unusable. The Polish aircrews and antiaircraft fire had taken a toll.

Canaris knew they had lost over 20 percent of the total German attacking aircraft. These were critical losses if the French and British decided to attack across the German frontier. Fortunately, there was no attack from the west, as yet. This meant there should be time to replenish men and equipment.

The current intelligence information from Canaris's agents noted that the French were massing on the Maginot Line, and the British were staging army units and Royal Air Force planes at French airfields.

With both the French and British readying their forces, Germany would face a far more organized enemy than they had found in Poland. However, with the two enemy forces standing on their borders taunting one another, the Western newspapers dubbed this series of battles the Sitzkrieg—the "Phony War."

The plan Canaris, von Greim, and Kammler had devised to prevent the potential American intervention was becoming more complicated too. Originally, the führer had advised them to be ready to act in early 1939. That date had come and gone.

Canaris paced in front of the window behind his desk. Snow was drifting lightly. The trees were almost pretty.

The führer had ordered that all be ready, but he cautioned that this wasn't to be a provocative attack. It was to be a quick and decisive defensive attack as soon as America declared war on Germany. But since that discussion, there had been delay after delay.

How much longer can we delay? Canaris wondered.

He stopped and spread his fingertips on the windowsill, leaning his weight forward. His forehead touched the frosted glass. All the components for the attack were in place. Only the pilots were still needed. He could send them to the area, but they could not launch the mission without the führer's order.

Canaris gazed out the window and shook his head. He was glad he had shipped over the bombs, aircraft, and supplies during the summer. After the attack on Poland, the United States had put shipping restrictions in place. Had they waited until now, it would have been nearly impossible to move the required equipment and get it stored in the mine in Michigan.

Turning to his desk, he opened his humidor and retrieved a cigar. He carefully trimmed and shaped the end, then struck a match. The flaring warmth of the flame briefly broke his reverie.

How long can the airfield and mine stay under the cover of this ruse?

His agent John Rogers had advised him that the Canadians had started to fortify their side of the great locks. It certainly wouldn't be long before President Roosevelt would also move to reinforce the American side.

Canaris was certain that America would eventually side with France and Britain and join the war. Word from his agents indicated that the United States was already ramping up wartime production with the intent to at least provide materials to France and Britain. Would that be enough for the führer to give the order?

As Canaris turned to the window again, he saw von Greim's car pull up to the curb in front of Abwehr headquarters. Kammler's driver pulled in behind. The two men got out, shook hands, and walked up the steps together for their meeting with Canaris.

"Gentlemen, our American attack plan, Poseidon, has been in place for several months," announced Canaris, trying for an optimistic start to the discussion. "Unfortunately, we still do not know when we will be allowed to launch the attack."

Von Greim and Kammler shook their heads in joint disgust.

"Are all the supplies in place in the mine?" asked Kammler.

"Yes, and the three aircraft are stored in the hangars at the airfield. We just need to stage the pilots without raising suspicions. General von Greim, do you have the pilots ready to send over?" Canaris blew out a stream of smoke from his cigar.

Von Greim hesitated, then admitted, "I had two slated for the assignment, but one was lost on a Deutsche Luft Hansa commercial flight to Brazil. The other pilot is his brother, Oberstleutnant Fritz Schmidt. He commanded an He 111 squadron in Poland."

"That's the kind of expertise we need," praised Canaris. "What about the other five pilots we determined we would need for the operation?"

"I already asked Oberstleutnant Schmidt to select five experienced pilots for a special mission. I've reviewed his selections and concur."

"Excellent!"

Maybe things will work out after all, Canaris thought.

"How soon can we get those pilots on their way to America?" interjected Kammler. "I understand the oberstleutnant is actually an American citizen. He should be able to return to America on a neutral country's ship, if we can free him up."

"I'm trying to get him on a Swedish vessel to America as soon as possible," responded von Greim. "If that doesn't work, we can get him to Mexico and work him up into the United States from there."

Canaris nodded his agreement. "I'll cut orders immediately for all six pilots to report to the Abwehr office in Berlin for a special assignment."

Two days later, six pilots reported to Canaris early in the morning.

"Gentlemen, you are entrusted with the most important mission to date in this war effort." Canaris paused for effect and watched the six men carefully before continuing. "This mission will take place within the borders of the United States."

Fritz looked directly at Canaris. The other five pilots exchanged glances. One squinted his eyes and looked back at the floor.

Canaris pursed his lips at the expected responses. "I understand you are all fluent in English and have a university background. In fact, one of you is actually an American citizen."

Canaris returned the look from Fritz.

"When you reach your destination, Oberstleutnant Schmidt will be in complete command. Is that understood?"

"Yes, sir," echoed the response.

"You'll all attend a briefing here tomorrow morning at oh seven hundred hours to receive instructions, clothing, and American money. This is top secret. You will not discuss this mission with one another or anyone else outside this room. Is that understood?"

Again, the stunned pilots quickly responded, "Yes, sir."

"Oberstleutnant Schmidt, you will remain here. The rest of you are free to go and return in the morning."

The five crewmen jumped to their feet, snapped their heels, said "*Heil, Hitler*" in unison, and marched out of the room.

"Oberstleutnant Schmidt, we need to discuss the details of your operation."

Fritz perched on the edge of his chair as Canaris began to reveal the details. Now that his family was gone, Fritz had no ties to Germany. He harbored a deep-seated anger with Elisa but had no way to respond. This special mission would be the perfect way to prove his loyalty to the führer.

"You will leave for New York City tonight on the Swedish vessel *Göteborg*. You will be well on your way before I brief the other pilots tomorrow. My agent John Rogers will meet you in New York and take you to your base of operations. As soon as America declares hostile intentions against Germany, the führer will give the order for your mission to begin. Your job is to lead your pilots to destroy key, selected military targets in America."

Fritz sat bolt upright and listened intently.

"Mr. Rogers has prepared an air base for this purpose in a remote area of the United States," Canaris continued. "The air base has an all-weather runway capable of handling a fully loaded Fw 200 bomber. In addition, weapons and armory personnel are already on-site. They are experienced Luftwaffe personnel and will help you succeed in this mission. The base has living quarters but is currently undercover as a mining operation." Canaris paused to ensure that his chosen leader was capturing all the details. "Any questions so far?"

"No, sir," Fritz replied.

Canaris smiled and nodded. He rather liked this young man. *It's too bad this will probably be a suicide mission*, he thought to himself.

"Here's your ticket for the ocean crossing." He handed an envelope to Fritz. "When you get to New York, my agent will need you to identify yourself by code. What would you like to use as your password?"

"I would like to stay with the call sign I've used in the Luftwaffe and from my days flying for Deutsche Luft Hansa: Condor One-Two-Three. That has been lucky for me so far," responded Fritz.

Lucky indeed. He had just spent a month in combat in Poland and had avoided death twice from antiaircraft fire. Several planes in his squadron had been shot down, but not Condor 123.

"Fine," acknowledged Canaris. "Good luck to you, Condor, and to your men. *Heil, Hitler*."

When Fritz arrived in Stockholm for his departure, he was pleased to see a massive Swedish flag painted on both the port and starboard sides of the *Göteborg* to ensure that German U-boats did not mistake the vessel and sink it.

The crossing was pleasant, but Fritz was hardly able to relax. Even though they were ultimately no match for the Third Reich, the Poles had fought hard and well. How would the Reich compare to a stronger adversary?

They were now on the brink of a world war, and fatigue, shock, and fear had already taken some of the edge off the National Socialism argument about Nordic superiority.

He blended in well on shipboard with the other Americans returning home from Europe. He enjoyed playing his undercover role as a civilian traveling on his American passport to escape from Europe at war. He also appreciated getting some much-needed rest before his next mission, not to mention an escape from his own domestic frenzy.

Immigration in New York was a simple process. Fritz passed through the gate to United States soil. He walked across the street to the small park where he had been directed by Canaris to meet his contact. He lit a cigarette, sat on a park bench, and paged through a magazine he had purchased on the passage. He tried to look nonchalant even though his heart was pounding.

As he finished his cigarette, a well-dressed man approached him and asked for a light. Fritz noted he was very fit and judged he was in his forties. Fritz lit a match and cupped it for the man, then lit a new cigarette for himself.

The man turned to watch the waterfront activity. "Looks like a good day for watching the seagulls," he said.

"Yes," replied Fritz. "I'm actually fonder of condors myself, though. Do you think we could see many condors in the area?"

John Rogers smiled, held out his hand, and introduced himself. "Let's grab a cab and get out to Floyd Bennett Field. I have a plane chartered for us. You're familiar with that airport, yes?"

Fritz nodded as he remembered his trip to New York last year and the meeting with his family.

"Yes, that's a very nice airport with excellent facilities."

When they arrived at the airport, Rogers quickly cleared the flight for takeoff, and they moved to the tarmac. A DC-3 marked Rogers Airfreight was already warming up.

"That's my freight company," Rogers said with a nod. "Actually, it's *our* freight company."

Fritz smiled at Rogers. *Hardly in the United States for an hour, and I already have a great cover. Things are looking up*, he thought.

As they settled into the cockpit, Rogers went over the flight plan he had filed.

"The flight will take about four hours. It's a little over eight hundred miles. It's important that we stay well within the borders of the United States. Canada has already started imposing flight restrictions due to the war. We don't want any trouble."

32.

HE DC-3 TURNED ON ITS FINAL APPROACH on a gorgeous late summer afternoon. The trees in Michigan's Upper Peninsula were just starting to hint at the coming fall. The maples had tints of yellow and red; the birches and poplars glistened silver in the fading sunlight. Fritz could see the crisp layout of the airport as they lined up for landing. The runway's bright black surface was lighted and marked perfectly.

The wheels touched down with a slight jolt. As they rolled down the runway, Rogers pointed out a building that looked like a large house.

"The pilots' quarters are in that building. You can take a room there. The rest of your team will join you soon."

The aircraft taxied to the end of the runway. Rogers directed Fritz's eyes to the large hangar, where he noticed two men standing just inside the doors. The doors gaped like a huge mouth. Inside he could see three Fw 200 aircraft standing side by side.

"This building is for aircraft storage and maintenance," Rogers explained. "As per the specifications, it's large enough to house three planes."

The ground crew rolled a stairway ramp to the door of the DC-3 for deplaning. The metal rungs of the ramp clanked loudly as Fritz and Rogers deplaned and walked out into the increasing dusk. Carrying his bag over his shoulder, Fritz marveled at the size of the hangar and the layout of the airport.

"The gray building on the other side of the pilots' quarters is where you'll get all your meals," said Rogers. "Hop in the jeep, and I'll take you over to drop your bag in your room. Then we'll take a run to the mine so I can show you the weapons magazine before dinner."

"Excellent," said Fritz. He was eager to see the rest of the operation.

After stopping at the pilots' quarters, Rogers took Fritz up to the mine site for the tour. He drove out the airport gate and down a paved road for about a mile before turning onto a gravel road that headed up into the trees. After winding through the woods for nearly two miles, they approached a gate with an armed guard.

Rogers introduced Fritz to the guard. "Corporal Heinrich, this is Oberstleutnant Fritz Schmidt. He is your new base commander."

The guard quickly came to attention and saluted Fritz.

"Corporal!" admonished Fritz. "Do not salute anyone here. This is a secret base. Do you not understand that?"

"Yes, sir," gasped the corporal apologetically.

"Please continue with your duties," instructed Fritz. "We will inspect the bunker now."

The corporal opened the gate for the jeep to enter the compound. Then he closed and locked the gate before returning to his place of concealment.

"I've been preaching to these men daily that they are not to salute anyone," Rogers said as he drove up to the mine entrance. "Apparently, they find it hard to maintain military decorum without saluting."

"We may be here for a while," said Fritz, nodding his agreement. "We don't want anything to cause someone to become suspicious of this area."

Climbing out of the jeep, Rogers pulled two flashlights from under his seat and handed one to Fritz. Rogers led the way into the mine and started his tour.

"Throughout the tunnel, we have electric lights that run on various generators. However, we try not to use the generator near the mine entrance very often. The Huron Mountain Club is just fifteen miles away, and we don't want anyone checking out unusual noises or lights."

Rogers flashed the light across the floor.

"As you can see, we have a narrow-gauge railway embedded in the tunnel floor, so we can easily transport the weapons in and out of the mine. The wooden beams provide additional support for the cave walls."

Rogers continued leading Fritz farther into the cave.

"There's a split in the tunnel just ahead. The rail leading to the right transports ore out of the working mine as a cover. The track to the left leads to the weapons bunker."

After they took the left fork, the track ended abruptly at a wooden-beam wall just fifty feet ahead. Fritz splashed his light around the tunnel walls and finally turned to Rogers.

"This is a bunker? I don't see any weapons."

Rogers smiled and placed his hand next to one of the beams, pressing a small dented rock. The movement of the wall startled Fritz.

"A bit of camouflage, Oberstleutnant," replied Rogers.

As the wooden wall shifted on a hidden hinge, Rogers's flashlight reflected on a steel door. A combination dial was embedded on the right side of the door. Rogers worked the combination, then pulled open the steel door with a slight rush of air.

Fritz could hear a generator pumping away deep in the cavern. The bright lights inside made him look away briefly to let his eyes adjust to the change. He could feel a slight breeze as the ventilation system tried to equalize the pressure with the steel door ajar.

"Come in and close the door, Oberstleutnant," Rogers said. "I'll go over the inventory with you."

Fritz turned off his flashlight and followed Rogers into the cavern, pulling the heavy metal door behind him. As his eyes adjusted to the interior lighting, he saw several racks of weapons. In addition, there were three cabinets and many labeled crates stacked around the perimeter of the cavern.

"We have twelve fourteen-hundred-kilogram bombs that can be dropped from any of the modified aircraft in the hangar." Rogers pointed to the nearest rack of weaponry. "In addition, there are large hollow-charge HEAT warheads that can be loaded into the cargo bay of any aircraft. And with our remote guidance systems, we can make that aircraft a flying bomb. We don't need an onboard delivery system to use that weapon."

Moving deeper into the cavern, Rogers pointed to a group of metal containers. "These are the new fuel-air bombs—you've received general information about them. Once the other five pilots arrive, I'll provide more-detailed information about how these should be delivered. In addition, we have three new red mercury bombs. They have a huge blast radius and would be useful for large-scale targets. These require special handling. They can be very toxic and explosive if mixed with water, so they must be kept dry. That's why they're kept in airtight, waterproof containers. You'll receive special instructions on these bombs from the technicians who just arrived from Germany."

Fritz stared at the collection of weapons. These were far more powerful than anything he had ever experienced. He wondered what Rogers meant by a "huge blast radius." He knew he had to learn quickly about his assignment. How would he need to change his unit's training on bombing tactics with these new weapons? And if there were significant revisions in the training, how much time would he have to complete that training?

Rogers continued his briefing. "In that far corner are four Henschel Hs 293 radio-controlled glide bombs. They've been improved with a new, larger five-hundred-kilo explosive warhead. As you know, those are similar to torpedoes. They can be dropped on a specific target from close range, then guided into place."

"The cabinets and crates contain an assortment of small arms for base defense, TNT blocks, as well as spare parts for the weapons and equipment needed to modify the Fw 200s for your mission. Finally, we have an area for secure radio communication. We have an Enigma machine that will allow us to freely communicate with Germany."

Fritz looked with pride at the stacks of weapons. "Only Germany could accomplish something this amazing and secretive in a foreign country," he gloated.

"The idea and financial backing came from Germany," responded Rogers. "However, the chief engineer for the airport portion was actually an American from Detroit. I think you may have heard of him."

"Oh, really?" Fritz cocked his head to the side.

"Yes," Rogers said with a laugh. "His name is Johann Schmidt. Your brother."

Fritz could not contain his surprise. "I can't believe that! But now that you mention it, when I met Johann in New York, he said he had a temporary job building an airport. Does he know its true purpose?"

"No," Rogers responded. "And he must *never* know its true purpose. Johann thought this airfield was a private field for mining operations. For our purposes, the site's designation will be Condor Base."

Fritz smiled at the use of his call sign.

Rogers continued. "If you hear a radio message 'Condor Base, proceed with Poseidon,' that will be your signal to strike your assigned targets."

Fritz glanced around at the weapons in the cavern and wondered how long it would be before that message was received.

As they made their way out of the bunker, Fritz noticed a radio dispatch on the table near the entrance. Scanning it quickly, he saw orders to provide updates on the Soo defenses. The dispatch was signed, "But wait for my command—AH."

My God, thought Fritz. *Could Hitler himself be running the show even here in the US?*

Within a month, Fritz was happily settling into Condor Base. He met frequently with his staff, and he received regular updates on the progress of the war in Europe. He kept up-to-date on other local and world activities by radio, newspapers, and magazines brought into the base.

Fritz was responsible for providing weekly updates on the base status to the German headquarters using the Enigma coding machine. The German device had over one billion different settings, so the code was thought to be unbreakable.

Rogers sent Fritz dispatches on the level of security now appearing at the Soo Locks, as reported by the Rogers Airfreight pilots who visually surveyed the locks during their flights.

Fritz couldn't help but wonder where Rogers got all this information and how he had gotten so well connected with the military, world governments, and industries. Fritz still had connections with the Luftwaffe, so he decided to start his own information gathering. As the Condor Base commander, he nonchalantly sent a few inquiries to learn more about Rogers.

The responses were intriguing. Rogers was born in America but had intimate connections with the Germans, all the way up the Gestapo and Nazi chains of command. He apparently had been a deep-cover German agent in the United States for some time.

However, the real word was that Rogers was a mercenary loyal to his own bank account, not a particular regime. He was very efficient. This mission was a success so far because Rogers had the contacts to gather resources quickly.

Fritz didn't trust mercenaries, but he was a long way from help if Rogers ever turned the tables. What would Rogers do if his plan didn't go according to schedule?

If I am truly in command of this base, Fritz assured himself, *the attack will go forward* only *when I'm ready!*

Fritz realized that his brother Johann had been a pawn in Rogers's game. Not wanting to fall under the same fate, Fritz needed more background on Rogers to protect himself and his men. Fritz contacted Rogers and invited him to meet for dinner. Perhaps a casual conversation about family would reveal some information.

The two men met at the Harbor Bar in Marquette at 6:00 p.m. Fritz ordered a cold Canadian Molson. Rogers loved scotch, straight up.

Fritz sipped his brew, then asked, "Do you have any family in the area?"

"I have a son, Francis William Rogers. He's doing very well in a boarding school in New York. He has political aspirations."

Fritz wondered how young Francis would deal with the knowledge that his father was a mercenary for the Nazis. Fritz filed that information away for possible later use.

Rogers finished his first scotch, raised a finger in the air, then changed the subject. "How are your pilots dealing with the delays on the project?"

A second scotch magically arrived. Fritz waved off the waitress when she asked if he too wanted another round. He planned to limit his drinking to the single beer in front of him.

Responding to Rogers's question, Fritz replied, "I've appointed Captain Ludvig Voss as my executive officer. That gives him more responsibility over the troops. In addition, the pilots have been paired up and assigned to particular aircraft. It gives them a chance to work together as they fly deliveries for Rogers Airfreight. I want them to get used to flying aircraft under various load distributions."

"An excellent idea," Rogers said, motioning for a third scotch. "I was pleased at how well you managed the turnover of airport duties to the new team who arrived last week."

"Thank you." Fritz pretended to sip his beer. "I've requested and just received some additional people for the base. The entire crew running the airport and control tower are now trained German intelligence agents. They've taken over control of airport operations to ensure the cover stays in place until the mission is completed," Fritz volunteered nonchalantly.

Rogers looked surprised to hear this news.

Good, Fritz thought. *He doesn't seem to know everything that's happening at the base. That's good for me to know. And it's good for him to know that I'm making my own decisions.*

Fritz felt the dinner had met its purpose. He had verified some vital new information, and Rogers now knew that Fritz controlled the mission.

Besides, the fish was wonderful.

The next morning, at the base, Rogers brought Fritz another list of potential targets from Admiral Canaris. Fritz needed to review all the targets and determine the most viable. He also had to ensure that the pilots could locate their specific targets using just map coordinates in case of inclement weather the day of the mission. The nearest target, the Soo Locks, was particularly prone to fog and bad weather.

Fritz requested aerial photographs of all the targets. The pilots took their Rogers Airfreight planes on practice flights near each of the potential targets. This allowed them to become familiar with the topography around each target from the air. Fritz reviewed the most important photographs with the crews to discuss exactly how to attack.

Only the pilots who spoke English were allowed to fly from the base for actual freight deliveries for Rogers Airfreight. The other pilots merely flew reconnaissance missions to practice their approach to the various targets.

The Luftwaffe ground troops were not allowed off the base, due to security concerns. Therefore, Fritz needed to bring entertainment to the troops restricted to the base. He ensured that Rogers Airfreight flights returned with American cigarettes, movies, and books. The men could also hike in the woods between the airport and the mine, and they could fish for trout in the streams running through the mining property that Rogers had secured for them.

Just as important as the attack plan was the escape plan, which would be enacted after the attack—or before, if the Americans discovered the base. Fritz set up predetermined sites to evacuate any remaining Fw 200s, pilots, and operational personnel. He would order them to destroy the bunker and any remaining weapons, codebooks, and the Enigma machine before they dispersed. Fritz purposely did not share any of this with Rogers.

As the weeks turned to months, winter came early to the Upper Peninsula. It brought with it heavy snow and blizzards with gale-force winds coming off the massive lake. Much of the troops' time was spent on maintenance and ensuring that the runways were clear. The Fw 200s were housed in the hangar, but the Rogers Airfreight DC-3 sat outside on the runway, ready for any possible shipments. They needed to ensure the aircraft engines and electronics would function in the cold for all the aircraft.

Fritz also busied the men with clearing and grooming trails for cross-country skiing. They also cleared a spot in the cargo hangar for doing calisthenics when the weather dipped into the double digits below zero. He made sure the returning flights brought skis and skates for their enjoyment.

Christmas and New Year's were festive for such an isolated outpost. Fritz managed to fly in all the trimmings for a true German holiday meal. They feasted on beef roast, potatoes, gravy, and turnips, plus hot apple strudel for dessert. Fritz also had the men cut fresh fir trees from the neighboring woods, and he ordered that decorations be shipped in. They spent Christmas Eve singing their native German carols and decorating the trees. One of the agents was a Lutheran deacon who led them in prayers to protect them in the coming year.

The new year of 1940 arrived with little change in the war situation and still no declaration of war between Germany and the United States. Months passed.

In April, Fritz was in the bunker when a startling news report came over the radio. The German army and air force had smashed into the Ardennes forest in Belgium, splitting the British and French armies. The British forces required evacuation by sea from Dunkirk, and they lost most of their supplies. In addition, the French had been forced to accept an armistice, allowing the Germans to occupy the northern half of France. German losses had been minimal. All this had happened in just ninety days.

Fritz was exuberant. "Germany is sure to win now!" he told the radio operator. "The French are defeated, and the English are stuck on their little island. Britain will have to accept Hitler's terms. There'll be no need for this mission—the United States won't have a base of operations on the European continent."

"It does look promising," responded the radioman with delight.

Fritz nodded his encouragement. *However*, he secretly thought, *I wouldn't count Churchill out. He's a fighter. You have to admit, the old boy's got balls!* But Fritz kept that suspicion to himself.

Fritz knew Hitler was determined to invade Britain and crush the Royal Air Force. But shortly after the reports of Nazi success, bad news came as the Battle of Britain raged on. Fritz started to travel to Marquette to read the American newspaper accounts of the battle. He found that the details received over the radio from Germany were starkly different from those the British and Americans were reporting. Fritz suspected that the truth lay somewhere in between.

The German aviators were at a distinct disadvantage when waging war over Britain. Their fighter planes didn't have enough fuel to stay with the bombers all the way to their targets and still return. If the mission extended far over enemy territory, the fighters often ended up in the North Sea or the English Channel. In addition, the British Spitfire and Hurricane fighters were also proving to match the German fighters. German pilots shot down over land were lost as prisoners of war.

By October, the Battle of Britain was over. Germany had failed to defeat the Royal Air Force. German losses were horrific. The Luftwaffe had lost 57 percent of its overall forces, including over half of its planes and pilots. Fritz learned that his old squadron had been almost completely destroyed during the Battle of Britain.

If I hadn't been transferred to Condor Base, thought Fritz, *I'd probably be dead by now!*

News of the losses spread across the base. Many of the men stationed there had lost friends or relatives. Fritz tried to bolster their courage by passing out whiskey and allowing them to drink toasts to their dead comrades.

Fritz continued to receive weekly updates from Rogers on the buildup of defenses at the Soo Locks. The Canadians had already fortified their side of the locks, and the US forces were rumored to be adding antiaircraft coastal artillery with searchlights. The incoming flights for Rogers Airfreight brought news that the searchlights were indeed a reality and could be seen from as far away as thirty miles. Defensive construction on the American side was moving at a fevered pace, putting in place nearly fifty antiaircraft guns around the locks. The locks would soon perhaps be too strong to attack.

Reports from Germany also indicated that military overloading of the Fw 200s had caused several to break up in flight. Fritz had known of this problem even before the war started, when some of the Deutsche Luft Hansa Fw 200s had crashed with structural problems. The aircraft at Condor Base had reinforced fuselages, but Fritz knew no one had truly tested the full weight they would need to carry to destroy the locks.

Fritz started calculating how to fit his Fw 200 for the task at hand. He planned to call a test for the ground crew to load his aircraft as they would for the actual mission—with one glide bomb under each wing and a larger, nearly 1,400-kilo bomb in the bomb bay. His total weight would be nearly 3,500 kilos.

That would be a proper test of the aircraft, or at least as accurate as they could get. The bombs would be unarmed during the test flight for safety. Also, he would need to land fully loaded after the test, whereas he did not anticipate any of the aircraft returning to base with armaments the day of the actual mission. For the test, he'd need to recalculate his runway touchdown zone to avoid an overrun.

The flight over the locks was only 250 miles round trip. Fritz carefully calculated his fuel requirements, allowing himself enough fuel without weighing himself down. That way, the weight would hopefully be well within reasonable limits for the aircraft.

He planned on taking along Dietrich, a copilot and trained recon photographer. That way, they could also get pictures of the construction at the locks and their defenses. With both the US and Canada fortifying the locks, time was not on their side, and Fritz wanted to get the real mission underway. This test flight would prove the airworthiness of a fully loaded Fw 200 as well as the efficiency of the crew in loading the armaments.

When the real attack would be called, Fritz would equip two Fw 200s in this same manner, followed by one additional Fw 200 carrying the new fuel-air bombs to complete the destruction. Perhaps it would also include at least one of the red mercury bombs to provide maximum destruction.

Checking the weather reports, Fritz spotted his chance. The next morning would dawn cloudless with light winds out of the west. He ordered the loading of the aircraft overnight and told Dietrich to be ready for takeoff at 0400.

Fritz did not sleep well that night. He tossed and turned in his bed. He couldn't stop thinking about everything that had gone wrong in the last year.

I've lost my brother Albert, my wife and sons, and so many friends and comrades. How will all this end? Will we all die here on this mission? If so, what are we truly dying for?

33.

"Rogers Airfreight, Condor One-Two-Three rolling," Fritz responded to the tower after receiving clearance.

He throttled up the aircraft. He was dangerously close to the end of the runway when he finally lifted off. He felt his pulse quicken. Dietrich glanced over nervously as the aircraft just cleared the tree line.

Fritz set his altitude at five thousand feet and headed into the still-dark skies east of the base. That would allow him to make his approach to the locks from the east just as the sun rose. The sun's glare would hopefully blind anyone on the ground from seeing the bombs hanging under the wings.

"Don't worry, Dietrich," he told his copilot, who still looked nervous. "We're just flying freight for all they know. We'll come in from the east to keep the sun out of your lens. You should be able to get some pretty good pictures."

Dietrich glanced out the window at the airport that suddenly looked incredibly tiny. Then he looked over his shoulder at the bomb under the wing on his side. Although he was a pilot, he was uneasy with the weight of the two bombs tucked under the wings, let alone the bigger bomb swaying in its belly. Taking off with that much weight was one thing. Landing a fully loaded aircraft was another thing altogether. He hoped Fritz was as skilled as the other pilots seemed to think.

Flying quietly in the growing morning light, Fritz once again began to ponder the war effort.

Germany is a cruel mistress. She's like a lioness who first dotes on then kills her own cubs. Only my brother Johann seems to have escaped the insanity.

Like the fabled phoenix, the blinding sun rose out of the massive lake as Fritz started his first turn. He had flown east across the Upper Peninsula, then banked across the northern tips of Lake Michigan and Lake Huron. Now he was starting the final banking maneuver toward the locks. The aircraft had performed well, and he was pleased with the weight distribution. The ground crew had done an excellent job following his orders and loading the aircraft for stability.

Approaching the locks, he radioed his intentions to avoid any unnecessary anxiety on the part of either the Canadians or the Americans.

"Soo Lock Central. Soo Lock Central. This is Rogers Airfreight, Condor One-Two-Three, requesting flyover of the locks area."

"Condor One-Two-Three, this is Soo Lock Central. Please identify your need for flyover permission."

"Soo Lock Central, Condor One-Two-Three. Rogers Airfreight is flying an emergency medical delivery for Houghton General Hospital and requests the shortest route."

"Condor One-Two-Three, Soo Lock Central. Permission granted. Please use a heading of two eight five on your flyover approach."

"Soo Lock Central, Condor One-Two-Three. Adjusting to heading two eight five. Condor One-Two-Three out."

Fritz was elated by the ease of gaining permission. This would be handy information for his pilots. He also considered passing the information on to Canaris. Maybe that would tip the scales in favor of initiating the mission sooner.

As they flew over the locks, Dietrich clicked pictures as fast as he could. He was excited at this opportunity to help the war effort and proud to have been handpicked by the obersteutnant.

Far below, the crews at the locks shaded their eyes as the plane approached. Flyovers of the locks were rare but not unheard of. The crews had seen similar aircraft that were part of a nearby airfreight company, but the wings looked heavier on this particular plane. Once the aircraft cleared the locks and headed across Lake Superior, they went back to work without much thought about the strange configuration.

Dietrich grinned in satisfaction and gave Fritz a thumbs-up. Fritz returned the sign and continued well out into Whitefish Bay. He would ensure he was out of sight of the lock before making his bank southwest and returning to Condor Base.

The German high command would be elated with this new information about passing over the locks. Fritz might even get a medal for his individual effort during this daring mission.

Fritz turned the aircraft for home. Just then, he felt a shudder. Quickly checking his gauges, he flashed an okay sign and what he hoped was a look of confidence to Dietrich, who was staring at him with wide eyes. Dietrich seemed to relax.

But once again, the aircraft shuddered. Then it started to vibrate. Fritz struggled to stabilize the plane. Suddenly, it stalled and started a sickening nose dive toward the gleaming surface of the big lake.

The aircraft struck the water hard, knocking both men unconscious. The weight of the plane easily cut a swath through the water. It settled slowly to the bottom of the bay in over two hundred feet of icy-cold water.

Fritz's grand mission was over. He had gone home after all.

Four hours later, Captain Ludvig Voss, executive officer at Condor Base, contacted Canaris with the news. Canaris was furious that Fritz had decided to fly a test mission on his own initiative. The return message received over the Enigma was not unexpected.

> *Destroy all traces of German occupancy at the airport. Arm and detonate the explosives in the bunker. Ensure the armaments, codebooks, and Enigma machine are destroyed with the bunker. Fly all Luftwaffe pilots to the Mexican extraction site and await pickup by U-boats. Advise the agents to disperse back to their earlier posts.*

The flurry of activity at the airport would have been suspicious if anyone had been watching the area. The remaining planes were rolled out and refueled. The two Fw 200s lifted off in just over two hours, carrying the Luftwaffe pilots and ground personnel to the designated landing strip east of Monterrey, Mexico.

The few remaining agents with US passports hastily split up. The larger group of Luftwaffe personnel destroyed all traces of their occupation at the airport. Two of the agents raced to the cave and set the timers on the destructive charges intended to destroy the cave and its contents. Then they all regrouped at the base and flew out on the DC-3. This flight carried only human cargo and would disperse the agents at locations in the United States, where they could fade back into their previous lives.

Moments after takeoff, a flash of light and a muffled explosion startled the deer in the Michigan woods bordering what had once been Condor Base.

The next day, the only flights over the Condor Base were an occasional murder of crows or flock of wayward seagulls.

Two weeks later, a DC-3 landed at the deserted airport. John Rogers stepped out of the plane and surveyed the scene. The airport looked as good as new. All traces of its true purpose had been removed. He trusted that the vestiges of the bunker had also been destroyed forever.

Rogers got back into the aircraft and took off. He had another plan.

There's always someone looking to build a good airport. Maybe even the US government for the Soo defense.

Rogers smiled at the irony. He could still make some money on this project.

— OKLAHOMA, 1969 —

34.

Bill's trip to Lawton went quickly—up I-35, then US 82, and finally I-44. The drive was only six hours. Less, actually, because he often let the big-ass engine of his new red Chevy convertible take over. Bill didn't call it the Rocket for nothing.

He was in his dress uniform as he approached the gate. The soldier at the gate wore an MP armband and saluted after quickly noting Bill's lieutenant's bars.

Bill returned the salute. "Can you direct me to the base administration?"

"Yes, sir. Just go straight ahead one-half mile, sir. The admin building is on your left, sir. You can park in any slot marked 'Officers Only,' sir." The MP saluted again.

Bill could only chuckle under his breath at the rapid-fire "sirs." He returned the salute and drove off as directed.

Bill reported to the adjutant's office with his orders. He was shown into the battalion commander's office for the formal transfer of command. He felt a bit foolish snapping to a salute, but after the greeting at the gate, he figured he had better get used to it.

"How was your drive up, Lieutenant?" Colonel Robert Fontaine, battalion commander, asked.

"Fine, sir. I hope I'll be allowed a vehicle on base. I parked where the MP directed me."

"No problem." The colonel smiled. "I saw that sweet red convertible and figured it must be the new guy." He picked up his phone and dialed a number. "Mark, pop into my office. Your new man is here."

Lieutenant Colonel Mark Stevens, the assistant battalion commander, knocked on the door.

"Enter!" Colonel Fontaine replied.

"Lieutenant O'Brien," said Stevens. He approached with his hand extended after an exchange of salutes. "It's a pleasure to finally meet you."

Bill shook hands with his new boss and sized him up. His blue eyes were intense but friendly. The handshake was casual, not that of a man with an ego to stroke.

This assignment could go all right, thought Bill.

"Why don't we head into my office? I'll give you the details on your new assignment, then get you assigned space in the bachelor officers' quarters. I suspect you'll want a base pass for that nice set of wheels."

Bill tried to hide his smile. *Did everyone see me drive in?*

"Yes, thank you, sir."

"O'Brien, we need you to give these new recruits as much realistic training as possible. You've had substantial field experience. You know that if anything can go wrong, it will. These men need to be taken down a peg and then built back up to be able to handle that pressure and make decisions under fire."

"Yes, sir," Bill responded.

"There are a lot of issues in this man's army now with drugs, protestors, and desertion, to name a few," Stevens continued. "Use your experience to convince them that they need to learn—and learn well—in order to survive. O'Brien, you have an outstanding record for a young officer. That's why you are here. You have proven your survival skills under extreme conditions. I believe you can instill that in your troops."

"Yes, sir. Thank you, sir. I'll do my best."

"Excellent. The transfer of command to the training battery will be tomorrow at eight hundred hours. You will be relieving Captain Sullivan, who is rotating to Germany. Check with the administrative assistant in the office by the door for assignment to your quarters and a parking pass."

Stevens stood up and reached across the desk to shake Bill's hand. Bill shook his hand, saluted, and headed for the door.

But then Stevens stopped him short when he barked, "O'Brien, you are out of uniform!"

Shaken, Bill spun around to face Stevens. "Sorry, sir. I don't understand."

Stevens handed him a small box. "Remove those lieutenant's bars, O'Brien. I need a captain for this command. You are now Captain William O'Brien."

Bill opened the box and saw his glistening new insignia.

Bill quickly settled into his role as commander of Battery A at the US Army Field Artillery School. The duty was quite light, compared to what he was used to. He commanded nearly 150 officers and enlisted men who were headed to Vietnam.

The officers were fresh from college ROTC units. The enlisted men were fresh from basic training. It reminded him of his first days at the base. He knew what they would face in Vietnam. He was told the officers would have more adjustment time when they got to Vietnam, which would be better than the "boots on ground, bullets overhead" indoctrination he had received. But he was still uneasy.

Each day, the Nixon administration edged closer to a drawdown of troops in Vietnam. The hope was that American involvement would end before too long. In the meantime, Bill's job was to ensure that all his troops received the best training possible.

Bill's focus was on precision in all aspects of the artillery training. He insisted on attention to detail—from accurate computer calculations for powder load, distance, and direction, to proper cleaning and care of the guns. It was *all* important, he thought, especially when you added the complications of jungle heat, dirt, vegetation, and the fact your own countrymen may be in the line of fire.

Map reading was at the top of Bill's list. The officers had to be able to quickly access, orient, calibrate, and call in shelling from their maps. Although the training zone was always the same acreage, Bill would throw in maps with different keys and in different languages just to keep them sharp. Proper map reading had saved Bill's life more than once. He could not stress that enough to the officers.

Bill's classes graduated officers every 120 days and enlisted men every 60 days. He never relished losing a well-trained squad and having to start over again, but he was getting used to the routine. He had to be careful not to make assumptions with one group just because he had covered the topic a couple of months ago with a different group. Each class needed to be sharp, and he needed to be sharp for them.

As each day drew to a close, Bill had paper work to complete. He reviewed the day's training and made notes about adjustments for this particular group. He also reviewed the news from Vietnam, paying particular attention when he saw the name of an officer or enlisted man who had gone through his training. The death of Americans in a far-off war was never easy, but recognizing a name made it more personal. It only hardened his hatred of the war.

The dreams visited Bill with regularity on the nights after he found a familiar name. These were his 3:00 a.m. nightmares, when the light of day would not come and sleep would not return. They revived the terror of his firefights in Vietnam. It felt as if he were reliving the battles over and over. He saw the faces of so many men who were killed and many he had killed himself. He saw those who had died saving his life—the young medic, the soldier who saved him from the land mine, and the boyish second lieutenant. Bill could not forget when the sparkle left his eyes as he bled to death.

On some nights, he saw the face of William Spiritlight Norman, his RTO, telling Bill he was safe. Bill wondered if it had anything to do with the man's Cherokee middle name. That man had saved Bill's life, and now his spirit was intent on doing it again. Bill sensed that his dead radioman was somehow giving him the power of second sight, or premonitions. Those feelings and visions had saved him in Vietnam, and he still trusted them now.

Other nights, Bill relived the battle where he had to take radio command and call in danger close firings. He had saved many men, but the ones he saw marching in sharp focus through his dreams were those killed by his friendly fire. On these nights, his only respite was a quick two fingers of Jameson. He tried to temper his drinking but was having limited success. The excuses to just have a short one happened more often than not.

Bill was getting better at controlling his habit of dropping to the ground at any loud, sharp noise. When he was training the troops, he did fine. He was getting used to the occasional car backfire and door slam. Actually, the last time he nearly hit the dirt was in the mess hall when someone dropped a metal cooking pot. He managed to cover his jump by grabbing his coffee cup and heading to the urn for a refill.

He also noticed he was more irritable since he got back from Vietnam. He had developed a very thin skin. He barked orders and doled out punishment if his demands were not met. Was the authority going to his head? Was he afraid they would blame him if his trainees were killed? Then he realized the only "they" that would blame him were his own internal demons. Still, he continued to be demanding and drove his men until they had the best scores of all the batteries at Fort Sill.

Even so, Bill continued to have trouble sleeping, and he experienced more and more pain from his leg and arm wounds. This only contributed to his irritability with junior officers who had the unlucky "opportunity" of screwing up an exercise.

Bill also was frustrated with his relationship with Susan. He traveled from Fort Sill to Fort Sam as often as he and Susan could arrange their schedules. But that became harder and harder not only because of Bill's duties but more so because of Susan's. Often, when Bill had time off, she said she was working or just that she had a "conflict."

And when they did get together, Susan was often disconnected and preoccupied. It was almost as if Bill weren't even there. One moment she would be bubbling over with energy, and the next she would get a distant look, as if dealing with a terrible loss. When he tried to talk to her about Vietnam, she would wave off the discussion. She was not ready to talk about what she had experienced. This was not helping their relationship. Bill was starting to wonder if there even was a relationship.

The last time Bill went down to see her, he caught her looking at an attractive older man. Bill guessed this was the Zack from Australia she had mentioned. She had been dating him quite regularly when she was working with Bill on his rehab. That seemed to end when Bill started dating Susan.

But seeing Susan flash a warm glance and bright smile at Zack triggered Bill's second sight. Susan and Zack must have picked up where they left off once Bill left for Fort Sill. Perhaps Bill's involvement had triggered more enthusiasm from Zack. Or perhaps it was just a matter of proximity for Susan, with Zack at Fort Sam, while Bill was several hours away. For all Bill knew, maybe they were serious and she was going to marry Zack. But why, then, didn't she just shut Bill down altogether?

One time when their schedules had aligned for a visit, Bill took Susan to lunch in the hospital cafeteria. Susan looked distracted, staring out the window. Bill asked a probing question.

"Susan, do you want to see me anymore? If not, just let me know. I expect you have men lined up around Fort Sam wanting to date you—doctors, high-ranking officers. So it would be no surprise to me if you were committing yourself to someone else. You have many better choices and opportunities with your time than I can provide. You are a truly beautiful and wonderful woman, and it's been great being with you for even this short time period."

Susan stiffened upright and turned her head to meet Bill's gaze. She looked concerned and hesitated briefly, trying to determine an appropriate response.

"Bill, I'm sorry, but I'm trying to resolve something. Right now, it's just difficult to see you as much as I would like."

Two weeks later, Susan was still "unavailable" every time Bill tried to see her. He more or less wrote off their relationship now. He left his last message for her, saying she could call him if she wanted to see him in the future. He laughed to himself with a sad realization that it had never been a relationship—just meals and discussion with a beautiful nurse treating a patient. They hadn't even been intimate with each other; Bill had sensed she needed her time and space.

Susan had saved Bill after Sara left, but he wondered why she had even bothered. Now she just seemed to be giving him breadcrumbs of her time and attention. He seemed to be wasting his time even when they were together. His problem, though, was that he did like her a lot.

For her part, Susan did have an issue she needed to resolve, and it was indeed with Zack.

Susan had dated a number of men during her first few months back from Vietnam. Some were doctors or officers. She really hadn't dated any civilians, due to her concern about the growing resistance to the military and the war.

It seemed that all these men she dated either just wanted sexual release or were scared off when she talked about her Vietnam experiences. They were tone-deaf to anything other than their own egos. No one could appreciate what she had been through. They just weren't willing to let her resolve any of her issues from the war.

She had hoped she and Zack could move on together, but she had reservations. He did listen a bit to her issues from the war, but he seemed more interested in the sexual portion of the relationship. He was a comfortable lover, but there was something missing. It was the depth of his commitment, the emotional depth, that she questioned. He said he loved her, but how deeply and completely?

Eventually, Susan would have to tell Zack her secret, the same secret she had told all the others who cared deeply for her. And as soon as she told them, every one, without exception, had moved away from her. What would Zack do?

In the meantime, she would leave Bill hanging, hoping he would still be there as a backup plan if Zack failed her. Bill had potential. She sensed something very different about him, how cautious he was with her, how he didn't make sexual advances, how polite and kind he was. She also assumed he didn't have a lot going on with other relationships. Perhaps she could keep him interested with only an occasional dinner or show for now.

Life was lonely for Bill, but it was different than the loneliness of Vietnam. He wasn't in combat anymore, which had kept his mind off the loneliness. Plus, everyone in Vietnam was lonely. Here at Fort Sill, he wasn't with a friend like Dale Patterson or his wonderful parents and of course not Sara.

No, he was in a military garrison that ran like a business. Many people went home at night to their families, girlfriends, or even their pets! Bill was by himself with only a few other single officers. There were also enlisted men, but by military regulations, Bill couldn't hang around with them. He had only himself, the officers' club, and his Jameson whiskey.

He was surprised and also so glad to get a letter from Sara. She must have remembered he would be at Fort Sill and had gotten his address. He was happy that he now had her address too. He was afraid to open the envelope and have the letter scream back at him the terrible loss that had occurred when she broke off their engagement. He rubbed his hands over the letter, trying to feel the tenderness of Sara's touch and the love he knew she still had for him. This love wasn't some breadcrumb. But it was a love she had to sacrifice out of her love and respect for her husband.

At last, Bill carefully and lovingly opened her letter. He could smell her perfume, that lovely smell he would never forget. He read the letter, and it made him terribly sad to learn that her husband was even more badly wounded than she had been told. He would never regain consciousness and would probably die from his wounds. Bill hated to think that if her husband died quickly, then perhaps she could come back. He would not wish that. He knew that would be hateful to her.

Her letter continued, saying she had thrown herself into her work when she wasn't sitting with her husband. It helped keep her mind off the decision she had made not only for her husband but for Bill as well. She signed it, "With sadness to the one I love most in this world—you, Bill. Sara."

Bill was almost willing to jump on the next plane to Boston but realized it would only be harder on Sara. He knew their parting at Fort Sam had torn her up emotionally, and he didn't want her to go through that again, particularly with this additional bad news about her husband's condition.

Immediately, he wrote a letter back to her, trying to be as encouraging as he could. He told her that if she wanted, he would come out and spend time with her, if that would help her deal with this situation. All she had to do was ask. He knew she would decline, but he wanted her to know he still cared for and loved her.

In the meantime, he had his duty to perform.

35.

A FEW DAYS LATER, LIEUTENANT COLONEL Mark Stevens asked Bill to come in for a talk.

Bill saluted as he entered the commander's office. "Sir, Captain O'Brien reporting, as ordered."

"Captain, please have a chair. I want to discuss a few things with you."

"Yes, sir. Thank you, sir."

Bill could only think that he had already used up a month's worth of "sirs" with this one meeting. He was reminded of his first encounter with the MP at the gate.

"Captain, you continue to do a fine job training the men. I couldn't be more pleased with their accomplishments."

"Thank you, sir." Bill was still unsure of the purpose of the meeting.

"I've noticed you limping more noticeably lately," Stevens said. "How are you feeling physically?"

"Sir, my leg and arm both bother me occasionally. The doctors said that with the extent of muscle damage, it might require more physical therapy to reduce the pain and improve my mobility. I just haven't had the time to do the necessary PT."

"How are you doing mentally?" the colonel pressed. "I've noticed you've been a bit sharp with some of the junior officers. Sometimes that's needed to help them experience the appropriate stress, but I'm concerned with how you are dealing with your Vietnam experiences."

Bill was embarrassed by the colonel's blunt statement. He thought he had been handling the pain and stress fairly well, considering.

"Well, sir, I haven't been sleeping well," Bill admitted. "I keep seeing the faces of my dead comrades. I've also been drinking more than I should. Maybe it's compensation."

"Captain, I'm glad you recognize those issues. Some men just try to bury their problems in excuses, and that doesn't work. I faced a similar issue from my Korean War experience. We had a long and disastrous retreat from the Yalu River, where I lost most of my command."

Colonel Stevens reached across his desk and handed Bill a business card. "There is someone in town I would like you to talk to. Here's his name and phone number. Give him a call."

"Thank you, sir," Bill replied with a sigh. "I'll give him a call right away."

"Very good, Captain. You're dismissed."

Bill saluted and left the office unsure of where this phone call would take him.

Bill did as he said and gave the number a call. He was answered by a kindly but gruff voice belonging to retired sergeant major Murphy O'Rourke. Bill explained that Lieutenant Colonel Stevens had referred him.

"Mark Stevens is a hell of a good man," O'Rourke said. "He must see a lot of promise in you to have you see me. I run a support group for former combat veterans. We'll be glad to include you, but there are five important ground rules," O'Rourke explained. "If you can't, or won't, follow them, we can't help you."

"Okay," Bill responded tentatively.

O'Rourke continued. "One, there is no rank here. Everyone is equal. Two, we use only first names. Three, you have to honestly share your issues, fears, and problems with the group. Four, you need to honestly listen and support the other group members. Five, nothing goes outside the group. This is entirely confidential." O'Rourke paused. "Can you agree to all that?"

Bill paused briefly, but there were no other options. "Yes, I can agree to that. When and where is your next meeting?"

A few days later, Bill parked the Rocket near an old storefront just off Main Street in Lawton. He shuffled into the building with his hands tucked in the back pockets of his jeans.

A man in a well-worn Stetson greeted him at the door. He looked like a character from a John Wayne cavalry picture. Murphy introduced himself. Bill knew instinctively that the sergeant major had spent a career listening to lame excuses from enlisted men and comical orders from officers. This man clearly knew bullshit when he heard it.

Bill was introduced to the group members. There were nine other Vietnam vets. They had served in a variety of units with an impressive amount of time in Vietnam. Several had endured multiple combat tours.

After the introductions, Murphy asked each man what was bothering him most that day. Bill tried to pass, claiming he was new and that he wanted to get used to the session first. The group got on him immediately about not being more open.

"I'm not able to sleep," Bill finally started. "I keep seeing the faces of men killed in my unit. One was my radioman, who gave his life to protect me. Another was a young medic who pushed me out of the way from a land mine and was blown to pieces while I received only some shrapnel wounds. Another soldier pulled me under cover after I had been hit by shrapnel from a mortar round. He was shot and killed as he dragged me to safety. Then there was a young second lieutenant who was only a week in-country and had no business in the field leading troops—he was shot by a sniper. I watched the light go out of his young, innocent eyes as he died. I had told him to seek better cover, but he just wouldn't listen. He thought it made him look afraid to his men. And some deaths were directly due to my actions, like when my danger close fire killed two of my own men near the Cambodian border."

Bill looked around cautiously. He saw only nods of agreement and understanding.

Feeling more confident, he added, "These memories are causing me to drink more than I should."

Gene responded first. "Man, that's bullshit, Bill. You need to force yourself to see the faces of the men who *lived*. You know, the ones you saved."

Bill was startled by this admonishment.

"The dead are gone," Bruce added. "Think only of the ones who lived. The lives they still have. The joy their loved ones feel because their son or brother or friend survived."

Bill sat in stunned silence at this revelation. He realized he was using the booze as a crutch. The frankness of this group slammed that into his face that night.

In the following weeks, the group meshed well together. Bill started feeling the emotional benefits of their special connection. He also joined the Saturday morning jogging sessions and noticed he was sleeping better and feeling less pain. He finally rose to the group's challenge to reduce his drinking—except coffee, of course.

Bill could definitely see and feel the benefits. He started working out with the heavy boxing bag at the base gym. This eased his shoulder pain as he improved the muscle tone in his arms. He even got into the boxing ring for some refreshers from his college days. He was developing a powerful punch and was improving his mobility and endurance. The result was deeper sleep at night with fewer and fewer dreams of combat.

The only thing that didn't seem to improve in his life was his relationship with Susan. She did eventually call Bill to get together again, but it seemed to be more of the same. She was still mostly unavailable. Now he was certain she was seriously dating another man, probably Zack.

Bill was dumb but not stupid. He knew she was stringing him along for some reason, most likely because she wasn't getting the desired results from the primary boyfriend. He had a feeling this would turn out just as it had with Barbara.

At least it had been different with Sara. Sara may have ended the relationship, but he was proud of her courage and honor to her husband. He must have been a remarkable man—one Bill would have loved to know and call a friend.

Still, there was a lot about Susan that made Bill want to dig in his heels and stay interested. He continued to travel to Fort Sam and see her whenever possible. With his second sight, he began to sense it wasn't as bleak as he initially thought.

Susan was an attractive and intelligent woman. He also knew from their brief conversations about Vietnam that she had gone through hell in the MASH unit. Bill had been through that unit twice and had seen enough to understand her experience better than most people.

Bill brought up Susan and their relationship at the next group meeting.

"She needs space," Gene said. "Don't crowd her. If you do, she'll close up, and you'll lose her. She sounds like a great lady, someone really worth waiting for. Don't do what some of us have done—don't try to bring things to the surface by confronting her."

The next time Bill saw Susan, he told her about his support group. "You should see if Fort Sam has a support program for nurses," he suggested.

Susan flipped her hair back and glared at him. "That's not for me," she replied.

"I understand it's not for everyone," Bill said. "But I just know how much it's helped me."

"Bill, just drop it!"

Bill flinched at the force of Susan's response and looked away briefly. He let out a soft sigh as he looked back at her. "I just want you to know I care about you. I'm always ready to listen if you want to talk."

"I'm sorry I snapped at you." She dropped her gaze to the floor. "Let me think about it."

Bill's unit continued to perform consistently above average. The base commanding general asked him to consider accepting a regular army commission and staying in the army as a career.

Bill did consider the offer, but he was honestly looking forward to ending his active service. He knew the army was starting to downsize its officer corps. Promotions would be difficult in the future. More importantly, he was tired of reviewing casualty reports from Vietnam. He was tired of the routine training. He was tired of fighting other people's battles. As a commissioned officer, he would be on call for the rest of his life if a national emergency occurred. However, he had personal battles to wage. He needed to resolve his relationship with Susan and deal with his uncle Sean.

Bill talked occasionally with Bradley Wilkerson, the attorney whom General Abrams arranged to delve into the situation with Sean. Wilkerson's initial review proved that Sean had knowingly used an outdated power of attorney. One of Sean's drinking buddies confessed to Wilkerson's investigator that Sean had told him about Michael and Helene granting Abrams the more recent power of attorney. But Sean felt that because he was family, he should be the one to direct the family affairs.

Wilkerson believed that Bill had an excellent chance of regaining control of M. O. Airfreight. He said his team was pursuing several other issues that might give Bill some financial recovery, but the details were sketchy at this point, so he did not elaborate. Their background work would take a couple of months.

The team was doing their best to work this pro bono case in with their other cases, but they did want to meet face-to-face with Bill as soon as he was available. Bill arranged to take leave from Fort Sill in a couple of months so he could go to Minneapolis for personal business.

Some good things seemed to be happening to him now, even if Susan was still stringing him along. At the very least, he could reestablish his life in Minnesota.

After many lonely nights and weekends at Fort Sill, Bill finally decided to get an apartment off-base to get away from the army during his free hours. Perhaps he could move on with his life and meet other women. At least it would be nice to find some company in his off-duty hours. He signed up for a business management class at the nearby community college. That gave him a reason to be unavailable too if Susan called.

Bill met Roberta Clark in his class. She was a bright twenty-three-year-old divorcée with shiny dark hair, pale-blue eyes, and a trim figure. Bobby, as she liked to be called, worked as a civilian contractor for the army. Her ex-husband was a drunk and abusive.

When Bill invited her for coffee after class, she told him immediately she wasn't interested in a long-term relationship, but she was happy to make a friend. They often met for dinner before class or coffee afterward. Bill thoroughly enjoyed Bobby's company and even asked her to a movie one Sunday afternoon.

When the class ended, Bill found out that Bobby had accepted a new job in Denver. Just when he thought things were going pretty well, she was leaving.

Just as Bobby left town, Bill's mail finally caught up with him from Vietnam. Surprisingly, he had another letter from Barbara. Much seemed to have changed in her life. She seemed more open and understanding than before. It was hard to sort out what that meant, but it piqued Bill's interest. Did Barbara of all people want to see him again? That was a most pleasant thought—one of the few he had received lately.

He wrote her a letter in response and said it would be interesting to see her again. He could perhaps meet with her during his trip to Minneapolis.

Bill decided he might even drop a hint about Barbara to Susan, just to see her response. He had little to lose.

First Bobby, now this letter from Barbara—it gave Bill new perspective. He thought about Bobby. She had been honest with him from day one with her declaration that she was interested only in friendship. That had been a nice change. It allowed Bill to relax and appreciate what a positive relationship could be like. He felt he was now better prepared to test his relationship with Susan again.

To Bill's surprise, Susan also seemed prepared to test the relationship. The next time they met for dinner, they began by sharing some small talk—including Bill's news about hearing from Barbara. But then, Susan suddenly opened up about Vietnam.

Susan cupped her hands around her wineglass. She swirled the liquid and smiled at Bill.

"Everyone had a patient they remembered," she said. "I remembered you because you kept coming through the ER. Each time, I wondered if you'd eventually be killed and I'd never see you again. That happened to so many of my patients. We would patch them up well enough so they could go back to the battle, only to be killed." She paused and reached for his hand. "Needless to say, I'm glad I was wrong about you!"

"Needless to say, I'm glad you were wrong too!" Bill said with a laugh.

Susan smiled and clasped his hand tightly before continuing. "When I first got on the airplane heading to Vietnam and saw that only one or two nurses were on board, it should have been a hint."

She shrugged her shoulders and set her glass down. She placed her other hand on his, leaned in, and drew him toward her.

"We were there to save lives, but there were so many of them and so few of us. When patients started rolling into the ER, I knew some would never make it. All I could do was sit nearby, write letters home for them, and watch them drift away in a morphine haze.

"There never seemed to be time to celebrate a happy moment, to feel that a job was well done. We lived on adrenalin, worked sixteen-to-thirty-six-hour shifts with little or no sleep, and always asked ourselves what *we* could have done to save that patient. We were so short staffed, and many of us were working in areas where we had little or no training."

Bill shifted in his chair so he could reach across the table and pull her hands toward him. He gazed directly into her eyes to ensure her that he understood what she was trying so hard to explain.

Susan's pained expression softened slightly with Bill's unspoken display of comfort.

"The soldiers were so young," she continued, "but they looked so old from the combat fatigue. They were just so . . . so damaged." Susan stopped to clear her throat. "Since the medevacs were so effective in reaching the wounded, we saw things nurses had never seen before in war. We saw badly maimed soldiers who in wars past would have died on the battlefield. Some were so badly crippled that it just tore your heart out, but you had to deal with it.

"We lived in Quonset huts with limited plumbing and couldn't even get basic female hygiene supplies. We had to ask our families to send us sanitary pads for our periods. We stayed together when we were off duty. We held our own little private parties because if we went to the officers' club, every rear echelon officer or doctor tried to get into our pants!

"Fortunately, Ruby, our head nursing officer was able to step in and make some things easier, like getting us PX supplies and protection from the aggressive officers. She had pull with the commanding general, and most of the men around the hospital were scared to death of her."

With that, Susan fell quiet. She sat in her chair, staring down at her wineglass.

Bill patted her hand reassuringly. He had his own experiences of the chaos of war. Now he was getting a true picture of what Susan had endured. He tried to comfort her with the encouragement his support group had provided him.

"But Susan, think of all those you *saved*. My God, you helped save ninety percent of the wounded. You all did a magnificent job! Focusing on the lives saved—not just on those lost—has certainly helped me adjust."

Susan took a deep breath and nodded. When she looked up at him, her eyes brimmed with tears. He knew only too well that she had been deeply scarred by the war.

Bill shifted his chair next to her and moved the wineglass out of the way. He hugged her tenderly, and she put her head on his shoulder. He could hear her sniffles as she fought back the tears from those terrible memories. She moved slightly back from his embrace so she could look into his eyes. She smiled.

"Thank you, William. I'm sorry I've been so distant from you for so long. You're the only person I feel comfortable talking to about these things. Thank you for being so kind. I want to see much more of you in the future."

He looked into her beautiful eyes, moved his lips, and kissed her very softly. They had clearly crossed a threshold in their relationship tonight. His second sight had been right once again.

But Bill couldn't help but also think, *Something must have happened between her and that other man she was seeing.*

Bill was correct. Something had happened between Susan and Zack.

She had thought Zack was different from all the other men, but he wasn't. He had seemed supportive, but he moved away as soon as she told him her secret. It was then plain to Susan that Zack was no better than the rest. All he had wanted was sex.

However, he had hurt her more than the others had. She had actually believed his professions of love—until he suddenly admitted he was engaged in Australia and would be married very soon. He was leaving the country in a few days. At the very least, he had been two-timing her.

She felt terribly foolish and used—but also so thankful that someone like Bill would still be there for her. The more she saw him, the more she appreciated him.

She knew she was fortunate that he still cared to be with her. Since Bill had moved off-base, she noticed he had often been unavailable to get together, perhaps because he was seeing someone else. She had also picked up on his comment about the letter he received from his college girlfriend. He described her in detail, and it was obvious she was a beautiful woman. Susan also remembered the great loss Bill had suffered that day she found him sitting on the bench outside the hospital. She suspected that was due to another beautiful woman—whom he still loved and who still loved him. Susan wondered if that relationship could rematerialize to take Bill away.

Susan was beginning to appreciate how strong Bill's attachments could be with people. No, she had underestimated that he had nothing going on, that there were no other women in his life. With the way she had strung him along, she knew she was awfully fortunate that he still cared for her. She questioned why she had been so gullible to believe Zack's statements of affection while ignoring Bill. She was not a young, stupid, naive girl in love for the first time.

She was determined this would not happen again.

It was time to see where this could go. She wouldn't tell Bill her secret quite yet, but she had a feeling this relationship would be different.

Late one Friday, Bill's mind flooded with thoughts as he pushed the Rocket past the speed limit as he headed to San Antonio. It had been a few weeks since the dinner when Susan had opened up. It seemed they had turned some type of corner in the relationship. There seemed to be no other boyfriend standing between them now.

Bill imagined he and Susan were two magnets. Depending on which poles were facing, they might attract or they might repel. Either reaction was equally strong. It gave them a strange relationship. At times, they seemed to really understand and meet each other's needs, even though they had not truly shared all the shadows from their pasts.

I wonder what love really means, he thought. *What do I know about true love? How does one define it? Hell, I've generally failed in all my relationships with women so far.*

He thought back to his relationship with Barbara. He wondered what she meant in her last letter. Did she now want to get back together?

But then again, he would never forget his relationship with Sara. He would never ever forget her. He knew he would never experience that kind of love again in his life from any other woman—a total, immediate, unselfish, and unrestrained love. It was a wonderful, brilliant gift from a beautiful woman to a war-weary soldier who had nothing and no one.

But there was definitely something more than just friendship with Susan, and she was special in her own right. Their last dinner together confirmed that. They just never seemed to have time or the setting to be together long enough for anything to really take shape.

That night at dinner, Bill told Susan he would be heading to Minneapolis on leave in a couple of weeks.

"Do you think I could come along and keep you company?" Susan asked. "Perhaps you'd like to meet my parents in Wisconsin too?"

Bill was surprised and delighted. "Of course! I'd love for you to join me," he said.

Susan smiled. "Great! I'll put in a leave request for the same period." She held up her glass for a toast.

Now this will either make or break the relationship, Bill thought as their glasses touched.

36.

WHEN BILL'S LEAVE TIME CAME THROUGH, he left the battery in the capable hands of his executive officer. He was excited to pick up Susan and head up to Minneapolis. But first, he had a special trip to make on his own.

Bill was heading to see the parents of RTO William Spiritlight Norman. They lived roughly fifty miles north of Lawton, in the town of Chickasha, Oklahoma. They were grateful that he wanted to make the visit and were eager to meet him.

Driving down the two-lane blacktop to Chickasha, Bill admonished himself for not making the visit earlier.

I've been only fifty miles away. The man saved my life. He's a hero. Yet it took me nearly a year to get around to a visit. Christ, O'Brien—what the hell is the matter with you! You should have come out here as soon as you arrived at Fort Sill.

He hit the steering wheel with the heel of his hand. Suddenly, he started to think this was a bad idea after all. Maybe he should just skip it.

"You already made the call, stupid," he told himself aloud. "They're expecting you. Suck it up!"

The Normans lived on a neatly kept hobby farm. It reminded Bill of his family farm in Minnesota, just a smaller version.

"Captain O'Brien," beamed Mrs. Norman as he stepped out of the car. "We are so proud to meet you."

"Please call me Bill, Mrs. Norman," he responded.

"My name is Bernice, and this is my husband, Ira."

As he shook hands with Ira, Bill felt the surprising strength of his grip. He met Ira's piercing dark eyes and noted the warmth of the gaze peering from the weathered face. Bernice wiped her hands on her apron and motioned Bill into their home.

"Please come and sit. I'll get some lemonade. You do like lemonade, don't you? I could make coffee otherwise."

"No—I mean, yes," Bill stuttered. "Yes, I like lemonade. That will be fine. Thank you." He looked sheepishly in Ira's direction and followed him into the dining room, where they both took chairs at the table.

Bernice came around the corner with glasses and a pitcher on a tray. Ira jumped up to help her serve.

"We're really delighted that you thought enough of William to come visit us," started Bernice.

"He saved my life, Mrs.—um, Bernice," Bill responded. "I can't forget him!"

"We received a Western Union telegram when Willie was killed," explained Ira. "So many men were being killed at that time that they couldn't visit each family in person. That fact, in itself, is overwhelmingly sad."

Ira continued. "We're proud members of the Cherokee tribe. We needed to deal with this loss by our customs. It was very stressful not to be able to prepare William for the Great Spirit immediately after his death."

Bernice concentrated on wiping the condensation on her glass with her finger.

"William was very proud of his family, his traditions, and his ability to serve," said Bill. "Ira, he mentioned you had served with distinction in World War II as a code talker. You kept the Japanese totally confused."

Both Ira and Bernice smiled warmly at Bill's praise.

"Yes," Ira said. "While I served in the war, Bernice worked as a schoolteacher. She taught English and Cherokee history to the children on the reservation."

Bill smiled at the specific reference to "Cherokee history." One would think history is history, right? You can't change the facts. However, Bill had often discussed history with his mother. There are all types of perspective, especially in history lessons. Perspective, not facts, is what caused so many issues between people.

Every time Bill found an article about a historical event, he paid close attention to the facts that were excluded. He knew the victors normally wrote popular history. The Cherokee had not been the victors in wars with the whites. He had never thought about Cherokee history, but he had no doubt it was every bit as real as any other.

Taking a deep breath, Bill knew it was time to tell Bernice and Ira about their son—and his death.

"I didn't know your son real well, but it did seem like a lifetime. We worked together for a few weeks before we were sent on the operation."

Bernice refilled Bill's glass, smiled appreciatively, and retook her seat.

"Your son was an expert radio operator. He could follow orders or call in artillery on his own, if needed. In fact, he was probably more knowledgeable than many of the officers who were forward observers."

Ira nodded, removed his glasses, cleaned them with his napkin, and returned them to his chiseled nose as Bill continued.

"Our job was to direct supporting fire from the local firebase. We supported a unit of American infantry and a local Vietnamese army battalion. We were dropped into an area that wasn't supposed to provide any resistance. It turned out otherwise."

Ira nodded knowingly, perhaps reliving his own demons. Bernice pursed her lips and blinked her eyes rapidly, fighting the inevitable.

"We were greatly outnumbered almost immediately. I had to call in artillery strikes. Our unit held its ground for a while, but the Vietnamese battalion turned and ran when the fighting became overwhelming. One of the shells I called in landed so close that I was knocked unconscious. When I finally came to, I was in the bottom of a foxhole with William spread-eagle in protection over me. He must have pulled me in. He was badly injured by the shell. He was also bayoneted."

Bernice let the tears trickle down her cheeks.

"When I was able to move, I realized the enemy forces had moved on in pursuit of the fleeing Vietnamese army battalion. In a sense, the cowardice of the Vietnamese and the fighting spirit of the small American unit saved us. William was still alive, and I tried to bandage him as best I could. When the medevacs and reinforcements arrived, I made sure he was one of the first to head to the hospital in Pleiku. I rode with him, but he died on the flight to the hospital."

Bill stopped to clear his dry throat. He sipped lemonade to make way for more words.

A single tear had settled on Ira's cheek. It hung on his sharp cheekbone, waiting for enough momentum to continue carving its path.

"I cannot express the depth of my sorrow for his death. He saved my life that day. I also wanted to let you know that I constantly feel his presence. It's very strange, but since his death, I seem to have this second sight, where I either anticipate something happening or understand what was happening much more clearly. To me, your son lives like my guardian angel. He seems to be with me always. I believe his presence has saved my life several times and helped me with many decisions. I hope that gives you some comfort."

Ira brushed the tear away and sat straight and proud in his chair. "Bill, we want to thank you for coming to see us. If our son had to die in the war, I'm glad to know he did so saving lives, including yours. He died as a warrior! That's the highest tribute any tribesman can receive. This will be a story we will retell to his relatives over and over. And Bill, we are glad that his spirit is with you. In many ways, you are very much like our son."

"Yes, Bill, thank you so much," Bernice added, blowing her nose and recovering her composure.

"I hope you've received the Silver Star I recommended for his actions in that battle," Bill said.

"We received the Purple Heart when his body was returned for burial," Ira responded.

"But that's all," Bernice added. "Maybe any other awards are tied up in paper work."

Bill frowned. That "tie-up" was probably thanks to the battery commander, who was in such a hurry to get his promotion to the Pentagon.

"I'll look into it," Bill stated. "I have some friends in high places, and they can make things happen. A medal is a small trade for a man's life, but you deserve it."

With that, he shook hands with the Normans, exchanged good-byes, and headed out to his car.

As much as he had initially dreaded his trip to Chickasha, Bill was buoyed by the experience. Just talking about Norman with his family had given him a release not unlike he felt with his support group. Maybe he was starting to turn that emotional corner.

And General Abrams will make short work of this Silver Star issue, he thought.

He backtracked a few miles to I-35 South, heading for San Antonio to pick up Susan. He had hours to go. He wanted to spend that time and energy thinking about what he would do in Minneapolis.

In addition to the appointment with the lawyers, maybe he'd drive past the old farmstead and visit Rudolph. Then perhaps he'd confront his uncle Sean, depending on what the attorneys had found out.

Bill pushed his James Taylor 8-track into the player and cranked the volume on "Fire and Rain." Thinking of an upcoming confrontation with Sean caused him to seethe. Every nerve said to go for an old Irish knock-down-drag-out brawl. Not very professional, but so satisfying! His brain, though, said he should listen to the attorneys. They were crafting ways to deal with a financial recovery. That would be satisfying too.

As he entered the city limits of San Antonio, he had other things to think about. He was glad he hadn't followed up with Barbara about a visit. While he did hope to see her again someday, this particular timing didn't feel right anymore, now that he and Susan were ready to explore their relationship.

They would have two weeks together. This would be the real test. Either they would grow closer together or further apart.

He popped the 8-track out of the player and pulled up to Susan's apartment with a mix of expectation and dread. He was happy with Susan, but that only made him hesitate. He had suffered his greatest personal losses when he had been the happiest.

Susan came dashing out with a suitcase and a huge smile.

Well, at least things were starting out well.

Bill turned the Rocket north on I-35 just as the sun was starting to set.

"We'll drive until we're tired," he said, "then we can find a place to stay. We'll head out again first thing in the morning."

Susan nodded in agreement.

Just south of Dallas, they found a hotel and ordered two separate but adjoining rooms. There was no sense asking for a single room, only to have a prudish desk clerk give them grief. A McDonald's provided dinner, which they took to go.

"My room will be the dining room," Susan said over her shoulder through the open separator door. "I packed a bottle of Jameson, in case you're interested. You'll have to go out and get the ice, though."

The ice machine was halfway down the hall. It seemed like miles before Bill slipped his key back into his door. He grabbed two tissue-wrapped plastic glasses off the counter in his room and joined Susan at her little table. She had the burgers and fries already laid out. She laughed at the sight of his plastic cups. Instead, she waved two cocktail glasses at him. Bill marveled that she had thought of packing those too.

Dinner was a quiet affair. They both finally agreed that they were eating for sustenance rather than enjoyment. Fast food was never Susan's favorite, no matter where it was from. When they were done, they gathered up the wrappers and filled the small wastebasket.

Bill picked up his glass and the bottle of Jameson and invited her to "the bedroom," as he called his room. As he turned to follow her, he noticed that the bed in her room was slightly mussed, as if it had been slept in.

So that's her plan: she'll make her bed look slept in to keep up the ruse of us sleeping in separate rooms. He grinned as he followed the "proper" Wisconsin farm girl into his room. *That woman thinks of everything.*

Bill's bed was a typical, well-used king-size mattress with defined hollows on both sides. They both fought their way to the high ground in the center. Bill reached out and pulled Susan to him, gently kissing her first on the cheek and then on the lips. He stroked her hair gently and tenderly. She wrapped her arms around him and pulled him to her with great passion. They were engulfed in the feeling of unity. It was the first time they had been intimate with each other.

The Jameson was forgotten, and the ice quietly melted away.

Afterward, they both slept more deeply than they had in months. Neither had nightmares of the horrors of Vietnam. No fears visited either of them that night. The warmth of their intimacy was like a blanket that held back the demons from their minds.

As they were packing up the next morning, Susan said, "Why don't we drive straight through tonight? We can take shifts. I can call ahead from here and get us a room in Minneapolis."

"You just want a chance to drive the Rocket," Bill joked.

"You got that right, buster," she replied.

"All right," Bill agreed. "Let's make reservations at the Thunderbird Motel, near the Minneapolis airport. It's kind of centrally located and has interesting ambiance."

Susan raised her eyebrows at "interesting ambiance," then called directory assistance, connected to the requested motel, and made the reservation for two nights.

Bill pulled his suitcase to the door and turned around, expecting to hold the door for Susan. "Let's grab breakfast and head out."

"Slow down, big boy," she said with a laugh. "Remember me, the 'girl next door'? We better shut and lock that adjoining door. Plus, I need to get my key and suitcase and remove the security chain from inside my door."

"Oh, we are being very proper today, aren't we?" Bill responded with an evil grin.

When she came out of her room, she hit him quite hard on his bad arm.

"Ouch, that hurt!" he grunted. "Are you trying to injure my driving arm? I'll need a nurse if this continues."

Susan smiled back and just waved at him to get moving. "First one to the car gets to drive!"

Bill had seen her racing around in her little car, a pastel-yellow Saab 99E Coupe he called the Pumpkin. It was better to just shut up and get moving.

They rolled into the Thunderbird a little after midnight. They had driven fifteen hours straight, stopping only to eat and change drivers. The conversation had been easy, but they stuck to fairly light topics. Still, they had enjoyed each other's company, and that was more than enough.

The hotel lobby held a marvelous collection of Native American artifacts from the Midwest. Susan noticed a few hokey, plastic tomahawks and Indian dolls in the gift shop, but the arrowheads and beadwork displays were authentic. They fascinated her.

She had once again reserved two rooms. *Things haven't changed much*, Bill thought, but he was grateful for the reservations. They were exhausted.

Bill crawled into bed first and dropped off to sleep. Susan undressed quickly. She kissed her snoring companion on his forehead and brushed his hair gently. His breathing only skipped a single beat.

She laughed quietly. *If the boys at the base knew you could go to sleep in sixty seconds while a beautiful, sexy woman was undressing in front of you, you would never live it down.*

She slipped under the sheet and cuddled up close to Bill. She just enjoyed the warmth of his body next to her.

She had been in many relationships over the years, but she was drawn to Bill now. He had shown such strength and tenderness when they made love the night before. It was way beyond what she experienced with those men who just craved sex. Bill was the strongest and sincerest lover she had ever been with.

She thought back to the woman who had broken his heart at Fort Sam that day. She wondered why she had left this man.

Susan was even more afraid now to tell him her secret. If he left her, it would be many times more painful than any other loss, including Zack. Yet she couldn't tell Bill why she had left him hanging for so long. How could she tell Bill she had pushed him aside because she had been so stupid to believe Zack? She had treated Bill with so little respect and consideration by not telling him up front about her concerns. Why wouldn't he think she would treat him that way again?

Despite her concerns, she too dropped off to sleep.

37.

AT BREAKFAST THE FOLLOWING MORNING, Bill asked Susan if she was sure she wanted to stay with him all day as he met with the lawyers, took a spin past the old farmstead, and visited Rudolph. Susan took a sip of her orange juice, then set the glass down carefully. "If you're comfortable with me accompanying you, I would be honored."

Bill just smiled in response. He was stunned by her reply. He didn't want to talk with his mouth full, but he couldn't quite swallow that bite of omelet around the other lump in his throat.

Bill parked the Rocket in the downtown Minneapolis ramp, as directed by Bradley Wilkerson. They took the elevator to the nineteenth floor of the Foshay Tower, where the law firm was headquartered. Susan admired the African mahogany and Italian marble details in the halls and the elevator. When the door opened, she gazed, mouth agape, at the silver-and-gold-plated ceiling in the hall.

"Susie, this is our floor," Bill said, breaking her reverie. "We can get out here."

A gold-lettered sign saying "Johnson, Abrams, and Wilkerson" was affixed above the reception desk. A neatly groomed woman with a welcoming smile sat perched in front of a typewriter. Behind her was a large window with a bird's-eye view of the Minneapolis skyline.

"Good morning. Welcome to Johnson, Abrams, and Wilkerson. How may I assist you?"

"Wow, that's quite a view!" answered Bill.

"I never get tired of it," the receptionist said. "It changes with the seasons, and I've got the best seat in town. Do you have an appointment?"

"Oh yeah. Bill O'Brien. We're here to see Mr. Bradley Wilkerson."

"I'll let him know you're here. Would you like a cup of coffee or water while you wait?"

Both Bill and Susan declined. They were more interested in gawking at the view. Neither of them even heard the elevator open.

"Good morning, Captain O'Brien," a voice boomed behind them.

Bill spun around and met a tall, lean man in his early thirties with his hand out. Bill clasped the hand and shook it firmly, then he introduced Susan as a "friend and interested party."

Wilkerson led them back to the elevator, where they rode down one level. The law firm also had that entire floor for office space. Wilkerson's office had an expansive window looking out over Minneapolis to the north.

"Wow, I might be able to see the old farmstead from here," Bill declared.

Susan smiled and took the seat Wilkerson held for her.

"We do enjoy the view! Can I get you any coffee or water?" Wilkerson asked.

This time, Susan accepted the offer of water. Bill declined. After sending an aide for the water, Wilkerson sat down, pulled out his Waterman pen, and laid it next to a pad of paper he picked up from the available stack on a side table.

"We've talked on the phone, but I should introduce myself briefly," Wilkerson said. "I worked for ten years as a lawyer for the judge advocate general's office. That's where I met General Abrams." Wilkerson paused and smiled at Bill. "By the way, General Abrams has very high regard for you. He made it abundantly clear that this case is to be done pro bono. Our group owes him a lot, so he knows he can count on us when he needs a favor. We're glad to help you out."

"I appreciate that," responded Bill, returning the knowing smile. He knew the general definitely kept his debts on an even keel. "By the way, the name Abrams is in the firm name—is that partner any relation to the general?"

"Sure is. It's Dean Abrams, the general's son," explained Wilkerson. "Dean is handling a complicated litigation right now, but I'll introduce you to him the first chance I get."

Wilkerson took a breath before continuing.

"So, we've done considerable research into Sean O'Brien and his holdings. We've kept our research totally confidential to this point. I wanted to meet with you before we put anything into action. I requested and received reports from the FAA, the FBI, the IRS, and the Interstate Commerce Commission. Our team met with representatives from all those organizations, and we agreed a confidential joint review was indeed warranted. I also received a copy of the current power of attorney document from General Abrams with the memo you signed indicating you have the original. Is that still in your possession?"

"Yes. I brought it along with me today, in case you need it," Bill said.

"I'll trade you my copy for the original and keep it with all the other official papers on the case. Before you leave, we'll make that transfer official and sign a receipt. We like to keep the paper trail clear."

Bill was feeling very comfortable with this firm.

"First, let's talk about the power of attorney document. As we discussed on the phone, Abrams's document is clearly dated after the one Sean used to adjudicate the estate of your parents, and we have proof that he knew it. Furthermore, when we reviewed the reports filed on your behalf with the courts, the amounts he reported for the sale of the property and the expenditure for your welfare just don't balance."

"I'm not surprised," interjected Bill. "He was very evasive when I asked him how much he got for the sale of the farm."

"Turns out he had good reason to be evasive—we cannot find any real estate sale for your homestead. It doesn't look like he ever truly sold the property. He did get some kind of contract for deed from the person currently living on the premises. But we did a title search last month, and Sean O'Brien is still listed as the legal owner."

"Seriously?" Bill glanced at Susan and frowned. "So what in the world did he do with the property? I know he was still living in his apartment in Saint Paul before I headed to Vietnam."

"He's actually living in a home on Lake Minnetonka now. He paid four hundred fifty thousand for it back in 1968. That's about ten times the average value of homes in the Twin Cities area," Wilkerson reported. "From what we can see, he agreed to a contract for deed on the farm with an old friend from Detroit. He gets next to nothing on that CD. His reported net income on his tax return is only fifteen thousand dollars a year from M. O. Airfreight. Kind of makes you wonder where the cash is coming from to support the mortgage."

Bill bristled at this new knowledge.

"Bill," Susan said calmly, noticing his reaction. "Let the lawyers handle it. I think they can make him squirm even more effectively than you can."

"Sorry. I was just imagining what I would do if he was right here in the room with us," Bill admitted. "But it sounds like the legal recourse will be more effective—and maybe just as painful."

Wilkerson smiled at his client's restraint. "The local IRS is currently auditing his tax returns for the last five years. He's in a world of hurt with them, but he doesn't even know it yet."

It was Bill's turn to smile.

"We also have a good relationship with the local FBI. Their latest report indicates Sean might be involved in some white-collar crime connected with M. O. Airfreight. They've received reports of lost shipments. Some of those shipments were high value and highly suspect, such as drugs, electronics, and medical equipment. The insurance company covering M. O. Airfreight requested a review and now has some insiders also taking a look at the losses.

"Preliminary reports show that Sean may be deliberately allowing the shipments to be hijacked and sold by gangs in Chicago, New York, and Los Angeles, to name a few locations. Word on the street is that Sean gets a kick-back of about thirty percent. Because of the air transport across state lines, the FBI, FAA, and ICC are also getting involved."

Bill sat in stunned silence. Susan reached over and gently caressed his shoulder. Wilkerson noticed the caress, glad that Bill had such a calming force.

"Obviously," Wilkerson said, "we need to keep the knowledge of the real estate dealings and the kickbacks confidential until the joint task force is ready to spring the trap. I think he'll be looking at a jail cell in a fairly short time after that."

"Gee, that's a shame!" exclaimed Bill. "So, what's next?"

"Captain, at this time, we can move forward on Sean's monetary holdings and his position at the business. We would like to file an injunction to set aside your father's will and the power of attorney used by Sean to gain access to the business and farmstead. With the details we have gathered so far, we can see an immediate return of about twenty thousand dollars in cash to you as well as the removal of Sean from any controlling interest or position at M. O. Airfreight. Since it's a privately held company and you are the sole heir, you would be named president and CEO from that date forward. At that point, you may do as you wish with the company."

Bill slumped back in his chair, suddenly taking in the enormity of his new role. He hesitated, then clasped his hands on the tabletop.

"Can I reconsider that glass of water?" Bill asked.

Wilkerson smiled and poured him a glass of water from the nearby pitcher, then continued.

"Our task force thinks Sean may be very eager to comply with you taking over the company, once he sees the other charges coming down the line at him. Because the company is Minnesota based, I would like to get that injunction and transfer done quickly to avoid any delays when the federal agencies file their charges."

"Let's go ahead," Bill agreed. "What do you need from me?"

"Just a signature." Wilkerson pulled out a document and put it on the table in front of Bill. "This gives us the authority to file the injunction on your behalf, to set up a trust fund in your name to hold the recovered funds, and to begin the ownership transfer of the business into your name."

As Bill reached to sign the document, Wilkerson raised his hand.

"A little more explanation before you sign that: you need to think about what you'll do with the company when it becomes yours. It could be a fairly rapid turnover, depending on the court ruling. I know your army tour is coming to an end, but you need to consider how to handle the company in the meantime.

"In addition, I'd like you to fly up here and be available for the court case. I'll let you know when it's on the docket. Generally, you can get personal leave fairly quickly for issues such as this. It'll only be a one-day case.

I think the judge would like to have you present in case there are any questions." Wilkerson smirked and added, "And I assume you'd like to be in the courtroom to see your uncle Sean squirm."

"That's for damn sure!" Bill said, signing his name with a flourish. He traded documents with Wilkerson and put the receipt in his briefcase.

Wilkerson stood and shook hands with Bill and Susan. "Okay. We're done for now. Give my regards to the general when you see him. I know he considers you another one of his sons."

"Thanks for all your hard work," said Bill, shaking the lawyer's hand firmly. Then he laughed. "By the way, if that's how the general sees me, then say hi to my 'brother,' Dean, for me. I look forward to meeting him when I come back for the court appearance."

In the elevator, Bill leaned over and gave Susan a kiss on the cheek.

She turned toward him with a smile. "What was that for?"

"Thanks for coming along. More importantly, thanks for offering your support when I was about ready to blow my cool."

"That's what friends are for," she responded.

"How about a celebratory late lunch at Murray's?" Bill asked. "It's just across the street, and the Silver Butter Knife Steak is to die for."

"So, you *are* going to feed me." Susan chuckled and took his arm.

After a filling lunch and just a single glass of the house merlot, Bill and Susan headed north to the farmstead.

"I won't do anything more than just drive by," Bill assured Susan. "I can't let Uncle Sean know that I'm in town or that I know he didn't sell the farm."

From the dirt road, they could see the white two-story farmhouse was in bad need of paint. One remaining shutter hung from a nail and rocked in the breeze. The barn and hangar had long since lost any sign of the red paint Bill had reapplied every other year.

What used to be the lawn—which Bill had mowed religiously—was now a beaten-down driveway with strips of swaying weeds. And the turf runway looked more like pasture. The wind sock flapped sadly at the south end, showing a northeast wind direction.

The one-acre garden was nearly invisible under weeds. *No loss there, though*, Bill thought as he reminisced about his weeding chores. But then he immediately admonished himself as he thought of the wonderful meals his mother had made with the produce from that garden.

Bill's hands tightened on the steering wheel. "If Wilkerson hadn't told me to keep this confidential and stay away from dear Uncle Sean," exclaimed Bill, "I'm afraid of what I would do to him."

Susan's eyes narrowed as she looked at the ruins of the farm home she knew Bill had loved. She was a farm girl herself. She knew what losing not only the property but also the animals and the way of life had meant to Bill. She was getting a better and better picture of what kind of grief he had suffered for so long, even before Vietnam.

Her heart went out to Bill—but right now, he needed to keep his temper in check. He needed to focus on the company takeover, which would happen soon. What would Bill do when he suddenly became the president and CEO of an airfreight business in Minneapolis? She wondered how this would impact his remaining service days.

Actually, she was also thinking about how it would impact their relationship. She was interested in continuing with Bill. Then again, her secret might destroy it all, regardless of what Bill decided to do with the company.

"Mind if we make one more stop before visiting Rudolph?" Bill asked, interrupting her deliberations.

"Sure. Where are we headed?"

"A place I haven't visited for a while," he responded as he pointed the Rocket south.

Bill stopped at a florist and then drove to Hope Lutheran Church. He parked the car near the cemetery gate and sat in silence. It had been nearly three years since he'd last visited the grave site. He was a bit ashamed that he hadn't made the effort when he'd first returned from Vietnam. There were always excuses.

Susan gazed out at the cemetery and assumed his family was buried here. "Do you mind if I go with you to visit the graves?"

"You're more than welcome, Susan. I could use the support."

Bill picked up the dozen white roses from the back seat. They were his mother's favorite. He held the door open for Susan, and they walked slowly arm in arm. The graves and surrounding area were neat, clean, and shaded by large oak trees. It was a pleasant and peaceful setting.

Bill remembered his plan to bury the family on the farm. Now seeing the serenity of the cemetery, he thought, *This may have been the only thing Uncle Sean did right for the family.*

A single headstone of brown-and-white-flecked marble stood with "O'Brien" deeply chiseled in its face. The names of his father, mother, sister, and brother were listed in a single line across the stone. Their birth dates were carefully detailed below. A single notation at the bottom stated an inclusive "Died June 27, 1962."

Rudolph had helped him select the stone. It seemed to fit perfectly with the serene cemetery setting. Yet it was a stark reminder of the end of such a happy family.

As they stood together over the graves, Bill said a silent prayer. This was one of the few times he had prayed since Vietnam. Bill held Susan's hand as he placed the flowers next to the headstone.

"When I bought these, I also arranged for the florist to put fresh roses on the grave on their birthdays and the day of their death. It's all I can do now to celebrate their lives."

Returning to the car, Bill held the door open. Susan's lips brushed a kiss on his cheek as she slipped onto the white leather seat. She was overwhelmed.

"Bill, I'm just stunned. I'm trying to understand how I would feel if my father, my mother, and my brothers had all been killed and buried together like that. Thank you for letting me come with you. It helps me understand you so much better."

"Thank you for coming. It means so very much to have you with me." He leaned over and kissed her on the lips.

"Where to next?" Susan asked. "You mentioned a Rudolph."

"Yes. He's my mother's cousin. I'd like to see if he's still around. He's the one who took me in and helped me get straightened out after my family's accident. He got me through my senior year in high school and through college. I'm not sure he was thrilled with my decision to join the army, but he still supported me."

"I'd love to meet him. He sounds like a marvelous man."

Bill was nervous as he drove up the driveway of Rudolph's small hobby farm. It was nearly 6:00 p.m., and the sun's light was beginning to fade.

"We haven't talked face-to-face in a couple of years. I hope he remembers me."

"I hope you at least wrote him a letter or two in that time, Bill!" Susan scolded.

"Me too," he answered with a sheepish grin.

Rudolph answered Bill's knock. He looked confused at first as he greeted the nice young couple at his front door. But then suddenly his eyes lit up.

"Oh, my God, William!" Tears glistened in Rudolph's eyes. "You're back in one piece! Come in, come in."

Bill and Susan followed Rudolph into the kitchen. He directed them to chairs around the table.

"Rudolph, this is a friend of mine, Susan Johnson. She's an army nurse down in San Antonio. Susan, this is my mother's cousin, Rudolph."

"Looks like a good friend, indeed." Rudolph winked at her. "How are you holding up, trying to deal with this hotheaded German Irishman?"

Susan laughed and just patted Bill on the back. "It's a challenge some days."

"Have you had dinner? I could rustle up a couple of sandwiches," Rudolph offered.

"Thank you, but we had an appointment downtown, then we stopped for a very late and very large lunch," explained Bill.

"I appreciate the offer, but I think we're stuffed," Susan agreed.

"Well then, how about a toast to friendship and the return of the warrior? I've got a bottle that's just crying to be shared," Rudolph said, but then he glanced at Susan, thinking he may have overstepped his invitation.

"That sounds like a great way to celebrate," she responded.

Bill didn't refuse.

As they clinked scotch glasses over the white laminated table, Rudolph said, "To friends—and relatives who only occasionally write letters."

Bill buried his head on the table under his arm. "I wrote when I could!" he whined.

"You poor baby," Susan said with a laugh, patting his head. "At least you didn't spill your drink when you groveled."

"Fair enough," said Rudolph. "I can't say I was Papa Hemingway myself, but I expected a bit more since you were such an avid writer before."

"Oh, really!" exclaimed Susan. "There's a news flash."

Bill clearly knew he was caught in the middle of this game. He also didn't care. These were the two people he cared for the most in the world. Their joyful bantering was like music to his ears.

Rudolph took another sip and cleared his throat. "William, I'm so glad you came to see me. I've been waiting for this day, hoping you'd come home safely so we could have this conversation. I have something your mother entrusted to me years ago. You were her eldest child, so she wanted you to have this when you were old enough to truly understand its contents. After their deaths and then your military service, I was afraid I'd never have this chance. I've kept it in my bedroom safe since she gave it to me. Give me a minute."

Bill and Susan exchanged puzzled glances as Rudolph disappeared into his bedroom.

Returning to the table, Rudolph set a stack of small books gently on the table, as if they were precious gems. His hand lingered over them. The little books were tied together with a frayed blue ribbon.

"These are a series of journals your mother kept while she was growing up in Germany and probably later when she worked for the OSS," Rudolph explained.

Susan was impressed by the reference to the OSS.

"Your mother kept adding journals as you kids were growing up—she said it was all just family stuff. I haven't read any of it out of respect to you and your family, but she said she wanted them to be part of the family inheritance. She didn't have a safe place to keep them, so she entrusted them to me."

"Huh. So my mother didn't trust Uncle Sean either. She was always a good judge of character," Bill said.

"Well, that's true," replied Rudolph. "I kept these secreted away even while you were living here after the accident. I didn't think you were truly ready at that time." Rudolph met eyes with Bill. "I swore to her I would make sure you got these once you were twenty-one. When you went to Vietnam, I was so afraid I'd never be able to fulfill my promise to her. Thanks for keeping your head down, son."

"He kept his head down, all right." Susan looked at Bill and laughed. "It was just the other parts of his anatomy I had to keep patching up at the hospital."

Bill groaned, but he also felt his eyes starting to water. He took a sip of his whiskey to hide his emotions.

Susan noticed and grabbed her own glass. "Here's to your mother and her great judgment of character," she toasted.

Bill and Rudolph laughed and clinked glasses with her before finishing the warming amber liquid.

Bill glanced at his watch. "Well, it's getting a bit late, and we've had a long day. I think we'll get out of your hair for the night." He paused. "Rudolph, I really appreciate everything you've done for me and my family. I promise to either write or visit again soon."

"I'll let you off the hook if you really follow through on that promise, William. Remember, I've got a witness here." He winked at Susan, and she smiled back warmly.

"I promise!" Bill whined in his best imitation of a two-year-old. He picked up the stack of journals gently.

"And I'll make sure he keeps that promise, Rudolph." Susan poked Bill in the ribs and followed him out to the car, where they locked his mother's precious gift in the Rocket's trunk.

The long day was over, but a romantic evening was just beginning.

38.

BILL WOKE TO LIGHT POURING THROUGH the open window curtain. Susan was already up and dressed. She had opened the door to her adjoining room and was sitting at her table reading the newspaper that had been left outside her door.

"Hey, sleepyhead," she said. "Thought I'd have to go to breakfast alone or maybe pick someone up in the restaurant."

"Damn, what time is it?" he mumbled, pulling the covers over his head to shut out the light.

"It's a little after eight," she responded.

"Eight a.m.?"

"Yup. That's zero eight hundred hours to you, Captain! There's an eight p.m. too. I'll introduce you later today."

Bill tossed off the covers and groaned as he rolled out of bed, making an attempt to straighten his hair and feel his beard.

"You'll need more than your paws to get that under control, Captain. How unmilitary," Susan said with a laugh. "I'm packed up. I'll take my suitcase and head down to the restaurant with the paper. Meet you there when you're ready."

"Unmilitary, my ass," was all he could muster. "Boy, that tour yesterday really did me in. Not to mention last night!"

Susan turned and gave him a playful smirk. "Poor baby. You're out of shape, dear." She laughed as she closed the adjoining door. Then he heard her room door close and her footsteps receding down the hallway.

Bill jumped up and headed to the bathroom. Today was Susan's part of their trip. After breakfast, they were heading to visit her family in Wisconsin for a couple of days.

As they drove down the new eastbound Interstate 94, their travel conversation took a decidedly more comfortable turn.

"Rudolph is really a good man," Susan said. "It sounds like he has a bit of an accent. Where is he from originally?"

"Rudolph was born and raised in Germany, as was my mother. He went through a lot in order to escape and come to the United States. He had an older brother here in Minnesota, who helped him get a new start. His brother died when I was really young. I never got to meet him. Rudolph's wife passed away about three years before the plane crash. I remember my mother visited him on many occasions after she dropped off us kids at school."

Bill paused for a second as memories flooded back.

"Rudolph took me in when my family was killed. I stayed with him while I finished school. He really became a father figure to me. He has a daughter, actually. I never met her until my high school graduation. She's three years older than me, so she was already off to college when I moved in with Rudolph. While I was in college, she and I crossed paths only a couple of times. On the Christmas holidays, I usually went on ski trips with my friends rather than go back home. So she and I seldom connected. I'm sorry for that, though. I hope to rekindle that little family connection when the dust settles with this legal battle."

"Is she still in the Twin Cities area?"

"Rudolph said she came back to the University of Minnesota to get a master's in business and transportation. The last I heard, she was working for Midwest Airfreight, handling their international freight. I always thought that was an interesting juxtaposition with my dad's business."

"What's her name?"

"Jessica," he responded. "She might be married by now, so I don't even know her last name." He felt guilty for not asking Rudolph about her when he had the chance.

"Anyway, tell me about your family." Bill had been in the spotlight long enough. "You've seen the kettle of fish I have for relatives."

Susan scrunched her nose and looked sideways at him. "My family is both loving and difficult. Maybe that's normal. I don't know." She sighed and looked out the window. "Take the Eau Claire exit up ahead," she said, pointing to the sign. "I'm the only daughter, and my mother is always on my case. I have four brothers, which is why I grew up as kind of a tomboy and got a lot of early nursing practice bandaging cuts and scrapes."

Bill grinned and looked at her. *Never thought of her as a tomboy*, he mused.

"My dad is great. He works hard on the farm with my two younger brothers. My two older brothers also have property nearby but probably won't be at my parents' place right now. Dad keeps everyone in line. The thing you need to know about my family is that they . . . well . . ." she hesitated, searching for the right words. "They ask some pretty pointed questions sometimes. They don't put a lot of thought into it, and they don't think about the impact. It can be very embarrassing. Sometimes I think they do it on purpose because I'm the girl. Other times, I just don't know where they're coming from."

Bill took the Eau Claire exit as directed, then looked out the left side window to cover his sly grin.

This should be interesting, he said to himself.

The Johnsons lived on a classic Wisconsin dairy farm. The white two-story farmhouse glistened as the centerpiece just to the left of a hayfield that went on as far as Bill could see. Across from the house was the barn and two machine sheds. One door was open, and Bill could see a man working on a tractor inside.

The pastures were neatly outlined with white fences. Bill could see the 150 head of milk cows dotting the landscape.

Bill parked the Rocket in the early-afternoon light, put up the convertible top, and followed Susan up the steps to the wraparound porch.

"We're here!" Susan announced, using her head nurse command voice.

A sprite of a woman came to the door, wiping her strong hands on a gingham apron tied tightly around her tiny waist.

"My dear Susie! I've been waiting all day. Where have you been? You look so thin. You're never going to get a man fading away like that."

"Oh, Mother, really," Susan said to cut her off.

She leaned down to give her mother a kiss on the cheek. Susan's smile looked strangely coy as she walked through the open door, leaving Bill to follow her past the Lilliputian tornado, who was now giving him the twice-over.

"Well, young man. We've heard a lot about you," she started. "You aren't married, are you? Susie is quite a catch, you know. Do you have a big family? Susie comes from a big family, if you count all the uncles and aunts and nieces and nephews." She stopped briefly for a breath. "You're a tall drink of water. You look like you need some more to eat too. Are you going to ask Susie to marry you?"

Bill cocked his head and smiled. *So, the game is afoot,* he thought.

"Maybe you should ask *Susie*," he replied in a singsong voice. "We haven't really had that conversation."

Susan groaned. "Don't call me Susie," she muttered, barely audible under her breath. She spun on her heels and came back to grab Bill by the arm and glare at him.

"Mom, this is Bill. He's a very good friend. We met in Vietnam. He's from Minneapolis and was kind enough to give me a ride. Bill, this is my mom, Julie, but you can call her Jewel."

With that, Susan rolled her eyes at Bill and this time mouthed *Don't call me Susie!*. She dragged him into the house to meet the tornado's family.

"Dad, I want you to meet a friend of mine from Minneapolis. Captain Bill O'Brien, this is my dad, Sam Johnson."

Bill reached out to shake the well-worn hand. The farmer had a tough but warm grasp, and his eyes held the same elfin glimmer Bill loved in Susan. She was definitely "daddy's girl."

A short, burly young man came running into the room. "Lima Bean, I didn't know you were back yet!" He grabbed Susan around the waist and whirled her in the air, setting her down suddenly as he noticed Bill nearby.

"Bill," said Susan, catching her breath, "this is my oldest brother, Steven."

Bill smirked at Susan's brother's excitement to see her. "Glad to meet you, Steven." Bill shook hands with the brother and then grinned at Susan. "Lima Bean, huh?"

"Long story." She shook her head, hoping to end the questions. "Where's Bobby?" she asked, trying to change the subject.

"He's out in the shed working on that cranky tractor," replied Sam. "Steve, why don't you tell him we've got visitors. Dinner is ready, anyways."

They all gathered around the table as soon as Bobby came inside and cleaned up. They bowed their heads obediently as Jewel ordered Sam to say grace. Then with Susan in tow, Jewel started bringing in the food.

It was a typical farm meal reminiscent of Bill's upbringing. First thing in was a large pot roast. Jewel presented Sam with the carving knife.

"Get busy carving before everyone dies of hunger."

Susan helped bring in the remaining dishes for them to pass around. Jewel had prepared fresh coleslaw from her garden cabbage and a fruit salad made from apples, blueberries, and strawberries picked that morning. She had real mashed potatoes and gravy, green beans, and corn on the cob, all products of her lush garden. And, of course, fresh baked bread and glasses of cold fresh milk.

Bill looked up as Susan helped pass out food. He smiled and thought about how much he loved her. Susan saw his smile and turned her head toward him, understanding what he was thinking. Her eyes glowed. It was an electric feeling.

When everyone was busy eating, Jewel picked up the conversation she had left at the front door. "Well, Susie, Bill looks like a fine young man. And he's a war hero to boot. When do you plan to get married?"

"Mom! Bill and I are just good friends. We haven't talked about marriage. Please don't embarrass him."

Bill smiled, sipped his milk, and enjoyed the repartee.

"Darling, you aren't getting any younger. I just don't want you to wait so long you can't have children."

"Mom!" Susan was exasperated.

Jewel shifted in her chair and next locked her gaze on Bill just as he was taking another drink of his milk. "How many children would you like to have, Bill? Two? Three?"

Bill coughed and snorted milk out his nose. "Sorry! I didn't mean to make a mess," he said as he wiped his shirt with his napkin.

Now it was time for Susan to smile.

"My darling Jewel, let the poor boy eat." Sam stepped in to save the day. "This is an excellent roast, as usual. You've really outdone yourself with this meal."

Jewel sat back to bask in the praise and lost her line of questioning.

When they were all bursting at the seams, Jewel called on Susan to help clear plates while she cut and plated slices of apple and blueberry pie. Once coffee was served, she handed Sam the ice cream scoop and a five-gallon tub of homemade ice cream.

"Time for dessert," Jewel announced.

With a brief break in the feast, Susan's youngest brother, Bobby, finally got the courage to address Bill. "Did you kill a lot of gooks in 'Nam?"

Bill slowly put his coffee cup down and looked across the table. Bobby had just graduated from high school and had missed the draft. Bill hoped the young man would be lucky enough to work on the family farm for the rest of his life and never have to do what Bill had to do in Vietnam.

"Well, Bobby, I was responsible for the deaths of many people, including some of my own men. It will always haunt me. I hope and pray you'll never have that on your conscience," he said sincerely.

Susan quickly shoved a piece of blueberry pie in front of Bobby, wincing at his intemperate question. She knew what terrible memories that question brought up for Bill—and herself.

Bobby bit his lip and picked up his fork to chase a blueberry around on the plate.

This could be a long two days, thought Bill.

After dinner, Sam asked Bill to have a drink on the porch. Sam and Jewel had been concerned about Susan's time in Vietnam. She hadn't told them about many of her experiences. But the ones she did talk about made them realize she had seen too much death and destruction to come out emotionally unscathed.

"I'm glad you're helping Lima Bean," Sam said, opening a bottle of Old Milwaukee for Bill. "You two seem good together. I know she's been through a lot, and Jewel and I just want to thank you for all you've done."

"Susan has been a godsend for me as well. I hope we can continue to build a long-term relationship." Bill took a sip of the cold beer. "Of course, if she heard me say that right now, she might just punch me."

Sam laughed. "William, I believe in telling people what I think. I like you a lot. I can already see you're a far better man than the boyfriend Susan brought home when she was in college. That guy, Larry Davis, had her wrapped around his finger. She would do anything for him without question. Frankly, a part of us was glad when she left for Vietnam so she wouldn't do something really stupid with him."

He shook his head as if shaking the man from his memory.

"I hope you two really do move on together. I can tell you have a lot of affection for each other, and you understand the hell the other went through. You can help each other deal with those demons you mentioned at the table. I know my daughter has them as well."

Bill was struck not only by Sam's understanding of the war's impact but also his insight on Susan and her past relationships.

"Say," Bill offered, "would you mind if I looked at that cranky tractor? I'm good with farm equipment, but I haven't had the chance to work with it for many years."

Sam smiled. He ducked inside to retrieve a pair of coveralls for Bill, and then they headed to the barn. Before long, they finally got the tractor running. They came back to the house with grease outlining the smiles on their faces.

"We left the coveralls in the barn, Mother," Sam announced.

Jewel looked up as they walked in the door. "Why did you get the boy all dirty? He's a guest, for heaven's sake. Show him where he can clean up!"

"Yes, Mother," Sam replied. He smirked as he led Bill in to clean up.

The last man Susan brought home wouldn't know what the inside of a tractor looked like, thought Jewel as she hid her smile. *This one's got potential.*

Susan came down the hallway as Bill headed for the bathroom. She just laughed at him.

"You look just like my dad and brothers right now," she said, pointing to the swath of oil across Bill's forehead.

"Susan, that is a very high compliment. You have a wonderful family."

With that, she went over to him, thinking no one was looking, and gave him a warm kiss on the lips.

But Jewel was watching. Beaming, she turned and looked at her husband, who was smiling too.

"Mother, Bill is an amazing young man," Sam said quietly enough for only her to hear. "You spend ten minutes with him, and you have to be impressed by his kindness, humility, and strength. My goodness, I'm glad our daughter is with him. I hope she never lets him get away. What a contrast to that creep Davis."

"Yes, dear, I agree. I have a feeling we'll be seeing a great deal more of William." Jewel tilted her head in thought. "He's a fine match for our beautiful but vulnerable daughter. She needs him, and he needs her. I hope she realizes that before he gets away from her and she winds up with another louse like Davis."

Jewel walked across the room to look out the window. "Any woman with a head on her shoulders would want to be with Bill. He has deep convictions, honor, and warmth. And he's great looking and a business owner to boot!"

Jewel turned to Sam and folded her arms across her chest. "Bill is so open and caring. I hope our Susan can see and appreciate that. She's had her issues. Even the first time she came home from Vietnam, I noticed she was strained. She doesn't show her emotions freely like she used to. Maybe Bill can help her through whatever is bothering her."

The remainder of the visit was less eventful. The next day, Susan wanted to drive into town to visit some friends, maybe eat lunch at the drive-in one of her former classmates owned. Bill was more than happy to drive her any-where. It was a pleasant afternoon.

"Steven is gay," Susan suddenly blurted as they were heading back to the farm. "I think that's why my mom is so vehement about me getting married and having children. For a while, she was afraid I was a lesbian because I wanted a professional career and to be an army nurse. She doesn't see anything wrong with the traditional housewife role. Not that there *is* anything wrong with it for some women, I guess. But it's just not me. Not me, not now."

Bill did not react to the revelation about Steven. People's orientation didn't really matter to him. But he thought Susan was selling her mother short.

"I think your mom loves you very much and just wants the best for you, Susan. You have a great family. I love your dad. We had a really good heart-to-heart." He sighed. "All families are a challenge. I really wish I'd had the chance to build the kind of relationship you have with your family. It was great fun to borrow them for a couple of days. It was a real joy to see the love you all have for one another. Now I can see why you told me so much about them when I first came to Fort Sam. They really are a treasure. And besides, if you want testimony on you not being gay, I'll be glad to offer it to your mother."

Susan looked at Bill with that half-angry squint of hers and smacked him on the arm. Then she laughed. "Billy boy, she is quite aware of that now!"

The next day, the good-byes were warm, loving, and overlapping.

"Don't forget to write."

"Drive careful."

"We'll miss you."

"Nice meeting you, Bill."

And then the one that made Susan roll her eyes: "Take good care of our little girl."

Finally, the Rocket cleared the driveway. Bill couldn't resist one more jab.

"Well, Lima Bean, that didn't go so badly."

Susan spun toward him. She narrowed her eyes and pursed her lips.

"Or would you prefer I called you Susie?" he finished.

With that, Susan smacked him on his sore shoulder.

In twenty-four hours of trading drivers, they arrived back in San Antonio. Bill dropped Susan off at her apartment, kissing her a long good-bye. He then turned the Rocket northeast for Lawton, Oklahoma.

With six hours to himself, he made a mental note to get the journals stored in his safe deposit box first thing in the morning. He recalled the pleasant trip with Susan and wondered how it would affect their up and down relationship.

Susan is such a kind and loving woman. I truly love being with her. Many times, we anticipate what the other is thinking just by a look. We finish the other's sentences as if we're made for a life together. I'm pretty sure she feels the same way about me too.

But even after several intimate nights together, she's still got a wall up for some reason. It seems to be stopping her from moving fully forward with our relationship. It's a wall I want to break down.

Bill knew he had his own wall—the death of his family and then the death of so many in Vietnam. He had lost so much. Even Sara. He feared that getting too close to someone would cause him to lose more. He didn't think he could deal with any more losses.

Yet he was trying to open up, and he hoped Susan could see that. Both she and her family were special.

Bill of course knew Susan had lost so many patients. She was reliving those deaths, just as Bill was working through his own shadows and fears. Maybe that was why she couldn't fully open up.

Perhaps we'll never be able to move on, he thought.

Or perhaps it was something else. He remembered what Sam had said about Susan's old boyfriend and the sway he seemed to have over her. Maybe she had a weakness to such men.

Is she still dating someone else at Fort Sam, unable to break free? he wondered. *Or does someone else still loom large in her emotions—maybe even this Davis?*

Despite the intimacy they had shared on the trip, Bill was reluctant to push that question with her, just as he would never bring up Sara with her.

Some feelings are just so personal that we can't share them, he thought. *I hope she'll tell me what the issue is when she's ready. I respect her too much to try and force that issue.*

Two weeks later, the issue forced itself.

Bill drove down to San Antonio for a visit. He hopped up the steps to Susan's apartment lobby and reached out to press her mailbox button. Just then, the security entrance door opened.

"Hey, aren't you Susan's friend?" A bubbly blond stood in the door.

"Yep, that's me," replied Bill. "I was just going to ring her."

"She's not back from her shift yet. They had a late meeting. Why don't you come on in?" She held the door open with one hand and extended the other to him. "I'm Vicky Benson, Susan's friend."

Bill accepted the offer of the open door and followed Vicky into the common area that contained a television, two plush couches, and two straight-back chairs. Vicky dropped into one of the couches, and Bill pulled up a chair.

Vicky opened up the conversation by saying, "Susan's been telling me that I'd remember you from the MASH hospital in Pleiku, and I do. How are you doing?"

"Oh, I'm healing up just fine. You can't keep an Irishman down for long." They both laughed.

"Susan and I attended nursing school together and then managed to serve together for a while in Pleiku," Vicky chattered on. "I got rotated back first and was really glad when she eventually got out too. I think she wanted to stay on because her fiancé, Larry Davis, had been shot down. It was really tough for her. I don't think she was ready to go home at first."

Oh, shit, Bill thought. He didn't move. He found himself holding his breath as Vicky continued to tell tales.

"I'm sure she's told you that he flew F-4s for the air force. Yeah. He went down two years ago north of the DMZ, in North Vietnam. He's been

335

listed as MIA since then. He was her first love. He proposed to her before he went to 'Nam. It was so romantic! They were going to be married about a year ago. Sure has been tough for her not knowing whether he's even still alive."

Bill nodded as if this were old news, letting her prattle on. But he felt as if he'd been kicked in the gut.

My God—I'm competing with a ghost, he thought. *No, not a ghost. Worse yet, he's an unknown. He could suddenly reappear. Just like Sara's husband.*

Why hasn't she ever told me about this? Obviously, this is why she won't fully commit. I don't see how any long-term relationship could work. Before, she was stringing me along because of that Zack. Now she's still stringing me along, only in a different way.

What would she do if Davis returned? Her father told me Davis had her wrapped around his finger. She did anything he asked. If he came back, would she just leave me, whether I was her boyfriend, fiancé, or husband? Could she be that cold and deceitful to keep such a secret from me?

"Oh, here she is now!" Vicky said.

Bill heard the click of the latch on the security door. He broke from his thoughts and looked up to see Susan's warm smile.

"Sorry I'm late. We had a big meeting I couldn't miss. I tried to call you, but you had already left. I hope Vicky was keeping you entertained."

"Yep. We were just trading war stories."

Bill jumped up to escort Susan upstairs before Vicky could correct him.

"I bet Vicky told you she's ending her service obligation soon," Susan said as they made their way to her apartment. "She's so excited. She'll be moving back home to Chicago."

Bill just nodded as Susan went on to tell him about a great little Mexican place she wanted them to try for dinner. Inside, Bill's mind raced. What he needed was time—time to come up with some gently leading questions that might nudge Susan to reveal this secret herself.

Bill was a bit concerned, though, that Vicky would mention their discussion about Susan's fiancé in the meantime. He was glad to hear Vicky would be moving soon. Hopefully, the two nurses would have other things to discuss.

Susan flitted about her apartment, getting ready for dinner. Bill did his best to smile. Now he knew why she had put up a wall. He was glad he hadn't pushed her on a relationship early. He couldn't help but feel for her and what she'd been through. He wasn't sure what he would do if Barbara or, God forbid, Sara were missing or had been killed.

39.

O N Monday morning, Bill called General Abrams. The general's aide answered the phone and transferred him over.

"William, so good to hear from you again," Abrams said as he came on the line. "Sorry to keep you waiting."

"Good to speak to you again so soon, sir. I wanted to let you know how much I appreciated the connection with Bradley Wilkerson in Minneapolis. He's been very helpful. It sounds like his team has a great plan in place."

"Good to hear, William. I also got a call from my son, Dean. He was sorry he missed you. He's done with his big case and will be helping Bradley a bit on the side for your case. He'll probably be at the court hearing, whenever they are ready for that. Bradley said you'll fly back up for the hearing too."

"Yeah. I agree with him that it would be good to be there in person. I want to look my uncle Sean in the face and prove to him I'm my father's son. We don't run from a fight."

"Glad to hear it."

Bill cleared his throat and shifted the phone to his other hand. He hesitated and struggled for the right words. First, he would address the commendation for his RTO Norman. Then he would address the even-more pressing question about the MIA Davis.

"General, I have a couple of other things I'd perhaps like some advice on."

"Go ahead. I told you I would help you any time I could."

"Well, these issues are more to help some friends, rather than me directly."

"Quit dancing around the issue and ask what you need!" Abrams said kindly but firmly.

Bill sighed and focused on his questions. "Okay. First, I need to know how I can find out what happened to a Silver Star commendation for the RTO who saved my life in 'Nam. I know the paper work was done, and I signed it. It just seems to have gotten lost in some Pentagon shuffle."

"What's the RTO's name?"

"William Spiritlight Norman. He's from the little town of Chickasha, Oklahoma. I stopped to visit his family when I drove home a couple of weeks ago. His folks got his Purple Heart, but they didn't even know he had been recommended for the Silver Star."

Bill could hear a pen scratching as Abrams took notes.

"I'll see what I can do. I'll let you know as soon as I get the paperwork and the medal. Since you have made contact with his family, I assume you'd like to present the medal to them as well."

"Yes, sir. I certainly would like that honor."

"No problem. What's the other favor?"

"I need to find out the status of Lieutenant Larry Davis. He went missing about two years ago, north of the DMZ. He's been listed as MIA. A friend of mine doesn't know whether he's dead or alive, and it's driving her crazy."

"That friend wouldn't be the Lieutenant Susan Johnson you're seeing, would it?"

Bill paused, then admitted, "As a matter of fact, it is. I just thought I'd try to find out what I could for her."

"I'll get my aide on it as soon as possible," the general assured him. "I'll let you know as soon as we have any information on the lieutenant, and I'll also get the Silver Star moving immediately."

Back at Fort Sill, Bill resumed his duties as the commanding officer of Battery A. He had a solid routine in place that provided a smooth and effective level of training for new artillery officers and enlisted men. He also had a good executive officer to fill in when he needed to be away. The men deserved continuity. They needed positive attitudes and clear heads when they faced deployment.

Bill's review of the casualty lists still haunted him, though. Despite the Vietnam-force drawdown the Nixon administration had initiated, men were still dying in a seemingly endless and purposeless war.

The mystery of Larry Davis continued to haunt him as well. Maybe if he could find out Davis's status, he could help Susan break down her wall and get on with her life.

Bill had given Susan ample opportunity with leading questions, but still she kept mum about her secret. He kept telling himself she would tell him when she was ready. But deep down, he wondered how much more emotional capital he could invest, especially now that he had set a plan in motion that could potentially lead to Davis's return, if he were discovered to be alive.

Am I just holding Davis's place until he's back? How could any man agree to that kind of relationship? I love her and want to help her through this if I can. But I can't do this forever.

The legal issues swirling around his uncle Sean were also still up in the air. He worried that even if the courts awarded him the possible $20,000 and ownership of M. O. Airfreight, the IRS might hold those assets to pay the penalties his uncle owed from his tax evasion. Bill might win the war yet come out empty-handed.

Thankfully, one issue on Bill's mind would resolve itself in a few months: his commitment to the army. His three-year active duty obligation would be up. He had already decided he would not re-up. As an officer, his next assignment would then be in the reserve forces. This would be for two more years, but he would only need to physically report once a month to his Army Reserve unit unless he was recalled.

Bill was looking forward to civilian life, yet he knew it would bring its own challenges. He had saved some money, but he would need to find a job. Or perhaps not—perhaps he'd suddenly find himself with an airfreight business to run. So much was still in flux.

Bill was trying hard to recreate himself as well. He was taking steps to reduce his involvement with his old Irish "friend" Jameson. He increased his workouts at the gym, which allowed him to sleep better and have more control over his nightmares and emotional struggles.

Even Susan joined the effort to take part in less-alcoholic pursuits. On dates, they tried to eat at family restaurants that didn't serve alcohol. They started taking walks at the zoo, attending plays, and catching a movie or two, where they could share popcorn instead of a morning hangover. They even tried jogging together—with mixed results.

As they enjoyed a quiet meal at a café near Fort Sam, Bill shared his thoughts about his army obligation coming to a close.

"I'm struggling to decide what I want to do when I leave Fort Sill. There aren't a lot of artillery jobs on the civilian side."

Susan smiled in agreement.

"I've chosen to serve in the Twin Cities Army Reserve unit. I'll be plenty busy back home," Bill admitted. "I'll have months of legal issues to resolve with good old Uncle Sean. And who knows—perhaps I'll have a business to run."

They shared a laugh.

"You're out a month before me," Bill said. "What are your plans?"

"I'll definitely stay in nursing, but not in the active military. I want to do rehab medicine with 'my guys,' the veterans. I've been in contact with the VA hospital in Milwaukee, but I haven't made any commitment yet. I've also put out feelers to a few private hospitals in the area."

"I agree you should stay in nursing—you truly have a gift!" he praised her. "What made you choose Milwaukee?"

Susan glanced down at her plate. When she looked up, she gave a little shrug. "It's not too far from my family."

"Say," Bill suggested, "have you considered applying to be a nurse at the VA in Minneapolis? The Twin Cities are only a little farther than Milwaukee is from your folks' place, so you could still easily see your family on weekends. I'm sure the Minneapolis VA would love to have you. And I'd love it if we were closer, rather than have another long drive to see each other."

Susan put down her fork and reached across the table to take his hand. "Bill, I don't really think that would be wise. I'm still not sure about us . . ."

Bill paused expectantly, thinking this was finally the moment she would reveal her secret about Davis. The missing lieutenant was obviously behind the wall she was putting up now. For all Bill knew, Davis was from Milwaukee, and that was why Susan was planning to move there. He decided to make his final plea and nudge.

"Susan, I want you to know I love you. And because I love you, I don't want to pressure you into a decision you might later regret. You seem to have a reason for going to Milwaukee. Me, I'm going to Minneapolis. But I want to keep you a part of my life, no matter what our relationship entails or where it takes us."

Susan pulled her hand away and straightened in her chair. "Bill, I'm not blind. I know you love me. But I'm sorry. I just don't think living in Minneapolis with you would work right now."

Bill had his answer. He had made his bid, giving her a chance to share her secret and be close to him, but she had accepted neither. It was another failure and loss.

Bill motioned for the check. "Well, I'm very sorry I mentioned this to you. I wish you well. I assume you'll no longer want to see me once you're in Milwaukee."

Susan cocked her head and smiled at him. "Milwaukee and Minneapolis are not that far apart. If you don't make an effort to see me, I'll be really pissed!" She picked up her fork to return to her meal, satisfied that the issue was resolved.

"Susan, you have no idea how far apart those cities seem right now."

Bill forced a smile and returned to his meal, but his appetite was gone. Susan watched him lay his fork and knife down and push his full plate of food away.

She knew she had slammed a door on him tonight. He had made a reasonable proposal to be near her. She had flat out rejected it—and him in the process.

Susan was angry at herself for being so strident. She didn't mean to reject Bill—far from it. She loved him very much. She wanted to be with him more than any man she had ever been with. He didn't deserve to be pushed away like that. Their trip to Minnesota had given her a much better understanding of the intense losses he had faced in life. And now she'd gone and added another.

She sensed he knew something was holding her back, that she had a secret. But he hadn't gotten angry, trying to force her to tell him. And he hadn't up and left her, as all the others had. Instead, he tried to move closer to her, quietly and pleasantly offering her a chance at commitment.

She knew she should tell him her secret, but this wasn't the right moment. If she shared the whole story now, in his present mood, she felt it would surely drive him away.

She hoped she could make it up to him that night, and they could somehow move on as before.

She put her hand on top of his on the table. "Any chance you booked a nice hotel room instead of the visiting officers' barracks tonight?"

Bill considered suggesting they not even bother, but instead he nodded and forced another smile.

"I did get a hotel room. I was anticipating a nice evening together."

The night at the Alamo Hilton was pleasant but uninspired. What did it prove? Bill was sure he had lost the fight to a ghost. She would go off to Milwaukee, waiting for her fiancé to maybe someday return so she could carry on with him. Bill would be just a pleasant sidebar memory for her.

He could only think what her parents would say if they knew she and Davis had gotten engaged and that she was now putting her life on hold to wait for his possible return. If they knew the truth, they maybe wouldn't welcome her home ever again. Bill hoped Davis was worth it. But then again, Bill decided he didn't care. That was up to Susan to decide. Either way, he was the loser again.

Bill had another dreary drive back to Fort Sill the next day.

40.

ILL FINALLY GOT SOME GOOD NEWS from Bradley Wilkerson. The preliminary ruling from the IRS conceded that M. O. Airfreight and the challenged $20,000 should be excluded from any federal recovery against Sean O'Brien. Both assets were in Sean's possession only due to the fraudulent use of power of attorney and should be returned to the rightful heir.

"It's not a final decision," Wilkerson warned Bill over the phone. "But if you take controlling interests before the IRS files liens against Sean's property, they will likely be exempted."

Bill sat back and smiled at this good news. For the first time, in a long time, something was finally looking encouraging.

"I would estimate a two-month window for the court case," continued Wilkerson. "The only extension would be if Sean were able to appeal. Our legal team is still digging for additional leverage. We'll keep you advised."

Before the end of the week, Bill also received good news from General Abrams. The general called to inform Bill that he had the Silver Star for Specialist William Spiritlight Norman.

First things first, thought Bill. He called the Normans and arranged to present the medal on Saturday. They wanted time to gather friends, family, and tribal members to celebrate their son and hear the story of his service once again. Bill was more than happy to oblige.

Bill stopped at the general's office late Friday. The general's aide handed Bill the medal and documentation.

"The general asked that you stop in to see him briefly, if you have time," the aide added.

"If *I* have time? I can make time for him!" Bill said with a laugh. He followed the aide to the general's office.

"I'm so glad you could drop in, Bill," the general greeted him. "I received a communication from the MIA personnel office. They have verified that Lieutenant Larry Davis is a prisoner of war in North Vietnam. Intelligence indicates he's still alive, but we don't know his condition. The air force said they notified the immediate family of his status when he was first reported missing. They wanted to know if someone else needs official notification now."

Bill glanced out the window. *Damn it,* he thought.

His last encounter with Susan hadn't ended well, and it looked as though they might be finished as a couple. Now this—her fiancé was alive.

This will really end our relationship. But Susan deserves to know about Larry. I love her too much to keep this from her.

"Yes, sir, there is. Lieutenant Susan Johnson was his fiancée. They planned to marry after their tours. They hadn't even told their families."

Abrams raised his eyebrows and looked carefully at Bill. The general had spent his career reading people—and Bill was an open book. He wanted to tell Bill how sorry he was. It broke his heart that this young man had to bear yet another disappointment. Instead, Abrams made him an offer.

"Seeing as this is a fairly sensitive issue, I could tell Lieutenant Johnson this news myself, if that is all right with you, Bill."

Bill shifted in his chair and looked at the floor. Finally looking up, he said, "Yes, sir. It would be good coming from someone at your level. I think this news that he's alive will come as a welcome shock to her—but learning he's being held captive will be difficult to hear. Regardless, she needs to be advised so she can make some decisions about her life." Bill paused and sighed. "I doubt she'll want to continue our relationship after this. She'll want to wait for Davis, if he should someday return. But I thank you for finding this information for her. You can tell her I wish her the best."

"All right," Abrams said with a nod. "You give my condolences to the Norman family, and I'll handle this issue with Lieutenant Johnson's notification."

Bill left the office with Norman's Silver Star in hand. He was thankful that he and Susan were each busy that weekend. That meant he wouldn't see her before she had a chance to meet with Abrams—he wouldn't have to hide his knowledge. Actually, Bill doubted he'd ever see her again. She was about to learn her fiancé was alive.

I hope this news helps her recover from her demons from the war, and I hope she and Davis can eventually move on together and be happy. She deserves that.

Bill was proud to present the medal at a tribal ceremony in a small arena near the Normans' home. The Normans and the elders of the tribe were dressed in brilliantly colored ceremonial regalia. Bill stepped forward in his full dress uniform. He retold the story of his RTO's final hours and heroism, then opened the box containing the Silver Star. He presented it to Ira. Bill then saluted the Normans, stepped back, and bowed his head in respect.

Ira reached out to shake Bill's hand. "Thank you for being there for our son and being here to celebrate his heroism. As you said, Bill, this is a small thing to trade for my son's life." Ira glanced down at the medal. "But he was a warrior, and we are grateful to receive it in his honor."

Back at home Saturday evening, Bill decided to refocus by applying for jobs in Minneapolis. He pulled out a list of companies he had earmarked. He figured he would go for a management position. Typing was not his forte, but he worked well into the night and had a healthy stack of letters ready for posting in the morning.

Sunday was a day for cleaning his quarters and checking his finances. He had about $9,000 in the bank. If he were careful in how he spent it, he could stretch it for a year. If the $20,000 ever materialized from the legal proceedings, then he'd be more comfortable financially. Still, even with the extra $20,000, Bill knew he'd go crazy without a job. He'd need something to fight the boredom once he moved to Minneapolis.

I may even need to follow up with Barbara after all to at least have some companionship when I get back to town, he thought.

On Monday morning, he woke early and called the two employment agencies he had been working with in Minneapolis. They each kept up the encouraging banter, but neither had any solid leads for him.

Next, he mailed his letters then stopped at his safe deposit box at Lawton National Bank to pick up his mother's journals. He planned to go through the journals now that his active duty was ending.

He was concerned that the journals were nothing more than the ramblings of a young girl so many years ago. If so, that wouldn't really interest him. However, his gut told him maybe they wouldn't be "ramblings" at all. Maybe his mother wrote these journals as an adult and with purpose. His mother had rarely done anything without a reason.

On Tuesday, Susan received a registered letter from the air force requesting she meet with General Abrams for information regarding her fiancé, Lieutenant Lawrence Davis.

She obviously knew of Bill's relationship with the general and how he had helped Bill start the legal proceedings in Minneapolis. But she had no idea about the general's relationship with her fiancé.

Susan arranged for a meeting on Thursday morning. General Abrams sent a car for her transportation. That gave her a little more time to calm her nerves and think through what this meeting might reveal.

The general's aide showed her into the expansive office, directed her to a chair, then left, closing the door behind him.

"Lieutenant Johnson," greeted Abrams, returning her smart salute. "It's great to meet you face-to-face. William has had nothing but good things to say about you. I was happy to help him cut through the red tape and get you the information you deserved about Lieutenant Davis."

Susan sat on the edge of her chair, confused. Was the general saying Bill knew about her fiancé?

Abrams noticed her stiff posture and continued in a fatherly fashion. "We have confirmation that Lieutenant Larry Davis is a prisoner of war in North Vietnam. We believe he is alive, but we don't know his condition. The air force didn't have record of your engagement to Lieutenant Davis," Abrams continued. "So when they advised the family of his status, they missed including you. I cannot even imagine the stress this has put on you. For that, I humbly apologize."

Susan blinked in response. She was still trying to reconcile what she was hearing. She had spent so much time assuming Larry was dead. This news that he was alive as a prisoner of war was overwhelming.

But what impact would this have on her relationship with Bill? She had intentionally kept this secret from Bill. She never told him about Larry because she was afraid he would back away—as did all the others who eventually learned her secret. No one wanted to compete with a ghost.

She'd been waiting for an appropriate time to tell Bill the truth without ruining their relationship. Somehow, though, he had found out on his own. Not only did he find out, but he had also gone out of his way to have Abrams investigate and let her know her fiancé was still alive.

Now Susan was worried. She suddenly realized she hadn't heard from Bill in several days. He was backing away, giving her the out he believed she wanted and needed. Bill no doubt assumed she would want to wait now for Larry, planning for a day when he would hopefully be released. And why wouldn't he think such a thing? She had just turned down Bill's offer to move to Minneapolis, saying she instead wanted to be in Milwaukee.

Susan gave a small smile. "General Abrams, Bill and I are very close friends, but I constantly underestimate him. He has been a godsend for me, helping me in ways he could never fathom, since my fiancé disappeared. I love him for that. But honestly, I didn't even know he was aware of Larry."

Abrams nodded and thought carefully about the minefield he was about to enter.

"William is like a son to me," he began. "I knew his father very well— William is just like him. Over the past years, William has dealt with losses that would cripple most people. Yet he has not only overcome his grief—he has used it to excel and succeed at everything thrown his way. I can assure you that he would do just about anything for you. I can see he loves you a great deal. I know you can trust him to help you deal with this difficult situation."

"I know that, sir," Susan said, nodding. "But now it's even more complicated. I didn't want Larry's uncertain status to hurt Bill, so I kept this secret. I kept pushing Bill away. And now this—now I know Larry is alive."

Susan swallowed, trying to find the courage to ask the question pressing on her mind. She had heard stories about POWs. Some had been in captivity for five years—and counting, as no one knew when this would all come to an end. Many had been tortured. Some had died.

Finally, she found the strength to speak, though quietly. "What are the chances of me ever seeing Larry again?"

Abrams bowed his head in thought. He knew much about how men in Larry's position were being treated. At this point, he truly had no information that would ease Susan's mind. He chose his words carefully.

"I don't know if, or when, Larry will be released. We can only pray to God that he will be." He stopped and cleared his throat, then met Susan's teary gaze. "Keep in mind, William is a strong man and is trying to support you. He's willing to help you deal with this by giving you time to understand the truth and determine what is right for you. He just wants you to be honest with him."

Susan nodded and clasped her hands in her lap. She needed to open up to someone, and the fatherly General Abrams seemed to be accepting.

"Can I tell you about Larry?"

"Please. I would be honored." The general sat back in his chair and crossed his arms on his burly chest.

"We were classmates in college. We met at a dance. I was a junior; he was a senior in the air force ROTC. He was my first true love. We corresponded while he trained as a pilot in the air force. I attended his graduation in San Antonio. That night, he asked me to marry him. I said yes immediately.

"He was my dream man—I thought he was so handsome, kind, and considerate. He wanted us to marry before he headed to Vietnam. I wanted to finish my nursing training and military obligation. We agreed to marry when we both returned from our tours. That was where we left it." She pulled a gold chain from around her neck, revealing a ring dangling at the end. "He gave me this ring, which I wore until I went to Vietnam. I couldn't wear it on duty, of course, so I put it on this chain to honor him."

Abrams smiled warmly, encouraging her to continue.

"I graduated from nursing school, signed up for the army nurse corps, and was sent to the hospital in Pleiku almost immediately." Susan then stopped and searched for the right words. "I thought Larry and I would maybe reconnect, now that we were finally in the same country again. I guess I was naive. He was shot down only two weeks after I arrived. One of his squadron members knew about us and came to tell me. He was Larry's wingman. He saw Larry's plane get hit, but he didn't know if Larry had ejected before it crashed. It was the hardest day of my life. My tour was almost unbearable."

Susan stared out the window, gathering her emotions. "Since that time, I've been living two lives. I've wanted to move forward with my life, but I've wanted to be faithful to Larry as well. Bill has helped me with all this, but I never even realized he knew what I was going through. I love him. I was seriously thinking of making a deeper commitment to our relationship. But with this information about Larry, I'm afraid he's left me now. He assumes I'll want to wait for Larry."

Abrams leaned forward. "Susan, you need to say these things to William." He paused to see her response. When she nodded slowly, he continued. "I think you care enough about William and your relationship that you can work this out together. Remember, he was the one who came to me with the request to investigate your fiancé's status so you could be notified. It was very hard for William to hear this news about Larry. He obviously loves you very much. He loves you so much he is willing to lose you for something you value. He is a brave and honorable man. You need to talk to him now and trust him. You may not decide to stay together as a couple, but you will have a most remarkable friendship for the rest of your life. I guarantee that."

Susan looked down at her hands clasped tightly in her lap. She had promised herself she wouldn't break down, but tears welled up in her eyes. It was simple advice. It was wise advice.

"Sir, you should have been a priest."

The general's hearty laugh broke the tension. "My God, no! The troops are likely to think I have more in common with that other fellow—the one guarding the lower realms."

Susan wiped a tear away and laughed at his bold self-assessment. General Abrams was more like a father than a military mastermind. She and Bill were very lucky to have been graced by his guidance.

The general was right. She had to talk to Bill. She would tell him everything and let the chips fall where they may.

41.

BILL WAS SURPRISED WHEN SUSAN CALLED HIM early Friday morning. He didn't think he'd ever hear from her again.

"I'm turning the tables and coming up to see you for a change," she said. "You've been putting enough miles on the Rocket. It's my turn to make the drive."

"Susan, I really don't want you driving that far by yourself. I know your little Pumpkin is new, but you shouldn't put all those miles on it."

"Really?" Susan wasn't used to men treating her in a condescending manner. "Remember who you're talking to, William," she reprimanded him. "Nurse's orders."

"Sorry—never mind," he apologized, catching the tone in her voice. "I'll get a nice hotel room and make some dinner reservations. Just drive careful! I love you," he added.

"Love you too."

As he replaced the receiver, Bill wondered if General Abrams had talked to Susan yet. If so, this visit would be an official farewell. *She probably wants to drive up here so she can leave as soon as she's done*, he thought grimly. *If she's angry, then she's angry. I took a chance, going behind her back like this to ask about Davis.*

Then again, she was very warm to him on the phone. That seemed strange, considering. Perhaps it would be a pleasant good-bye, but a good-bye nonetheless. *Whatever happens, happens*, he thought. *Besides, it will be wonderful to see her again, one last time.*

Susan backed the Pumpkin out of the parking lot, then shifted into first gear. She loved the control of the manual transmission and the nimble handling of her first new car. "It's a chick car," Bill had kidded her, but he secretly liked it as much as the Rocket.

Susan pushed in her Joni Mitchell 8-track and headed north. "Big Yellow Taxi" appropriately boomed from the speakers and set her in the right frame of mind for the six-hour drive. She had plenty of time to think through what the general had told her.

She didn't want to lose Bill. But in all fairness, she had to be sure she was ready to let Larry go.

I'm so glad Larry is still alive, she admitted. She'd seen too many eighteen- and nineteen-year-olds die in the last few years, with all the promises of their lives unfulfilled. Some of them had girlfriends back home who were still waiting, not knowing.

Larry's being alive was good news, yet even Abrams couldn't guarantee she would ever see him again. She couldn't fathom what Larry and the other POWs were going through. They too might have girlfriends and other loved ones back home waiting. The POWs needed to know people still loved them. They needed to know someone still cared. They were going through hell.

But Bill and I have been through our own hells, Susan reminded herself. *Bill especially.*

Bill had lost every loved one in his life—every one! He struggled with terrible loneliness. He struggled too with the killing he had witnessed and committed in Vietnam.

Yet despite all that, he put her needs before his own by inquiring about her loved one's status. It took special courage for Bill to risk losing someone he loved. Larry never would have done that. No one she'd ever known would have done that.

As the landscape rushed by her window, Susan contemplated her options. *What will I do when—if—Larry is released? Do I want to go back to him?*

Susan had changed so much since their engagement. She was no longer the wide-eyed young girl who'd been swept off her feet by a Prince Charming in uniform. She was a very different person now. She could only imagine Larry was too. People simply grow apart with time and different life experiences—particularly when those experiences are so traumatic.

As she looked back, she saw her relationship with Larry in a new light. Certain things had seemed so wonderful about Larry then, but she didn't like them now. Her values had changed. She had a much greater appreciation for honor, integrity, courage, and compassion.

Larry didn't have those values. In fact, her parents had always been critical of him, but she hadn't listened. But Bill did have those values, and Susan knew her parents saw this in him as well.

Susan was indeed a different person than the college coed who'd gushed yes at an officer's proposal. She had experienced death on its own ugly terms. She had learned that life was precious, unpredictable, and often short. You couldn't live in the past—that only caused you to miss opportunities in the present and the future. There was not enough love in the world—or in anyone's life, for that matter—to waste any opportunity for it.

Several mile markers later, Susan made her decision.

She popped in the *Clouds* 8-track and declared aloud, "I do love you, Bill—you sneaky, kind, loving bastard! I need to tell you everything so we can move forward. If Larry is released, we'll deal with it together."

She felt empowered as "Both Sides, Now" soothed her mood. She knew she'd been given an almost unbelievable gift from a man who had suffered so much in his short lifetime. She would do her best now to never hurt him again.

Carpe diem, she told herself. *Seize the day.* She smiled in anticipation. She would seize more than that on this visit.

But first, she'd have some fun making Bill sweat a little.

Susan rolled up to the guard gate at Fort Sill. She saluted, showed her credentials, and was directed to park in the Battery A visitors' lot.

"Go through the front door to the ready room, Lieutenant. Captain O'Brien will meet you there."

They exchanged salutes again, and she headed for the parking lot.

When she walked into the ready room, the enlisted company clerk jumped to his feet and saluted. She was a first lieutenant now. As a woman, she was always amused at the intensity of the gaze behind the salutes.

"At ease, Corporal," she saluted in response.

Bill had seen her pilot the Pumpkin through the gate. He came out of his office, ready to head for dinner. She snapped to a quick salute, and he returned it, inwardly smiling.

As they walked out of the battery headquarters, he said, "I got you a room at the Lawton Hilton. Do you want to ride with me?"

"No, I know where it is, Captain. I'll meet you there."

Susan smiled and climbed back into the Pumpkin. She headed out the gate, leaving Bill standing in the visitors' lot looking confused.

When Bill got to the hotel, Susan had already checked in.

"She said to send you up," the clerk responded. "She's in room 803."

Bill thanked the clerk and took the elevator up to the room. Before he knocked on the door, Susan opened it and struck a Scarlett O'Hara pose.

"Captain, dear Captain. Whatever can I do for you?"

Her Southern accent was corny, but he liked the question and went in.

Susan followed her initial greeting by using the Vietnamese vernacular and a phrase men commonly heard in Vietnam: "You number one GI."

Maybe this will be a nice weekend, Bill thought. *At least she didn't punch me at the door.* He wandered to the window and pulled back the curtain to take in the view from the eighth floor.

Susan cleared her throat. "Bill, I had a chance to visit with General Abrams last week."

Bill spun away from the curtain, catching it around his arm. He shook himself loose with a surprised look.

"Oh, General Abrams? How is the general?"

"He was just fine." She raised her eyebrows and linked her arms across her chest. "He had some information for me—that you requested."

Bill immediately clenched his hands in front of him and studied the burn mark on the nearby table. "What did the general have to tell you?"

"I think you know," she replied.

Susan tried hard to keep a straight face as she watched her victim squirm. She could tell Bill was dangling on the edge. Finally, she let him off the hook.

"Bill, I'm sorry. I should have told you about Larry long ago."

She walked across the room, wrapped her arms around his neck, and gave him a long and welcomed kiss. Stepping back, she asked, "How did you find out about Larry?"

Bill was pretty sure this was a good time to be vague and protect his source. "I overheard something about him a while ago. I didn't want to bring it up unless you did. I understand how long it takes to deal with such a loss."

Bill knew Susan would assume this was a reference to the loss of his family. Actually, though, he meant the loss of Sara. Bill would never recover from that. That was his secret, one he couldn't disclose to Susan now and hopefully would never have to.

Susan kissed him lightly on the cheek. "I really appreciate your patience. You've been unbelievably kind and understanding. More than anyone I've ever met. You were willing to do the greatest thing anyone can do for a loved one—let them go."

Bill put his hands around Susan's waist and pulled her toward him. "I love you, Susan. I want to spend the rest of my life with you, if you'll let me. I'll do whatever I need to do to make that happen. But I don't expect you to make a commitment to me unless you are ready. I assume you may want to wait for Larry, so maybe someday he'll be released and you can go on with him."

Susan looked at Bill sternly, still trying to keep him off guard. Then she broke into a smile. "No, Bill. I am ready and willing right now. I don't want to wait on this. You are too special, and I love you. Whatever happens in the future with Larry, we will deal with it together as a married couple."

"Are you proposing to me?" Bill asked with a smile.

"Only if you're accepting my offer," she responded.

They sealed their engagement with another long kiss.

"What time are the dinner reservations?" Susan asked when she came up for air.

Bill checked his watch. "Right now, actually."

"Well, I'm starving after driving all the way up here. You promised me dinner!"

"Let's go celebrate with a champagne dinner. Or do you want room service instead?" Bill asked.

"We'll be together for a very long time, darling. We'll have plenty of time for room service. Right now, I'm hungry," replied Susan. "Besides, at dinner we need to discuss how to announce this to my parents. I can't wait to see my mom's face!"

They closed the door and went to a dinner they would both remember for a long time. Bill insisted they sit side by side instead of across the table. They held hands in the candlelight and sipped their champagne. He ordered steak and lobster for two. She squeezed his hand or leaned in to give him frequent kisses. He surprised her with Baked Alaska for dessert.

After dinner, Bill suggested a walk down the promenade to shop for an engagement ring before the stores closed. He wanted potential suitors to know of their commitment.

For Bill, money was no object. For Susan, practicality was just as important as the symbol. They chose a thin diamond-studded gold band with an interlocking gold wedding band. Susan knew she'd have to take it off when she worked with patients. She planned to put this ring on her gold chain. At her first opportunity, she'd put Larry's ring in an envelope in her jewelry box. She'd keep it to return to him if he was released.

That night in the hotel was a joyous one for them both. Susan was no longer burdened by her secret, and Bill was able to show fully his love for her. There were no more pretenses of separate rooms. There would not be a need again.

Bill was elated, but again he had to caution himself. After all, his engagement with Sara had ended in disaster. And with a similar situation. Sara's husband, presumed dead, suddenly resurfaced. What would Susan do if her first fiancé returned?

What Susan didn't know was that Bill had gotten some information from the fraternity Larry had belonged to at the University of Wisconsin. Larry was a very rich and handsome man. His father owned a manufacturing company in Milwaukee that specialized in new inventions. Were he to reappear, Larry could provide everything Susan could ever want. Bill could not match those material things.

Larry was also used to having his own way, and he was a real charmer, according to his fraternity brothers. Bill wondered how Susan would—or whether she could—stand up to that kind of power.

And what would Larry be like after so many years in captivity? What if he were injured, sick, or tortured? With her nurse's heart, would Susan be moved to care for him? Would that destroy her ability to resist him? Would she confuse caretaking for love?

With so many unanswered questions about Larry, Bill knew there were great risks ahead. But at least he wouldn't be surprised if he found himself facing them. In addition, he would be facing them with Susan, as a married couple. He wouldn't be powerless, as he had been with Sara.

Suddenly, Bill couldn't help but wonder how he himself would react if Sara suddenly reappeared, even after he and Susan married. How strong and fair would he be with Susan then?

42.

SUSAN HEADED HOME ON SUNDAY with a wonderful glow Bill wanted never to be apart from again. She proudly displayed her new ring to anyone who cared to see it—and to a lot of men who were not happy to see it.

Inspired by his future as a husband and perhaps even a father, Bill committed to reading his mother's stack of journals. Bill knew his mother's maiden name was Bahr and that she was originally from Germany, but he knew nothing more about her past. *Hopefully, these journals will give me a clue to her background,* he thought as he stirred cream into his coffee.

As he read the first journal, he found himself confused. It wasn't his mother's journal at all. It was written by a young woman named Freda Fromm. A quick glance revealed the other journals were in the same handwriting. Who was this Freda, and how had his mother gotten her journals?

Reading the entries was like eavesdropping on a stranger. The first journal appeared to have been written in England during the war.

I was born in 1919 in Heidelberg to Rolf and Margarette Fromm. My father is an archaeologist and a professor. I often accompany him on digs to various sites in Asia and Africa. I attend his classes when I can, sitting in the back and watching proudly as his students hang on every word.

Bill remembered his mother saying she took classes from a famous Professor Fromm in Germany. She must have met Freda during one of her classes.

The journal continued:

I have married a young pilot named Albert Schmidt. Albert emigrated from America to Germany with his brother in 1935 to fly for Deutsche Luft Hansa. He is a loving and caring man.

Freda's weekly entries detailed her life with Albert and the birth of their daughter, Katrina. She also described the work her husband and his brother Fritz were doing with Deutsche Luft Hansa.

The tone shifted drastically in the second journal. Freda noted the changes in society while Hitler created his perfect Germany.

The third journal ended abruptly in late 1939. Albert had managed to spirit Freda, Katrina, and the elder Fromms out of Germany just before the war started. Sadly, though, the escape didn't go as planned. As Bill read the heartbreaking report, he could tell that Freda had loved Albert much the same as he loved Susan.

After Katrina and I made it safely to South Africa, my dearest Albert disappeared in an airplane crash off the coast of Argentina while flying for Deutsche Luft Hansa. He was the love of my life, and he hated the Nazi regime. He was trying to get our family to safety in South America when he disappeared.

The fourth journal read like a classic spy novel. The only difference was, this was real life. Although the entries described events beginning in 1940, Freda apparently wrote it after the war, when she lived in Detroit. Bill wondered if perhaps Freda reconnected with his mother in Detroit at that time.

Then suddenly Bill read something that shocked him. He spilled coffee on his lap.

I changed my name from Freda Fromm to Helene Bahr after my husband disappeared. It was for Albert and my daughter that I took a

position working for British intelligence to help defeat the Nazis. The
British provided me with a background story and a means to fight. I
secretly parachuted into Germany as an SOE agent to gather intelli-
gence for the Allied war effort.

I am still looking for Katrina. The agency said she was sent to
Canada during the Blitz, while I was working in Germany. But the
records office was bombed, and all records of the children were lost.

Bill sat back in his chair, stunned at this revelation. *This Freda is Mom? Mom*
was previously married? And I have a stepsister somewhere in Canada? Holy shit.
The journals confirmed what General Abrams had said about his mother
being a British spy. But Bill doubted even Abrams knew about his mother's
double identity!

Bill quickly calculated. This Katrina would be in her mid-thirties—if
still alive. He wanted more than anything to find this lost thread to his past
and share these journals with her.

The next entry made the hair stand up on Bill's neck.

During my last trip to Berlin in 1939, I managed to make a copy
of Hitler's plans for the invasion of the Soviet Union. Unfortunately,
Joseph Stalin did not believe the information we provided.

Bill let out his breath in a whoosh. "Holy crap! My quiet, gentle mother was
making copies of Hitler's plans?"

Helene also documented helping her sister-in-law Elisa escape to
Sweden with her twin boys, Adolf Petra and Otto. She then was able to get
her parents to Sweden as well.

In late 1940, I helped my parents reach Sweden and join up with Elisa
and her boys. It is a comfort having them all together. Elisa needed to
disappear to a place where the Gestapo could never find her and the boys.
I barely escaped arrest by the Gestapo myself. If I had been captured, I
would surely have been tortured and killed.

Bill whistled out loud. "Wow. This is better than a history book!"

After settling her family in Sweden, and afraid her identity had been compromised to the Gestapo, Helene took a position at Bletchley Park, working in the code-breaking division. Bill knew about this group. They had cracked the code of the Enigma machines found on U-boats and in German bunkers seized in commando raids. This also confirmed what General Abrams had told him.

Helene's journal entries continued.

While working as a code breaker in 1940, I kept seeing references to "Condor Base" and "Operation Poseidon." Our initial radio triangulation placed the Nazi base somewhere in the Huron Mountain area near here, in the Upper Peninsula of Michigan. The intermittent signals lasted only a little over a year, then stopped abruptly.

There is no mistake that "Condor 123" was Elisa's husband, Fritz, but there was no follow-up. There were bigger issues, such as the potential invasion of Britain. America was not yet in the war, so the threat seemed minor. The coordinates are included in this diary for future reference.

My God, thought Bill. *My mother's brother-in-law was involved in a top-secret Nazi mission on US soil. It sure seems there was a lot happening up there in the Michigan wilderness in 1940 that never made the history books.*

Bill scanned the coordinates his mother had noted for the possible base in Michigan. The land and cabin General Abrams had held in trust for Bill was fairly close to the area. When he had a chance, Bill vowed to do a little exploratory hiking.

The fifth journal started on a happier note:

In the fall of 1943, while working at Bletchley and with the OSS, I met a young American pilot named Michael O'Brien. He was flying for the US Army Air Force. I found him to be such an open, happy, and loving man. Despite my feelings for Albert, I fell in love with Michael. I did play hard to get for some time and dated several other pilots in Michael's squadron. Finally, Michael asked me to marry him. I accepted.

The only resistance I noted was the reaction of Michael's brother, Sean. From the beginning, he did not seem to like me, or at least he disliked the idea of Michael marrying a non-Catholic. I did not think my religion would be an issue, considering the life-and-death struggles we were involved with each day at the time.

Life is just too short and unpredictable to pass up love. I resigned my position in London and moved to Detroit when Michael completed his combat tour.

But then an entry near the end of the fifth journal caused Bill's gut to churn.

I still haven't told Michael about the final intercept I translated. I checked it multiple times. It was about Sean O'Brien—yes, my new husband's brother. Sean was working on the ground crew for the US Army Air Force. He never passed the flight checks and always seemed jealous of Michael. The message proved that Sean was providing information about Allied air missions to the German agents in England. I did not want to disgrace Michael, but I had to stop Sean. When I told my superiors, the agency arranged to have Sean quietly removed from the air force unit and sent home with a general discharge.

The final entry in the fifth journal, apparently written after the family moved to Minneapolis, added to Bill's discomfort.

Sean found out why he had been unceremoniously returned home during the war. He hates me for it. Since coming to Minneapolis, I have been using my resources to build a dossier on Sean's activities, just in case he tries to retaliate. I discovered he has been involved in criminal activities in Minneapolis.

In addition, I have gathered strong evidence that Sean killed a man in a dispute over stolen property, although it was never proven. The victim was a known criminal, so the authorities had little interest in pursuing the case. These may be the same people he was involved with in Detroit before Michael invited him to Minneapolis.

The sixth journal was even more alarming.

> *Somehow Sean found out about the dossiers I had prepared on the German scientists and intelligence officers brought to the US under Operation Paperclip. These are serious Nazi Party members and war criminals given whitewashed backgrounds. I vetted many of them before I left England. I was not happy to see this program exist. I approached my former OSS contacts with my concerns, but I was overruled. These people have blended into American society. Many of them, or their families, would not want it known that they were Nazi Party members. If Sean has discovered any of their identities, this may be a threat to our family.*
>
> *I write in this journal at Rudolph's house now after I drop off the kids at school. I don't think my journals would be safe at the farm, since Sean has been spending time there working with Michael on the plane.*

Tucked neatly in the back of the journal were press clippings and a list of dates, events, and other documentation that implicated Sean in illegal activities.

> *I have tried to talk to Michael about potential issues with Sean. So far, he sees Sean as family in need of assistance. I cannot share all I know quite yet. Michael does not know my life as Freda. I just wanted to start fresh when we met. It seemed easier.*
>
> *I have convinced him to file a new power of attorney naming his friend General Wallace Abrams as executor. This will replace previous documents done a few years earlier naming Sean. Michael had insisted that Sean be given those responsibilities, despite my objections. He felt Sean was up to the challenge and wanted to keep the responsibility within the immediate family. Michael always had a blind spot when it came to Sean.*
>
> *I am glad to finally have a trusted person responsible for our precious children in case we are unable to care for them. I lost one child during the war. I do not want our children to lose what we have built for them. We fly to San Antonio tomorrow to meet with Abrams and sign the papers.*

Toward the end of the sixth journal, Bill noted this bittersweet entry.

> *My life in America and with Michael has been a storybook. I love him*
> *so deeply that it's not possible to express in writing. We have a lovely*
> *family of two boys and a girl. Michael has a job he loves. I am a proud*
> *American citizen. We have a lovely farmstead north of Minneapolis,*
> *where the children can play, mature, and learn responsibility. My only*
> *regret is that I have not been able to find my daughter Katrina. I hope*
> *she is safe and happy with her own family. Maybe someday we can find*
> *Katrina and we can be reunited.*

The last entry was dated June 1962.

> *Sean was at the farm today, helping Michael tune up the plane for our*
> *family trip out west tomorrow. John and Jackie are excited. Bill is con-*
> *flicted. I told him to decide whether he wants to travel with the family*
> *or work and save for school. I think he has made the right decision. I*
> *am so proud of him.*

Bill gasped and swallowed hard. *This is like a voice from the grave. I'm so sorry I didn't go with you, Mom.* Deep inside, though, it was good to know she had been proud of him.

Bill knew he needed to call Wilkerson immediately. They now had the trigger to push Sean to settle the estate case. They also had information for the police about a murder that had been a cold case for many years.

"Sean," Bill muttered under his breath as he grabbed the phone, "Now you'll finally get what you deserve."

Wilkerson could not believe this gift of evidence. "Send us a copy of a few of the more damning pages from the journal," he suggested. "We'll get all the wheels greased and set up a face-to-face meeting with Sean and his attorneys. Once we get them in the room, we'll show them the evidence. We'll tell Sean we'll give this information and more to the FBI and the local police unless he releases all his claims on M. O. Airfreight and the twenty thousand dollars of your inheritance without appeal."

Within two weeks, Wilkerson arranged for Bill to fly to Minneapolis and attend a meeting with the lawyers and Uncle Sean. Bill and Wilkerson met the day before the scheduled meeting to prepare their multilayered attack.

"Don't talk to Sean before the meeting," Wilkerson warned. "I don't want him or his attorneys to know the true purpose of the meeting. We want to drop the evidence on them cold. And honestly, even if Sean decides to play ball with us, I have a feeling a judge will still probably use the evidence to hold Sean for future criminal proceedings."

Bill readily agreed. It was good to use this evidence as leverage, yet he had no intention of letting Sean off the hook for anything. He wanted to pursue an investigation into Sean's connection with his family's death, as Wilkerson could pass the information to the FAA and FBI. Since Abrams had the wreckage stored in a hangar in Colorado, he could give the go-ahead to look for sabotage.

Bill stayed in the Radisson downtown. He had a quiet dinner in the Flame Room. It was a far more pleasant meal than the last one he had there with Barbara. Sipping an after-dinner cognac, he wondered if she was still in town living with her parents. He decided he'd call their house after his meeting the next day. He hoped she was around so he could let her know about his engagement.

Perhaps it's my time to rub it in, he thought.

43.

BILL WAS ALREADY SEATED IN THE NINETEENTH-FLOOR conference room of Johnson, Abrams, and Wilkerson. He had his briefcase on the table in front of him, ready for phase one. He sat with his back to the window. He wanted no distractions. His uncle's face was the only thing he would be concentrating on.

Wilkerson escorted Sean and his attorney into the room. "Coffee? Water? Juice?" he offered.

"Orange juice would be great—thanks," said Sean, licking his lizard lips. He turned his attention to Bill. "Well, Bill, glad to see you're still alive. Sorry we have this little dispute that requires high-priced lawyers." He cocked his head and looked slowly around the room, setting his sights on the stunning view out the window behind Bill. "I know they charge by the minute, so I want to do my best for you, as usual."

Bill could feel his face tighten, his temperature rise, his muscles contract. Sean looked older, fatter, and even more abrasive than before.

"Uncle Sean, we're here today to see that justice is done."

"Excellent!" Sean smiled a toothy grin. "Whatever it is, let's settle it quick."

"Gentlemen," Wilkerson announced as he took his seat, "let's begin."

Sean sipped his orange juice with a satisfied slurp.

With that, Wilkerson began systematically laying out the evidence. As he passed more documents to Sean and his attorney, Sean's face flushed redder. His eyes bulged, making him look like the fruit fly checking out the remaining orange juice in his glass.

Bill wondered if Sean might just stroke out in front of him. Bill actually took some joy in that thought but did his best to hide his feelings.

"You ungrateful fool!" Sean roared at Bill. "Look at all I did for you when your parents died! *I* got your family sent back here and buried them. *I* settled the estate. *I* stepped up for you!"

Wilkerson gestured to Bill to take over.

Bill took a measured breath. "Uncle Sean, I promised these gentlemen and my fiancée that I would be civil today, and I will." He sounded calmer than he felt. "But you enriched yourself at my expense, and you settled very little that benefited me. We are here today to rectify that. Actually, Rudolph arranged to have my family's bodies sent home. Rudolph is the one who stepped up for me. You, all you did was siphon money from the business, my inheritance, and even my home. As you have seen, we have the proof."

Sean looked down at the papers covering the table, then looked at his attorney with a bewildered look of a frightened animal. Sean had not seen this coming.

"What do you want?" he stammered.

"I want control of M. O. Airfreight. I want at least twenty thousand dollars of my inheritance. And I want you to sign over the contract for deed for the farmstead right now!"

Bill sat forward and stared at Sean, letting him digest what he had just said. After a moment, he continued.

"I had Mr. Wilkerson draw up the appropriate papers for your signature. Your attorney can review them here, but we are not leaving until we have your signature. Otherwise, as we said in Vietnam, there'll be hell to pay." Bill folded his hands on the table and glared at Sean.

Sean's attorney held up his hand to keep his client from overreacting any further. He read the documents carefully page by page. When he was done, he sighed, turned the pages toward Sean, and handed him a pen.

"You don't have a leg to stand on, Sean," the attorney admitted. "I recommend you sign now and hope for the best."

Sean gripped the pen so hard he nearly broke it in half. He glanced out the window, then glared back at Bill before he put pen to paper. He signed the document relinquishing all rights and title to M. O. Airfreight. In addition, he signed the document agreeing that a bank draft in the amount of $20,000 be sent to Bradley Wilkerson at the law firm the following day, along with the outstanding CD for the farm property.

When he was done, Sean jumped up and threw open the conference room door with volatile fury. He left without looking back. The condensation from his glass dripped down to the walnut table.

Bill sat quietly in his chair. He was still trying to grasp the enormity of what had just happened. He wondered what their next move would be.

Wilkerson slapped Bill on the back. "You did it! Your mom's journal was the deciding factor."

Bill nodded and smiled briefly to accept the congratulations.

"Now we'll start on phase two, as we discussed," Wilkerson said. "From what our team has found, we should be able to reclaim the farm for you and remove the present tenant quickly. He has only a month left on the CD from Sean, and he doesn't have an option to buy the property. Any payoff will come to you. We'll also have our investigator visit the property and ensure that the present tenant doesn't do any damage before he leaves. Our investigator can be a mean bastard, when needed. In addition, I'll have Dean call his dad and arrange for the FAA to review the wreckage in Colorado."

Bill nodded again, then turned to gaze out the window. He was having a difficult time understanding how his uncle could be so callous and hurtful to his own family. Sean was obviously not very bright, but the hatred he had shown to Bill's loved ones was unforgivable.

Wilkerson broke into Bill's thoughts. "How about a celebratory luncheon over at Murray's?"

"Sounds like a good idea," Bill responded. He stood up, gathered his copies of the signed documents, and put them in his briefcase.

First we celebrate, he thought, *then we stick the knife in a little deeper and twist it.*

As soon as Bill got back to his hotel room, he called Susan to give her the good news.

"Oh, Bill!" she exclaimed with delight. "I never doubted it for a minute! I wish I could have been a mouse in the corner watching Sean squirm. Sounds like you kept your cool, though. I'm so proud of you!"

"Lima Bean, this is good news for you too—now you know I won't be some deadbeat husband living off your salary!"

"Nice to know, but you know how much they pay nurses. If we had to live off my salary, we'd be eating a lot of oatmeal! Now go to work and make me proud."

Bill's next call was to Rudolph. "Well, I managed to get control of M. O. Airfreight and twenty thousand dollars to boot," he reported happily. "Next, my attorney will initiate the FAA investigation on Dad's plane."

"I knew you could do it, Bill!" Rudolph replied. "I am so happy for you.

"Thanks for all the support you've given me over the years. Now that I'm a business owner, I'll have to head over to the office tomorrow and see what I got myself into. I'm not sure how I'm going to run this on a day-to-day basis from Oklahoma for the next several months until my tour of duty is over. For now, I'll have to do some quick checks on the personnel already in place. I'll have to see who has some abilities versus who was in lockstep with Uncle Sean and needs to be jettisoned."

"Sounds like you need some help," said Rudolph.

"Are you offering?"

"Me? What do I know about running a business?" Rudolph laughed. "I do have a suggestion, though."

"I'm open to suggestions!"

"Remember my daughter, Jessica?" asked Rudolph.

"Sure. She's working somewhere in Minneapolis, isn't she?"

"Yep, and not too happily. I talked to her yesterday. She's working for Midwest Airfreight. She's not too thrilled with her boss right now," Rudolph explained. "Apparently, she brought up some concerns about several procedures, and her boss just said she could always find a different job if she didn't like it there. They have a problem with assertive women."

"Wow—sounds like I should reconnect with my distant cousin!" exclaimed Bill. "What's her number?"

Minutes later, Bill called Jessica. They hadn't seen each other or spoken in years, and even then, he'd never known her all that well. As they reconnected this time, though, he instantly liked her strong business experience and personal confidence.

After some brief family talk, Bill got right to the point, explaining the M. O. Airfreight takeover and the possible mess he had wrestled from Sean.

Without skipping a beat, Jessica got right to the point too. "And now you need help."

Bill could detect a smirk in her voice.

"Yes. I need someone with airfreight and management experience who can come in and do the necessary review of personnel, procedures—the whole nine yards."

"Sounds interesting," she responded with a laugh. "What title are you planning to bestow on the sucker who takes you up on this offer?"

"I'm thinking 'Executive Vice President and Chief Operations Officer,' " responded Bill, hoping it would impress her. "Your first job would be to write your own job description. I won't be on-site, so you would be working on your own. I'll be available by phone if you have questions, but it would be your baby."

"Hmm," she responded. "Job descriptions and swim lane process charts are all my current boss thinks I can handle."

"Swim *what* charts?"

"Never mind," she said, laughing again. "Can we meet for dinner tonight and discuss the details? Dad said you are at the Radisson downtown. I can be at the hotel by six, if that works for you."

"Sounds great. We'll have dinner at the Flame Room. I've grown to like that place."

Next, Bill called his commanding officer back in Oklahoma and requested an additional week of leave. He explained the court case and its result.

"I need to take formal control of the airfreight company tomorrow, then get some management in place," Bill said. "I already have someone in mind to run it for me. I'm interviewing her tonight over dinner."

"*Her?*" his commanding officer repeated. "That was fast."

"She really has the skills I need. I just hope she'll accept. I want to take her over to the headquarters tomorrow, if possible."

His request for additional leave was granted.

It had been several years since Bill and Jessica had seen each other. He remembered her at his college graduation, holding Rudolph's hand. Her dark hair was tied tightly in a ponytail, and her dress was a bit frumpy, if he remembered. He also recalled thinking of her as a tomboy.

Now she was a vision. At thirty-three, she was graceful, athletic, and very much in control of herself and her surroundings. She definitely had a presence that would work well in the man's world of airfreight.

Again, they started with some small talk, then he came right out and asked if she would take on the business.

"It needs an experienced person to run it, thanks to all the problems Sean caused. I can honestly say I'm not sure how deep the corruption might go. You'll be free to hire and fire as you see fit. You'll be responsible for all operations. And I'll more than match your present salary."

Jessica smiled. What Bill didn't know was that as soon as they finished their chat earlier that afternoon, she'd immediately resigned at Midwest Airfreight. She was ready for a new challenge. Still, she wanted to leave him hanging a bit longer.

"You're probably a tough guy to work for, even from a distance," she commented, doing her best to keep a straight face.

Bill squirmed a bit in his chair. He tried to think of some way to sell this woman on what he hoped would be the opportunity of a lifetime for them both.

"Um, no, not really. Some people say I have bountiful charm," he added with a smile. It was a pretty dumb answer, but it was all he could muster.

"Well, in that case, I accept," she said, unable to hold back her laugh anymore.

Bill let out a sigh of relief, then returned her laugh. He lifted his glass. "Here's to the new M. O. Airfreight team—I hope it lasts a long time and builds the company back to my father's dream."

"Hear, hear," Jessica agreed as she touched her glass to his. "In fact, let's visit the headquarters tomorrow to survey the damage as a team," she directed, stepping right into her new role. "But first, let's talk about that salary!"

Bill was amused by her forthright approach. "Yes, cousin. Let's get right to it!"

Back in his hotel room later that night, Bill suddenly got the urge to call Barbara. As he suspected, she was back in town living with her parents.

"I was surprised to hear from your letters that you were back in Minneapolis," Bill said.

"Well, my relationship with Robert didn't pan out," she admitted. "He wanted to get married, but it seems he expected a wife to be ornamental. She could share his bed when he was home, but she was to wait quietly as he went off with a lot of other bedmates, if you know what I mean! That just wasn't worth it. I wanted to pursue acting and the women's movement."

Bill felt bad for her. It sounded as though she was still trying to find herself.

"I'm sorry it didn't work out for you in California," he said. "You deserve better than that."

"How about you?" she asked. "What have you been up to since being back?"

Bill explained the news about Uncle Sean, the company, and how he'd be moving back to Minneapolis soon. Barbara listened with rapt interest, asking questions.

"I also recently got engaged," he added.

Barbara hesitated. "Oh," she finally said. "That's great, Bill. I'm happy for you," she added in earnest. She did seem pleased to hear Bill was moving on with his life.

He considered describing Susan and how they first met in Vietnam. Then he decided against it. He had lost all interest in rubbing anything in.

"I'd like to stay in touch, if that would be okay," she said hopefully.

"Yes, let's. Perhaps when I get settled in the Cities, you can call me at the company and we can have dinner."

"Okay, Bill. I'd love that."

"I want to thank you for your letters," Bill said. "They helped me get through some hard times in Vietnam. And I always remembered our time together at the university. Thoughts of those wonderful times really helped me."

As they said their good-byes and hung up, Bill could only think just how much they had drifted apart since that walk in the park after graduation. It seemed a lifetime ago. *My God, we were so innocent then*, he thought. *So naive.* But her beautiful memory was one of the good things he would never forget. It would be nice to see her again.

Bill turned out the light and went to sleep. He had to be sharp for his first day walking in as owner of M. O. Airfreight.

44.

A FTER HIS EXTRA WEEK OF LEAVE, Bill returned to Fort Sill to complete his final months of duty. True to his word, he kept his finger on the pulse of M. O. Airfreight but left the running of the company up to Jessica. She was more than capable.

A few months later, Susan left San Antonio for her new position at the Veterans Administration hospital in Minneapolis. She had applied to multiple VA hospitals and was pleased when both Milwaukee and Minneapolis offered her a position.

Her plan to move to Milwaukee and wait for Larry seemed like a distant memory. But now with her and Bill's upcoming marriage, Minneapolis was of course a better fit. She would find an apartment and set it up for the both of them, so it would be ready when Bill arrived. The plan was to officially tie the knot once things settled down in Susan's new job and once Bill had a handle on salvaging his father's business.

Susan told Bill how excited she was for the new job. "I want to keep helping my guys," as she called the veterans. She was sure her time in the rehab unit at Fort Sam would help her adjust in Minneapolis.

Before heading to Minneapolis, however, she detoured to the farm to see her family. She made sure her ring was off. This visit wasn't to announce the engagement; she and Bill would do that together sometime. For now, Susan needed to stay mum about the engagement—that and the fact that she and Bill would soon be living together. Jewel would have much to say if she knew about those plans.

Jewel met her at the door, wiping her hands on her apron. "Susie, you look tired and hungry. Are you feeling well?"

"Oh, Mother—I'm fine. I'm not hungry right now. Let's just sit and talk." Susan took her mother's arm and led her back into the kitchen.

"I'm glad you stopped in before heading to Minneapolis to start your new job," Jewel noted. "Why did you decide on that VA hospital, rather than one closer to home?"

"Mother, do you remember Bill? I'm still seeing him," Susan explained. "He'll be in Minneapolis, so it will be more convenient for us."

"Daughter, of course I remember him, and I want to see him out here soon! I'm glad you're moving on with him. He's a real keeper. Are you serious with him now?" Jewel bubbled. "Have you made any plans?"

Susan tried to sound nonchalant. "Oh, Mom, we're just friends. We enjoy each other's company."

Jewel accepted that explanation—on the surface. But she knew her daughter very well. She knew they were a lot more than "just friends." Jewel was silently overjoyed.

She teased her daughter now. "Well, Susie, you better be careful. Bill's a great catch for someone. He owns a business now and is a wonderfully kind and caring man. And great looking. He'll make a wonderful father."

Susan just nodded her agreement. Out of everything, the fatherhood part made her roll her eyes. Of course her mother would start pushing for grandkids already.

"Once I'm in Minneapolis, I may be a bit hard to reach on the phone, Mom," Susan explained. "I'm not sure what my shifts will be with the new job. I have an answering machine, so just leave me a message, and I'll call you back as soon as I can."

Now Susan just had to train Bill to let the phone ring through to the machine.

Susan arrived in the Twin Cities and picked an apartment close to the VA hospital. She called Bill from their new home.

"You better get up here fast, sweetie. Our long-distance charges will go through the roof these next few weeks," she joked. "I'm already lonesome!"

Next, she went to the VA and saw Joyce, the chief nursing supervisor, who was responsible for all nursing hires.

Joyce was a pleasant older woman. She was glad to have Susan on staff, but she was clear on the issues surrounding care delivery at the VA. Susan sat in silence as Joyce laid it all out.

"Susan, the VA is facing major problems delivering care to an ever-increasing veteran population. The World War II population is reaching an age where their medical needs are skyrocketing. On top of that, we are getting many new patients from the Vietnam War. We are understaffed, underresourced, and often unappreciated by our patients. They believe they deserve better care—and they're right! You'll be required to work long shifts, but we just can't spread ourselves any thinner.

"You'll work with many patients who've lived with illness or disability for a long time. This is particularly true of the World War II veterans. Many of them know they won't get better, and they take their anger out on others. In addition, many of them abuse alcohol and exhibit multiple disorders—in some cases, mental illness. They can often become aggressive and verbally abusive. You need to be careful to protect yourself." Joyce paused for effect. "Do you still want the job?"

Susan was stunned by Joyce's frankness. It left Susan concerned if she could in fact render proper care. However, she was here, and she would do her best. If worst came to worst, she wasn't stuck, as she'd been in Vietnam. She could leave and find a different position.

"I'll do my best," she promised. "When and where can I start?"

"We'll want you to work initially in the outpatient rehab unit. This is our area of highest demand and volume. You may also need to spend time in the inpatient wards, depending on our staffing and census levels. I'll have the floor supervisor meet you now so you can coordinate your starting date with her."

Joyce called the floor supervisor, Dorothy, who took Susan down to the outpatient ward for a quick tour. Dorothy was an experienced forty-year-old nurse. She had a pencil stuck in her hair and walked with a rolling gait.

She was supportive of the care they were giving but also very aware of the dangers Susan might encounter in the job.

"I like to be called Dottie," she said as they walked. "It keeps our relationship a bit more informal. But keep in mind—we have some serious ground rules that must be followed for your safety and that of the patient. First, never see a patient alone. Always have at least one other nurse with you or a male attendant."

Dottie waited for Susan to acknowledge rule one, which she did with a nod.

"Second, never turn your back on a patient. Third, avoid certain doctors—we'll help you learn which ones make a practice of trying to bed good-looking nurses like you. Fourth, do the best you can with the equipment available. We don't have enough, and some of it needs repair. Any questions?"

"No, Dottie, not right now. I appreciate that the staff will point out the problem doctors. I'm engaged, so I don't have any time for that crap."

Dottie glanced down at Susan's résumé. "Looking at your skill set, you'll know how to provide the care needed for these guys. I'm really glad you're here. Let me know if anything comes up later. Will starting Monday work for you?"

"Absolutely," Susan replied.

Finally, three weeks later, Bill turned Battery A over to the next commander, packed up, and drove the Rocket away from Fort Sill for the last time. He had warned Susan he would arrive late after an almost-nonstop drive. He knocked on her door at 2:00 a.m. Saturday morning.

"I'm not sure I should let you in," she joked with the chain still holding the door ajar. "It's kind of late. I think my fiancé might object."

"Open the door, lady," Bill responded in his best gangster tone. "I'm comin' in!"

She was happy to oblige. Bill closed the door, dropped his bag, and reached out to Susan, pulling her to him. They warmly kissed as Susan ran her fingers through Bill's hair. Despite the early hour and Bill's fatigue from the drive, neither wanted to break the spell. They lingered intertwined for many minutes, then she led him to the bedroom of their first home together. She would save her excitement about her new job at the VA for the next day. Now they had other catching up to do.

After a short but wonderful night together, Susan regaled Bill about her new job over breakfast. Bill was very proud to hear how well she was doing.

"Speaking of new jobs," Bill said, "I better call Jessica to let her know I'm in town for good."

Bill gave her a ring at home. "Hmm, no answer," he said with a shrug. After a second, it dawned on him. "Why don't we drive out to the freight office to see if anything is happening on a Saturday?" he said with a wink.

"I'd love to see your company—and meet this mystery lady who is turning it around!"

As it turned out, Jessica was working on the weekend as well as working wonders on the business.

"I think we've turned the corner," she reported. "Revenues are up fifteen percent, we have three new customers, and I have a couple of salespeople shaking the bushes for more."

As she explained to Bill and Susan, it hadn't taken her long to complete her review of all the employees and make appropriate adjustments. The company was near bankruptcy, but she was already turning things around with her knowledge of the airfreight industry. She laid off the people who seemed to be sucking the life out of the company and replaced them with new hires or reassigned the jobs to current employees.

Bill was glad to see the spark in Jessica's eyes. She truly loved the job and the freedom to make a difference. She was an assertive, knowledgeable, and spunky woman.

Thank God for that, Bill thought.

"I just wanted to stop by to let you know I'm in town for good now, but I'm not here to make any changes," he assured her. "I'm here only to see if you need any help."

"I think I have everything in order, but I'd really like a professional opinion about taxes. I'm not an attorney, and filing could be really tricky this first year. I'm not sure what kind of games Sean was playing with the books."

Bill was pleased. Jessica could handle so much of the business, yet she was willing to admit when she was in uncomfortable waters. He too had been thinking about the upcoming tax filing.

"I know just who to call," he said. "Start with Bradley Wilkerson at Johnson, Abrams, and Wilkerson in Minneapolis. They helped me out when I needed to wrestle this company away from Sean. I think it'd be a good idea to give them some business in return."

"I'll give him a call first thing on Monday. Thanks, boss."

Jessica grinned when Bill blushed.

Susan was also very impressed with Jessica. As she walked out to the Rocket locked arm in arm with Bill, she commented, "Jessica has really done a great job with your company. It's a good thing she's a relative, otherwise I might be jealous."

"Really?" Bill laughed. "But green isn't your color."

Over the next few weeks, life together in Minneapolis started to take on a normalcy neither of them had experienced for a long time.

Susan enjoyed her work in the outpatient therapy unit, working with wounded veterans from the Korean War, World War II, and the Vietnam War. This was despite the staff shortages, equipment problems, funding shortfalls, and some verbally abusive patients. She felt she was giving back to those who needed it the most.

Working with the vets made Susan think about Larry, though. Some of the older vets had been POWs. Seeing their struggles filled her head with concerns about her former fiancé and what he might be going through. Sometimes she was flooded with guilt—was he thinking about her, holding on to the hope of reuniting with her one day?

She kept these thoughts to herself. For the moment, she was still very happy with her life with Bill and still looking forward to marriage. But there was a part of her that just didn't know what would happen if Larry reappeared in her life.

As for Bill, he loved having Jessica calling the shots at M. O. Airfreight so he could take on the role of customer service troubleshooter and goodwill ambassador. Jessica assigned him the toughest customers and those who needed special handling. Many were his father's old customers who had been neglected by Sean.

"We never saw that Sean fella," one customer recalled. "He never returned phone calls. Just didn't care about our once-a-month shipping needs. Guess we weren't big enough for him to bother with."

Both Jessica and Bill understood that there really wasn't a lot of money to be made with small shippers. However, Jessica managed to work those customers into monthly schedules, where she could combine several shipments and make the run worthwhile. It was just a matter of thinking outside the box. She could do it better than anyone Bill had met.

Bill's role in it all had him traveling a great deal. Both he and Susan found their time apart manageable, though, seeing as they each had so much to do.

Bill also still had some duties as a reserve officer with a Fort Snelling–based army reserve unit. Fort Snelling was only a few minutes' drive from their new home. He was the executive officer of a base engineering company. He didn't have a lot to do, seeing as he was required to be on base only once a month for formation. With Bill's record, no one seemed to care if he showed up or not.

The chief benefit, however, was Bill's ability to work out in the Fort Snelling base gym. He could exercise any time he wanted to continue his rehabilitation. He also took advantage of the boxing ring to recapture his skills. He enjoyed the sparing matches with the other soldiers. In fact, he was proud of his ability to move and punch. He was also improving his upper-body strength, easily bench-pressing more than his weight.

When he was home, Bill enjoyed being out at the old farmstead. The contract for deed had been paid to Bill, and the old tenant hadn't damaged the property. However, Bill still found that the old house needed to be gutted down to the studs and refurbished. At least the outbuildings were virtually untouched, so Bill could use the barn as a temporary workshop.

Being out at the farm made Bill think about starting a family. "Your mom wants grandchildren," he teased Susan. "Maybe six or seven!"

"I won't be pregnant for the next ten years, buster," she grumbled. "Thanks for that!"

"Well, maybe we can settle on perhaps two kids in the not-too-distant future," he concluded with a laugh.

Susan laughed along, but on the inside, she remained firm. She had no expectations for children for an extended period of time. Right now, they both had new jobs that required their full attention.

And truth be told, Susan was overwhelmed just thinking about the commitment it took to start a family. It meant agreeing to a certain future, when there were so many variables that could come into play. Maybe she'd want to pursue a new direction with her career. Or maybe Larry would show up on her doorstep one day. How would she face those choices if she and Bill had children?

Because of these unknown variables, Susan had started taking birth control pills—something Bill wouldn't be advised of. Right now, she felt it was her decision to make.

At last, Bill and Susan made plans for their wedding. They decided to marry in the fall.

First, however, they needed to make a pilgrimage to see Susan's family and make the engagement formal. They couldn't keep dodging her mother's frequent phone calls without risking a slipup. So Susan called to say *they* were coming for a visit.

"I think you need to ask my mother, not my father, for the blessing," Susan joked as they headed down 94 toward Eau Claire, Wisconsin.

"I agree, but that would be properly unconventional. I think she would short-circuit!" Bill replied, laughing at her suggestion.

"How about we just *tell* them, instead of asking them for their blessing? Either way, it'll be a great surprise for them. Mom has been trying to get me hitched since I graduated from high school."

As they turned onto the road leading up to the farm, they saw Jewel and Sam standing on the front porch. The parents shielded their eyes from the sun and watched the Rocket approach.

Bill winked at Susan as he pulled the car to a stop. Then he hopped out and raced around to ceremoniously hold the door for Susan. They walked up to the porch arm in arm.

"Well, I declare . . ." started Jewel. She made a mistake of taking a breath.

Before she could say anything more, Bill and Susan said in unison, "We're getting married in the fall."

"So there!" Susan added.

"Well, it's about time," Jewel just said. "Now, what about my grandchildren?"

Susan groaned, but Sam laughed and shook Bill's hand.

Despite Jewel's attempt to make the wedding into a Lutheran pageant, Susan and Bill married that fall in a quiet ceremony at the Johnsons' small country church. Susan was stunning in her white wedding dress. It was enough to make any man fall in love with her.

Jewel was appalled that they didn't take a romantic Hawaiian honeymoon. They explained that perhaps they would visit Hawaii in the future. They had each already been there—sort of.

Instead, Bill and Susan opted to use their honeymoon as a chance to check out the rustic cabin Bill had inherited in the wilds of Michigan's Upper Peninsula. They were both glad Bill's parents had entrusted the deed to General Abrams. If Sean had gotten his hands on it, he would have sold it.

Susan declared it her "happy place." "It's so nice to watch the sunrise out on the porch and listen to the world wake up around you," she commented. "Sure, it's a long drive, but it's well worth it!"

They enjoyed the peace and quiet and loved to spend the cool mornings on the deck with a cup of coffee. A late-afternoon hike along the lakeshore was relaxing and a great way to work up an appetite for fresh trout for dinner—and all that followed.

Bill definitely did not want to drive the Rocket out on the dirt roads, so he talked his new friend Jeff from nearby L'Anse out of a camouflage-painted jeep.

Susan was appalled. "I'm not riding around in an army vehicle," she vowed. "We have left that life behind us, mister!"

After a trip to the hardware store, Susan made the vehicle acceptable to them both. Bill's side was left in its original camouflage. Her side sported a bright-yellow smiley face on the door.

The newlyweds made time for a day trip north to Copper Harbor, then another trip south to the museum at the Ford sawmill in Alberta. While talking with the locals during their outings, Susan heard that electricity was being run down the gravel road to the cabin.

"Sign us up," she ordered. "We're going on the grid as soon as possible."

As the honeymoon came to an end, Bill looked out at the wilderness and wondered if his mother's journals were right. Had there been a Nazi base nearby? Someday he'd have to investigate. But now, he had a new life to start with Susan.

45.

RETURNING FROM THEIR LITTLE HONEYMOON GETAWAY, both Bill and Susan found themselves quite busy. There was much to juggle—and that was in addition to two careers and the everyday demands of married life.

As promised, General Abrams requested an FAA in-depth analysis of the O'Briens' plane wreckage. A team of five individuals would comb the wreckage for any evidence of sabotage. Bill flew out to Colorado to meet George Donovan, the chief inspector, at the storage site.

"Mr. O'Brien, General Abrams sure raised hell with the head of the FAA," George said. "You've got the A team out here for this review. When the chief of staff of the air force speaks, we jump. You must be very special to him."

"General Abrams has known my family since World War II," Bill explained. "My father and the general flew together in B-24s. They were like brothers." Bill smiled, then grew more serious. "We have strong suspicions that the plane crash was not caused by pilot error or weather. We believe it was due to mechanical problems or sabotage. That's what we want you to consider in your review."

"Bill, I can assure you, we will leave no stone unturned," George stated. "I checked the initial crash review reports. The air force recovery team picked up the wreckage and returned it, but no one asked for a detailed review at that time, so they assumed either weather-related issues or pilot error. But now we'll look at every square inch of the wreckage. If there's any evidence of tampering, we'll find it."

While the inspection got under way in Colorado, Sean's problems continued back in Minnesota. If anything, they had gotten worse. The first case to hit Sean was in federal court. The IRS had completed an audit of his finances and tax returns. They determined he had underreported his true earnings by about $400,000 over the last six years.

With the IRS ruling, Sean was now broke. The IRS slapped a lien on his lakefront home in Minnetonka and on his remaining bank accounts and indicted him for tax evasion.

So, that helps explain how he managed to buy a mansion when the airfreight company was turning such a small profit, Bill thought. He could only shake his head.

But there was more. The next case proved even more how Sean had been able to afford his luxuries. It was a federal case for racketeering and the organized theft of M. O. Airfreight customer shipments. A number of Sean's loyal accomplices turned as witnesses. Many had known Sean in Detroit. They testified that he had orchestrated the hijacking of shipments and received a 30 percent kickback.

Sean was held in the Hennepin County jail while awaiting the charges, seeing as he couldn't cover his bail. When the case concluded, he was found guilty on all counts and sentenced to ten years in the federal prison in Sandstone, Minnesota.

Bill almost felt sorry for his uncle. *Almost.* He had always thought Sean to be slow and devious, but he really never thought he could be such a thief.

And now Bill waited to see if the most personal charges would be filed. Would the FAA find any evidence that Sean had a hand in the crash that killed his family?

While Sean faced justice, Bill continued his efforts to restore the legacy Sean had kept from him for so long. Work on the old farmstead was starting to show benefits. He had set up a workshop in the shed and had replaced worn siding. The roofing was next on his agenda. He knew he needed to ensure the buildings were weatherproof as soon as possible.

But deep in his heart, Bill knew he would never be able to live there with Susan. On a practical level, it was a long commute to their jobs in Minneapolis.

More importantly, there were just too many memories. Sure, some of them were good family memories, but they were always overshadowed. Whenever a thunderstorm rose in the distance, he would remember that night alone worrying about his family. Whenever the phone rang, it would bring back that call from the FAA in Denver.

Even though Bill knew he didn't want to make it his and Susan's home, he still wanted the farmstead to have some special purpose. This was part of his legacy, which he had fought hard to reclaim.

"I finally decided what I'm going to do with the farmstead," he told Susan over dinner in their apartment one night.

"Oh? What?" she asked carefully.

She too had concluded that the farmhouse wasn't for them. But she decided it would be better to hold off any discussions until Bill was ready. She spiked a piece of meat loaf with her fork and waited.

"I'm going to turn it into a private flying club. When my dad first moved to the area, he joined a club and really enjoyed the camaraderie. It would be a good way to provide flying lessons for local kids and continue my dad's interest in aviation."

"Wow, that's a good idea," Susan said. She chewed and swallowed before continuing. "Are *you* planning to take flying lessons?" she asked with a bit of trepidation.

"Probably not. I think one plane crash in a family is enough for anyone to deal with." He cocked his head to check her reaction, then he raised his wineglass in a toast. "But I think a flying club would be a wonderful, lasting memorial to my mom and dad."

"Then I love that idea!" Susan raised her glass to meet his halfway. "You could call it the Michael and Helene O'Brien Flying Club."

"Now there's a great idea!" he responded. His eyes lit up as more ideas began tumbling out of his mouth. "I want to set up the club as soon as possible. Maybe I can get some guys out here to help with refurbishing the runway. The barn and outbuildings could be used for aircraft maintenance. We could have fly-in breakfasts."

"Whoa, Chuck Lindbergh! Take a breath," Susan cautioned. "I know you could sell ice cubes to an Eskimo, but this won't happen in a week. Right now, you need to get some help finishing the house—the 'clubhouse,' that is. Maybe you should talk to Bradley Wilkerson about any legal issues and see if his firm can help draw up the paper work. If you offer lessons to kids and get people to donate their time and aircraft to the cause, you might be able to even make it a nonprofit organization."

Bill laughed. "So now who's taking this idea to the moon?"

He was glad Susan was as excited as he was about the idea. It would make a great legacy for his parents. They had both given so much. It was time to give back.

Weeks quickly turned into months. M. O. Airfreight was gaining stability, and the flying club was far past the conceptual phase. Bill and Susan decided it was time to look for a house and put down some more permanent roots.

So they pooled their money for the down payment with a VA loan and started packing up their apartment. After several trips with a real estate agent, they found a new two-story house just west of Penn Avenue and Old Shakopee Road in Bloomington, a nice up-and-coming suburb. The home was near the airport, the Minneapolis VA, and Fort Snelling.

Bill and Susan were excited to finally have a house to call their own. They could decorate, buy and arrange furniture, and enjoy the peace and quiet of suburban life. They only had to please each other. Of course, that proved harder than they initially thought. They still had to learn how to live together and deal with the typical squabbles of a newly married couple.

For instance, having a home meant having more housework. Susan stated that it only seemed fair to split the workload. And so, the exchanges began.

"Bill, when are you going to mow the grass?"

"Soon, dear."

"Susan, when you put the dishes in the dishwasher, it helps to add soap and actually start the machine. They don't wash themselves."

"Yes, darling smartass."

One day, Susan came home to see the shed in the backyard painted a hideous shade of blue.

"Bill, why did you paint the shed that ugly color?"

"The hardware store gives away premixed gallons of paint that other people return. They're free because they can't resell them. So I got a gallon of dark blue and a gallon of off-white, and I just dumped them together to make two gallons of light blue." He shrugged. "It's just a shed."

"Yes, dear. But if you ever paint again without checking with me about color, I'll confiscate your paintbrushes forever."

"If only I could be that lucky!" Bill said with a grin.

However, one time when Bill returned from a weeklong trek for business, he was met with a surprise of his own.

"Susie, I'm home!" he said in his best Desi Arnaz imitation as he stepped in the door.

He headed into the dining room, where Susan was setting the table, but then he stopped right in his tracks. The dining room was now sporting bright floral wallpaper.

"Welcome back!" Susan replied. "What do you think?" She spread her hands and gestured to the walls.

Bill's smile disappeared. He gagged quietly.

"Um . . . it'll take some getting used to," was all he could think to say.

With a pattern like that, at least you can't tell if it gets dirty, Bill admitted to himself.

Being away for a week at a time was common for Bill. His work with M. O. Airfreight still required a lot of travel. At first, Susan relished the weeks when Bill was away on business. She loved when he was home, of course, but she had so much more freedom when he was gone.

She cooked what she wanted to eat instead of having to placate Bill's meat-and-potatoes appetite. She could watch *The Carol Burnett Show* instead of *Gunsmoke*. She could paint the walls, shop for quirky antiques, and live in a space devoid of shoes in the middle of the floor and pants draped over the bedroom chair. She could also take extra shifts at the VA, as she still loved working with the vets in the rehab ward.

When Bill was home, he just wanted to crash in his sweat pants and watch his Westerns. Not the most romantic sight. He could also be dangerous around appliances when left unsupervised. Susan returned home from work one night to the wail of smoke alarms.

"What happened?" she yelled, holding her hands over her ears.

Bill was waving a towel, trying to coax the smoke out an open window in the kitchen.

"I got a little distracted when I was heating up some spaghetti sauce for a snack. It burned on a little."

"A *little*?" Susan cringed. "Where's the pan."

"In the sink."

Susan glanced at the scorched pan and cringed again. "That's the saucepan from the set my parents gave us for a wedding gift!"

"Maybe," Bill responded with a shrug. To himself, though, he added, *Oh, shit.*

"Oh, Bill—you bonehead!" Susan shook her head at the disaster. "I should crack you on the head with this pan, but it would only dent the pan." She rolled her eyes and left the room.

While Bill continued dissipating the smoke with his towel, he glanced at the pan. Some of the sauce still looked edible. He dipped his finger in and tentatively tasted the sauce.

Hey, not bad. Just like old army food.

After the saucepan incident, Bill was banned from cooking. In fact, Susan took over the meal planning as well. She was determined to eat healthy. No more meat and potatoes.

"Eat what is placed in front of you," Susan declared each night.

To Bill's dismay, Susan loved to visit the farmers' market and experiment with all sorts of new vegetables. Something unusual appeared on his plate at each meal. Kohlrabi, zucchini, eggplant—the list went on and on. Bill cut the vegetables on his plate into small pieces and washed them down with a swallow of wine. He had taken to buying cheap wine lately, mostly just to wash down vegetables. It was hard to justify using the good stuff for that.

When tofu made the menu, he finally objected.

"Okay," negotiated Susan. "You learn to cook without scorching a pan, and we'll trade off. If you cook, I do the dishes. If I cook, you do the dishes. We can alternate every other day."

That sounded like a good plan to Bill, so he redoubled his efforts to learn to cook. In addition, he got a small television in the kitchen so he wouldn't need to leave the room for *Gunsmoke* and *Rawhide* reruns. Since Bill's days were less structured than Susan's, he tended to be home earlier and eventually became the chief cook. Susan was relegated to "bottle washer."

While trying to adjust to married life, Susan also poured herself into her career. She was finally rewarded with a promotion to senior rehabilitation nurse at the VA. She was glad her hard work had been recognized, and she enjoyed the new challenges.

Her new position required shifts in the inpatient areas of the hospital in addition to her continued outpatient rehab work. She found herself working extra hours. Suddenly, she missed Bill when he was out of town so much. She missed sleeping with him and being able to talk to him about the demands of her new job.

The new duties were frustrating at times, but she just had to remind herself and her staff to compare the patients' current status to their status at intake. Unfortunately, there was often little progress, particularly with older patients with severe, long-standing injuries. But some patients did show progress, even occasionally those with the worst injuries. Attitude played a huge part. Susan knew that many of them had little likelihood of reclaiming their previous lives, yet she kept reminding herself they were all just finding their "new normal." Just as she and Bill had done.

Even though she was trained not to get too close to her patients, some of her cases became more personal. One such case was a young man in his early twenties who had lost both arms in a grenade explosion. Susan was helping him learn to write with his feet. One day, he finally managed to print his first name, Tom.

"Look at that, Nurse O'Brien," he exclaimed. "Pretty soon I'll be able to write Mom and Dad a letter!"

Susan smiled at his optimism and praised his penmanship. But as he struggled to next print his last name, she had to excuse herself. The nursing supervisor, Deb Nelson, found Susan drying her red eyes in the bathroom a few minutes later.

"Susan, you cannot get personally involved with these patients."

Deb absently tucked a strand of her dark hair back under her cap while she gathered her thoughts. She was shorter than Susan but stocky. Her no-nonsense attitude always got attention, but her nurses knew she was always there for them. Deb reached out and put her hands on Susan's shoulders to make sure Susan understood her sincerity.

"You're working long hours, and you're noticeably tired. You need to take care of yourself first. If you're not alert, you could make a mistake with a patient or a patient could harm you. I've seen it happen."

Susan dabbed her eyes with some tissue. "Thanks, Deb. I'll keep that in mind. But I think I'm okay. I used to pull nearly twenty-four-hour shifts in Vietnam."

Deb was only two years older than Susan and had served a rotation in Vietnam before Susan. With their common experiences, they had become fast friends.

"This isn't Vietnam," Deb said knowingly. "Some of these patients are dangerous, some are on drugs, and some have mental disorders. And we don't always have enough people to protect the staff. You need to stay sharp at all times, and being emotional like this just doesn't help."

Susan nodded, stood straight, and checked her makeup in the mirror. She went back to work with a warier attitude.

But how could she not get emotional? She was trying to follow Bill's advice—she tried to balance each life she saved or helped against those she had been unable to help in Vietnam. That was reassuring at times, but it was also taking a toll on her. Working with these men was heartbreaking at times. So many seemed beyond her help, and some even lashed out at her.

She'd been pushed and slapped many times by patients who were frustrated and in pain. She even thought of the Korean War veteran who swore angrily whenever he had to wait for his appointment. He had swung his cane menacingly at her a few times. Despite her desire to help him, all she or anyone could do was review his stride and adjust the prosthesis that replaced his right leg. She felt that even this small service was of benefit, yet she had to endure his harsh treatment.

She was working more and more shifts at the hospital, and she knew she didn't have the same energy or acute awareness as when she started. She seemed to be curt with patients when they weren't willing to follow her instructions. She also snapped at her staff and sometimes her superiors.

And after a long, tough day, she often came home to an empty house. Bill was having enormous success with the company and was gone two to three weeks each month. When he was home, it was almost as if they had to reacquaint themselves. To Susan, Bill's work was dominating their lives. (Though Bill would argue the opposite, that Susan's work was the dominating factor.) At times, she felt as if Bill had left her, at least mentally. She didn't sleep well when he wasn't home, and she had no one to turn to when she needed a sympathetic ear.

So she started stopping in for a few drinks with her fellow nurses at the Thunderbird after work. Some cocktails and conversation helped her unwind.

But more than just nurses gathered for happy hour. Susan had attracted a new admirer by the name of Dr. Herman Bahl. The nurses called him "Handy Herman." He was one of the doctors she had been warned about when she started.

Herman often showed up at the Thunderbird too. He bragged about his conquests, claiming he did his best work when women had a few drinks in them. Whenever he appeared, the nurses just scattered to avoid being trapped and groped. He was particularly interested in Susan, however. She constantly rejected his advances, but he just would not go away.

Early one Thursday morning, Bill and Susan were having a rare breakfast together before Susan headed to work. As usual lately, they both sensed an underlying and unspoken tension, yet they were actually enjoying a few moments together when the phone rang.

Susan wiped her lips carefully with her napkin so she didn't mess her lipstick, then she grabbed the phone. "Hello. O'Briens."

"Is Bill O'Brien available?" came the response.

"Sure. May I tell him who's calling?"

"This is George Donovan of the FAA."

"Yes, just a minute!" Susan put her hand over the receiver. "Bill, it's the FAA inspector!"

Bill jumped up, knocking his knife, spoon, and napkin on the floor. Susan noted that all three had been in the exact spots where she had placed them when setting the table. Bill hadn't used any of them.

"Yes, George—this is Bill." He hoped he didn't sound as anxious as he felt.

Susan started quietly clearing plates from the table and loading the dishwasher.

George took a deep breath. "Bill, I wanted to let you know we definitely found evidence of tampering with the aircraft. There are two issues. First, our metallurgist discovered that some of the parts used in the steering mechanism were nonaviation grade. His metal-fatigue analysis confirmed that the replacement rods and cabling would have never survived the stress of a prolonged flight. At some point, they broke or came loose, and the plane was uncontrollable.

"Second, the internal cabling for the elevator and rudder were frayed. On one side, they had broken. The other side was intact but showed signs of being partially cut. Your dad was a good pilot. He would have checked the movement of the elevator and rudder in his preflight, but these cables were cut inside. You can only see them by removing the wing housing."

Bill was stunned. He thought back to the morning his family had taken off on the ill-fated flight. His dad had checked the weather and verified his route to see if he needed to adjust his flight plan. Bill had walked around the plane, chatting with his father about the trip. He knew his father had his clipboard and had carefully checked off items as he reviewed the plane.

"But there's more, Bill," George said. "We issued a search warrant for Sean's house and found similar nonaviation-grade steering mechanism parts in the garage. Credit card receipts signed by your uncle were right in the boxes too. We also found tools that could have been used to cut the cables. Our team is testing the tool marks to see if there's a match. I'm not sure why he kept all that, but I'm glad he did."

Bill's knees buckled. Even though he had suspected Sean was involved somehow in the plane crash, this was too much to take.

"I'll get this evidence written up for the federal attorney by tomorrow," George continued. "It'll be up to him to decide what, if any, charges can be leveled."

Bill thanked the inspector and hung up the phone. He remained motionless for several seconds, holding the kitchen counter for support.

"Bill?" Susan asked. "What did he say?"

"He's got evidence of sabotage from Sean. If they can make a case, it would probably put him away for life."

Susan hesitated. "I'm kind of conflicted. I'm happy they found the evidence but sorry you had to lose your family to this scumbag."

"Yeah," Bill mumbled.

As much as Bill disliked his uncle, he couldn't fathom that Sean would have deliberately taken steps to kill the entire family. Yes, Sean had always been jealous of Michael, but they were still brothers. They had a close bond. Was Sean that evil, to kill his own brother and his brother's family? And if Sean had done it, had he been so dumb as to hang on to the parts and tools that caused the plane crash?

Had someone else been involved in this?

Finally, Bill broke out of his thoughts. He went over to give Susan a kiss on the cheek so as not to muss up her lipstick.

She smiled briefly, then left for work.

46.

SUSAN'S INCREASED WORKLOAD AT THE VA made it nearly impossible for her to get away for an excursion to their cabin. She had two weeks of vacation time available, but she couldn't—or wouldn't—use it.

So Bill often headed up to the cabin alone. The quiet and seclusion helped him think, and there was always routine maintenance to keep him busy. One time it was a plumbing leak, then a bird took out a window, then some siding needed replacing. He also helped the contractor wire the house for electricity.

After years of abandonment, the house also needed painting. As they discussed it back home in Minnesota, Susan convinced Bill to call the trusty contractor for that task.

"I don't want you on a ladder, painting a two-story house with no contact or assistance within twenty miles!" Susan admonished him. "Besides, I know your track record with paintbrushes."

Truthfully, Bill was happy to hire out the painting. That meant he didn't have to buy a big ladder, and it would save him plenty of time for exploring the hiking trails near the Huron Mountains.

On one of his solo trips, Bill readied his backpack for a springtime hike, this time with a topographic map in hand. He had marked the coordinates of the base his mother mentioned in her journals. He packed plenty of water and food—well, his kind of food. It was mostly snacks. He tossed in a fleece jacket, a rainsuit, a compass, binoculars, a flashlight with fresh batteries, a rope and tarp for an impromptu tent, and his jackknife. He also threw in a can of bear spray, even though Dale Patterson had warned him that it didn't really deter bears as much as tenderize the user's flesh when it blew back.

He drove the jeep over Big Eric's Bridge and followed the marked snowmobile trails several miles from the cabin. Finding a turnout near the top of the Huron Mountains, he parked and set out hiking northeast along the trails.

Most of the trails were merely animal paths. He scared up a whitetail doe with twin fawns as he came around a bend. They were grazing happily in tall grass next to the path.

Where there are deer, there are usually wolves or coyotes. Pulling off his backpack, Bill retrieved the bear spray and put it in his pocket.

I wonder if this works on wolves any better than on bears, Bill thought. In any event, it was his only weapon, so he figured it might be worth keeping handy.

A pile of scat on the trail reminded Bill this truly was bear country. He decided to make some noise so he wouldn't startle them as he came around the bends. He started singing the Beatles' hit "Drive My Car" at the top of his lungs. He particularly liked the "beep, beep" chorus. The deer didn't appreciate it and moved on.

The woods in early spring were cool and crisp, not at all like the jungles of Vietnam. Bill was tracking to coordinates, just as he had done with his compass in 'Nam, but here no one was shooting at him.

He neared the coordinates a little over five miles down the trail. Stopping for a sip of water and a handful of raisins and cashews, he scanned the area with his binoculars.

Across a small gorge, he could see through the bare tree limbs. A leveled spot at the top of the gorge looked out of place. Towering trees surrounded it, but only small poplar saplings sprouted in the leveled area. He estimated they were maybe only twenty years old.

He saw a deer path heading down into the gorge and up the other side. Tossing the backpack over his shoulder, he headed out to check the area. Climbing up the side of the gorge, he saw a solid base of gravel on the level spot.

Actually, those saplings must be older than twenty years if they worked their way through this, he mused.

He could also see the mouth of a large cave. It was nearly twelve feet high with a jumble of rocks just inside the opening. Bill thought the cavern had collapsed, but on further investigation, he found there was an opening at the top. He scrambled up to the top of the rock pile, pulled off his backpack, and prepared to slide in.

He came to his senses just before ducking his head under. What was he thinking? Where there are dark caverns, there are usually bears.

He checked the surrounding rocks for bear scat. Nothing.

"Hey, bear!" he yelled into the opening.

"Hey, bear!" echoed back out.

Bill shrugged, turned on his flashlight, and pushed his pack ahead of him through the opening. As he slid down the backside of the rock pile, he scanned the cave walls with the flashlight beam. To his left were smooth walls of sandstone reinforced with large timbers. There was a similar support system to the right as well.

As his flashlight illuminated the beams on the right, he saw a carving. He scooted over to check it out. A large bird with outspread wings had been artfully carved into the beam. Lettering below it was mostly hidden by a boulder.

Bill put the flashlight down on his backpack beside him. *I wonder if I can get that baby to move out of the way*, he thought as he gazed at the boulder.

He braced himself on the rock pile and pushed against the boulder with his feet. The boulder shifted. Suddenly, Bill realized that perhaps the whole rock pile might shift with the boulder and send everything down upon him.

"Ah, what the hell," he said out loud. "Nothing ventured, nothing gained."

He gave the boulder a harder push. It tumbled down the pile, landing at the base in a cloud of dust. Nothing else shifted.

Grabbing his flashlight, he scanned the carving on the beam again. The lettering was as carefully done as the bird: CONDOR.

Definitely the right place, he announced to himself and grinned.

Bill scampered down the side of the rock pile to the floor of the cave, dragging his backpack behind him. As he cast the flashlight back and forth, he saw the remnants of a railroad track sloping up from the opening into the dark recesses. The track near the opening was rusted, but farther up the slope, the rails were uprooted and tossed at angles, leaning against rockslides.

Okay, O'Brien, he said to himself, *let's see what kind of cojones you have. This whole place could crash down at any time!*

He realized Susan wouldn't be pleased if he called her from the hospital in Marquette. That is, if he could somehow manage to get himself to Marquette. If something were to happen, he'd likely be trapped. No one knew he was there or that this place existed.

Hell, Susan wouldn't be pleased if she knew he was in the cavern in the first place, even if he eventually escaped unharmed. Then again, considering how things had been between them lately, he felt maybe she wouldn't really care.

Bill hesitated briefly, then resigned himself to his adventurous side. He turned and took one more look at the daylight streaming through the cave opening before heading deeper into the abyss.

Bill followed the railroad tracks, stumbling over rocks and overturned ties. At one point, he tripped and went down on his right knee. He dropped the flashlight, and it flicked off, plunging him into the darkest dark he had ever experienced.

"Goddamn, that hurt!" he cursed aloud.

He waited a few moments, hoping his eyes would adjust enough to retrieve the flashlight. But there was no light whatsoever in the cave.

So he struggled out of the backpack straps and carefully felt the ground around his legs. Finally, he felt the cool metal of the flashlight casing.

"Come on, baby," he said hopefully, clicking the button on the side.

The rocks once again illuminated around him. He heaved a sigh of relief.

Damn. Now I know what it's like to be blind!

Limping from his injured knee, Bill slowly made his way to the back of the cave, watching his footing very carefully. He came to a fork in the tunnel.

The fork to the right had a dirt floor and seemed to go on forever. The one to the left was partially blocked by a rockslide that looked about six feet high.

He had gotten over the rocks at the cave mouth; in theory, he could get over these as well. He wasn't entirely convinced by his own logic, but he was never one to take the easy way. Scrambling up the new obstruction, he slid down the other side, splashing light around the scattered rocks and upended railroad ties.

Just four feet away was a heavy wooden door hanging precariously from its hinges. Bill kicked a few rocks out of the way, grabbed the leading edge of the door, and tugged at it. It swung open with a loud creak. Behind it was a steel door with a combination lock.

"What the fuck?" he exclaimed.

He listened as his words echoed back at him through the cave.

What in the world could require a steel door and combination lock at the end of an underground cavern? And how could he ever figure out the combination?

Rubbing his hands together, he decided to do the first thing anyone would do: he grabbed the door handle and pulled. No problem—it opened. The door wasn't even locked! It was stiff, and he had to move a few more fallen rocks, but he was in.

He stepped into a huge vault. At first glance, he could discern some shelving and metallic shapes that looked oddly familiar. His flashlight carved out the definitions on all sides as he carefully moved in a circle.

The air was dank and close, but it seemed breathable, at least for a while. He could feel an inflow of air from the mouth of the cave, so the circulation would help some.

He moved the light around the vault slowly, trying to decipher the shapes as they came into view. A few chairs were overturned near a desk and a table to the left. The desk contained what looked like radios. Some books and papers were scattered on the desktop and on the floor.

On the right was machinery that looked like a generator and maybe an air pump. That made sense. Whoever was there would have wanted light and fresh air.

He moved closer to the generator, thinking perhaps he could get it going for some light. That's when he noticed the labeling was in German.

My God, Mom! You were right! The Germans were right here in this cave during the war!

He moved to a series of tall cabinets on the right side of the vault. Opening one of the cabinets, he saw stacks of automatic weapons, pistols, and ammunition. In another were tools, although he had no idea what they were for. The third held small radio parts on the top shelves. The bottom shelf housed electronics parts similar to what he had seen his father using on the plane.

Deeper in the vault cavern were large freestanding racks. They reminded him of the wine cellar racks he had seen when he toured a California winery. But these racks didn't hold kegs of fermenting wine. These held rocket and bomb casings.

To the left of the racks were boxes of explosives. One of them was open, and he peered inside.

That's TNT! he silently exclaimed. *Damn—if that stuff is deteriorated, this whole place could go up!*

Time to make a hasty retreat.

He grabbed a couple of German Luger pistols and a machine gun off the shelf as souvenirs. Next, he quickly flipped through the papers on the desk. The verbiage was all in German, but the formatting was remarkably similar to orders he had seen at the firebase in Vietnam. Other papers looked like flight plans. He pulled together as much of the paper work as he could find.

As he crammed it into his backpack, three small leather-bound books caught his eye. He found they were handwritten journals in English.

Worst case, it'll make interesting reading material, he thought as he added them to his backpack as well.

Bill retraced his steps, carefully climbing the two rock piles and navigating over the railroad ties without tripping. Outside, he munched another handful of raisins and nuts and drank water to clear the dust from his throat.

What was once a gravel road led away from the cave mouth. He decided to see where it went. Grasses and small trees shot up through the gravel, trying to reclaim what had once been wilderness. Again, whitetail deer spooked as they watched him picking his way down the deteriorated road.

As he hiked, he vowed to give General Abrams a call when he got back to civilization. Bill was sure the general would be more than interested in this stash. Besides, the weapons and explosives needed to be cleared out by the authorities, not by treasure hunters.

Bill raised his eyebrows and shifted his overflowing pack a little higher on his shoulders.

Yeah, treasure hunters like me.

As he followed the road down a hill, he caught glimpses of a large flat prairie in the distance. A bull moose wandered aimlessly through the tall grasses, stomping a path across a black expanse and revealing some metallic reflections on the ground as he went. The trees on the edge of the prairie were obviously not as old as those on the outskirts. It looked like an abandoned tree nursery.

The road circled down the hillside for about two miles before Bill came to the prairie edge. That's when he discovered it wasn't a prairie or a nursery. He was standing on the end of a very long, very old blacktop runway, complete with crumpled and rusting landing lights.

At the other end of the runway were several rundown buildings and storage sheds. From the distance, one of the buildings looked like a control tower. It must have been quite an airport in its time.

Bill released a loud "Wow!"

It didn't take a genius to make a connection between an abandoned airport and a nearby stash of weapons from the 1940s. The Nazis must have been planning something right here in Michigan.

A light mist started to fall as Bill headed back up the road. He crossed into the gorge, hiked to the parking turnout, and drove the jeep back to the cabin as the light was beginning to fade. He was glad the jeep had a roof to protect him from the mist.

Contemplating the mist, Bill decided to pack up and be on the road to Minneapolis first thing in the morning. In the Upper Peninsula, you never know if winter is officially over—until it's officially over. Bill realized that a light mist could quickly become rain or even a late-spring snowstorm. With the lake effect, they could get twelve to fifteen inches overnight. The snow would melt as quickly as it had come, but Bill still wanted to get out ahead of it.

At the cabin, Bill sipped a bit of Jameson on the rocks as he sorted through the papers he had grabbed from the cavern. Those in German went in one pile. They did Bill little good. Someone on Abram's team would need to deal with those. Bill's conversational German was one thing, but reading the language was a whole different skill set. All he could make out was that several papers documented shipments through Rogers Airfreight, based in Detroit, Marquette, and New York.

He hit pay dirt, though, with several of the papers scribbled in broken English. They seemed to be translations of radio transmissions. They provided details for a plot to attack the locks near Sault Ste. Marie. Bill sorted the transmissions by date and scanned through them before setting the pile aside.

Next he opened one of the leather-bound journals. They were all written by Fritz Schmidt, who was apparently the commander of the base.

Bill leaned back in his chair. Could this really be the same Fritz that was his mother's brother-in-law? He read the journals well into the night.

Early the next morning, Bill hid the two Lugers, the machine gun, and the German papers in the crawl space under the cabin. He put Fritz's journals in his backpack, then hopped in the Rocket.

Driving the thirty miles to L'Anse for breakfast at the Nite Owl Café, he was still contemplating the journal entries. Based on his mother's journals and the family connection with this Fritz Schmidt, he wanted to see where these new journals led him before he decided to hand them over.

After a hearty breakfast, Bill called General Abrams from a pay phone.

"Want to come up to Michigan for a trout fishing excursion? I've got a little sideshow for you too," he teased.

47.

WO WEEKS LATER, SPRING HAD TRULY COME to the Upper Peninsula. Jeff in L'Anse assured Bill that the steelhead and rainbow trout were indeed running.

The general met Bill at the air force base at Wold-Chamberlain Field in Minneapolis. His son, Dean, also joined them, as he had some time off from the law firm.

General Abrams wasn't up for the seven-hour drive between Minneapolis and the cabin, even in the Rocket. He arranged for a jet to fly them to the base at Marquette in just over an hour. A rental car would be waiting for them there.

"The drive to the cabin from Marquette will probably take longer than the flight," Bill joked.

They hiked to the Huron River mouth first thing in the morning. The Abrams family proved to be excellent fishing company. It didn't take long to fill their creels with large keepers.

"Looks like it's trout for dinner tonight!" Bill commented.

Abrams laughed heartily. "Yep, and since Dean caught the biggest one, he can do the cooking."

They headed back to the cabin to clean the fish and put them on ice. As they grabbed a little lunch, Bill suggested they take an afternoon hike.

"As I told you, I have something you really need to see," he added.

Dean laughed and looked at his father. "Think you're up for a hike?"

"Hell, yes," Abrams said. "After sitting on my can in meetings at the Pentagon day after day, I need some exercise."

"You ride in front, Dad. I'll take the back seat," Dean offered as Bill backed the jeep out of the garage.

Abrams skirted around to the passenger side. "What the hell is that?" he exclaimed when he spotted the big yellow smiley face.

"Sorry, General—that's my concession to Susan," Bill explained. "If I want a camouflage jeep, she gets to decorate her side."

Abrams climbed in and slammed the door. "Son of a bitch—I'm riding in a fucking hippie's sunshine-mobile."

Bill laughed as they headed down the back roads, over Big Eric's Bridge, and beyond. As they finally pulled out of the trees and traversed a sandy plain, Bill found the parking area and pulled the jeep off the trail.

"We'll walk in from here," he announced.

"Good thing," responded the general, unfolding his bulky frame from the seat and stretching after the rough ride over the rutted roads. He took a deep breath of refreshing air.

"You lead, William. I haven't had this much fun in years. This is a good day to die!" he joked.

Dean just shook his head. He knew his dad had more moxie than men half his age. A little hike wouldn't be a problem.

Bill led the way to the tunnel and scrambled up the rock pile at its mouth. He glanced back and saw Abrams hesitate briefly to turn on his flashlight, then clamor up after him. Dean followed closely. Ducking under the cave roof, Bill flipped on his flashlight and scampered down the other side. He turned around and played his light on the rocks to help the others pick their way down.

"Watch your footing in here," he warned. "The rocks are everywhere, and the rails are slippery."

When Abrams finally landed on the cavern floor next to Bill, he commented, "William, you owe me a hell of a big scotch if we don't find something pretty terrific stuffed in this cave."

Bill continued down the passageway to the left fork and over the second pile of rocks. When Abrams and Dean were safely beside him, he pulled the wooden door back carefully. The steel vault door was visible.

"Want to guess what that is?" he asked, trying to hide his excitement.

"Looks like a door to me," responded Dean in earnest.

Bill and Abrams both played their lights into Dean's eyes.

"He gets that part of his smarts from his mother's side," quipped Abrams. "My dear son, what do you think a damn door is doing here in a cave?"

Dean buried his face in his hands, both to shut out the glare of the lights and from embarrassment.

Abrams turned back to the door. "Okay, William—let's see what the hell is behind door number one."

"Yes, sir!" Bill pulled the vault door open and stepped inside.

As their flashlights illuminated the various corners of the vault, Bill heard the general gasp.

"Jesus Christ Almighty! This is Nazi equipment! There are bombs, explosives. And over there—that's an Enigma machine!" Abrams was finally speechless as he continued to take inventory of the cavern.

Abrams wandered over to the desk and put his hand on the Enigma. "This is one of the most sophisticated communication devices used by the Nazis during World War II. Many ships were sunk by coded messages sent on these back in the forties."

He mulled over the discovery.

"I'll get a bomb-disposal team on this ASAP. We better get out of here before we disturb the wrong rock and have this place go up in smoke around us." Abrams was now thinking out loud. "But how in the hell did they get all this stuff in here? We're in the middle of nowhere."

Bill looked at the general. "Sir, there's an old abandoned airport down the hill. It's about two miles away. That has to be how they got it in here."

"A lot of these abandoned airports were used by the army during the war," responded Abrams. "They used them to protect the Soo Locks. I'll have to see if that airport was one of them. Maybe we can find out who built it too."

With one more glance around the chamber, Abrams herded the boys out and carefully pushed the vault door back in place.

Back at the cabin, Bill went down in the crawl space and retrieved the Lugers, the machine gun, and the papers he had gathered on his first excursion.

"General, I have a few souvenirs for you. I picked them up the first time I was in the cave."

Bill saw the general's startled expression.

"I figured if the place went up in smoke before you could see it, at least I'd have proof of what was there," Bill quickly explained. "If all I had was just my story, you'd probably chalk it up to a lonely man in a backwoods cabin sipping a bit too much Jameson!"

Abrams's expression softened. "Okay, William—I see your point. I guess it's best to have something as proof. But you better stick to that story if anyone asks why you have an arsenal in your crawl space!"

The general scanned the documents, then handed them to Dean. "Put your German language education to use, son."

Dean sorted through the papers to put them in some semblance of order. "It looks like it was a secret Nazi base set up in 1938 or '39," he started to explain. "The mission seems to have been a strike on selected war production points in the United States—in the event we joined the war against Germany. According to this, the key target was the locks at Sault Ste. Marie."

Dean shuffled some more of the papers and scanned a bit further.

"Looks like the weapons were smuggled in before World War II started in Poland. There are even references to three Fw 200 bombers." Dean flipped back through the sheaf of paper. "Wait a minute. This stack has control tower messages. Looks like an Fw 200 was cleared as a Rogers Airfreight run for a flight over the Soo Locks in late 1940—but it never returned."

Abrams had been sitting on the edge of his chair. The healthy scotch Bill had poured him was forgotten on the table.

"What the hell?" he exclaimed. "I've studied the development of air travel for years. But I don't know of any missing planes in this area from that era. Or any unexplained crashes, for that matter. I wonder if that baby went into the lake and no one even realized it!"

While Dean continued translating the documents, Bill cooked a fabulous trout dinner with all the trimmings. When their plates were clean and stomachs full, Abrams decided they had better cut their visit short.

"Let's head over to the base in the morning," he said. "I'll check in with the local commander and connect up with the coast guard in Marquette. I want to start the weapons cleanup and see if any plane wreckage has ever been detected in the Whitefish Bay area."

Bill nodded and poured one more after-dinner round. "Thanks for joining this 'fishing' expedition. Hope the trout and the weapons met your expectations!"

48.

S USAN HARDLY REALIZED BILL HAD RETURNED from Michigan. One
day she saw him unpacking, and the next she saw him packing
again, this time for a business trip.

Not that Bill's comings and goings really mattered to Susan.
She was still busy working extra shifts. Her job was her entire life now. She
knew the long hours were draining her, but it was better to be at the hospital
trying to help her guys than to be in an empty house with no husband.

But then it happened. One night, she was straightening up an empty
bed, ticking through her long mental to-do list for her shift. Suddenly she
was struck from behind by something hard. In an instant, she was thrown
on top of the bed.

Lying there stunned, she could feel the attacker trying to rip off her clothes.
He slapped her hard several times, trying to subdue her. He tore her blouse and
began reaching under her skirt to rip off her panty hose and underwear.

Susan let out a blood-curdling scream and flailed at the attacker with
all her might.

Hearing her scream, a male ward attendant burst into the room. As
fast as everything had begun, it was over. The ward attendant yanked the
attacker off Susan and forcefully led him out of the room.

Susan was dizzy from the blow to her head and bleeding from several abrasions on her face and arms. She tried to stand, but instead she just
leaned against the bed and began to sob.

The on-duty supervisor rushed in. "Susan—my God! I heard the commotion. What happened?"

Susan could only continue to sob as the supervisor helped her to the nurses' lounge. As the supervisor and other nurses tended to Susan's injuries, word came in that the attacker was a man from the psychiatric ward. He had managed to stray through an accidentally unlocked door.

Susan was angry at the lack of security that allowed a mental patient to end up in her ward. She was also angry that Bill wasn't home to comfort her. He would be gone on business for two more days, and the house would be empty.

Mostly, though, Susan was angry with herself for being caught unaware. Deb and the others had warned her about this. She decided it was her fault. She told herself she had to dig down and try even harder.

When Susan assured everyone she was feeling better, her supervisor gently ordered her to go home and rest. So Susan changed clothes, left the hospital, and headed over to the Thunderbird for a drink. More than one, actually. Anything to avoid going to an empty house that hadn't offered any comfort for some time.

When Bill arrived home late on Friday night, he was surprised that Susan was already in bed. He was concerned, since she had been suffering insomnia recently, but he let her sleep. The next morning, he finally saw the deep scratches and bruises on her arms and her cheek.

"How in the world did you get the bruises?"

She hesitated before replying. "Oh, I ran into something at work. It's nothing. I'm fine."

Bill was not convinced. His boxing training made him well aware of wounds caused by someone's fists. He pressed further.

"Susie, I'm worried about you. Are you sure you're all right?" He set a cup of coffee on the table for her. "Something's wrong here. I never get to see you anymore. Can you cut back on the hours at the VA? You work late and go out afterward for drinks."

Exasperated, Susan looked up at him. "Bill, you're almost never here! What am I supposed to do, sit around an empty house? I never complain when you're out traveling for a week. Besides, I have a duty to my patients." She picked up the cup and sipped it like a barrier between them.

"I agree, but maybe we could find a happy medium. I'm worried that you're working too hard. It seems to be dominating your time and interests. You seem tired and frustrated. I never know what to expect when we try to talk. And now you have these bruises. I know you didn't run into something. Those are from someone's fists. I can't stand seeing you injured. Who did this to you?"

Susan slammed the cup on the table and stood up. "I think I'm the best judge of what's best for me."

She stormed out of the room, leaving Bill bewildered and searching for answers.

As two weeks passed, Susan became even more withdrawn and angry. She would yell at the neighborhood children crossing their yard and get mad and throw things in the kitchen. Worst of all, she never smiled. She seemed very angry at almost everything Bill tried to do around the house. Her glow had just disappeared.

Bill was determined to find out what was going on, but he knew he had to tread lightly. He thought a social outing might cheer her up. Bill knew Susan and Deb were good friends. Perhaps if they went out with Deb and her husband, Bill could start building a bridge from Susan's work life to her home life. Plus, Bill wanted a chance to talk to Deb alone. If anyone knew what was going on, it would be Deb.

So that afternoon, he followed Susan into the bedroom and leaned against the doorframe.

"Susie, why don't we have dinner at the Ranch House Restaurant with Deb and her husband? I could make reservations for tonight."

"I doubt they'd be available at such short notice," she responded with her back turned.

"Give her a call. You never know."

After more prodding, Susan finally gave in and called her friend. Deb accepted the invitation quickly.

"Stuart and I would be glad to join you. I think we could all use a nice quiet night out, Sue."

During dinner, Susan was quiet and looked tired. She didn't take part in the conversation. When addressed, she replied only with brief statements. She pushed her food around on the plate and appeared anxious to have the meal over as soon as possible.

Toward the end of the meal, Susan got up to use the restroom. This gave Bill the opportunity to ask Deb about Susan.

Deb checked over her shoulder to make sure Susan was out of earshot, then she sighed.

"Bill, she's working too many hours. She gets angry with any staff who dare ask her to slow down. And I have to admit," Deb continued, "I've noticed alcohol on her breath in the afternoons. Some people have told me they've seen her taking amphetamines, probably to allow her to keep working those long hours. Amphetamines cause irritability and hostility. They also cause a loss of appetite and insomnia. Over a long time, this can lead to depression and anxiety."

Bill sat back in his chair, trying to understand all he was hearing. He glanced at Stuart, who was staring intently at his wineglass.

My God, thought Bill. *Am I the last one to hear about this? How could I not see this coming?*

"In addition," Deb continued, "she's been at the Thunderbird almost every night and drinking too much. As you know, Bill, alcohol is a sedative and amphetamines are stimulants. Mixing the drugs and alcohol may cause her to lose track of both of them, resulting in alcohol poisoning."

Deb shook her head in concern for both Susan and Bill.

"We've all been worried about her since the attack."

Bill glanced up and locked eyes with Deb. "What attack?"

"Heavens, Bill—didn't you know? She was attacked and nearly raped by a mental patient. You were on a business trip, so we did our best to help her through it. I assumed she told you when you noticed the bruises."

Bill was close to tears. "She told me she ran into something at work. She lied to me. I just knew someone hit her. But to learn she was also nearly raped—what kind of hell is this job turning into? What the hell can we do about this?"

"Patients can be nasty at times and sometimes dangerous. But this is way beyond the norm, even for the VA. The nursing supervisor who helped her after the attack said it was quite brutal. It's a good thing Susan could fight the guy off as much as she did, or she could have been very severely injured."

Deb reached across the table and put her hand on Bill's clenched fist.

"She needs all the help you can get for her, Bill. She's on the edge. An attack like that is one of the most traumatic experiences a woman can ever endure. She has not been the same since."

Bill saw Susan heading back to the table and struggled to regain his composure. The weight was almost too much to bear. She'd been attacked and nearly raped. And he hadn't been there to support her. She had to spend two nights alone because he was out of town. He was gone when she most needed him. She turned to drugs and alcohol for her support. He was ashamed. No wonder she was angry with him.

They drove home quietly. Susan headed straight to bed, but Bill called out to her.

"Susan, wait."

She stopped but kept her back turned to him. He could see her shoulders tense.

"Deb told you, didn't she?" Her voice was as tense as her body.

"Yes. She's your friend, and she's concerned for you." He paused. "I'm concerned for you. My God—you could have been killed! Why don't you get another job or at least take some extended time off? You've earned it with all the hours you've been working."

She spun around, her hands balled in fists at her sides. "Don't tell me what to do! Since we've been married, I've taken a back seat to your business, but you don't hear me telling you what to do!"

It was the truth, and it hurt. He didn't know what to say, so he focused back on Susan.

"I would never tell you what to do. I never have. I love and respect you too much to do that. I'm just asking you to take a look at what's happening. I just don't want you to get hurt again. This job is too dangerous."

Susan shook her head. For a moment, the anger in her eyes turned to despair. "Look, it was nothing. It was my fault. I wasn't alert. I was tired and not doing my job properly. Deb warned me about something like this when I started. I just have to do a better job." Then her eyes hardened again. "But the VA work is what I set out to do, and I'm going to do it. Nursing is my life!"

With that, she turned on her heel and disappeared into the bedroom, leaving Bill to wonder where and how he fit into her life.

Bill had many questions but no answers. Susan headed off to work on Monday without exchanging a glance, let alone a word, with her husband. As her car pulled out of the garage, Bill called Dr. Rob Nelson, a psychiatrist he had met at a business luncheon at Murray's. Dr. Nelson had a practice in the Medical Arts Building in downtown Minneapolis. Bill luckily caught him at a good time, before his appointments started for the day.

"Dr. Nelson, I was hoping you could perhaps help me sort through an issue my wife is facing. I want to help her, but I'm not sure where to start."

"Describe Susan's symptoms and history for me," the doctor began.

Bill highlighted Susan's experience in the MASH unit in Vietnam, her fiancé's POW status, her stressful work at the VA, and the attack at the hospital. He also explained that Susan was using alcohol and amphetamines in order to deal with her day-to-day activities.

"For as long as I've known her, she's struggled at times. But she's really struggling now."

"Until I can examine Susan, I can only guess," the doctor explained. "But I think she may be suffering from an illness called post-traumatic stress disorder, or PTSD. It affects women more than men. From what I've read, PTSD can really be a problem with nurses, as it seems to attack their caring instincts. On top of that, something like a near rape could be a prime stressor for PTSD."

Bill was grateful the doctor had taken the time to explain the syndrome. "So what course of treatment do you recommend?"

"Again, it's a bit early to talk treatment before I see the patient," Dr. Nelson cautioned. "I'd like to see Susan and discuss her drug and alcohol use. That is separate from the PTSD diagnosis and treatment."

Bill nodded silently, knowing that Susan wouldn't be willing to admit to a problem. For her, admitting she had a problem was the same as admitting she had failed.

"As far as the other issues," Dr. Nelson continued, "we have a treatment called cognitive processing therapy, or CPT, that works quite well for people with PTSD. It's a process that identifies a person's 'stuck' points. These are areas where victims can't accommodate the information about a trauma, since it doesn't fit into their existing beliefs or memory schemes. The idea is to get the victim to develop a new understanding of the trauma, and then we focus on the victim's beliefs about the meaning and implications of the trauma. Sometimes there's fairly rapid progress, particularly if the trauma has been recent. But other people require long-term treatment, and even then, it may not be totally successful."

After thanking Dr. Nelson and saying his good-byes, Bill had much to consider. He knew how Susan felt about support group therapy from her comments back at Fort Sam. What would she think about more formal treatment, such as CPT?

Bill didn't know how to answer that question right now, but he did know one thing: he needed time and freedom. He needed to be home.

Next, he called Jessica. "You have to fire me," he told her.

"What in the world are you talking about?"

"It's hard to explain, but I need some time away. Susan is in rough shape, and we'll never find our way out of it unless I'm here at home to support her."

Jessica immediately grew serious. "Absolutely, Bill. What do you have in mind?"

"I've got the big trip to Ford Motor Company in Detroit coming up in a few days. I'm meeting with the vice president responsible for shipping. After that, I'd like to clear my schedule. Could you find someone to fill in for me for a while?"

"I'm on it," Jessica said.

Before Bill could even thank her, she hung up. And before he even knew it, she was ringing him back later that afternoon.

"You are temporarily fired," she said.

Bill could only smile when he heard that her father, Rudolph, was willing to handle Bill's customer service duties as long as necessary.

49.

Susan's silent treatment was continuing with no end in sight. By breakfast the next morning, she still wasn't speaking to Bill. In an attempt to break the ice, he decided to tell her about discovering the military base in the Huron Mountains. Even as he told her about his daring adventure through the cave, she never once looked up from her untouched plate of food.

Undeterred, he showed her Fritz's journals. "I was thinking maybe we could delve into the details together, comparing these journals to my mother's. Together, we might just solve a mystery!"

Susan nodded absentmindedly as she gathered her purse and car keys, getting ready to leave for work. "Mm-hm."

At least it's a response, he thought to himself. *It's a start.*

He pressed a little further. "Maybe we can get started tonight. I'm home for a few days now before I head to Detroit. But once I'm back, I'm going to be home for a while. Won't it be nice to have more time together?"

He smiled expectantly, hoping to see some reaction, some acknowledgment of how important it was for them to reconnect.

Susan ignored nearly every word. "I can't tonight—I'll be home late." She headed for the door. "Don't wait up on me," she added as the door closed behind her.

Bill just sat there at the table, staring down at the two sets of journals. Silence echoed throughout the house. The only thing he could think to do was open the journals and begin reading.

Fritz Schmidt held a rank equivalent to an American lieutenant colonel. His call sign, as documented by Helene, was Condor 123. That tied to the Condor references Bill had seen carved in the cave's support beam.

Per Helene's journal, Fritz had two brothers, Albert and Johann. That was also noted in Fritz's journal in one of the last entries.

I miss my wife, Elisa, and sons, Otto and Adolf. I fear I have been assigned a suicide mission here and will never see them again. Rogers has mentioned my brother Johann in Detroit but warned me never to contact him. Perhaps that is best.

Albert is gone. I probably will not see my parents, Otto and Emma Schmidt, again. They are living happily in nearby Detroit. It is best I do not contact them either.

My comrades are gone, killed in the Battle of Britain. I am alone, and I truly doubt that Hitler is building a better Germany, as he promised.

Looks like Fritz was up to his neck in this plan, Bill thought to himself. *I wonder where he is now—if he made it out alive.*

Bill reread the entry again, this time lingering at the name Rogers. He recalled a Rogers Airfreight from the German documents he gave General Abrams. He'd have to check with the general to see if they'd found any connection between the Nazis and this Rogers.

He continued to read Fritz's journal to the last entry:

I have made a mistake by returning to the United States for this mission. I fear my prior beliefs cost Elisa's parents their lives. I did not realize the Gestapo would go to such lengths.

My flight tomorrow may be my last, even though it is only a test flight to make sure the planes can handle the weight of the bombs. The defenses at the locks are being strengthened. They may even shoot us down on this test flight. I fear if I tell Dietrich, he may refuse to accompany me to take the pictures. This flight is being done under my authority and not under Rogers's.

Bill closed the journal with a sad heart. Gazing out the window, deep in thought, Bill looked as though he were in another world.

Both Fritz and Bill's mother told of such sorrows. War tore the Schmidt family apart. Bill wanted to find his lost stepsister, Katrina, in Canada. He wanted to find Elisa and her children and share Fritz's journals with them. He knew those diaries would mean as much to them as his mother's meant to him. It would be cathartic for them all. Or perhaps he could find Johann.

Wait a minute, Bill thought. *Johann Schmidt . . .*

Suddenly he remembered a Johann Schmidt at his family's funeral. Johann had represented the Ford family; he was an executive with Edsel and Henry Ford II. And even Jack Patterson, Dale's father, had mentioned him just a few years ago. Maybe he was still around in Detroit.

Bill immediately called the personnel office at the Ford Motor Company.

"Hi, my name is Bill O'Brien, and I'm with M. O. Airfreight. I have a meeting this week with Harold Dugan. But in addition, I'm trying to connect with an executive who may have retired a few years ago from your corporation. His name is Johann Schmidt. I believe he worked closely with Edsel and Henry Ford II. He was a friend of my father's."

"Hold on. Let me check our retiree files, sir," a perky sounding woman responded. After a few moments, the perky voice provided a phone number and address in Detroit.

Bill was nervous as he dialed the number, rehearsing what he would say to this distant relative.

"Hello?" a man answered.

"Hello, is this Johann Schmidt?"

"Yes, may I help you with something?"

Bill took a breath. "I don't know if you remember me. My name is William O'Brien. My father was Michael O'Brien."

"The O'Brien who started M. O. Airfreight?" was the astonished response.

"Yes. You were kind enough to attend my family's funeral in 1962."

"Yes, yes. I knew your father. I was terribly sad to hear of the death of your family."

"Mr. Schmidt, I'd like to meet with you and share some information about your own family—information you may not be aware of."

"Really?" Johann was even more astonished now. "I'm very interested. Do you get to the Detroit area often?"

"Actually, I'll be there on Wednesday. I've taken over ownership and customer service for M. O. Airfreight. One of my largest customers is Ford Motor Company, and I have an upcoming meeting there."

"Maybe we can get together at the Detroit Athletic Club around one o'clock for a late lunch?" Johann suggested.

"I would be honored."

"Very good. I'll make the reservations and look forward to seeing you then."

Bill was extra excited now for his trip to Detroit, yet he was nervous about leaving Susan alone. He had one more call to make—this time to Wisconsin.

"Bill!" Jewel greeted when she picked up the phone. "What a surprise! I hope you're calling me to let me know I'm going to be a grandma," she added with a laugh.

On his end, Bill gave a sad smile. *If only it were that simple . . .*

"Actually, I'm calling because I need your help with Susan."

Immediately, Jewel's tone changed. "Bill, what's wrong?"

He took a breath, then launched in, telling her everything. At the mention of Susan nearly being raped, Jewel broke down sobbing.

"She blames herself for the attack," Bill continued. "She says she should have been more aware, more careful. She's overworking herself. She isn't receptive to my suggestions to find another nursing position. I've also heard she's drinking too much and might be taking drugs to help her work long hours. A lot of it may be a reaction to her time in Vietnam and the traumas she's faced."

Bill could hear Jewel still sniffling and crying.

"The hardest part is, she's shutting me out. I was away on business when the attack happened. I will forever blame myself for not being there that night." He stopped and cleared his throat, giving himself a moment.

Jewel composed herself, letting out a deep sigh. "Bill, what can we do to help you both?"

"I've put all my involvement with the business on hold, except for a trip this week to Detroit. I need to meet with our biggest customer and then handle some personal business. While I'm gone, I was wondering if you could stay here so Susan sees a loving face when she comes home from work."

Bill never doubted what answer he'd receive.

"We'll drive up tomorrow and 'surprise' you both," she stated. "We'll be there before you leave, and we'll stay as long as we're needed. You tell Susan we called today to let you know we planned a little vacation to Minneapolis."

Bill smiled gratefully at the deviousness of his mother-in-law.

When Susan arrived home from work, Bill was checking the refrigerator for something for dinner. He looked up and smiled.

"Hey, Susie—your mom called. She said they're taking a short vacation. They're coming up tomorrow to visit for a couple days. I'm sorry I'll miss them because I have that trip to Detroit. But I bet it'll be nice for you to see them again."

Susan tossed her coat on a nearby chair. "I don't have time to look after my parents right now!" Then her eyes narrowed, and she glared at him. "Bill, they never take vacations. What did you tell her?"

"What? I . . ." Bill stammered.

Susan flushed. "Damn it! You had no right to get them involved in this situation." She grabbed her coat and purse and headed out the door. "Cook your own damn dinner! I'm heading to the Thunderbird. I may be home late . . . or maybe not at all!"

Bill closed the refrigerator door and stood in stunned silence as he heard Susan's car door slam. The roar of the engine faded in the night.

Later that night, Bill heard Susan stumble into the guest bedroom. When he was sure she was asleep, he went in and covered her with a blanket.

He stood there and watched her sleep. He knew she'd leave for work the next morning without a word. He'd wait for her parents to arrive, explain the latest situation to them, then leave for the airfield for his flight to Detroit.

50.

BILL'S MEETING WITH THE SHIPPING REPRESENTATIVE at Ford went well, as he expected. It was more of a courtesy call, but Bill knew how important it was to stay in touch with customers. It was hard, though, to keep from checking his watch every few minutes. He was anxious about his lunch with Johann.

After the meeting, he took a taxi to the Detroit Athletic Club. He asked for Mr. Schmidt and was led to a nice table by the window, where a smartly groomed man in his early sixties stood to greet him.

"Good afternoon, William. I hope your meeting was a success."

"Yes, it was. Thank you. And thank you so much for arranging a late lunch at such a great location."

"I always like to eat here now," Johann said with a chuckle. "When I was younger, I couldn't afford it."

The two men ordered the whitefish special. Johann selected a bottle of white wine to accompany the meal.

"Tell me what you've been doing since I saw you at the funeral. That's been—what, ten years?"

"Yes. Actually a little over ten years," Bill responded.

He quickly summarized his service in Vietnam, his marriage, and the issues with his uncle. He couldn't call them highlights, just events.

Johann shook his head. "William, war is a tragedy. Very little good ever comes from it. Several of my family members were caught up in World War II and never heard from again. I'm so happy you came out of Vietnam in one piece physically and that you have a wife to help with the remainder of the healing."

Bill winced a bit, thinking about his wife and healing. He quickly moved on.

"Speaking of your family, Mr. Schmidt—"

"Please, call me Johann."

"All right, Johann. I have some information about your family that I think you'll be amazed to hear. You and I are actually related through my mother."

As lunch was served, Bill started his narrative.

"My mother was actually married to your brother Albert. She kept a diary during their marriage, and she expressed her love for him so many times. After Albert disappeared while flying from Johannesburg to Rio de Janeiro in 1939, she changed her name from Freda Fromm to Helene Bahr. Albert actually disappeared the day Hitler invaded Poland, and Freda needed to hide with her daughter."

Johann glanced away for a second, trying to piece it all together. "Are you saying Helene O'Brien was actually Albert's wife, Freda?" He shook his head in disbelief. "And to think I attended her funeral, even though I wasn't aware of our relationship. It means more to me than you could know to make that connection."

Johann picked up his wineglass and took a sip to settle the lump in his throat.

"There's more," Bill said, taking a quick sip of his wine as well. "You have a niece you've never met. Freda and Albert had a daughter named Katrina. Freda fled with Katrina to England. From there, Freda—now Helene—worked for the British Special Operations Executive, or SOE, parachuting into Germany. Katrina was sent to Canada by the British government, but all information on her location was lost when London was bombed. I believe she's still living in Canada, and I'm hoping to find her."

Johann sat back in his seat in shock, trying to take it all in.

But Bill wasn't finished with his story. "And then there's Fritz."

Johann leaned forward again. Something in his expression changed. "Do you have information about Fritz? The last time I saw him, he met our family in New York in late 1938. He had just made a historic trans-atlantic flight."

It was Bill's turn to be surprised. "I didn't know that. It makes sense, though. Fritz was a lieutenant colonel in the German air force. According to my mother's journals, Fritz was dedicated to the Nazi movement, initially. He and his wife, Elisa, had twin sons. But in 1939, Elisa took the boys and fled Berlin. So you have two nephews you don't know about too. I hope I may someday find them as well."

Bill paused and briefly glanced down at his whitefish still untouched on his plate. There wasn't time to take even a bite, though.

"In late 1939, Fritz was sent on a special mission to the United States to command a Nazi military base near the Huron Mountains."

"Wait a minute," exclaimed Johann, interrupting. "I helped design and build an airport in the late thirties in that area. Was that part of this Nazi base?"

Bill paused at this new revelation. "It may be the same airport. It's abandoned now, and there's a munitions bunker a few miles up in the hills west of the airport."

"That was the ore mine!" Johann stated incredulously. "That's why they were guarding it so intently. A man named John Rogers of Rogers Airfreight hired me. His flights came in and out of that airport on a daily basis while I was there."

Bill couldn't believe it. Like a puzzle, the pieces were all coming together.

"Did you know Fritz was at that base in 1939?"

"No," Johann replied sadly. "I moved back to Detroit with my family that summer. I must have just missed him." He paused and brushed away a tear at the thought of being so close—yet so far—from his own brother.

Bill reached in his briefcase and placed Fritz's leather-bound journals gently on the table.

"Johann, we really don't know for sure what happened to Fritz. These are his journals, where he detailed his mission to strike key targets if the US had joined the war. But Fritz came to feel betrayed by the Nazis. The loss of his family was hard on him. He started to question all he had come to believe, and he admitted his mistakes. He was sad that he wouldn't see you or his parents again."

Bill slid the journals toward Johann.

"We aren't sure what happened to him. He wrote in his journal that he was taking a test flight near the Soo Locks, but there was nothing further. In the end, he was a very brave and honest man."

Johann turned toward the window. He could not hold back the tears. When he composed himself, he turned back to the table and placed his hand on the journals.

"My parents died a few years back. I wish they could have known what happened to Fritz. So much of our family is gone. It has been difficult wondering what happened to them. Thank you for giving me some closure. I'm excited to count you as family, and I'm excited by the idea that we have family we may yet embrace."

Bill nodded, tears now forming in his eyes as well. "It also gives me a bit of peace for the losses I've suffered. I haven't had peace for many years. It's like the return of the light after a long period of darkness."

Johann raised his wineglass in a toast. "To our family—may the search continue."

Bill raised his glass in return.

Johann was quiet for a moment, looking down at his plate intently. When he finally looked up, Bill could almost detect a hint of a smile.

"William, I would like you to have dinner with my wife, Ann, and me tonight at our home. Will you still be in town?"

"Yes. I don't catch my flight home until tomorrow morning. I'd love to meet your wife and have dinner."

"Great. Let me give you our address." Johann wrote on the back of a business card and handed it to Bill. "How is seven o'clock for you?"

"That will be fine."

The newly reunited family enjoyed the light lunch as they continued trading stories.

Bill arrived a little early for dinner. He was always eager for a good meal when traveling.

Johann greeted him at the door. "Good evening, William. Please come in. Ann is waiting in the study. We can have a drink before dinner." He led the way with a sly smile. "Actually, there's someone else I'd like you to meet. I think you'll find him interesting."

Entering the study, Bill saw a lovely woman he estimated to be in her late fifties. Standing near the large corner window was a dapper man with a glass in his hand.

Johann first introduced his wife, Ann, then extended his left hand toward the man.

"William O'Brien, I would like to introduce my brother Albert—your mother's first husband."

Bill was speechless. Johann, Ann, and Albert laughed at the shock on Bill's face.

"How is this possible?" Bill said when he finally recovered. "My mother's journals said you crashed in the ocean and there were no reports of survivors."

"First, William—it's so wonderful to meet you," Albert said, reaching out to shake his hand.

"Please, call me Bill."

Johann handed Bill a scotch as Albert began to tell his story.

"It's true that my plane went down. I was severely injured. I held on to a piece of wreckage until it became waterlogged and sunk, then I spotted an inflated life raft bobbing nearby. I managed to climb on board. I floated for several hours in a raging storm. I kept looking for other survivors but never found anyone. I don't remember anything else. I was told that a freighter spotted the raft several days later and picked me up.

"They took me to a hospital in Rio de Janeiro. I didn't have any identification, so the hospital personnel had no way to connect me with Deutsche Luft Hansa. When I was released from the hospital several weeks later, I went to the American consulate in Rio. I tried to contact my wife—your mother—in South Africa. But Freda and Katrina were nowhere to be found. I even tried to contact Deutsche Luft Hansa for any forwarding address. But with the start of the war, I got no reply. Finally, the consulate helped me get back to the United States."

Albert paused and glanced out the window before continuing.

"I came back to Detroit to be with Johann and my family just before the United States entered the war. At first, the US Army Air Force was reluctant to let me to join, since I had been so involved in German aviation. Eventually, they reconsidered, as they needed my experience. I was able to get a commission. I flew a B-17 on submarine patrols in the Atlantic and also a B-24 in Italy. We bombed the oil fields in Romania. I actually spent a good deal of the war as a flight instructor here in the United States."

Albert gestured to his brother. "After the war, Johann and I started an aircraft-parts company. We've been quite successful. I never remarried, though, and I never gave up trying to find my Freda. I prayed to God I would find her again. It's sad knowing she is dead. But your news of Katrina has given me hope."

Tears welled as he smiled at Bill.

"And most importantly, it's wonderful to meet a stepson after all these years. From what Johann has told me, and from what I can see meeting you, you have your mother's fire and determination. I couldn't be prouder of you if you were my own son."

Unable to speak as tears formed in his eyes as well, Bill simply lifted the remaining scotch in his glass in a toast. This was another amazing story of family survival.

Albert toasted Bill back, finishing his scotch. "I want to join you in searching for Katrina and the rest of our family. We all need to know their fate."

Bill returned to Minneapolis filled with the warmth of a newly found family and optimism for the future. He was eager to tell Susan all the wonderful news. His enthusiasm was dampened, however, by the fact that his in-laws were his only audience when he arrived home.

51.

J EWEL'S FACE WAS TAUT WHEN SHE AND SAM met Bill at the door. "Susie headed over to the Thunderbird," she said, clearly upset. "Apparently it's someone's birthday. She left not too long ago. You just missed her. I tried to talk her out of it, reminding her you'd be home soon. Let's just say she didn't appreciate my input."

Bill grimaced. Even under normal circumstances, Susan was often short with her mother. He could only imagine how she'd treated Jewel tonight. He glanced at Sam, who just shook his head and frowned.

"I'm sorry to put you both through all this," Bill said with a sigh. "How was she the last few days?"

"She was gone a lot," Jewel reported. "And when she was home, she didn't say much. I'd ask her about work, trying to coax something out of her, but she'd get angry or change the subject. But this morning at breakfast, she seemed different. Better, I think. We started talking about the farm and her brothers. She seemed to relax a bit. She even volunteered some things about her job, saying she was tired of all the hours. I can tell she's struggling, and she knows something has to change. But then suddenly she clammed up again and was out the door."

Bill nodded. "Maybe it's a start," he said hopefully. "I'm just glad she had someone here with her while I was away. I thank you for both of us."

"We just want to help," Sam replied, putting a comforting hand on Bill's shoulder.

"Would you like some supper?" Jewel asked.

"Thanks, Mom, but I better head over to the Thunderbird. I need to see my wife."

Jewel just smiled when Bill called her Mom. Since the first time Susan brought him home, Jewel had considered him one of her own sons. She could think of no one she'd rather see by her daughter's side through these hard times.

Susan found her VA friends sitting in a booth toward the back of the bar. From the looks of the glasses on the table, they were a few rounds in on rum and Cokes. When the waitress came to the table, her friends ordered another round and one for Susan.

"Actually, just a Coke, please, for me. No ice," Susan said.

"What's the deal? You on the wagon?" came the reply from one of the friends.

"No," Susan quickly said. She shrugged. "I just want a Coke tonight."

She looked away, hoping to end the line of questioning.

"That doesn't sound like much fun. Wanna dance, then?" the friend asked.

Susan shook her head. "No. I'm just tired. Go ahead—I'll watch your purses."

Her friends moved to the center of the floor and started dancing. Susan watched them, but her mind wandered.

Her mother was right—she shouldn't have gone out tonight. Before her mother even said a word, Susan knew she should have stayed home. But it was her friend's birthday . . . and it was hard to take that first step in a new direction.

Well, at least I ordered a Coke, she thought. *That counts for something.*

She glanced down at her watch. Bill was due home by now. She had so much to tell him. So why was she here instead? Maybe she wasn't sure what to say. Maybe she was afraid he wouldn't listen.

Out on the dance floor, some men had joined her friends. Some were fellow VA staffers, but a few were complete strangers, most likely hot to try their best pickup lines. Susan sipped her Coke and let out a small sigh. Every woman was flattered to get a little attention from the opposite sex. But with some men, the constant onslaught and pressure was overwhelming.

Just then, as if someone had heard her thoughts, Susan felt a presence. Before she could fully turn around, someone slid beside her in the booth, instantly pinning her into the corner. Without even looking, she knew who it was. Handy Herman.

"Herman, leave me alone!" she ordered, elbowing him and trying to scramble out of the booth.

Nearly every day, she had to fight him off either at work or here at the Thunderbird. But this time, he had her trapped. He writhed against her, pinning her tighter and placing a hand on her thigh.

"Come on—tonight's the night," he said with a leer. "We're going to have a good time."

"Like hell we will, you lousy bastard! Let me out of here!" she screamed.

Handy moved in for a French kiss and a grope of her breast. He kept his hand there even as Susan delivered a punch to his exposed belly.

Susan suddenly sensed another presence—a powerful one next to the booth. Then she heard a familiar voice overwhelm the pounding music.

"Get your fucking hands off her!"

Handy leaned in closer to Susan, then glared over his shoulder at the man. "Beat it, buddy. She's mine."

Susan twisted away again and saw Bill. As Handy shifted for a new position, Bill reached across the table and grabbed him by the throat. Bill leaned into Handy's face. Susan could see the cold rage in Bill's eyes. She had witnessed this before in Vietnam. Soldiers would be so overwhelmed by the death of their comrades that they only wanted to return to the battlefield to kill more of the enemy.

Bill squeezed tightly and pulled Handy right over the top of the table. The clattering and crashing of glasses made everyone in the bar turn to the commotion. Bill's upper-body strength was impressive, making quite an impression on Handy most of all.

With Bill still gripping Handy around the throat, Susan gasped and jumped to her feet. She was sure Bill would kill Handy.

"Bill, don't! The son of a bitch isn't worth it!"

Bill seemed to ignore her plea as he kept his hand around Handy's neck. But then Bill "persuaded" Handy toward the back door.

"You can't do this to me!" Handy railed, fighting against Bill's tight grip. His fists flew wildly, some making contact. "I'm a doctor! I'll sue you!"

In response, Bill yanked Handy's head back and whispered something in his ear. Immediately, Handy froze and turned pale. Susan gaped and watched as Bill kicked open the back door and disappeared with Handy into the dark alley. The door slammed loudly behind them.

Everyone inside the bar could hear garbage cans crashing and clanking in the alley, then finally silence. When the door opened again, Bill came sauntering in alone, and cheers erupted. Even the bar staff smirked and nodded at Bill. They knew Handy Herman all too well. Surprisingly, this was the first time he'd been thrashed by an intervening husband. The staff was glad someone had tossed that creep out into the trash, where he deserved to be.

Despite the accolades, Bill didn't smile. This was no cause for celebration. He wasn't entirely unscathed. Handy had somehow managed to land one good punch to his ribs.

Bill gently massaged his rib cage, but more importantly, he was upset at himself for losing his temper.

But how could he not lose it? He came in looking for his wife, only to find her with some guy's hands and mouth all over her. It looked as though she had been fighting him off. And that punch she threw looked real. But it was hard to say.

Plus, the table had been covered in empty booze glasses. Who knows how many she'd had. Maybe she encouraged the guy. Maybe this was what happened every night at the Thunderbird: she'd get drunk, come on to some random guy, but then not have the wherewithal to keep it from going too far.

Given everything else that was happening, Bill wouldn't be shocked in the least if Susan were having an affair. Booze, drugs, an affair—why not? It would explain why she was pushing Bill away and showing such anger whenever he wanted to be close to her. Maybe Bill had caught her red-handed tonight, so she pretended to fight the guy just to put on the innocent act.

Bill didn't know what to believe. All he knew was that the moment he saw them, he lost all control. His temper, his marriage, his life—he had no control over any of it.

Bill's hands were still clenched in tight balls as he walked up to Susan, who stood there staring at him with wide eyes even as her friends crowded around her in excitement.

Bill met Susan's eyes, then glanced around at the growing crowd. "That's enough fun for one night," he told her. "Your boyfriend is out back licking his wounds if you want to see him. I'm going home." His voice was mixed with as much sadness as anger.

"Bill, wait," Susan pleaded, reaching out to stop him. "It's not what you think—"

But Bill pivoted and headed for the door, turning down drink offers from many VA staffers who rushed over to congratulate him.

On the drive home, Bill's mind raced faster than the Rocket. When he pulled into the garage, he turned off the engine, lowered the door behind him, then sat in the seat awhile, trying to make sense of the incident. Finally, he got out and headed for the door leading to the kitchen.

He felt as helpless as he had the day his family died, as lost as he had the day Sara left him.

Suddenly, rage again overtook him. He smashed his fist into the garage wall, creating a twelve-inch hole in the Sheetrock. The nails in the wall ripped his skin, drawing blood. But the impact and pain only increased his rage.

Next he stumbled over to the heavy boxing bag hanging from the garage rafters. Over and over, faster and faster, he pounded the bag bare-handed with both fists. His hands, forearms, and elbows screamed in pain. His hands bled profusely now.

Finally exhausted, he wrapped his arms around the bag and cried as he swayed in the dim garage light. He was glad his in-laws were sleeping upstairs. He didn't want them to see him like this. He held his hands in front of him as if they belonged to someone else. At least two fingers on his left hand appeared to be broken.

Just then, the garage door opened, and Susan drove the Pumpkin into its spot. She looked in horror as she opened her door.

"My God, Bill! What the hell happened? Are you all right?" She rushed over to examine his hands.

He couldn't reply. He tried, but no words came out of his mouth.

Susan wiped the tears from his cheeks and put her arm under his shoulder. Holding him close, she ushered him into the house.

"Come sit in the kitchen so we don't wake the folks. Let me take a look at you." She somehow managed a smile as she settled him into a chair at the table. "It's been a while since you were my patient. At least this time you don't have bullet holes in you."

Bill could only shake his head. He still couldn't clear his throat to speak. He tried to wipe his tears on his arm. He looked pathetic and felt like a fool.

Susan once again gently wiped his eyes, then went to retrieve the first aid kit. She cleaned the cuts on his hands and wrapped his two broken fingers together. When she was done, she sat down facing him.

The wall she had built between them in the last few months was crumbling. Seeing him enraged at the Thunderbird and now broken and bloodied, she understood how emotionally vulnerable her husband had become. Until now, she'd never thought of him as vulnerable in any way, even when he'd been a patient under her care in the MASH unit. He'd always been strong and resilient.

But now she saw that Bill's enormous courage and strength had its limits—especially when he thought he had lost his wife to work, booze, drugs, and maybe even another man. Susan knew she needed and wanted to bring him back to her. She had to make him understand how much she loved him. For the first time in a long time, she was ready to let it all out.

"Want to talk?" she began.

"You go first," he said with a sniff.

"First of all," she said, "let's talk about tonight's featured bout, which will be forever known as 'Handy in the Trash.'"

Bill looked at her quizzically, partly because he didn't understand and partly because he thought he detected a twinkle in her eyes that he hadn't seen in weeks.

"Handy?" he repeated.

He listened quietly as she told him about the good doctor's reputation at the VA and how he had trapped her in the booth and tried to have his way with her.

"For the record, that jackass is not a friend. I'm not having an affair with anyone, though I'm sure you're wondering." Susan dropped her head a bit. "And I wasn't drinking tonight. It was just Coke, no booze. I'm not taking those amphetamines anymore either. I stupidly used them a couple of times, thinking they would help me work longer. All they did was give me really bad side effects."

She looked up at Bill with a small smile.

"Actually, these changes are all because of a new nurse supervisor named Ruby. She was one of my commanding officers at the Seventy-First Evac in Pleiku too. She helped keep top brass from harassing us nurses. Her career goes back to the Korean War, so she's seen so much. She suffered some of the same problems I did in Vietnam and at the VA.

"Anyway, she approached me the other day. Deb and the other nurses told her about my drinking and drug use and about the attack. Ruby leads a support group after work for nurses, and she invited me to join them. I went yesterday, and it wasn't too bad. Several of the nurses described similar or worse encounters than mine. Going to group seems to help them—and I know how much your support groups helped you. I know it's only been one session, but I'm really enthusiastic about the group. They've already helped me realize that I need to make some changes. Cutting out booze and drugs is just the beginning."

She gently reached over to take Bill's right hand—without the broken fingers—in her own hands.

"I'm starting to understand that I haven't failed the VA. To a large degree, the VA has failed me. I see now that I've done all I can for my guys. But I can't let it take over my whole life anymore. I'm thinking of getting a new job. I've talked to our friend Dr. Tom Johnson at the University of Minnesota Hospital, in the pediatrics department. I've had lots of experience dealing with children. First, my brothers, then my husband." She winked and laughed again.

Bill could hardly believe his ears or his eyes. She had the old twinkle back, the old banter and humor. He should have known she was stubborn and smart enough to find her own method of dealing with her problems. He also knew she was lucky to have Deb, Ruby, and the nurse support group.

She nodded her head down the hallway, toward the guest room. "By the way, thank you for calling Mom and Dad. I don't think I was the most hospitable hostess, but honestly, it was nice to see them and have them here. I promise I'll make it up to them before they leave. I understand now that they're worried about me—just as you have been."

Susan's eyes shined as they filled with tears. "I'm so sorry for the grief I've caused all of you. I know now that changes have to be made. And they will be. I want a career, yes, but I also want a husband. Maybe a family—someday, that is!" she quickly added. "Don't let Mother Jewel hear that!"

As she laughed and her eyes crinkled, her tears gently slipped out.

"But right now, all I want is to love and be loved by my husband."

Bill squeezed her hand as hard as he could without reopening the cuts she'd just tended. Tears came to his eyes as well.

"Lima Bean, if you promise never to hit me with a punch like I saw you throw tonight, I'll love you forever."

Susan once again let out a laugh. "Okay—but on two conditions. First, you tell me what you said to Handy before you tossed him in the trash. Whatever it was, it must have been good. Second, you get over here and kiss me right now. And then you make up for lost time in bed tonight—despite your paws being damaged."

"Isn't that three things?" Bill replied. "But who's counting?"

He stood, bringing Susan to her feet too. Then he grabbed her around the waist with his right hand and pulled her close.

"All I said to Handy was, 'No one fucks with my family.' I guess he understood."

"Bill, how very poetic of you," replied Susan. "Now, let's get on with the rest of the conditions."

Neither of them needed further prodding.

— WASHINGTON, DC, 1972 —

52.

ICHIGAN FBI AGENTS DANIEL HOGAN AND Glenn Bauer landed at Washington National Airport, grabbed a rental car, and drove through the typical DC rush-hour traffic. They were heading to the Pentagon.

During dinner the evening before, Hogan had received a call from the Michigan coast guard regarding images taken by the *Spirit of Superior* research vessel. While in the Whitefish Bay area, the crew had come upon a wreckage. It was clearly a four-engine aircraft.

That very morning, Hogan and Bauer were ordered to forward the information to the CIA, and they were booked on the next flight to Washington. That was all they knew.

But you don't question a meeting at the Pentagon. You just get there a little early, if possible, to make a good impression.

Hogan and Bauer passed through security and were ushered into a conference room. There, a group of senior air force brass and CIA staff had already gathered. The two Michigan agents sat as directed. A CIA agent named Mitchell reached into his black leather briefcase and pulled out a file labeled "Top Secret—Eyes Only."

"General, here are the details," he said, handing the file to General Abrams.

Abrams opened the folder and scanned the briefing page. He flipped through the attached photographs in silence. His face registered concern. He knew exactly what this was.

"What's our status?" he finally asked the Michigan agents. "Who knows about this?"

Senior Agent Hogan addressed the group. "No one—as far as we know, sir. A storm has kicked up in Lake Superior, so there is no possibility of anyone tampering with the site today. Even the *Spirit of Superior* is currently held in harbor."

"Good," stated Abrams. He turned next to his staff.

"Let me be very clear! We need to secure that site as soon as possible with our own people before some sport divers find the wreck," Abrams commanded. "This must be the Fw 200 that went missing from the Condor Base we've been cleaning up. If so, it might be carrying live bombs. They might even be the red mercury bombs that have proven to be very nasty. They're like dirty bombs," he added. "If there are bombs on that plane, they must be secured properly. If not, we risk a huge contamination issue in the lake. And if any of the bombs detonate, the blast area could be massive."

Abrams carefully scanned the faces in the room. Everyone was intent and grim—especially Hogan and Bauer, who were just now understanding what they were up against.

"Let's get to work," Abrams ordered.

Everyone nodded in agreement.

Abrams started the ball rolling. He personally made a call to the secretary of the navy to ask that resources be sent immediately to the coordinates provided with the photographs. They needed to dispatch a deepwater dive vessel and get close-up pictures of the aircraft. They also needed to have an underwater demolitions expert on board.

The *USS Recovery*, a navy dive and recovery ship, was in Lake Michigan and could reach the site in a day. Captain Hankinson was told to run at flank speed to the crash site to evaluate and investigate as soon as the storm cleared. After steaming through the night, the *Recovery* reached the coordinates provided by the *Spirit of Superior*.

The aircraft wreck was beyond normal scuba-diving depth, so a special diving unit was required. As the *Recovery* moved into position, two of the crew helped Specialist Cragan don the one-man JIM suit for deep diving. He looked like an astronaut in the bulky suit, but it would protect him from the high pressure at the extreme depths.

Cragan was lowered into the water for initial recon. Thirty minutes later came the first radio contact from the diver.

"Mother, this is Deep Dive One. Mother, this is Deep Dive One. Over."

"Deep Dive One, this is Mother. What do you see? Over."

"Mother, this is Deep Dive One. I'm on the bottom in just over two hundred feet of water. There is definitely an aircraft here. It's a four-engine craft. The configuration matches the old German Fw 200. It's lying slightly on its side but upright. The tail section is sheared off about midway. I'll turn on the camera so you can see what I'm seeing."

Cragan reached up to turn on the camera. Captain Hankinson leaned in and stared at the fuzzy images as they began to appear on the screen. It was clearly an aircraft nestled in the sand on the bottom.

"The lettering on the side says 'Rogers Airfreight,' " Cragan continued. "I'm going to grab a picture with my still camera so we can make out the details for later analysis."

A few minutes later, Cragan returned to the radio. "Okay, Mother, got the still pictures." Cragan moved his position again to view the wings. "There are attachments under each of the wings. They appear to be . . . well, for lack of a better description . . . they appear to be bombs." The diver repositioned himself to peer through the hole created by the sheared-off tail section. "There also appears to be a large bomb inside the fuselage. Are you getting good video of this? Over."

"Deep Dive One, this is Mother. We copy that and have good picture. Can you determine if those bombs can be detached and brought to the surface safely? Over."

"Mother, this is Deep Dive One. The one that broke loose is lying a few yards away from the fuselage. That one can be brought up for sure by an underwater demolition team. I think the other two can also be safely retrieved. Upon closer inspection, they don't appear to have fuses, so they are not armed. I don't see any other bombs in or near the aircraft's fuselage. It does not appear that the red mercury weapons were on board the aircraft."

"Deep Dive One, this is Mother. Copy that. That is good news. We will notify headquarters. Can you reposition and check the cockpit for any remains? Over."

"Mother, this is Deep Dive One. Repositioning to the cockpit. Over."

The picture went black while the diver slowly repositioned to the front of the aircraft. After five minutes, the radio stuttered back to life.

"Mother, this is Deep Dive One. I'm turning on the video again so you can see the cockpit interior. It looks like two well-preserved bodies in military-style flight suits with dog tags floating in front of them. There also appears to be a metal cylinder clipped to the dash that may contain some documents. The windshield is broken out. Do you want me to try to retrieve the cylinder? Over."

"Deep Dive One, this is Mother. Copy that. See if you can grab the cylinder first. Then try to get the dog tags off the bodies. Bring up whatever you can retrieve. Over."

"Mother, this is Deep Dive One. Copy that—attempting a retrieve."

Captain Hankinson leaned closer to the screen as he saw Cragan extend the probe through the open space where the windshield should have been. The probe grabbed the cylinder, then retracted so Cragan could deposit the cylinder in the hold basket attached to the chest plate of his suit.

The probe extended again. This time, it took several attempts to grab the chain that held the copilot's dog tags. But as Cragan pulled the probe back through the windshield, the chain slipped from its grasp and drifted out of view. Cragan backed up slowly and tilted down. The dog tags were lost in the sand at the bottom of the deep lake.

"Mother, this is Deep Dive One. Sorry—lost that one. Do you want me to try for the other one? This probe arm is just not calibrated for something that small. Over."

"Deep Dive One, this is Mother. Give it a try. It doesn't matter if it's buried in the sand or left dangling where it is. Either way, we can't read it unless it's up here, so give it a shot. Over."

"Mother, this is Deep Dive One. Roger that. Moving back in to try the pilot's tags. Over."

It seemed like an eternity. The crew members held their collective breath as they watched the huge probe try to thread the needle and remove the small chain from the pilot's neck. This time, Cragan clamped the probe directly to the tags, rather than the chain. As he slowly withdrew the probe, the chain broke and slipped off the tags into the interior of the aircraft. But the tags remained locked in the jaws of the probe and were safely deposited into the retrieval basket.

Thirty minutes later, Cragan surfaced and was brought to the deck of the *Recovery*. Captain Hankinson reached into the retrieval basket and pulled out the metal dog tags. Only a number was punched into the metal, no name. After all that effort, the dog tag appeared to be of no help.

"Damn," Cragan said, voicing the entire crew's frustration. "Don't German dog tags have names?"

"Apparently not," Hankinson said. "But hold on. Let's see what we have here."

With that, Hankinson opened the cylinder and scanned the documents lying inside. They detailed the planned mission and clearly identified the pilot as Fritz Schmidt, Oberstleutnant, Luftwaffe.

General Abrams was pleased with the news. The next day, the underwater demolition team retrieved the three unarmed bombs from the wreckage. The bodies of Fritz Schmidt and his copilot—presumed to be Dietrich, according to Fritz's journals—were left in the aircraft, where they had been found. The location would now be treated as an official grave site.

Abrams now had the documents and munitions from the cavern, the information O'Brien had shared from his mother's journals, plus the information Johann Schmidt had revealed to Bill about John Rogers's involvement in building the airfield for the Nazi attack mission. In addition, military records showed that the army had paid a John Rogers $50,000 for the deserted airport previously known as Marquette Private Field.

Little did the general realize that later that year, this information would go a long way in eliminating the political aspirations of Francis William

Rogers, a narcissistic senator from the great state of New York. He would quietly withdraw his name as a nominee for president of the United States.

For now, though, Abrams sat at his desk in deep thought. It was hard to fathom how all of this had come together—how Bill had happened to unravel this great mystery.

With a small smile, the general picked up the phone to call Bill. He had to let him know the plane had been found and that only the bodies of Fritz, Dietrich, and their Fw 200 were left to bear witness to the attack on America that never happened.

EPILOGUE

THE COLD GRAY OF ROLLING WAVES on Lake Superior had risen to three to four feet, eroding and redepositing parts of the sandbar twenty yards offshore. The sound of the waves brought Bill back from his reverie reflecting back on years past.

The sand washed in and out with the fickle waves. The waters on the shore side of the sandbar were coppery brown in the early-morning sun. The waters farther out were dark navy and steel gray with whitecaps breaking the surface. The Canadian shoreline was two hundred miles away, across this lake that looked more like an ocean. It was a daunting place for small boats.

Early spring was arriving in the Upper Peninsula of Michigan. Everything was slowly awakening this morning. After two days of rain, it was good to see the sun creeping across the eastern horizon. The crackling fire and the comfort of his Jameson-fortified coffee allowed Bill to relax.

His gaze wandered to the fireplace mantel, where he saw his favorite black-and-white picture he had taken of his family. His father, Michael, had his arm tightly around his wife's waist, pulling her close to him. They exchanged a loving glance, rather than look at the camera. Bill's younger brother, John, stared intently at the camera. Young Jackie clung to her father's other hand and looked coy.

Bill smiled and moved to the mantel to pick up the photograph. Passing his fingertips gently over the faces in the image, he thought about these precious individuals in his life. Bill hoped he had become as loving and patient as his father.

Bill knew there had been times when lying or running away from issues would have made his life easier. But his father had taught him to be honest and to face up to his problems. For instance, he could have tried to avoid Vietnam, but he had felt it was his duty. He had taken risks to help others. He had been mentally and physically injured because of some of his decisions, but he was proud that he had learned from his mistakes and moved on.

Bill glanced out the window again. He finished his coffee and sighed deeply, reflecting on the growing distance from the black-and-white picture to his present reality. Replacing the picture on the mantel, he scanned the other photos next to it.

He saw Susan's formal graduation picture from nursing college contrasted next to the grainy snapshot of her working in the MASH unit in Vietnam. Both symbolized the strength and care she had provided to all the veterans. The only colored picture on the mantel was their wedding portrait. Susan's glowing smile and simple white gown with a draped train still took his breath away.

No more darkness today, Bill thought. *I'm a lucky guy.*

He finally had the great fortune to have a beautiful, loving, and wonderful woman as his wife. It had been a struggle, but he was finally starting a true family. For a moment, he pondered why Susan hadn't gotten pregnant yet. She had said she wanted children. Perhaps soon.

He shrugged. *One step at a time. For now, I'm just joyful to be with her.*

But for a moment, he also wondered about Sara. What had happened to her? How had she changed? Had she found happiness? Would he ever see her again? He admitted that she was a ghost, not unlike Larry for Susan. Was Larry still alive? Would he ever come back from Vietnam?

To help chase away these thoughts, Bill poured another cup of coffee and topped it with Jameson again. As he plopped down in a recliner by the window, he contemplated shaving and showering. But it was still too early. And he was too comfortable and too content with his coffee.

The merganser family he had been watching for a while paddled out of view. He watched the eagle course down the shoreline, looking for a meal.

Hopefully, the mergansers would duck under the surface in time to avoid losing yet another member. The lake trout had already claimed one of them.

The hummingbirds were returning this morning, and they were hungry. Bill kept the feeders full so he could watch their aerial battles. This morning, one female guarded the feeder on the east side. She sipped nectar quietly, next to her mate. If another tried to feed, though, she would chirp and attack, driving it away. Bill never tired at watching their tenacity and ability to hover, dart to and fro, and even fly backward. They demonstrated such a desire to help their mates.

Bill reached over and cranked open the window to allow the cool, crisp air into the cabin. It was invigorating. He shifted back to a comfortable position and propped his feet on the windowsill. His thoughts were a million miles away.

Susan seemed to be recovering. She was finally happy. He knew that if he had lost her, the light in his life would be gone forever.

He still needed to call Johann and Albert in Detroit to discuss the search for Katrina. Then, of course, there were the clues they were still following about Elisa and the twins. Not to mention the open questions about the sabotage on his dad's plane. Bill's mood clouded at that thought.

On a happier note, Bill's old army buddy, Dale Patterson, had promised to visit in the not-too-distant future. Dale hadn't seen the O'Brien camp, and he wanted to meet Susan. He said he had his own announcement that he thought Bill would appreciate.

So much had happened in such a short time, with so much left to experience. Bill could only wonder what the next revelation would be. But right now, he could again see the bottom of his cup. It was time for a refill.

He dropped his feet to the floor and stood up to get more coffee. He decided to start the marinade for the steaks as well. Just then, he heard stirring up in the loft.

"Dear, are you making breakfast or not?" Susan called down to him.

Bill loved that Susan had a robust appetite these days. A good sign. She had barely picked at her food for weeks.

"Yes, dear." He looked up at the loft, where his wife was leaning coyly over the balcony rail. "What would you like, my darling wife, other than the toast I just burned?"

"Oh, Bill!" she admonished over the wafting odor of yet another burnt offering. "Are you still at war with the appliances?"

Susan pulled on her robe and trotted down the stairs, looking a little frumpy. He couldn't resist repeating a comment she had made about his appearance on their first trip to Minneapolis many months ago: "Dear, you really look *unmilitary* today."

"Oh really?" she replied, yawning. "But remember, I'm a civilian now, buster. Where's my breakfast?"

He smiled as she contemplated her real choices for breakfast. He loved cooking now—as long as she did the dishes.

Susan saw the glint of the rising sun as it returned from its nightly eclipse and warmed the huge lake surface. "What a beautiful sunny day this will be," she exclaimed. "I think it's the most beautiful day we've had in a very long time. Maybe forever!"

Susan smiled at Bill. It was wonderful to have him as her husband and to be in this remote cabin alone.

There was peace here—peace for their minds, bodies, and their souls. It was a beautiful day indeed.

AUTHOR'S NOTE

THE LOCKS AT SAULT STE. MARIE, MICHIGAN, also known as the Soo Locks, were some of the most heavily defended locations in the United States for the first three years of World War II. The American and Canadian governments recognized that damage to or closure of the locks would be a crippling blow to American steel production, seeing as 90 percent of America's iron ore flowed through them.

At one time, 7,300 soldiers were stationed at the locks. In addition, underwater steel antitorpedo nets were installed both above and below the locks to prevent torpedo or bomb damage. A coastal artillery battalion was put in place with fifteen sixty-inch searchlights, eighteen barrage balloons, and nearly fifty antiaircraft guns. Radar sites were established in Ontario, Canada, to guard against enemy aircraft. Combat air patrols ranged as far north as Hudson Bay. It was not until 1944 that the defenses were reduced.

Although the locks were never attacked, the potential threat was very real.

ACKNOWLEDGMENTS

WRITING HISTORICAL FICTION IS LIKE taking a journey in a time machine. It allows you to travel to the past in an instant and return to the present in a heartbeat. It allows you to relive the past with all its glorious possibilities, options, and successes along with all its heartbreaking losses and fears. Historical fiction permits you to creatively build characters and plot, yet requires you to respect the limits of the time and place.

Like any journey, it is never traveled alone. Along your writing journey, the people you meet, choices you make, and events beyond your control will influence and guide you. They will help you describe how history affects the human condition.

My writing journey has allowed me to express the elements of my experience. My parents encouraged my love of reading. Their untimely deaths made me face loneliness and homelessness at an early age. Vietnam forced me to deal with fear—and at times terror—and accept the suddenness of violent death. My long marriage has allowed me to understand love and commitment.

I have overcome many trials on my journey, and so I have tried to build strength in my characters in this novel. These men and women are normal people who struggle and sometimes fail. But like the real soldiers and nurses I have known, they refuse to give up. If they had not held to their resolve, they would not have survived.

This novel would not have been possible without the direct support and assistance of so many people. My wife, Nancy, has been my primary support and first editor. Thankfully, she took time to transcribe my hand-written manuscript into crafted prose.

I also want to thank the creative people at Beaver's Pond Press in Edina, Minnesota—Hanna, Margarita, Athena, Laurie, and many others behind the scenes—for their tremendous support.

Thanks also to my wonderful editor, Angela Wiechmann, A. M. W. Editing. Her professional expertise and wonderful sense of humor allowed us to move through months of detailed edits while still having fun.

Last but not least, thanks to my website developer, Echo Martin, who created a beautiful, unique, and functional author site for me.

Many thanks to you all. You have made this novel possible.

ABOUT THE AUTHOR

A LIFELONG STORYTELLER AND WORLD TRAVELER, Michael Dardis specializes in twentieth-century European history, American history, and military history. After receiving a degree from the University of Minnesota in history and geography, Michael went on to serve in the United States Army during the Vietnam War. He was awarded a Purple Heart and the US Army Commendation Medal for Valor.

When not writing fiction, Michael stays involved in national and local government activities, serving on several commissions for the City of Bloomington, Minnesota, where he and his wife, Nancy, have lived for forty-two years of marriage. He is a member of the Committee on Foreign Relations Minnesota, the Military Order of the Purple Heart, the University of Minnesota Alumni Association, and the Minnesota Historical Society. Michael also works with Volunteers Enlisted to Assist People, Cornerstone Advocacy Service, and the University of Minnesota Foundation to provide academic scholarships.

Michael's first book, *The Dark Side of the Sun*, is a historical fiction novel.